MY BOOK HOUSE
THROUGH FAIRY HALLS

THROUGH FAIRY HALLS

LO! here are airy halls and fairy halls
  Where life and joy and all true splendour reign,
And be it shining creature with bright wings,
  Or but a little man or queer old dame,
Or talking beast who doth appear to guide,
  Pray let him lead you hither to these halls.

Through
FAIRY HALLS
of
MY BOOKHOUSE

EDITED BY

Olive Beaupré Miller

PUBLISHERS

The BOOKHOUSE for CHILDREN

CHICAGO   TORONTO

Publishers of

My BOOKHOUSE
Six Volumes

My TRAVELSHIP
Three Volumes

My BOOK *of* HISTORY
Six Volumes

LIST OF STORIES AND POEMS

LIST OF STORIES AND POEMS

LIST OF STORIES AND POEMS

(*Translated by William Makepeace Thackeray*)

LIST OF STORIES AND POEMS

THE ASSEMBLING OF THE FAYS

They come from huts of leafage green,
They creep from the mullein's velvet screen,
Some on the backs of beetles fly,
From the silver aspen moon-touched trees.
Where they swing in their cobweb hammocks high,
And rocked about in the swaying breeze.
And now they throng the moonlight glade,
Above—below—on every side,
Their little minim forms arrayed
In the tricksy panof fairy pride.

— *Joseph Rodman Drake.*

THE ASSEMBLING OF THE FAYS

They come from beds of lichen green,
They creep from the mullein's velvet screen;
   Some on the backs of beetles fly
From the silver tops of moon-touched trees,
Where they swung in their cobweb hammocks high,
And rocked about in the evening breeze;
And now they throng the moonlight glade,
Above—below—on every side,
Their little minim forms arrayed,
In the tricksy pomp of fairy pride.

—*Joseph Rodman Drake*

The Story of Fairyfoot*
FRANCES BROWNE

ONCE upon a time there stood far away in the west country a town called Stumpinghame. It contained seven windmills, a royal palace, a market place, and a prison, with every other convenience befitting the capital of a kingdom. A capital city was Stumpinghame, and its inhabitants thought it the only one in the world. It stood in the midst of a great plain, which for three leagues round its walls was covered with corn, flax and orchards. Beyond that lay a great circle of pasture land, seven leagues in breadth, and it was bounded on all sides by a forest so thick and old that no man in Stumpinghame knew its extent; and the opinion of the learned was, that it reached to the end of the world.

There were strong reasons for this opinion. First, that forest was known to be inhabited time out of mind by the fairies, and no hunter cared to go beyond its borders—so the west country believed it to be solidly full of old trees to the heart. Secondly, the people of Stumpinghame were no travellers—man, woman, and child had feet so large and heavy that it was by no means convenient to carry them far. Whether it was the nature of the place or the people, I cannot tell, but great feet had been the fashion there time immemorial, and the higher the family the larger were they. It was, therefore, the aim of everybody above the degree of shepherds, and such-like rustics, to swell out and enlarge their feet by way of gentility; and so successful were they in these undertakings that, on a pinch, respectable people's slippers would have served for panniers.

Stumpinghame had a king of its own, and his name was Stiffstep; his family was very ancient and large-footed. His subjects called him Lord of the World, and he made a speech to them every year concerning the grandeur of his mighty empire. His

*Taken from *Granny's Wonderful Chair.* 12

queen, Hammerheel, was the greatest beauty in Stumpinghame. Her majesty's shoe was not much less than a fishing-boat; their six children promised to be quite as handsome, and all went well with them till the birth of their seventh son.

For a long time nobody about the palace could understand what was the matter—the ladies-in-waiting looked so astonished, and the king so vexed; but at last it was whispered through the city that the queen's seventh child had been born with such miserably small feet that they resembled nothing ever seen or heard of in Stumpinghame, except the feet of the fairies.

The chronicles furnished no example of such an affliction ever before happening in the royal family. The common people thought it portended some great calamity to the city, the learned men began to write books about it; and all the relations of the king and queen assembled at the palace to mourn with them over their singular misfortune. The whole court and most of the citizens helped in this mourning, but when it had lasted seven days they all found out it was of no use. So to cheer up the queen's spirits, the young prince was sent privately out to the pasture lands, to be nursed among the shepherds.

The chief man there was called Fleecefold, and his wife's name was Rough Ruddy. They lived in a snug cottage with their son, Blackthorn, and their daughter, Brownberry, and were thought great people, because they kept the king's sheep. Moreover, Fleecefold's family were known to be ancient; and Rough Ruddy boasted that she had the largest feet in all the pastures. The shepherds held them in high respect, and it grew still higher when the news spread that the king's seventh son had been sent to their cottage. People came from all quarters to see the young prince, and great were the lamentations over his misfortune in having such small feet.

The king and queen had given him fourteen names, beginning

with Augustus—such being the fashion in that royal family; but the honest country people could not remember so many; besides, his feet were the most remarkable thing about the child, so with one accord they called him Fairyfoot and the boy never had another name throughout the pastures. At court it was not thought polite to speak of him at all. They did not keep his birthday, and he was never sent for at Christmas, because the queen and her ladies could not bear the sight. Once a year the undermost scullion was sent to see how he did, with a bundle of his next brother's cast-off clothes; and, as the king grew old and cross, it was said he had thoughts of disowning him.

So Fairyfoot grew in Fleecefold's cottage. Perhaps the country air made him fair and rosy—for all agreed that he would have been a handsome boy but for his small feet, with which nevertheless he learned to walk, and in time to run and to jump, thereby amazing everybody, for such doings were not known among the children of Stumpinghame. The news of court, however, travelled to the shepherds, and Fairyfoot was despised among them. The old people thought him unlucky; the children refused to play with him. Fleecefold was ashamed to have him in his cottage, but he durst not disobey the king's orders. Moreover, Blackthorn wore most of the clothes brought by the scullion. At last, Rough Ruddy found out that the sight of such horrid jumping would make her children vulgar; and, as soon as he was old enough, she sent Fairyfoot every day to watch some sheep on a wild, weedy pasture, hard by the forest.

THROUGH FAIRY HALLS

Poor Fairyfoot was often lonely and sorrowful; many a time he wished his feet would grow larger, and all the comfort he had was running and jumping by himself in the wild pasture, and thinking that none of the shepherds' children could do the like, for all their pride of their great feet.

Tired of this sport, he was lying in the shadow of a mossy rock one warm summer's noon, with the sheep feeding around, when a robin, pursued by a great hawk, flew into the old velvet cap which lay on the ground beside him. Fairyfoot covered it up, and the hawk, frightened by his shout, flew away.

"Now you may go, poor robin!" he said, opening the cap; but instead of the bird, out sprang a little man dressed in ragged blue, and looking as if he were a hundred years old. Fairyfoot could not speak for astonishment, but the little man said:

"Thank you for your shelter, and be sure I will do as much

DONN P. CRANE

for you. Call on me if you are ever in trouble; my name is
Robin Goodfellow;" and darting off, he was out of sight in an
instant. For days the boy wondered who that little man could
be, but he told nobody, for the little man's feet were as small
as his own, and it was clear he would be no favorite in Stumpinghame. Fairyfoot kept the story to himself, and at last mid-
summer came. That evening was a feast among the shepherds.
There were bonfires on the hills, and fun in the villages. But
Fairyfoot sat alone beside his sheepfold, for the children of his
village had refused to let him dance with them about the bonfire.
He had never felt so lonely in all his life, and remembering the
little man, he plucked up spirit, and cried:

"Ho! Robin Goodfellow!"

"Here I am," said a shrill voice at his elbow; and there stood
the little man himself.

"I am very lonely, and no one will play with me, because
my feet are not large enough," said Fairyfoot.

"Come then and play with us," said the little man. "We
lead the merriest lives in the world, and care for nobody's feet;
but all companies have their own manners, and there are two
things you must mind among us: first, do as you see the rest
doing; and secondly, never speak of anything you may hear or
see, for we and the people of this country have had no friendship
ever since large feet came in fashion."

"I will do that, and anything more you like," said Fairyfoot;
and the little man, taking his hand, led him over the pasture
into the forest, and along a mossy path among old trees wreathed
with ivy (he never knew how far), till they heard the sound of
music, and came upon a meadow where the moon shone as bright
as day, and all the flowers of the year—snowdrops, violets, prim-
roses, and cowslips—bloomed together in the thick grass. There
were a crowd of little men and women, some clad in russet colour,

but far more in green, dancing round a little well as clear as crystal. And under great rose-trees which grew here and there in the meadow, companies were sitting round low tables covered with cups of milk, dishes of honey, and carved wooden flagons filled with clear red wine. The little man led Fairyfoot up to the nearest table, handed him one of the flagons, and said, "Drink to the good company!"

Then the boy forgot all his troubles—how Blackthorn and Brownberry wore his clothes, how Rough Ruddy sent him to keep the sickly sheep, and the children would not dance with him; in short, he forgot the whole misfortune of his feet, and it seemed to his mind that he was a king's son, and all was well with him. All the little people about the well cried:

"Welcome! welcome!" and every one said: "Come and dance with me!" So Fairyfoot was as happy as a prince, and drank milk and ate honey till the moon was low in the sky, and then the little man took him by the hand, and never stopped nor stayed till he was at his own bed of straw in the cottage corner.

Next morning Fairyfoot was not tired for all his dancing. Nobody in the cottage had missed him, and he went out with the sheep as usual; but every night all that summer, when the shepherds were safe in bed, the little man came and took him

17

away to dance in the forest. Now he did not care to play with the shepherds' children, nor grieve that his father and mother had forgotten him, but watched the sheep all day singing to himself or plaiting rushes; and when the sun went down, Fairyfoot's heart rejoiced at thought of meeting that merry company.

The wonder was that he was never tired nor sleepy, as people are apt to be who dance all night; but before the summer was ended Fairyfoot found out the reason. One night, when the moon was full, and the last of the ripe corn rustling in the fields, Robin Goodfellow came for him as usual, and away they went to the flowery green. The fun there was high, and Robin was in haste. So he only pointed to the carved cup from which Fairyfoot every night drank.

"I am not thirsty, and there is no use losing time," thought the boy to himself, and he joined the dance; but never in all his life did Fairyfoot find such hard work as to keep pace with the company. Their feet seemed to move like lightning; the swallows did not fly so fast or turn so quickly. Fairyfoot did his best, for he never gave in easily, but at length, his breath and strength being spent, the boy was glad to steal away, and sit down behind a mossy oak, where his eyes closed for very weariness. When he awoke the dance was nearly over, but two little ladies clad in green talked close beside him.

"What a beautiful boy!" said one of them. "He is worthy to be a king's son. Only see what handsome feet he has!"

"Yes," said the other, with a laugh that sounded spiteful; "they are just like the feet Princess Maybloom had before she washed them in the Growing Well. Her father has sent far and wide throughout the whole country searching for a doctor to make them small again, but nothing in this world can do it except the water of the Fair Fountain, and none but I and the nightingales know where it is."

"One would not care to let the like be known," said the first little lady, "there would come such crowds of these great coarse creatures of mankind, nobody would have peace for leagues round. But you will surely send word to the sweet princess!— she was so kind to our birds and butterflies, and danced so like one of ourselves!"

"Not I, indeed!" said the spiteful fairy. "Her father cut down the cedar which I loved best in the whole forest, and made a chest of it to hold his money in; besides, I never liked the princess—everybody praised her so."

When they were gone, Fairyfoot could sleep no more with astonishment. He did not wonder at the fairies admiring his feet, because their own were much the same; but it amazed him that Princess Maybloom's father should be troubled at hers growing large. Moreover, he wished to see that same princess and her country, since there were really other places in the world than Stumpinghame.

All the next day Fairyfoot was so weary that in the afternoon he fell asleep, with his head on a clump of rushes. It was seldom that any one thought of looking after him and the sheep; but it so happened that towards evening the old shepherd, Fleecefold, thought he would see how things went on in the pastures. The shepherd had a bad temper and a slick staff, and no sooner did he catch sight of Fairyfoot sleeping, and his flock straying away, than shouting all the ill names he could remember, in a voice which woke up the boy, he ran after him as fast as his great feet would allow; while Fairyfoot, seeing no other shelter from his fury, fled into the forest, and never stopped nor stayed till he reached the banks of a little stream.

Thinking it might lead him to the fairies' dancing-ground, he followed that stream for many an hour, but it wound away into the heart of the forest, flowing through dells, falling over mossy rocks, and at last leading Fairyfoot, when he was tired and the night had fallen, to a grove of great rose-trees, with the moon shining on it as bright as day, and thousands of nightingales singing in the branches. In the midst of that grove was a clear spring, bordered with banks of lilies, and Fairyfoot sat down by it to rest himself and listen. The singing was so sweet he could have listened forever, but as he sat the nightingales left off their songs, and began to talk together in the silence of the night:

"What boy is that," said one on a branch above him, "who sits so lonely by the Fair Fountain? He cannot have come from Stumpinghame with such small and handsome feet."

"No, I'll warrant you," said another, "he has come from the west country. How in the world did he find the way?"

"How simple you are!" said a third nightingale. "What had he to do but follow the ground-ivy which grows over height and hollow, bank and bush, from the lowest gate of the king's kitchen-garden to the root of this rose-tree? He looks a wise boy, and I hope he will keep the secret, or we shall have all the west country here, dabbling in our fountain, and leaving us no rest to either talk or sing."

Fairyfoot sat in great astonishment at this discourse, but by and by, when the talk ceased and the songs began, he thought it might be as well for him to follow the ground-ivy, and see the Princess Maybloom, not to speak of getting rid of Rough Ruddy, the sickly sheep, and the crusty old shepherd. It was a long journey; but he went on, eating wild berries by day, sleeping in the hollows of old trees by night, and never losing sight of the ground-ivy, which led him over height and hollow, bank and bush, out of the forest, and along a noble high road, with fields and villages on every side, to a great city, and a low old-fashioned gate of the king's kitchen-garden, which was thought

too mean for scullions, and had not been opened for seven years.

There was no use knocking—the gate was overgrown with tall weeds and moss; so, being an active boy, he climbed over, and walked through the garden, till a little fawn came frisking by, and he heard a soft voice saying sorrowfully:

"Come back, come back, my fawn! I cannot run and play with you now, my feet have grown so heavy;" and looking round he saw the loveliest young princess in the world, dressed in snow-white, and wearing a wreath of roses on her golden hair; but walking slowly, as the great people did in Stumpinghame, for her feet were as large as the best of them.

After her came six young ladies, dressed in white and walking slowly, for they could not go before the princess; but Fairyfoot was amazed to see that their feet were as small as his own. At once he guessed that this must be the Princess Maybloom, and made her an humble bow, saying:

"Royal princess, I have heard of your trouble because your

feet have grown large; in my country that's all the fashion. For seven years past I have been wondering what would make mine grow, to no purpose; but I know of a certain fountain that will make yours smaller and finer than ever they were, if the king, your father, gives you leave to come with me, accompanied by two of your maids that are the least given to talking, and the most prudent officer in all his household; for it would offend the fairies and the nightingales to make that fountain known."

When the princess heard that, she danced for joy in spite of her large feet, and she and her six maids brought Fairyfoot before the king and queen, where they sat in their palace hall, with all the courtiers paying their morning compliments. The lords were very much astonished to see a ragged, bare-footed boy brought in among them, and the ladies thought Princess Maybloom must have gone mad; but Fairyfoot, making an humble reverence, told his message to the king and queen, and offered to set out with the princess that very day. At first the king would not believe that there could be any use in his offer, because so many great physicians had failed to give any relief. The courtiers laughed Fairyfoot to scorn, and the pages wanted to turn him out for an impudent impostor, but the queen, being a prudent woman, said:

"I pray your majesty to notice what fine feet this boy has. There may be some truth in his story. For the sake of our only daughter, I will choose two maids who talk the least of all our train, and my chamberlain, who is the most discreet officer in our household. Let them go with the princess; who knows but our sorrow may be lessened?"

After some persuasion the king consented, though all his councillors advised the contrary. So the two silent maids, the discreet chamberlain, and her fawn, which would not stay behind, were sent with Princess Maybloom, and they all set out after dinner. Fairyfoot had hard work guiding them along the track of the ground-ivy. The maids and the chamberlain did not like the brambles and rough roots of the forest—they thought it hard to eat berries and sleep in hollow trees; but the princess went on with good courage, and at last they reached the grove of rose-trees, and the spring bordered with lilies.

The chamberlain washed—and though his hair had been grey, and his face wrinkled, the young courtiers envied his beauty for years after. The maids washed—and from that day they were esteemed the fairest in all the palace. Lastly, the princess washed also—it could make her no fairer, but the moment her feet touched the water they grew less, and when she had washed and dried them three times, they were as small and finely shaped as Fairyfoot's own. There was great joy among them, but the boy said sorrowfully:

"Oh! if there had been a well in the world to make my feet large, my father and mother would not have cast me off, nor sent me to live among the shepherds."

"Cheer up your heart," said the Princess Maybloom; "if you want large feet, there is a well in this forest that will do it. Last summer time, I came with my father and his foresters to see a great cedar cut down, of which he meant to make a money chest. While they were busy with the cedar, I saw a bramble branch covered with berries. Some were ripe and some were green, but it was the longest bramble that ever grew; for the sake of the berries, I went on and on to its root, which grew hard by a muddy-looking well, with banks of dark green moss, in the deepest part of the forest. The day was warm and dry, so I took off my scarlet shoes, and washed my feet in the well; but as I washed they grew larger every minute, and nothing could ever make them less again. I have seen the bramble this day; it is not far off, and as you have shown me the Fair Fountain, I am very eager to show you the Growing Well."

Up rose Fairyfoot and Princess Maybloom, and went together till they found the bramble, and came to where its root grew, hard by the muddy-looking well, with banks of dark green moss, in the deepest dell of the forest. Fairyfoot sat down to wash, but at that minute he heard a sound of music, and knew it was the fairies going to their dancing-ground.

"If my feet grow large," said the boy to himself, "how shall I dance with them?" So, rising quickly, he took the Princess Maybloom by the hand. The fawn followed them; the maids and the chamberlain followed it, and all followed the music through the forest. At last they came to the flowery green. Robin Goodfellow welcomed the company for Fairyfoot's sake, and they danced there from sunset till the grey morning, and nobody was tired. But before the lark sang, Robin Goodfellow took them all safe home, as he used to take Fairyfoot.

There was great joy that day in the palace because Princess Maybloom's feet were made small again. The king gave Fairyfoot all manner of fine clothes and rich jewels; and when they heard this wonderful story, he and the queen asked him to live with them and be their son. In process of time Fairyfoot and Princess Maybloom were married, and still live happily. When they go to visit at Stumpinghame, they always wash their feet in the Growing Well, lest the royal family might think them a disgrace, but when they come back, they make haste to the Fair Fountain; and the fair-ies and the nightin-gales are great friends to them, as well as the maids and the cham-berlain, because they have told nobody about it, and there is peace and quiet yet in the grove of rose trees.

LULLABY FOR TITANIA
WILLIAM SHAKESPEARE

You spotted snakes with double tongue,
　Thorny hedgehogs, be not seen;
Newts and blind-worms, do no wrong;
　Come not near our fairy queen.

Weaving spiders, come not here;
　Hence, you long-legg'd spinners, hence!
Beetles black, approach not near;
　Worm nor snail, do not offence.

REFRAIN

Philomel, with melody,
　Sing in our sweet lullaby;
Lulla, lulla, lullaby; lulla, lulla, lullaby!
　Never harm,
　Nor spell nor charm,
　Come our lovely lady nigh;
　So, good-night, with lullaby.

The Sleeping Beauty

A long time ago there lived a King and Queen who said every day, "Ah, if only we had a child!" but for a long time they had none. So, when a beautiful little daughter came to them, the King could scarcely contain himself for joy and ordered a great feast to celebrate the event. He invited not only his kindred, friends and acquaintances, but also the fairies who give gifts to children. There were thirteen of these in his kingdom, but as he had only twelve golden plates, one of them was not invited.

The feast was held with all manner of splendor, and when it came to an end the fairies bestowed their gifts on the baby. One gave her virtue, another good nature, a third wisdom, a fourth beauty, and so on with everything that is good. But when eleven had said their say, suddenly the thirteenth who had not been invited presented herself at the door. She was an ugly old woman whose gifts to children were always evil, so the father of little Briar-rose had done well to find no place for her at the feast. But now everyone fell back in a fright before her, so she forced her way into the hall in a fury to think she had not been invited, and went straight up to the baby's cradle.

"This is my gift to the King's daughter," she cried. "In her fifteenth year she shall prick her finger with a spindle and die!" With these spiteful words, she tossed her head and stormed out of the hall.

The King was left in a panic; the Queen was left in a panic and all the guests were struck dumb with terror. But just at that moment, the twelfth fairy stepped forth, for she had not yet made her promise for the child.

"Nay," she said gently, "the Princess shall not die, but fall into a deep sleep."

Now the King was so anxious to guard his dear child from misfortune that he thought the best way would be to remove all

26

spindles out of his kingdom, and then she would never be able to prick her finger. So he gave orders the very next day that every spindle should be burned to ashes and never another one made or used throughout the length and breadth of the land.

Meantime, the gifts of the fairies were plenteously fulfilled in the young girl, for she was so beautiful, modest and kind that all who saw her loved her. But it happened on the very day when she was fifteen years old, that the King and Queen, being now quite at rest about their daughter, since they thought they had put all danger out of her reach, went away from home, leaving Briar-rose all alone. No sooner were they gone, than the Princess began to feel a great desire to go poking about the palace into all the strange places she had never visited before. So she went into all sorts of great, echoing halls and queer little chambers, and at last she came to an old stone tower, with a narrow stair that went winding upward. Up the rickety steps she started. She climbed and she climbed and at last she came to a little old door with a queer old rusty key in the lock. When she turned the key, the door sprang open. There in a dusty little room, sat a little old woman in gray, and she was working busily.

"Good-day, good dame," said Briar-rose, "what are you doing?"

"I am spinning," said the woman, nodding her head. And she drew out a thread of flax, twisting it deftly between her fingers.

"And what is that little thing you send twirling around so merrily?"

"A spindle! A spindle!"

"Ah!" cried little Briar-rose, "I have never seen anything merrier!" And she crept up closer and closer. At last, as she watched the twisting and twirling, she grew so anxious to try it herself that she said, "Good dame, pray let me try to spin."

The old woman smiled till the curves of her mouth went way up under her long hook-nose, then she handed Briar-rose the distaff and the spindle. The Princess tucked the distaff under her left arm as she had seen the old woman do, and started to pull out a thread. But alas! she knew nothing of spindles, nor had she ever been taught how to handle one properly, so at the very first turn, she clumsily thrust the point into her hand and pricked her finger.

In an instant spindle and distaff dropped to the floor; little Briar-rose sank upon a bed and lay there in a deep sleep which spread over all the castle. Then the little old woman in gray disappeared and the room in the tower was quiet and still.

Down below, the King and Queen, who had just returned to the great hall of the castle, went to sleep on their thrones and all their courtiers with them. The horses went to sleep in their stables, the dogs went to sleep in the yard; the pigeons went to sleep on the roof; the flies went to sleep on the wall. Even the fire on the kitchen hearth stopped flaming and slept in its embers; the great iron kettle above left off boiling, and the cook, who was just going to pull the hair of a careless scullery boy, let him go and sank down fast asleep. The wind fell, the flowers and grasses sank down on the earth and on the trees before the castle not a single leaf stirred again.

Round about all there began to grow a hedge of thorns; snow fell with ice and sleet. So years passed by and every year the hedge grew denser and higher, till at last it hid every tower from sight. Nothing at all could be seen of the castle, not even the flags on its roof. And over the spot, year in and year out, it was always frozen winter.

But the story of the beautiful Princess, sleep-bound in her castle, still went abroad through the land.

From time to time, Kings' sons came and tried to force themselves in through the thorny hedge to awaken her. All these the hedge used sadly. The thorns held fast together as if they had hands and tore their fine clothes, and scratched and pulled and kept them tight caught as if in a net. And Briar-rose slept on.

At last and at last, after many, many years, there came to the land a certain King's son to whom an old man told the tale of the Princess and how sadly the Kings' sons had fared who tried to do battle with the hedge. But this youth said, "I am

DONN P. CRANE

not afraid of the hedge. The hedge is nothing to me. I shall go and awaken the beautiful Princess."

The good old man did all in his power to dissuade the Prince, but the youth would not listen to his words. Off he set toward the frozen castle. As he drew near he felt its icy breath, he saw the snow over all and the giant thorn hedge that rose threatening before him. But he strode confidently on, and when he came square upon those dark bushes, lo! they turned suddenly fresh and green, blossomed with large and splendid flowers, and parted of their own accord to let him safely through. Above, the snow stopped falling; beneath his feet, ice melted, flowers and grasses lifted up their heads. By the time he reached the castle yard, all signs of winter had fled, the earth was in bloom about him. He saw the horses and dogs asleep, the pigeons on the rooftop still with heads buried under their wings. When he entered the castle, the flies were still asleep on the wall, the fire still slept in its embers, and the cook was still holding out her hand as though to cuff the scullery boy.

Within the great hall, the King and Queen lay asleep on their thrones with their whole court sleeping about them. All was so quiet everywhere that a breath could have been heard. At last the King's son came to the stone tower with the narrow stair that went winding upward. Up the rickety steps he climbed and opened the door of the little chamber. There before him on the bed lay Briar-rose asleep. Her cheeks were faintly flushed, her hair was like gold, and her clothes were all quaint and old-fashioned, like those his great great grandmother had worn. So beautiful was she that the King's son could not turn his eyes from her. As he looked, he stooped down and gently gave her a kiss. The moment she felt his kiss, Briar-rose opened her eyes and awoke. Then she looked at him sweetly and slowly rose from her couch. Hand in hand, down the stairs together they went. When they entered the great hall of the castle, the King awoke and the Queen and the whole court, and all looked at each other astonished. The horses in the courtyard stood up and shook themselves; the dogs jumped up and wagged their tails; the pigeons on the roof awoke and flew away into the open country; the flies on the wall crept again; the fire on the kitchen hearth flickered and flamed up; the great iron kettle began to boil, and the cook soundly boxed the ears of the scullery boy.

The very next day the marriage of the King's son with Briar-rose was celebrated with all manner of rejoicing, and inside the castle and out was the life and bloom of the spring.

SONG ON MAY MORNING
JOHN MILTON

Now the bright morning star, Day's harbinger,
Comes dancing from the East, and leads with her
The flowery May, who from her green lap throws
The yellow cowslip and the pale primrose.
Hail, bounteous May, that doth inspire
Mirth, and youth, and warm desire;
Woods and groves are of thy dressing,
Hill and dale doth boast thy blessing.
Thus we salute thee with our early song,
And welcome thee, and wish thee long.

MR. MOON*
BLISS CARMAN

O Moon, Mr. Moon,
When you comin' down?
Down on the hilltop,
Down in the glen,
Out in the clearin',
To play with little men?
Moon, Mr. Moon,
When you comin' down?

O Mr. Moon,
Hurry up your stumps!
Don't you hear Bullfrog
Callin' to his wife,
And old black Cricket
A-wheezin' at his fife?
Hurry up your stumps,
And get on your pumps!
Moon, Mr. Moon,
When you comin' down?

O Mr. Moon,
Hurry up along!
The reeds in the current
Are whisperin' slow;
The river 's a-wimplin'
To and fro.
Hurry up along,
Or you'll miss the song!
Moon, Mr. Moon,
When you comin' down?

O Mr. Moon,
We're all here!
Honey-bug, Thistledrift,
White-imp, Weird,
Wryface, Billiken,
Quidnunc, Queered;
We're all here,
And the coast is clear!
Moon, Mr. Moon,
When you comin' down?

O Mr. Moon,
There's not much time!
Hurry, if you're comin',
You lazy old bones!
You can sleep to-morrow
While the Buzbuz drones;
There's not much time
Till the church bells chime.
Moon, Mr. Moon,
When you comin' down?

O Mr. Moon,
When you comin' down?
Down where the Good Folk
Dance in a ring,
Down where the Little Folk
Sing?
Moon, Mr. Moon,
When you comin' down?

Prince Harweda and The Magic Prison*
ELIZABETH HARRISON

ITTLE Harweda was born a prince. His father was King over all the land and his mother was the most beautiful Queen the world had ever seen and Prince Harweda was their only child. From the day of his birth everything that love or money could do for him had been done. The very wind of heaven was made to fan over an aeolian harp that it might enter his room, not as a strong, fresh breeze, but as a breath of music. Reflectors were so arranged in the windows that twice as much moonlight fell on his crib as on that of any ordinary child. The pillow on which his head rested was made out of the down from humming birds' breasts and the water in which his face and hands were washed was always steeped in rose leaves before being brought to the nursery. Everything that could be done was done, and nothing which could add to his ease or comfort was left undone.

But his parents, although they were King and Queen, were not very wise, for they never thought of making the young prince think of anybody but himself, so, of course, he grew to be selfish and peevish, and by the time he was five years old he was so disagreeable that nobody loved him. "Dear, dear! what shall we do?" said the poor Queen mother and the King only sighed and answered, "Ah, what indeed!" They were both very much grieved at heart for they well knew that little Harweda, although he was a prince, would never grow up to be a really great King unless he could make his people love him.

At last they decided to send for his fairy god-mother and see if she could suggest anything which would cure Prince Harweda of always thinking about himself. "Well, well, well!"

*From *In Storyland*. Used by special arrangement with the author.

exclaimed the god-mother when they had laid the case before her—"This is a pretty state of affairs! and I his god-mother, too! Why wasn't I called in sooner?" She then told them that she would have to think a day and a night and a day again before she could offer them any assistance. "But," added she, "if I take the child in charge you must promise not to interfere for a whole year." The King and Queen gladly promised that they would not speak to or even see their son for the required time if the fairy god-mother would only cure him.

"We'll see about that," said the god-mother. "Humph, expecting to be a King some day and not caring for anybody but himself—a fine King he'll make!" With that off she flew and the King and Queen saw nothing more of her for a day and a night and another day. Then back she came in a great hurry. "Give me the prince," said she; "I have his house all ready for him. One month from to-day I'll bring him back to you. Perhaps he'll be cured and perhaps he won't. If he is not cured then we shall try two months next time. We'll see, we'll see." Without any more ado she picked up the astonished young prince and flew away with him as lightly as if he were nothing but a feather or a straw. In vain the poor Queen wept and begged for a last kiss. Before she had wiped her eyes, the fairy god-mother and Prince Harweda were out of sight.

They flew a long distance until they reached a great forest. When they had come to the middle of it, down flew the fairy, and in a minute more the young prince was standing on the green grass beside a beautiful pink marble palace that looked something like a good-sized summer house.

"This is your home," said the god-mother, "in it you will find everything you need and you can do just as you choose with your time." Little Harweda was delighted at this for there was nothing in the world he liked better than to do as he

pleased, so he tossed his cap up into the air and ran into the lovely little house without so much as saying "Thank you" to his god-mother. "Humph," said she as he dis-appeared, "you'll have enough of it before you are through with it, my fine prince." With that off she flew.

Prince Harweda had no sooner set his foot inside the small, rose-colored palace than the iron door shut with a bang and locked itself. For you must know by this time that it was an enchanted house, as all houses are that are built by fairies.

Prince Harweda did not mind being locked in, as he cared very little for the great, beautiful outside world, and the new home which was to be *all his own* was very fine, and he was eager to examine it. Then, too, he thought that when he was tired of it, all he would have to do would be to kick on the door and a servant from somewhere would come and open it,—he had always had a servant ready to obey his slightest command.

His fairy god-mother had told him that it was *his* house, therefore he was interested in looking at everything in it.

The floor was made of a beautiful red copper that shone in the sunlight like burnished gold and seemed almost a dark red in the shadow. He had never seen anything half so fine before. The ceiling was of mother-of-pearl and showed a constant chang-ing of tints of red and blue and yellow and green, all blending into the gleaming white, as only mother-of-pearl can. From the middle of this handsome ceiling hung a large gilded bird cage containing a beautiful bird, which just at this moment was singing a glad song of welcome to the Prince. Harweda cared, however, very little about birds, so he took no notice of the songster.

Around on every side were costly divans with richly embroidered coverings, on which were many sizes of soft down pillows. "Ah," thought the prince, "here I can lounge at my ease with no one to call me to stupid lessons!" Wonderfully carved jars and vases of wrought gold and silver stood about on the floor and each was filled with a different kind of perfume. "This is delicious," said Prince Harweda. "Now I can have all the sweet odors I want without the trouble of going out into the garden for roses or lilies."

In the center of the room was a fountain of sparkling water which leaped up and fell back into its marble basin with a kind of rhythmical sound that made a faint, dreamy music very pleasant to listen to.

On a table near at hand were various baskets of the most tempting pears and grapes and peaches, and near them were dishes of all kinds of sweetmeats. "Good," said the greedy young prince, "that is what I like best of all," and therewith he fell to eating the fruit and sweetmeats as fast as he could cram them into his mouth. But strange to say, the table was just as full as when he began, for no sooner did he reach his hand out and take a soft mellow pear or a rich juicy peach than another pear or peach took its place in the basket. The same thing occurred when he helped himself to chocolate drops or marshmallows or any of the other confectionery upon the table.

When Prince Harweda had eaten until he could eat no more he threw himself down upon one of the couches and an invisible hand gently stroked his hair until he fell asleep. When he awoke he noticed for the first time the walls, which, by the way, were really the strangest part of his new home. They had in them twelve long, checkered windows which reached from the ceiling to the floor. The spaces between the windows were filled in with mirrors exactly the same size as the windows, so that the whole room was walled in with windows and looking glasses. Through the three windows that looked to the north could be seen the far distant mountains Beautiful, as they were called, towering high above the surrounding country; sometimes their snow-covered tops were pink or creamy yellow as they caught the rays of the sunrise; sometimes they were dark purple or blue as they reflected the storm cloud. From the three windows that faced the south could be seen the great ocean, tossing and moving, constantly catching a thousand gleams of silver from the moonlight. Again and again, each little wave would be capped with white from its romp with the wind. Yet, as the huge mountains seemed to reach higher than man could climb, so the vast ocean seemed to stretch out farther than any ship could possibly carry him. The eastern windows gave each morning a glorious vision of sky as the darkness of the night slowly melted into the still, gray dawn, and that changed into a golden glow and that in turn became a tender pink. It was really the most beautiful as well as the most mysterious sight on earth if one watched it closely. The windows on the west looked out upon a great forest of tall fir trees and at the time of sunset the glorious colors of the sunset sky could be seen between the dark green branches.

But little Prince Harweda cared for none of these beautiful views. In fact, he scarcely glanced out of the windows at all, he was so taken up with the broad, handsome mirrors, for in each of them he could see himself reflected and he was very fond of looking at himself in a looking glass. He was much pleased when he noticed that the mirrors were so arranged that each one not only reflected his whole body, head, arms, feet and all, but that it also reflected his image as seen in several of the other mirrors. He could thus see his front and back and each side, all at the same time. As he was a handsome boy he enjoyed these many views of himself immensely, and would stand and sit and lie down just for the fun of seeing the many images of himself do the same thing.

He spent so much time looking at and admiring himself in the wonderful looking-glasses that he had very little time for the books and games which had been provided for his amusement. Hours were spent each day first before one mirror and then another, and he did not notice that the windows were growing narrower and the mirrors wider until the former had become so small that they hardly admitted light enough for him to see himself in the looking-glass. Still, this did not alarm him very much as he cared nothing whatever for the outside world. It only made him spend more time before the mirror, as it was now getting quite difficult for him to see himself at all. The

windows at last became mere slits in the wall and the mirrors grew so large that they not only reflected little Harweda but all of the room besides in a dim, indistinct kind of a way.

Finally, however, Prince Harweda awoke one morning and found himself in total darkness. Not a ray of light came from the outside and, of course, not an object in the room could be seen. He rubbed his eyes and sat up to make sure that he was not dreaming. Then he called loudly for some one to come and open a window for him, but no one came. He got up and groped his way to the iron door and tried to open it, but it was, as you know, locked. He kicked it and beat upon it, but he only bruised his fists and hurt his toes. He grew quite angry now. How dare any one shut him, a prince, up in a dark prison like this! He abused his fairy god-mother, calling her all sorts of horrid names. Then he upbraided his father and mother, the King and Queen, for letting him go away with such a god-mother. In fact, he blamed everybody and everything but himself for his present condition, but it was of no use. The sound of his own voice was his only answer. The whole of the outside world seemed to have forgotten him.

As he felt his way back to his couch he knocked over one of the golden jars which had held the liquid perfume, but the perfume was all gone now and only an empty jar rolled over the floor. He laid himself down on the divan but its soft pillows had been removed and a hard iron frame-work received him. He was dismayed and lay for a long time thinking of what he had best do with himself. All before him was blank darkness, as black as the darkest night you ever saw. He reached out his hand to get some fruit to eat, but only one or two withered apples remained on the table. Suddenly he noticed that the tinkling music of the fountain had ceased. He hastily groped his way over to it and he found in place of the dancing, running stream stood a silent pool of water. A hush had fallen upon everything, a dead silence was in the room. He threw himself down upon the floor and lay there for a long, long time.

At last he heard, or thought he heard, a faint sound. He listened eagerly. It seemed to be some tiny creature not far from him, trying to move about. For the first time for nearly a month he remembered the bird in its gilded cage. "Poor little thing," he cried as he sprang up, "you, too, are shut within this terrible prison. This thick darkness must be as hard for you to bear as it is for me." He went towards the cage and as he approached it the bird gave a sad little chirp.

"You must need some water to drink," continued he as he filled its drinking cup. "This is all I have to give you."

Just then he heard a harsh, grating sound, as of rusty bolts sliding with difficulty out of their sockets, and then faint rays of light not wider than a hair began to shine between the heavy plate mirrors. Prince Harweda was filled with joy. "Perhaps, perhaps," said he softly, "I may yet see the light again. Ah, how beautiful the outside world would look to me now!"

The next day he was so hungry that he began to eat one of the old withered apples, and as he bit it, he thought of the bird, his fellow-prisoner. "You must be hungry, too, poor little thing," said he as he divided his miserable food and put part of it into the bird's cage. Again came the harsh, grating sound, and the boy noticed that the cracks of light were growing larger. On going up to one and putting his eye close to it as he would to a pinhole in a paper, he was rejoiced to find that he could tell the greenness of the grass from the blue of the sky. "Ah, my pretty bird," he cried joyfully, "I have had a glimpse of the great, beautiful outside world and you shall have it, too."

With these words he climbed up into a chair and loosening the cage from the golden chain by which it hung, he carried it carefully to the nearest crack of light and placed it close to the narrow opening. Again was heard the harsh, grating sound and the walls moved a bit and the windows were now at least an inch wide. At this the poor Prince clasped his hands with delight. He sat himself down near the bird cage and gazed out of the narrow opening. Never before had the trees looked so tall and stately, or the white clouds floating through the sky so lovely. The next day as he was carefully cleaning the bird's cage so that the little creature might be somewhat more comfortable, the walls again creaked and groaned and the mirrors grew narrower by just so many inches as the windows widened. But Prince Harweda saw only the flood of sunshine that poured in, and the added beauty of the larger landscape. He cared nothing whatever now for the stupid mirrors which could only reflect what was placed before them. Each day he found something new and beautiful in the view from the narrow windows. Now it was a squirrel frisking about and running up some tall tree trunk so rapidly that Prince Harweda could not follow it with his eyes; again it was a mother bird feeding her young. By this time the windows were a foot wide or more. One day as two white doves suddenly soared aloft in the blue sky the poor little bird who had now become the tenderly cared for comrade of the young Prince, gave a pitiful little thrill. "Dear little fellow," cried Prince Harweda, "do you also long for your freedom? You shall at least be as free as I am." So saying, he opened the cage door and the bird flew out.

The Prince laughed as he watched it flutter about from chair to table and back to chair again. He was so much occupied with the bird that he did not notice that the walls had again shaken and the windows were now their full size, until the added light caused him to look around. He turned and saw the room looking almost exactly as it did the day he entered it with so much pride because it was all his own. Now it seemed close and stuffy and he would gladly have exchanged it for the humblest home in his father's kingdom where he could meet people and hear them talk and see them smile at each other, even if they should take no notice of him. One day soon after this, the little bird fluttered up against the window pane and beat his wings against it in a vain effort to get out. A new idea seized the young Prince, and taking up one of the golden jars he went to the window and struck on one of its checkered panes of glass with all his force. "You shall be free, even if I can not," said he to the bird. Two or three strong blows shivered the small pane and the bird swept out into the free open air beyond. "Ah, my pretty one, how glad I am that you are free at last," exclaimed the prince as he stood watching the flight of his fellow-prisoner. His face was bright with glad, unselfish joy over the bird's liberty. The small, pink marble palace shook from top to bottom, the iron door flew open and the fresh wind from the sea rushed in and seemed to catch the boy in its invisible arms. Prince Harweda could hardly believe his eyes as he sprang to the door. There stood his fairy god-mother, smiling and with her hand reached out toward him. "Come, my god-child," said she gently, "we shall now go back to your father and mother."

Great indeed was the rejoicing in the palace when Prince Harweda was returned to them a sweet, loving boy, kind and thoughtful to all about him. Many a struggle he had with himself and many a conquest, but as time passed by he grew to be a great and wise king, tenderly caring for all his people and loved by them in return.

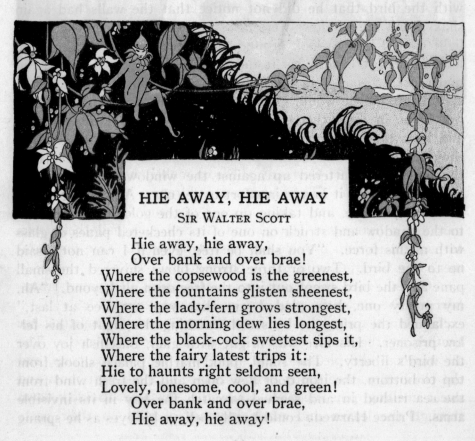

HIE AWAY, HIE AWAY
Sir Walter Scott

Hie away, hie away,
Over bank and over brae!
Where the copsewood is the greenest,
Where the fountains glisten sheenest,
Where the lady-fern grows strongest,
Where the morning dew lies longest,
Where the black-cock sweetest sips it,
Where the fairy latest trips it:
Hie to haunts right seldom seen,
Lovely, lonesome, cool, and green!
Over bank and over brae,
Hie away, hie away!

Hansel and Grethel*

Once upon a time there lived in a little cottage on the edge of the Black Forest in Germany a broom-maker, named Peter, and his wife, Gertrude. They had two children, a boy, Hansel, and Grethel, a pretty little girl. Now Peter and Gertrude worked hard for a living and Hansel and Grethel each had their tasks to perform to help provide for their daily needs. One fine summer's day Gertrude said to the children:

"Go out into the forest, my dears, and pick some strawberries that our table may not be bare for supper."

So Hansel took a basket from the wall, and Grethel took her brother by the hand, and off they went into the woods. The air was cool and pleasant, the little birds sang in the trees, and the children walked along over a carpet of thick, soft moss and sweet-smelling pine needles, while the sunshine trickled down through the leaves and made blotches of gold on their path.

*Adapted from the opera, *Hansel and Grethel*, by Humperdinck.

45

Farther and farther into the forest they wandered, picking strawberries and gathering flowers, of which they made garlands and nosegays. At last Hansel cried joyously:

"See our basket! It is full! We shall all have berries for supper."

But just at that moment the cry of a cuckoo sounded near at hand, echoing through the forest.

"Cuck-oo! Cuck-oo!" cried Grethel, imitating the cry of the bird. "Cuck-oo, thou stealer of eggs!"

"Cuck-oo! Cuck-oo!" answered Hansel roguishly. "Cuck-oo, thou stealer of *strawberries!*" And he stole a strawberry out of the basket and sucked it into his mouth as though he were a cuckoo sucking the egg he had found in another bird's nest.

"Ho! Ho!" cried Grethel, "I can do that, too! Just watch me!" And she took a berry also and sucked it into her mouth. Then the cuckoo in the forest cried again.

"Cuck-oo! Cuck-oo!" mimicked Grethel, and Hansel laughed and cried as before, "Cuck-oo! Cuck-oo! thou stealer of strawberries!" This time, however, he stole not one berry, but a whole handful to eat, and Grethel, not to be outdone, took just as many as he. So the children played the game of the cuckoo, turn and turn about, till they grew so excited over their play, they began to snatch the basket back and forth and quarrel over who should have it. Hansel was stronger than Grethel and finally he jerked it out of her hands. In a twinkling he poured all the rest of the berries into his mouth and greedily swallowed them, every one.

"What have you done? What have you done?" cried Grethel. Then she began to weep for she saw what they had done. "We have eaten up all the berries and there will be nothing at all for mother and father for supper!"

At that, Hansel also stood still and was sorrowful and repentant.

"We must gather more," he said, but now as the children looked about, they saw that while they had been eating and quarreling, the sun had sunk in the west. Dull gold gleamed the sky through the pine trees, the songs of the birds were hushed, and about them was dim, gray twilight.

"Nay, we cannot see to gather berries now," cried Grethel and she crowded up close to her brother. Hansel squared his shoulders, threw up his head and took his sister by the hand.

"Come," he said, "I shall find the way out of the forest."

On they wandered and on, but they could no longer see the path. The farther they went, the deeper they lost themselves in the wood. And now all the light had faded out of the sky. It was dark, quite dark. Black loomed the giant pine trees, ghostly gleamed the little white birches, the woods were filled with strange night sounds, over the marshes white mists arose, and hither and thither before them darted the gleaming fire of the will-o'-the-wisp. Still Hansel held his shoulders square and strode sturdily forward, holding his sister fast by the hand. But at last the two were both wearied out. Not another step could they plod. So they stopped in a little glade and said their evening prayer together. Then they laid themselves down on the moss and fell fast asleep with their arms about each other.

By and by a bird twittered in the trees, the sun came streaking through the leaves—it was morning. Grethel stretched herself and awoke. "Wake up, Hansel," cried she, and when he, too, had opened his eyes, they set off once more through the forest.

They had gone some little distance when lo! they came on a queer little house. Both stood still in amazement,—the cottage was all made of frosted cake. Its roof was of tarts and cookies and its windows of transparent sugar. Around it stood a fence of life-sized gingerbread girls and boys. The children thought they had never seen anything so inviting.

"Ah," cried Hansel at once, "this will be something for us! We will have a good meal!" And he ran forward and broke

off a little piece of trimming from the house, while Grethel helped herself to a cooky shingle from the roof. Then there was heard a little voice from within the cottage:

"Nibble, nibble, little mouse,
Who nibbles at my little house?"

But the children paid no heed. Hansel seized a whole frosting balcony and Grethel wrenched off a tart. Then was heard again the little voice from within the cottage:

"Nibble, nibble, little mouse,
Who nibbles at my little house?"

Still the children turned a deaf ear and went on cramming

themselves. Now Hansel boldly broke off a great piece of the house itself and Grethel pushed a whole round pane out of one of the windows. Then all at once the door opened, and out of the sugary-pugary cottage, came an ugly old witch. Hansel and Grethel were so astonished that they dropped what they held to the ground. But their first alarm was soon lulled to rest, for the old woman said in a voice as sweet as honey:

"Ah, my dear, sweet little children, who brought you here? Come in and stay with me! I will feed you full of sweetmeats."

She took them by the hand and, thinking only of what more they might find to eat within, they followed her into the house. A nice dinner she set before them, pancakes and sugar, syrup and honey, and soon Hansel and Grethel were so greedily stuffing themselves that they forgot entirely to be on their guard against the old witch. She called them by such pet names as Sugar Plum and Sugar Dolly and said she loved such sweet little dears

—loved them so much she could just eat them up! But Hansel and Grethel paid no heed. After dinner, she showed them two little white beds in which they slept through the night.

But early in the morning before Hansel and Grethel were awake, the old witch got up, went over to a great oven in one corner of the house and lit a blazing fire under it.

"Sweet little dears. They will be dainty morsels. They will make beautiful gingerbread children," she said, for this old syrup and honey witch lured children with sweetmeats to her sugar cottage. Then she popped them into the oven and turned them to gingerbread.

When the fire was going, she seized Hansel right out of bed with one bony hand and carried him wriggling and squirming off to a cage that stood behind the house. Here she locked him up and left him, though he shook the iron bars as hard as he could, and shrieked to her boldly to let him loose. After that she came back and rudely awakened Grethel.

"Get up, little lazy bones!" she cried. "Get up and set the table. Lay out on the cloth my little plate and my little knife and my little napkin to wipe my mouth, and do it all quickly— I'm to have a delicious gingerbread boy for my breakfast."

Now Grethel began to suspect that the witch was not as sweet as she seemed. She saw Hansel shut up in the cage and heard the noise he was making, and there she must lay out the little plate and wonder what was to be eaten on it, and lay out the little knife and wonder what was to be cut with it, and lay out the napkin and wonder, wonder, wonder. When the table was laid, the old witch called to Grethel.

"Creep into the oven, little sweetie, and see if it is properly heated. If it is, then we'll put in our dough."

She meant when Grethel had crawled in to bang the door shut, and have a gingerbread girl as well as a boy for her breakfast. But by this time Grethel guessed what the old woman intended. So she answered:

"I don't know how to get into the oven."

"Ah, my dear little Sugar Dolly," cried the witch. "Just crawl in. The opening is big enough,—I could even do it myself."

As she spoke, she hobbled up and poked her head into the opening. Quick as lightning Grethel gave her a shove and sent her head first, sprawling, into the oven. Then Grethel banged the door and bolted it and ran off to the iron cage. In a twinkling she had set Hansel free and the two hurried out of the cottage.

There, all about the house, they saw the row of gingerbread children turning pink and rosy, beginning to yawn and stretch themselves and move their arms and legs. They had all become real children again, set free from the old witch's charms when Grethel popped her into the oven. Joyously they thronged around Hansel and Grethel as soon as they awoke. Then all in a body they went into the house to peep into the oven and see what had become of their enemy. There, lo and behold! was no witch at all but just a huge ginger cake! But the children had no more desire to eat sweeties, you may believe, so they left the ginger cake and ran, laughing into the forest.

They had not gone far, when Hansel and Grethel heard voices calling, and in another moment there came Peter and Gertrude to meet them. The children ran and threw themselves into the arms of their father and mother. Long had Peter and Gertrude searched for their little ones, and now they held them close and covered them with kisses. Then they turned with glad cries and started off once more to lead all the children back to their homes. As they walked through the woods, Hansel and Grethel filled their basket with strawberries and when they returned to their own humble cottage, they all shared the simple supper and great was their rejoicing.

The Princess on the Glass Hill*
Sir George Webb Dasent

ONCE on a time there was a man who had a meadow, which lay high up on the hill-side, and in the meadow was a barn, which he had built to keep his hay in. Now, I must tell you there hadn't been much in the barn for the last year or two, for every St. John's night, when the grass stood green-est and deepest, the meadow was eaten down to the very ground just as if a whole drove of sheep had been there feeding on it over night. This happened once, it happened twice; so at last the man grew weary of losing his crop of hay, and said to his sons—for he had three of them, and the youngest was nicknamed Boots, of course—that now one of them must go and sleep in the barn in the outlying field when St. John's night came, for it was too good a joke that his grass should be eaten, root and blade, this year, as it had been the last two years. So whichever of them went must keep a sharp lookout; that was what their father said.

Well, the eldest son was ready to go and watch the meadow; trust him for looking after the grass! It shouldn't be his fault if man or beast got a blade of grass. So, when evening came, he set off to the barn, and lay down to sleep; but a little on in the night came such a clatter, and such an earthquake, that walls and roof shook, and groaned, and creaked; then up jumped the lad, and took to his heels as fast as ever he could; nor dared he once look round till he reached home; and as for the hay, why it was eaten up this year just as it had been twice before.

The next St. John's night, the man said again it would never do to lose all the grass in the outlying field year after year in this

*From *Popular Tales from the Norse*, published by G. P. Putnam's Sons.

way, so one of his sons must just trudge off to watch it, and watch it well, too. Well, the next oldest son was ready to try his luck, so he set off, and lay down to sleep in the barn as his brother had done before him; but as night wore on there came on a rumbling and quaking of the earth, worse even than on the last St. John's night, and when the lad heard it he got frightened, and took to his heels as though he were running a race.

Next year the turn came to Boots; but when he made ready to go, the other two began to laugh, and to make game of him, saying,—

"You're just the man to watch the hay, that you are; you who have done nothing all your life but sit in the ashes and toast yourself by the fire."

But Boots did not care a pin for their chattering, and stumped away, as evening drew on, up the hill-side to the outlying field. There he went inside the barn and lay down; but in about an hour's time the barn began to groan and creak, so that it was dreadful to hear.

"Well," said Boots to himself, "if it isn't worse than this, I can stand it well enough."

A little while after came another creak and an earthquake, so that the litter in the barn flew about the lad's ears.

"Oh!" said Boots to himself, "if it isn't worse than this, I daresay I can stand it out."

But just then came a third rumbling, and a third earthquake, so that the lad thought walls and roof were coming down on his head; but it passed off, and all was still as death about him.

"It'll come again, I'll be bound," thought Boots; but no, it did not come again; still it was and still it stayed; but after he had lain a little while he heard a noise as if a horse were standing just outside the barn-door. He peeped through a chink, and there stood a horse feeding away. So big, and fat, and grand a horse, Boots had never set eyes on; by his side on the grass lay a saddle and bridle, and a full set of armour for a knight, all of brass, so bright that the light gleamed from it.

"Ho, ho!" thought the lad; "it's you, is it, that eats up our hay? I'll soon put a spoke in your wheel; just see if I don't."

So he lost no time, but took the steel out of his tinder-box, and threw it over the horse; then it had no power to stir from the spot, and became so tame that the lad could do what he liked with it. So he got on its back, and rode off with it to a place which no one knew of, and there he put up the horse. When he got home his brothers laughed, and asked how he had fared?

"You didn't lie long in the barn, even if you had the heart to go as far as the field."

"Well," said Boots, "all I can say is, I lay in the barn till the sun rose, and neither saw nor heard anything; I can't think what there was in the barn to make you both so afraid."

"A pretty story!" said his brothers. "But we'll soon see how you have watched the meadow." So they set off; but when they reached it, there stood the grass as deep and thick as it had been over night.

Well, the next St. John's eve it was the same story over again; neither of the older brothers dared to go out to the outlying field to watch the crop; but Boots, he had the heart to go, and everything happened just as it had happened the year before. First a clatter and an earthquake, then a greater clatter and another earthquake, and so on a third time; only this year the earthquakes were far worse than the year before. Then all at once everything was as still as death and the lad heard how something was cropping the grass outside the barn-door, so he stole to the door, and peeped through a chink; and what do you think he saw? Why, another horse standing right up against the wall, and chewing and champing with might and main. It was far finer and fatter than that which came the year before, and it had a saddle on its back and a bridle on its neck, and a full suit of mail for a knight lay by its side, all of silver, and as grand as you would wish to see.

"Ho, ho!" said Boots to himself; "it's you that gobbles up our hay, is it? I'll soon put a spoke in your wheel;" and with that he took the steel out of his tinder-box, and threw it over the horse's crest, which stood as still as a lamb. Well, the lad rode this horse, too, to the hiding-place where he kept the other one, and after that he went home.

"I suppose you'll tell us," said one of his brothers, "there's a fine crop this year, too, up in the hayfield."

"Well, so there is," said Boots; and off ran the others to see. There stood the grass and thick and deep, as it was the year before; but they didn't give Boots softer words for all that.

Now, when the third St. John's eve came, the two elder still hadn't the heart to lie out in the barn and watch the grass, for they had got so scared at heart the night they lay there before, but Boots, he dared to go; and, to make a long story short, the very same thing happened this time as had happened twice before. Three earthquakes came, one after the other each worse than the one which went before, and when the last came, the

lad danced about with the shock from one barn wall to the other; and, after that, all at once, it was still as death. Now when he had lain a little while he heard something tugging away at the grass outside the barn, so he stole again to the door-chink, and peeped out, and there stood a horse close outside—far, far bigger and fatter than the two he had taken before.

"Ho, ho!" said the lad to himself, "it's you, is it, that comes here eating up our hay? I'll soon stop that—I'll soon put a spoke in your wheel." So he caught up his steel and threw it over the horse's neck, and in a trice it stood as if it were nailed to the ground, and Boots could do as he pleased with it. Then he rode off with it to the hiding-place where he kept the other two, and then went home. When he got home his two brothers made game of him as they had done before, saying they could see he had watched the grass well, for he looked for all the world as if he were walking in his sleep, and many other spiteful things they said, but Boots gave no heed to them, only asking them to go and see for themselves; and when they went, there stood the grass as fine and deep this time as it had been twice before.

Now, you must know that the King of the country where Boots lived had a daughter, whom he would only give to the man who could ride up over the hill of glass, for there was a high, high, high hill, all of glass, as smooth and slippery as ice, close to the King's palace. Upon the tip-top of the hill the King's daughter was to sit, with three golden apples in her lap, and the man who could ride up and carry off the three golden apples was to have half the kingdom, and the Princess to wife. This the King had stuck up on all the church-doors in his realm, and had given it out in many other kingdoms besides. Now, this Princess was so lovely that all who set eyes on her fell over head and ears in love with her whether they would or no. So I needn't tell you how all the princes and knights who heard of her were eager to win her and half the kingdom beside; and how they came riding from all parts of the world on high prancing horses, and clad in the grandest clothes, for there wasn't one of them who hadn't made up his mind that he, and he alone, was to win the Princess.

So when the day of trial came, which the King had fixed, there was such a crowd of princes and knights under the glass hill that it made one's head whirl to look at them; and every one in the country who could even crawl along was off to the hill, for they were eager to see the man who was to win the Princess. So the two elder brothers set off with the rest; but as for Boots, they said outright he shouldn't go with them, for if they were seen with such a dirty lad, all begrimed with smut from cleaning their shoes and sifting cinders in the dusthole, they said folk would make game of them.

"Very well," said Boots, "it's all one to me. I can go alone, and stand or fall by myself."

Now when the two brothers came to the hill of glass the knights and princes were all hard at it, riding their horses till they were all in a foam; but it was no good, by my troth; for as soon as ever the horses set foot on the hill, down they slipped, and there wasn't one who could get a yard or two up; and no wonder, for the hill was as smooth as a sheet of glass, and as steep as a house-wall. But all were eager to have the Princess and half the kingdom. So they rode and slipped, and slipped and rode, and still it was the same story over again. At last all their horses were so weary that they could scarce lift a leg, and in such a sweat that the lather dripped from them, and so the knights had to give up trying any more. So the King was just thinking that he would proclaim a new trial for the next day, to see if they would have better luck, when all at once a knight came riding up on so brave a steed no one had ever seen the like of it in his born days, and the knight had mail of brass, and the horse a brass bit in his mouth, so bright that the sunbeams shone from it. Then all the others called out to him he might just as well spare himself the trouble of riding at the hill, for it would lead to no good; but he gave no heed to them, and put his horse at the hill, and went up it like nothing for a good way, about a third of the height; and when he got so far, he turned his horse round and rode down again. So lovely a knight the Princess thought she had never yet seen, and while he was riding she sat and thought to herself—

"Would to heaven he might only come up, and down the other side."

And when she saw him turning back, she threw down one of the golden apples after him, and it rolled down into his shoe. But when he got to the bottom of the hill he rode off so fast that no one could tell what had become of him. That evening all the knights and princes were to go before the King that he who had ridden so far up the hill might show the apple which the Princess had thrown, but there was no one who had anything to show. One after the other they all came, but not a man could show the apple.

At even the brothers of Boots came home, too, and had such a long story to tell about the riding up the hill.

"First of all," they said, "there was not one of the whole lot who could get so much as a stride up; but at last came one who had a suit of brass mail, and a brass bridle and saddle, all so bright that the sun shone from them a mile off. He was a chap to ride, just! He rode a third of the way up the hill of glass, and he could easily have ridden the whole way up, if he chose; but he turned round and rode down, thinking, maybe, that was enough for once."

"Oh! I should so like to have seen him, that I should," said Boots, who sat by the fireside, and stuck his feet into the cinders as was his wont.

"Oh!" said his brothers, "you would, would you? You look fit to keep company with such high lords, dirty fellow that you are sitting there amongst the ashes."

Next day the brothers were all for setting off again, and Boots begged them this time, too, to let him go with them and see the riding but, no, they wouldn't have him at any price.

"Well, well!" said Boots; "if I go at all, I must go by myself. I'm not afraid."

So when the brothers got to the hill of glass, all the princes and knights began to ride again, and you may fancy they had taken care to shoe their horses sharp; but it was no good—they rode and slipped, and slipped and rode, just as they had done the day before, and there was not one who could get so far as a yard up the hill. And when they had worn out their horses, so that they could not stir a leg, they were all forced to give it up as a bad job. So the King thought he might as well proclaim that the riding should take place the day after for the last time, just to give them one chance more; but all at once it came across his mind that he might as well wait a little longer, to see if the knight in brass mail would come this day too. Well, they saw nothing of him, but all at once came one riding on a steed far, far braver and finer than that on which the knight in brass had ridden, and he had silver mail, and a silver saddle all so bright that the sunbeams gleamed and glanced from them far away. Then the others shouted out to him again, saying he might as well hold hard, and not try to ride up the hill, for all his trouble would be thrown away; but the knight paid no heed to them, and rode straight at the hill, and right up it, till he had gone two-thirds of the way, and then he wheeled his horse round and rode down again. To tell the truth, the Princess liked him still better than the knight in brass, and she sat and wished he might only be able to come right up to the top and down the other side; but when she saw him turning back she threw the second apple after him, and it rolled down and fell into his shoe. But as soon as ever he had come down from the hill of glass, he rode off so fast that no one could see what became of him.

At even, when all were to go in before the King and the Princess, that he who had the golden apple might show it, in they went, one after the other, but there was no one who had any apple to show, and the two brothers, as they had done on the former day, went home and told how things had gone, and how all had ridden at the hill and none got up.

"But, last of all," they said, "came one in a silver suit, and his horse had a silver saddle and a silver bridle. He was just a chap to ride; and he got two-thirds up the hill, and then turned back. He was a fine fellow and no mistake; and the Princess threw the second gold apple to him."

"Oh!" said Boots, "I should so like to have seen him, too, that I should."

"A pretty story!" they said. "Perhaps you think his coat of mail was as bright as the ashes you are always poking about!"

The third day everything happened as it had happened the two days before. There was no one who could get so much as a yard up the hill; and now all waited for the knight in silver mail, but they neither saw nor heard of him. At last came one riding on a steed, so brave that no one had ever seen his match; and the knight had a suit of golden mail, and a golden saddle and bridle, so wondrous bright that the sunbeams gleamed from them a mile off. The other knights and princes could not find time to call out to him not to try his luck, for they were amazed to see how grand he was. So he rode at the hill, and tore up it like nothing, so that the Princess hadn't even time to wish that he might get up the whole way. As soon as ever he reached the top, he took the third golden apple from the Princess' lap, and then turned his horse and rode down again. As soon as he got down, he rode off at full speed, and was out of sight in no time.

Now, when the brothers got home at even, you may fancy what long stories they told, how the riding had gone off that day; and amongst other things, they had a deal to say about the knight in golden mail.

"He just was a chap to ride!" they said, "so grand a knight isn't to be found in the wide world."

"Oh!" said Boots, "I should so like to have seen him; that I should."

Next day all the knights and princes were to pass before the King and the Princess—it was too late to do so the night before, I suppose—that he who had the gold apple might bring it forth; but one came after another, first the princes, and then the knights, and still there was no one who could show the gold apple.

"Well," said the King, "some one must have it, for it was something that we all saw with our own eyes, how a man came and rode up and bore it off."

So he commanded that every one who was in the kingdom should come up to the palace and see if they could show the apple. Well, they all came, one after another, but no one had the golden apple, and after a long time the two brothers of Boots came. They were the last of all, so the King asked them if there was no one else in the kingdom who hadn't come.

"Oh, yes," said they, "we have a brother, but he never carried off the golden apple. He hasn't stirred out of the dust-hole on any of the three days."

"Never mind that," said the King; "he may as well come up to the palace like the rest."

So Boots had to go up to the palace.

"How, now," said the King; "have you got the golden apple? Speak out!"

"Yes, I have," said Boots; "here is the first, and here is the second, and there is the third, too;" and with that he pulled all three golden apples out of his pocket, and at the same time threw off his sooty rags, and stood before them in his gleaming golden mail.

"Yes!" said the King; "you shall have my daughter and half my kingdom, for you well deserve both her and it."

So they got ready for the wedding, and Boots got the Princess to wife, and there was great merry-making at the bridal-feast, you may fancy, for they could all be merry though they couldn't ride up the hill of glass; and all I can say is, if they haven't left off their merry-making yet, why, they're still at it.

The Pert Fire Engine*
GELETT BURGESS

There were many fire engines, members of the Fire Department of the City o' Ligg, but of all the number, the most ill-behaved was the disreputable little Number Four. He was known all over the city as the black sheep of the flock, and every one knew the stories of his mischief.

In spite of his evil deeds he was a very handsome machine, wearing a pretty coat of enamel, and all his fittings were nickeled, so that they shone like silver buttons. He always had silken hose, too, for he was very rich. But he usually was the last engine at the fire, and he was always sure to shirk. He would hold back when he was signalled to "*Play away, Four,*" and he would squirt a stream strong enough to drench the Chief, when

*From *The Lively City o' Ligg*. Reprinted by special arrangement with the publishers, Frederick A. Stokes Company.

he should have held back. He consumed an enormous amount of the most expensive fuel, and he wheezed and puffed till the air shook with vibrations. He could have been the best engine in the fire department if he had wanted to, but he didn't.

So the people of the City o' Ligg were not very much surprised when they heard that Number Four had run away. They hoped only that he would stay away, for they could get along much better without him. "He's more trouble than he's worth," said an old ladder-cart. "I've been tempted more than once to fall on him and break his boiler for him. He wouldn't even have his hose darned, because he prefers to leak all over the street!"

For a few weeks Number Four enjoyed his truancy. He spent most of his time down by a lake, a little outside the city, and there he amused himself by going in swimming, and squirting water over himself like an elephant, till he shone brilliantly in the sunshine. When he was tired of that, he went around to the farm houses, and sucked all the water out of their wells, and flooded their cellars. The stables were all very much afraid of him, but dared not complain, though they told their fences to catch him if they could.

Another favorite game of his was to fill his tank with water, and squirt it at the windmills, playing on their sails so as to make the wheels spin backwards. This made many of the windmills so dizzy that they had to stop pumping for weeks.

But at last Number Four grew tired of this mischief in the country, and he began to cast about for something more exciting to do. So one night he loaded himself with water and rolled into the City o' Ligg.

He drew up before a two-story house that was not painted, but only whitewashed, and began to squirt water all over her. The poor little house shut all her doors and windows, but even then she was drenched to the skin, and after an hour or so, almost all the whitewash was soaked off, and she stood cold, dripping and shivering in the night air, with her naked boards streaked with white. The naughty fire engine laughed brutally at her distress, and went back to the lake to concoct more mischief.

Every night after that, Number Four went into the town and drenched the houses, laughing, as he poured streams of cold water down their chimneys, breaking their windows, washing away their foundations, and splashing them all over with muddy water.

At last it got to be altogether too much to endure, and the houses consulted together to see how Number Four could be caught and punished. They could think of no way, however, and so, after the fire engine had showered a very old and respectable church, and given it a severe cold, they applied to the telegraph office to help them.

The telegraph office was by far the cleverest building in the City o' Ligg, but it took him some time to think of a remedy for this trouble. He consulted, by wire, with all the offices around Ligg, and at last they decided upon a plan.

Notice was sent to all the telegraph poles to strip off their wires and come into Ligg for further orders. The next day the houses were surprised to see a procession of long, naked telegraph poles march into town, each with a roll of wire on his arm. They marched up to the telegraph office that night and received their instructions.

As soon as it was dark, the poles separated this way and that, going some to one part of the town, and some to another, till the whole city was surrounded. For several hours, while the houses slept in peace, the poles worked, going in and out with the wires till they had woven a fence all round the town. At the principal entrances, they left the streets free for the fire engine to get in; but they contrived big V-shaped traps here and there, which could be closed by the poles at a moment's notice. It was by this time twelve o'clock, the hour when Number Four usually appeared, and when all the town was quiet the poles waited for the bad engine to come.

At last they heard the rumble of wheels on the road from the lake, and in the dark they saw a bright light approaching; it was the fire in the naughty engine, who was puffing his way into the town, chuckling to himself over the fun he was to have with the Town Hall that night; for he had planned to fill the whole of the third story with water before he came back.

Number Four came up to the city gate, with no suspicion of what was awaiting him, and boldly rolled up the main avenue, past the double line of sleeping houses. There was one house that was snoring with a rough noise, and the fire engine turned with a laugh and sent a stream of water through the window.

Suddenly the telegraph poles closed round him; they waved and towered over his head, they lay on the ground across his road, they threatened to fall upon him. The poor engine was terrified out of his senses. He backed and jumped, he whistled and groaned, and he spouted a black column of smoke out of his funnel, and sent streams of water in every direction. Suddenly seeing an opening, he darted back toward the gate, but he soon found hinself walled in by the wire fences. He tried another way and another, but there was no escape; the wires hemmed him in on all sides, till he finally was stuck so fast that he could not move, and he stood panting, waiting to see what would happen next.

His wheels were tied, and his fires put out, and the next morning the poor, shame-faced engine was pulled into town past the lines of houses, who jeered at him scornfully. He was led into the Park in the center of the City o' Ligg, and there, where all the principal buildings could see, he was severely scolded

by the Mayor. It was a long lecture, telling all the story of his wickedness, and ending with the sentence that was to be inflicted upon him as a punishment. One by one they took off his bright red gold wheels, they took off his pole, and whipple trees, his seat-cushions, and tool-box, and then they dug a deep hole in the middle of the Park, by the side of a well, put him in, covered him with dirt, and sodded over the burial place.

And now when the tourists in the City o' Ligg compliment the Mayor upon the beautiful fountain that plays night and day in the middle of the Park, sending up a straight stream of water a hundred feet in the air, the Mayor says:

"Oh, yes; quite so, quite so! That is the naughty fire engine, little Number Four, working out his time of punishment. He was put in for twenty years, but if he behaves well, we're going to let him out in nineteen!"

The Marvelous Pot

J. CHRISTIAN BAY*

Out where the land was poor there stood a small cottage. The roof was so low that one could hardly see it from the road. In this cottage lived a man and his wife. They were so poor that they couldn't afford to keep more than one cow and yet they were honest and worthy. Times became worse and worse, they sold their furniture and lived on the bare floor. An ugly old man in town bought their poor little things, but refused to pay for them,—that was his way of treating poor people. He cheated them, too, by putting saw dust in the flour that he sold them, and he took their very last cent for sugar so mixed with salt that it would not sweeten anything.

The poor people didn't know what to do, for their children had to go hungry. At last they made up their minds to sell the cow, and the man started for town leading Bossy by a rope. As he walked along the road, a stranger hailed him, and asked if he wanted to sell the cow.

"I'll take twenty dollars for her," answered the man.

"All my money's gone," said the stranger, "but look here— I have a little thing which is worth more than twenty dollars. Here is a pot. I'll give you that for your cow." And he pulled forth an old iron pot with three legs and a handle.

"A pot!" said the poor man. "What good would that pot do me and my family when we have nothing to put into it? Do you think one gets anything out of a pot with-out putting something into it?"

Just then the three-legged pot began to talk.

"Take me! Take me!" it said. "I'll get food enough for you and all your family."

When the poor man heard this, he thought that if the pot could speak it might do even

*Author of *Danish Fairy and Folk Tales.*

69

more. So he closed the bargain, took the pot, and brought it home.

When he returned to the cottage he first went to the stall where the good old cow had stood, for he was sorry that he had lost her. He then tied the pot where the cow had been, and went on into the house.

"Did you sell the cow?" asked the wife.

"Yes," said he.

"That is well," remarked the wife. "The money you got will last a long time, if we can get some honest flour and sugar of the rich merchant."

Then the man had to confess that he had received no money for the cow.

"Dear me!" said the woman. "What did you get, then?"

He told her to go and look in the stall.

When the wife saw the iron pot she scolded her husband roundly.

"What a blockhead!" she cried. "Why didn't I take the cow to town myself! I never heard of such foolishness—to sell a good cow for an old iron pot."

"Clean me, and put me on the fire!" cried the pot all at once.

The woman was dumb for wonder.

"Can—can you speak? A-a-are you alive?" she asked at last.

"Come and see!" said the pot.

So the woman took the pot, scrubbed and cleaned it, and put it on the fire.

"I skip, I skip!" cried the pot.

"How far do you skip?" asked the woman.

"To the rich man's house, to the rich man's house," cried the pot. "Here I go—

lackady, lackady, lackady, lackady,"

and off it went on its three small legs, up the road.

70

THROUGH FAIRY HALLS

The rich merchant lived in the middle of the town, in a great house. His wife was in the kitchen, baking bread, when the pot came pattering in, jumped on the table and stood there, stock still.

"Well," exclaimed the rich man's wife, "I call that luck. I just need you for the pudding I am going to bake." So she put all kinds of good things into the pot,—fine flour, sweet sugar, a lot of butter, raisins, almonds, and a good pinch of spices for flavoring. At last, when the pot was full of rich and savory dough, she tried to take it by the handle, to put it into the oven,—but

lackady, lackady, lackady, lackady,

went the three short legs, and the pot was soon out of the door.

"Dear me!" screamed the woman. "Where are you going with my fine pudding?"

"To the poor man's home, to the poor man's home," said the pot, and off it went in earnest.

When the poor people saw the pot as it skipped into their room, with the pudding, they were very glad. The man asked his wife if she didn't think the bargain turned out pretty well, after all. She said she was pleased indeed, and begged pardon for the hard words she had used. They made a fine meal of the pudding, and the children had all they could eat.

Next morning the pot again cried, "I skip, I skip!"

"How far do you skip?" asked they.

"To the rich man's barn, to the rich man's barn," it shouted, and off it went.

When it came to the rich man's barn, it stopped at the gate. There were some men inside, threshing wheat.

"Look at that black pot!" they said. "Let us see how much it will hold!" And so they poured a bushel of wheat into it. The pot held it all, and there was still space left. Another bushel went in, but even this did not fill the pot. So they threw in every grain of wheat they had. When there was no more left, the legs began to move, and

        lackady, lackady, lackady, lackady,

the pot was off up the road.

"Stop!" cried the men. "Where do you go with all our wheat?"

"To the poor man's home, to the poor man's home!" cried the pot, and off it went on its way.

Next morning the pot once more skipped up the old road. The sun was out, the birds bathed in the brook, and the air was so warm that the rich merchant had spread his money on a table near an open window to prevent the gold from becoming tarnished.

All at once the pot stood on the window-sill, and as the man counted his money, it made a skip and a bound and stood right beside him. He could not imagine where the pot came from, but thought it would be a good place to put his money as he counted it. So he threw in one handful after another until all was there. At that the pot made another skip and a bound and landed on the window-sill.

"Hold on!" shouted the rich merchant. "Where are you going with my money?"

"To the poor man's home, to the poor man's home," answered the pot, as it jumped from the window, and it skipped down the road so merrily that the money danced within it. In  the middle of the poor man's house it stopped and turned a somersault. The money rolled all over the floor, and the poor people could scarcely believe their eyes. Then the little pot cried:

"As much for you as is your due, and the rest for the other poor people in town from whom the rich man stole it."

"Many thanks, little pot," said the man and his wife. "We'll keep you well cleaned and scoured for this!"

Next morning the pot again said it was ready to skip.

"How far do you skip?" asked the farmer's family.

"To the rich man's house, to the rich man's house." And off it was. It never stopped until it stood right in the middle of the rich man's office. As soon as he saw it, he cried:

"There is the black pot that carried off our pudding, our wheat, and all our money!—Here you! Give back all the things you took from me!"

"You took it from the poor people all over town," answered the pot. "Now it goes back to whom it belongs. Make your money honestly, and you'll keep it—Good-bye."

The three short legs began to move.

"Hold on!" yelled the merchant, and he flung himself squarely on the pot to hold it. But the pot kept on moving.

"I skip, I skip!" cried the pot.

"Skip to the North Pole, if you wish," shrieked the merchant. At that, the pot skipped down the road, and the man now found himself stuck to it fast and carried along by force. He tried hard, but could not free himself. He saw the doors of his neighbors' houses rushing past, and yelled for help, but nobody heard him. The pot ran faster and faster. It passed the poor people's little cottage, but never, never stopped.

And nobody ever saw hide or hair of the rich merchant who mixed his flour with sawdust and put salt in the sugar, until some wise men one day climbed way up to the top of the Earth and discovered the North Pole. There sat the rich man rubbing his nose with both hands, for it was purple with cold.

Daniel O'Rourke

Adapted from T. CROFTON CROKER

PEOPLE may have heard of the renowned adventures of Daniel O'Rourke, but few there be who know that the cause of all his perils, above and below, was neither more nor less than his having slept under the walls of the Pooka's Tower. An old man was he at the time he told me the story, with gray hair and a red nose; he sat smoking his pipe under the old poplar tree, on as fine an evening as ever shone from the sky.

"I am often *axed* to tell it, sir," said he. "The master's son, you see, had come from beyond foreign parts in France and Spain as young gentlemen used to do, and, sure enough, there was a dinner given to all the people on the ground, gentle and simple, high and low, rich and poor.

"Well, we had everything of the best, and plenty of it; and it was in the wee small hours o' the morning that I left the place. Just as I was crossing the stepping-stones of the ford of Bally-ashenogh, hard by the Pooka's Tower, and was looking up at the stars, whistling to keep awake, I missed my foot, and souse I fell into the water. '*Begorra!*' thought I. 'Is it drounded I'm goin' to be?' However, I began swimming, swimming, swimming away for dear life, till at last I got ashore, somehow or other, but never the one of me can tell how, on a *desarted* island.

"I wandered and wandered about, without knowing where I wandered, until at last I got into a big bog. The moon was shining as bright as day, and I looked east and west, north and south, and every way, and nothing did I see but bog, bog, bog. So I sat upon a stone, and I began to scratch my head, for, sure and certain, thinks I, here's the end o' Daniel O'Rourke. And

74

THROUGH FAIRY HALLS

I began to sing the *Ullagone*—when all of a sudden the moon grew black, and I looked up and saw something for all the world as if it was moving down between me and it, and I could not tell what it was. Down it came with a pounce, and looked at me full in the face; and what was it but an eagle?—as fine a one as ever flew from the kingdom of Kerry. So he looked at me in the face, and says he to me, 'Daniel O'Rourke,' says he, 'how do you do?'

" 'Very well, I thank you, sir,' says I; 'I hope you're well;' wondering out of my senses all the time how an eagle came to speak like a Christian.

" 'What brings you here, Dan?' says he.

" 'Nothing at all, sir,' says I, 'only I wish I was safe home again.'

" 'Is it out of the bog you want to go, Dan?' says he.

" ' 'Tis, sir', says I.

" 'Dan,' says he, after a minute's thought, 'as you are a decent sober man, who never flings stones at me or mine, my life for yours,' says he; 'get up on my back, grip me well, and I'll fly you out of the bog.'

" 'I am afraid,' says I, 'your honour's making game of me; for whoever heard of riding a-horse-back on an eagle before?'

" ' 'Pon the honour of a gentleman,' says he, putting his right foot on his breast, 'I am quite in earnest; and so now either take my offer or starve in the bog!'

"I had no choice; so, thinks I to myself, faint heart never won fair lady. 'I thank your honour,' says I, 'for the kind offer.' I therefore mounted on the back of the eagle, and held him tight enough by the throat, and up he flew in the air like a lark. Little I knew the trick he was going to serve me. Up, up, up—God knows how far he flew. 'Why, then,' said I to him—thinking he did not know the right road home—very civilly, because why? I was in his power entirely; 'sir,' says I, 'please your honour's glory, and with humble submission to your better judgment, if you'd fly down a bit, you're now just over my cabin, and I could be put down there, and many thanks to your worship.'

" '*Arrah*, Dan,' says he, 'do you think me a fool? Hold your tongue, and mind your own business, and don't be interfering with the business of other people.'

" 'Faith, this is my business, I think,' says I. 'Where in the world are you going, sir?'

" 'Be quiet, Dan!' says he, and *bedad* he flew on and on.

"Well, sir, where should we come to at last but to the moon itself. Now you can't see it from here, but there is, or there was in my time, a reaping-hook sticking out of the side of the moon.

" 'Dan,' says the eagle, 'I'm tired with this long fly. I had no notion 'twas so far!'

" 'And my lord, sir,' says I, 'who in the world *axed* you to fly so far—was it I? Did not I beg and pray and beseech you to stop half an hour ago?'

" 'There's no use talking, Dan,' said he; 'I'm tired bad enough, so you must get off, and sit down on the moon until I rest myself.'

" 'Is it sit down upon that little round thing?' said I. 'Why, then, sure, I'd fall off in a minute and be split and smashed entirely. You are a vile deceiver—so you are.'

" 'Not at all, Dan,' says he; 'you can catch fast hold of the reaping-hook that's sticking out of the side of the moon, and 'twill keep you up.'

" 'I won't then,' said I.

" 'Maybe not,' said he, quite quiet. 'If you don't, my man, I shall just give you a shake, and one slap of my wing, and send you down smash to the ground!'

" 'Why, then, I'm in a fine way,' said I to myself, 'ever to have come along with the likes of you;' and so, telling him plain to his face what I thought of him (but in Irish, for fear he'd know what I said) I got off his back with a heavy heart, took hold of the reaping-hook, and sat down upon the moon.

"When he had me there fairly landed, he turned about on me, and said, 'Good morning to you, Daniel O'Rourke,' said he; 'I think I've nicked you fairly now. You robbed my nest last year and in return you are freely welcome to cool your heels dangling upon the moon.'

" 'Is this how you leave me, you brute, you?' says I. 'You ugly, unnatural *baste!*' 'Twas all to no manner of use; he spread out his great wings, burst out a-laughing, and flew away like lightning. I bawled after him to stop; but I might have called and bawled forever, without his minding me. Away he went and I never saw him from that day to this. You may be sure I was in a disconsolate condition, and kept roaring out for the bare grief, when all at once a door opened right in the middle of the moon! creaking on its hinges as if it had not been opened

for a month before—I suppose they never thought of greasing them—and out there walks—who do you think but the man in the moon himself? I knew him by his bush.

" 'Good morrow to you, Daniel O'Rourke,' says he, 'how do you do?'

" 'Very well, thank your honour,' says I. 'I hope your honour's well.'

" 'What brought you here, Dan?' said he. So I told him all the whole terrible story.

" 'Dan,' said the man in the moon, taking a pinch of snuff when I was done, 'you must not stay here.'

" 'Indeed, sir,' says I, ' 'tis much against my will that I'm here at all; but how am I to go back?'

" 'That's your business,' said he; 'Dan, mine is to tell you that you must not stay, so be off in less than no time.'

" 'I'm doing no harm,' said I, 'only holding on hard by the reaping-hook lest I fall off.'

" 'That's what you must not do, Dan,' says he.

" 'Faith, and with your leave,' says I, 'I'll not let go the reaping-hook, and the more you bids me, the more I won't let go—so I will.'

" 'You had better, Dan,' says he again.

" 'Why, then, my little fellow,' says I, taking the whole weight of him with my eye from head to foot, 'there are two words to that bargain; and I'll not budge!'

" 'We'll see how that is to be,' says he; and back he went, giving the door such a great bang after him (for it was plain he was huffed) that I thought the moon and all would fall down with it.

"Well, I was preparing myself to try strength with him, when back he comes, with the kitchen cleaver in his hand, and without saying a word he gives two bangs to the handle of the reaping-hook that was holding me up, and *whap*, it came in two.

'Good morning to you, Dan,' says the blackguard, when he saw
me cleanly falling down with a bit of the handle in my hand,
'I thank you for your visit, and fair weather after you, Daniel.'
I had no time to make any answer to him, for I was tumbling
over and over, and rolling and rolling, at the rate of a fox-hunt.
'God help me!' says I. 'But this is a pretty pickle for a decent
man to be seen in at this time o' night. I am now sold fairly.'
The word was not out of my mouth, when, whiz! what should
fly by close to my ear but a flock of wild geese, all the way from
my own bog of Ballyashenogh, else how should they know *me?*
The *ould* gander, who was their general, turning about his head,
cried out to me, 'Is that you, Dan?'

" 'The same,' said I.

" 'Good morrow to you,' says he, 'Daniel O'Rourke; how are
you in health this morning?'

" 'Very well, sir,' says I, 'thank you kindly!' drawing my
breath, for I was mightily in want of some. 'I hope your honour's
the same?'

" 'I think 'tis falling you are, Daniel,' says he.

" 'You may say that, sir,' says I.

" 'And where are you going all the way so fast?' said the

gander, so I told him all the whole, terrible story and never the once stopped rolling.

" 'Dan,' says he, 'I'll save you; put out your hand and catch me by the leg, and I'll fly you home.' Well, I didn't much trust the gander, but there was no help for it. So I caught him by the leg, and away I and the other geese flew after him as fast as hops.

"We flew, and we flew, and we flew, until we came right over the ocean. 'Ah, my lord,' said I to the goose, for I thought it best to keep a civil tongue in my head, 'fly to land, if you please.'

" 'It is impossible, Dan,' said he, 'for you see, we are going to Arabia!'

" 'To Arabia!' said I. 'Oh! Mr. Goose, why, then, to be sure, I'm a man to be pitied among you.'

" 'Whist, whist, you *impident* rascal,' says he, 'hold your ongue. Arabia is a very decent sort of place.'

"Just as we were talking a ship hove in sight, sailing so beau-.tiful before the wind. 'Ah, then, sir,' said I, 'will you drop me on the ship, if you please?'

" 'We are not fair over it,' said he; 'if I dropped you now you would go splash into the sea.'

" 'I would not,' says I, 'I know better than that, so let me drop at once.'

" 'If you must, you must,' said he; 'there, take your own way;' and he opened his claw, and, faith, he was right—I came down plump into the sea! Down to the very bottom I went, and I gave myself up, then, for ever, when a whale walked up to me, scratching himself after his night's sleep, and looked me full in the face, and never the word did he say, but, lifting up his tail, he splashed me all over again with the cold salt water till there wasn't a dry stitch on me! And I heard somebody saying —'twas a voice I knew, too—'Get up, you lazy *vagabone!*' With that I woke up, and there was Judy with a tub full of water, splashing, splashing all over me.

"'Get up,' says she, 'and to work. Late out o'nights, no reason for *shlapin'* late o' morning. Off with you after the pigs!'

"*Begorra!* of all the places in the parish, there I'd been fast asleep under the *ould* walls of the Pooka's Tower. And what with eagles, and men of the moon, and ganders, and whales, driving me through bogs, and up to the moon, and down to the bottom of the ocean, I never again took forty winks on the road coming home from a party—leastwise not under the Pooka's Tower!"

HER DAIRY*

"*A milkweed, and a buttercup, and cowslip,*" said sweet Mary,
"*Are growing in my garden-plot, and this I call my dairy.*"
—Peter Newell.

*From *Pictures and Rhymes*, published by Harper & Brothers.

The Wise Men of Gotham

Three wise men of Gotham,
They went to sea in a bowl,
And if the bowl had been stronger,
My tale had been longer.

In old days the village of Gotham was known throughout all merry England, for that its men were wondrous wise.

On a time, twelve wise men of Gotham went a-fishing. Some went into the water and some fished on dry land. As they ambled home at nightfall, says one to the others, "We have been venturesome this day, comrades, a-wading in the brook. A marvel is it if none of us was drowned!"

"Aye, marry!" says another. " 'Twere well to count ourselves, lest, peradventure, one be left behind! Twelve of us did come from home!"

So every man did count the others, man by man, and did never count himself!

"Lauk-a-mercy-on-us!" they all began to cry. "Here be but eleven. One of us is drowned!"

So they ran back to the brook, and looked up and down, and here and there with outcries and loud lamentations.

Anon, came riding by a gentleman. "Save you, sirs," says he. "Why all this dreadful dole?"

"Alas, good master," cried the wise men. "This day there came twelve of us to fish in this brook, and one of us is drowned!"

"Bless me!" says the gentleman. "Count yourselves, then, man by man!" And each did count eleven and never count himself.

" 'Twere pity of my life if one among so wise a company were lost," says the gentleman. "I pray you, what will you give me an I find the twelfth man?"

"All that is in our wallets," said the men of Gotham.

So they gave the gentleman all the money they had; then he began with the first and gave him a whack on the shoulders with the flat of his sword, that he shrieked aloud. "That is one, by your leave!" says he, and he served them all likewise, counting them man by man. But when he was come to the last, he gave him a most dreadful whack, that he scarce held his footing. "By my faith!" cried he. "Here is your twelfth man!"

"Marvelous!" cried all the company. "Marvelous past the wit of man! You have found our neighbor that was lost!"

The next day but one, there went to market to Nottingham to buy sheep, a certain man of Gotham, and, as he crossed over Nottingham bridge, he met another man of Gotham going home.

"Where are you going?" asked he that came from Nottingham —Dobbin by name.

"Marry," says Hodge that was going to Nottingham. "I am going to buy sheep."

"And which way will you bring them home?" says Dobbin.

"Over this bridge," says Hodge.

"Not so, neither," says Dobbin. "I like not to have sheep cross over this bridge."

"Beshrew me!" says Hodge, "but I will bring them over the bridge an I choose!"

"By my life, but you will not!"

"I will!"

"You will not!"

"Rascal!"

"Rogue!"

And they fell a-beating their staves one against another as if there had been an hundred sheep between them.

"Have a care!" cried Hodge. "What with all this noise, my sheep will jump off the bridge!"

"It matters not!" shrieked Dobbin. "They shall not cross!"

"If thou makest so much to do, I'll put my fist in thy face!"

"And I'll put my staff on thy pate!"

As they were thus at contention, there came by another man of Gotham with a sack of meal on his horse. Seeing his neighbors thus at strife about sheep when there were no sheep between them, he said, "How now, stupid fellows, will you never learn wisdom? Peace! Peace!" Then he took down the sack of meal from his horse, went to the side of the bridge, opened the mouth of the sack, and shook all his meal out into the river.

"Look you, sirrahs," says he. "How much meal is there in my sack?"

"Marry!" said they. "None at all!"

"By my faith," says he. "There's even as much meal in my sack as wit in your heads, to be at strife about nothing! Let this be a lesson to you!"

And he went on his way with his empty sack, looking most marvelous wise.

THROUGH FAIRY HALLS

When the summer was come, the men of Gotham found a cuckoo in a hawthorn-brake, singing a rare, enchanting song.

"Ho," said they, "we will take this wondrous creature into the midst of our village where all may hear it sing, and build a hedge about it, that we may keep it with us all the year."

So they fetched the cuckoo into the town and built a high hedge about it.

"Sing there now all the year," said they. At that, up sprang the cuckoo and flew away.

"A murrain on us for stupid fellows," cried the men of Gotham. "We should have built our hedge higher!"

WILD FLOWERS*

"Of what are you afraid, my child?" inquired the kindly teacher.
"O sir! the flowers, they are wild," replied the timid creature.

—*Peter Newell.*

*From *Pictures and Rhymes*. Harper & Brothers, Publishers.

Where Sarah Jane's Doll Went*

MARY E. WILKINS FREEMAN

In the first place, Sarah Jane had no right to take the doll to school, but the temptation was too much for her. The doll was new—it was, in fact, only one day old—and such a doll! Rag, of course—Sarah Jane had heard only vague rumors of other kinds—but no more like the ordinary rag doll than a fairy princess is like a dairymaid. The minute that Sarah Jane saw it she knew at once that there never had been such a doll. It was small—not more than seven or eight inches tall—not by any means the usual big, sprawling, moon-faced rag baby with its arms standing out at right angles with its body. It was tiny and genteel in figure, slim-waisted, and straight-backed. It was made of, not common cotton cloth, but linen—real, glossy, white linen—which Sarah Jane's mother, and consequently the doll's grandmother, had spun and woven. Its face was colored after a fashion which was real high art to Sarah Jane. The little cheeks and mouth were sparingly flushed with cranberry juice, and the eyes beamed blue with indigo. The nose was delicately traced with a quill dipped in its grandfather's ink-stand, and though not quite as natural as the rest of the features, showed fine effort. Its little wig was made from the fine ravellings of Serena's brown silk stockings.

Serena was Sarah Jane's married sister, who lived in the next house across the broad, green yard, and she had made this wonderful doll. She brought it over one evening just before Sarah Jane went to bed. "There," said she, "if you'll be a real good girl I'll give you this."

"Oh," cried Sarah Jane, and she could say no more.

Serena, who was only a girl herself, dandled the doll impressively before her bewildered eyes. It was dressed in a charming frock made from a bit of Serena's best French calico. The frock was of a pale lilac color with roses sprinkled over it, and was cut with a low neck and short puffed sleeves.

"Now, Sarah Jane," said Serena admonishingly, "there's one thing I want to tell you: you musn't carry this doll to school. If you do, you'll lose it; and you won't get another very soon. It was a good deal of work to make it. Now you mind what I say."

"Yes, ma'am," said Sarah Jane. It was not her habit to say ma'am to her sister Serena, if she was twelve years older than she; but she did now, and reached out impatiently for the doll.

"Well, you remember," said Serena. "If you take it to school and lose it, it'll be the last doll you'll get."

And Sarah Jane said, "Yes, ma'am," again.

She had to go to bed directly, but she took the new doll with her—that was not forbidden, much to her relief. And before she went to sleep she had named her with a most flowery name, nothing less than Lily Rosalie Violet May. It took her a long time to decide upon it, but she was finally quite satisfied, and went to sleep hugging Lily Rosalie, and dreamed about her next day's spelling lesson—that she failed and went to the foot of the class.

It was singular, but for once a dream of Sarah Jane's came true. She actually did miss in her spelling lesson the next day, and although she did not go quite to the foot of the class, she went very near to it. But if Sarah Jane was not able to spell *scissors* correctly, she could have spelled with great success *Lily Rosalie Violet May*. All the evening she had been printing it over and over on a fly-leaf of her spelling-book. She could feel no interest in scissors, which had no connection, except a past one, with her beloved new doll.

Poor Sarah Jane lived such a long way from school that she had to carry her dinner with her, so there was a whole day's separation, when she had only possessed Lily Rosalie for a matter

of twelve hours. It was hard. She told some of her particular cronies about her, and described her charms with enthusiasm, but it was not quite equal to displaying her in person.

The little girls promised to come over and see the new doll just as soon as their mothers would let them, and one, Ruth Gurney, who was Sarah Jane's especial friend, said she would go home with her that very night—she didn't believe her mother would care—but they were going to have company at tea, and she was afraid if she were late, and had to sit at the second table, that she wouldn't get any currant tarts.

Sarah Jane did not urge her, but she felt deeply hurt that Ruth could prefer currant tarts to a sight of Lily Rosalie.

She was rather apt to loiter on her way home. There was much temptation to at this time of the year, when the meadows on either side of the road were so brimful of grass and flowers, when the air was so sweet, and so many birds were singing. There was a brook on the way, and occasionally Sarah Jane used to stop and have a little secret wade. But to-night neither nodding way-side flowers nor softly rippling brook had any attraction for her. Straight home, her little, starched, white sun-bonnet pointing ahead unswervingly, her small, pattering feet never turning aside from the narrow, beaten track between the wayside grasses, she went to Lily Rosalie Violet May.

She found her just as beautiful as when she left her. That long day of absence, filled in with her extravagant childish fancy, had not caused her charms to lessen in the least.

Sarah Jane ran straight to the linen chest, in whose till she had hidden for safety the precious doll, and there she lay, her indigo blue eyes staring up, smiling at her with the sweet cranberry-colored smile which Serena had fixed on her face. Sarah

GLEN KETCHUM

Jane caught her up in rapture. Her mother told Serena that night that she didn't know when she'd seen the child so tickled with anything as she was with that doll.

"She didn't carry it to the school, did she?" said Serena.

"No. I guess she won't want to, as long as you told her not to," replied her mother.

Sarah Jane had been always an obedient little girl; but— she had never before had Lily Rosalie Violet May. Her mother did not consider that.

Sarah Jane did not have a pocket made in her dress; it was not then the fashion. Instead, she wore a very large-sized one, made of stout cotton, tied around her waist by a string under her dress skirt. The next day, when Sarah Jane went to school, she carried in this pocket her new doll. She was quite late this morning, so there was no time to display it before school commenced.

Once, when the high arithmetic class was out on the floor, she pulled it slyly out of her pocket, held it under her desk, and poked Ruth Gurney, who sat in the next seat.

"Oh!" gasped Ruth, almost aloud. The doll seemed to fascinate everybody. "Let me take it," motioned Ruth; but Sarah Jane shook a wise head, and slid Lily Rosalie back in her pocket. She was not going to run the risk of having her confiscated by the teacher. But when recess came Sarah Jane was soon the proud little centre of an admiring group.

"Sarah Jane's got the handsomest new doll," one whispered to another, and they all crowded around. Even some of the "big girls" came, and two or three of the big boys. Sarah Jane was one of the smallest girls in school, and sat in the very front seat. Now she felt like a big girl herself. This wonderful doll raised her at once to a position of importance. There she stood in the corner by the window, and proudly held it. She wore a neat cotton dress cut after the fashion of Lily Rosalie's, with a low neck and short sleeves, displaying her dimpled neck and arms. Her round cheeks were flushed with a softer pink than the doll's, and her honest brown eyes were full of delight.

One and another of the girls begged for the privilege of taking the doll a moment and Sarah Jane would grant it, and then watch them with thinly veiled anxiety. Suppose their fingers shouldn't be quite clean, and there should be a spot on Lily Rosalie's beautiful white linen skin! One of the girls rubbed her cheeks to see if the red would come off, and Sarah Jane wriggled.

Joe West was one of the big boys who had joined the group. Years after, he was Joseph B. West, an eminent city lawyer. Years after that, he was Judge West of the Superior Court. Now he was simply Joe West, a tall, lanky boy with a long, rosy face and a high forehead. His arms came too far through his jacket sleeves, and showed his wrists, which looked unnaturally knobby and bony. He went barefoot all summer long, and was much given to chewing sassafras.

He offered a piece to Sarah Jane now, extracting it with gravity from a mass of chalk, top strings, buttons, nails, and other wealth with which his pocket was filled.

Sarah Jane accepted it with a modest little blush, and plumped it into her rosy mouth.

Then Joe West followed up his advantage. "Say, Sarah Jane," said he, "lemme take her a minute."

She eyed him doubtfully. Somehow she mistrusted him. Joe West had rather the reputation of being a sore tease.

"She's just the prettiest doll I ever saw," Joe went on. "Lemme take her just a minute, Sarah Jane; now do."

"He's just stuffing you, Sarah Jane; don't you let him touch it," spoke out one of the big girls.

"Stuffing" was a very expressive word in the language of

the school. Sarah Jane shook her head with a timid little smile, and hugged Lily Rosalie tighter.

"Now do, Sarah Jane. I wouldn't be stingy. Haven't I just given you some sassafras?"

That softened her a little. The spicy twang of the sassafras was yet on her tongue. "I'm afraid you won't give her back to me," murmured she.

"Yes, I will, honest. Now do, Sarah Jane."

It was against her better judgment; the big girl again raised her warning voice; but Joe West adroitly administered a little more flattery, and followed it up with entreaty, and Sarah Jane, yielding, finally put her precious little, white linen baby into his big, grimy, out-reaching hands.

"Oh, the pretty little sing!" said Joe West then, in an absurdly soft voice, and dandled it up and down. "What's its name, Sarah Jane?"

And Sarah Jane in her honesty and simplicity repeated that flowery name.

"Lily Rosalie Violet May," said Joe, after her, softly. And everybody giggled.

A pink color spread all over Sarah Jane's face and dimpled neck; tears sprang to her eyes. She felt as if they were poking fun at something sacred; her honest, childish confidence was betrayed. "Give her back to me, Joe West!" she cried.

But Joe only dandled it out of her reach, and then the bell rang. The children trooped back into the school-room, and Joe quietly slipped the doll into his pocket and marched gravely to his seat.

Every time when Sarah Jane gazed around at him he was studying his geography with the most tireless industry. She could hardly wait for school to be done; when it was, she tried to get to Joe, but he was too quick for her. He had started with

GLEN KETCHUM

his long stride down the road before she could get to the door. She called after him, but he appeared to have suddenly grown deaf. The other girls condoled with her, all but the big girl who had given the warning. "You'd ought to have listened to me," said she, severely, as she tied on her sun-bonnet in the entry. "I told you how it would be, letting a boy have hold of it."

Sarah Jane was not much comforted. She crept forlornly along towards home. Joe West's house was on the way. There was a field south of it. As she came to this field she saw Joe out there with the bossy. This bossy, which was tethered to an old apple-tree, was cream-colored, with a white star on her forehead and a neck and head like a deer. She stood knee-deep in the daisies and clover, and looked like a regular picture-calf. If Sarah Jane had not been so much occupied with her own troubles, she would have stopped to gaze with pleasure at the pretty creature. Joe stood at her head and appeared to be teasing her. She twitched away from him, and lunged at him playfully with her budding horns.

"Joe! Joe!" called quaking little Sarah Jane.

Joe West gave one glance at her; his face flushed a burning red; then he left the bossy and went with long strides across the fields towards his home. The poor girl followed him.

"Joe! Joe!" called the little despairing voice, but he never turned his head.

Sarah Jane got past his house; then she sat down beside the road and wept. She did not know how Joe West, remorseful and penitent, was peeping at her from his window. She did not know of the tragedy which had just been enacted over there in the clover-field. The bossy calf, who was hungry for all strange articles of food, had poked her inquiring nose into Joe West's jacket pocket, whence a bit of French calico emerged, had caught hold of it, and, in short, had then and there eaten up Lily Rosalie Violet May. Joe had made an attempt to pull her by her silken wig out of that greedy mouth, but the bossy calmly chewed on.

It was just as well that Sarah Jane did not know it at the time. She had enough to bear—her own distress over the loss of the doll, and the reproaches of Serena and her mother. They agreed that the loss of the doll served her right for her disobedience, and that nothing should be said to Joe West. They also thought the affair too trivial to fuss over. Lily Rosalie even in her designer's eyes was not what she was to Sarah Jane.

"If you'd minded me you wouldn't have lost it," said Serena. "I am not going to make you another."

Sarah Jane hung her head meekly. But in the course of three months she had another doll in a very unexpected and curious way. One evening there was a knock on the side door, and when it was opened there was no one there, but on the step lay a big package directed to Sarah Jane. It contained a real, bought doll, with a china head and a cloth body, who was gorgeously and airily attired in pink tarlatan with silver spangles. The memory of Lily Rosalie paled.

There was great wonder and speculation. Nobody dreamed how poor Joe West had driven cows from pasture, and milked, and chopped wood, out of school-hours, and taken every cent he had earned and bought this doll to atone for the theft of Lily Rosalie Violet May.

Sarah Jane's mother declared that she should not carry this doll, no matter whence it came, to school, and she never did but once—that was on her birthday, and she teased so hard, and promised not to let any one take her, that her mother consented. At recess Sarah Jane was again the centre of attraction. She turned that wonderful pink tarlatan lady round and round before the admiring eyes; but when Joe West, meek and mildly conciliatory, approached the circle, she clutched her tightly and turned her back on him.

"I'm not going to have Joe West steal another doll," said she. And Joe colored and retreated.

Years afterwards, when Joe was practicing law in the city, and came home for a visit, and Sarah Jane was so grown-up that she wore a white muslin hat with rosebuds, and a black silk mantilla, to church, she knew the whole story, and they had a laugh over it.

IN THE LANE*

MADISON CAWEIN

When the hornet hangs in the hollyhock,
  And the brown bee drones i' the rose,
And the west is a red-streaked four-o'-clock,
  And the summer is near its close—
It's—Oh, for the gate and the locust lane
  And dusk and dew and home again!

*Used by the courteous permission of Madison Cawein, son of the author, and the publishers, The Macmillan Company.

KIDS*
WITTER BYNNER

"Hey, I've found some money-wort,
Some day I'll be rich!
Or I wonder if it's checkerberry?
I don't know which is which.

"Look, don't touch that blade of grass,
Just keep away from it!
For see that frothy, bubbly ball?
That's snake-spit!

"Cover your lips, the darning-needle
Loves to sew 'em up!—
Who likes butter? Lift your chin—
Here's a buttercup.

"She loves me—she loves me not—
I wish that I knew why
It always comes a different way
Every time I try.

"How many children? Here you are—
You can have three blows—
And you don't want many children,
For you have to buy 'em clo'es.

*Quoted by the courteous permission of the Author and the Publishers, Frederick A. Stokes Company.

THROUGH FAIRY HALLS

"Now we can take the stems, see,
And wet 'em into curls
And stick 'em in our hair and run
And make believe we're girls.

"D'ye ever whistle a blade of grass?
Look, I got a fat one . . .
You slit it, see?   Here's one for you—
There's no snake-spit on that one.

"Aren't big people funny
That they don't want to play?
And some of 'em don't like ice-cream—
I couldn't be that way.

"They just sit round and talk and talk—
O'course their hands are clean.
But they make us wash ours all the time,
I couldn't be that mean.

"No, honestly I couldn't,
Could you?   I'd sooner die.
We'll dig some worms tomorrow
And go fishin'!   Goo'-by!"

A Credit to the School*

DIKKEN ZWILGMEYER

Translated from the Norwegian by Emilie Poulsson

Johnny Blossom was walking home from school. He carried his head high; his turned-up, freckled nose was held proudly in the air; his cap hung on the back of his head. Both hands were in his pockets, and his loud whistling waked the echoes as he strode through Jensen Alley. Perfectly splendid monthly report! Of course he knew it, word for word, and he said over to himself again, as he had many times:

"John has lately been more industrious. With his excellent ability he is now a credit to the school."

This was signed with nothing less than the Principal's name. Not just a teacher's—no, thank you! A credit to the school. The whistling grew louder and more piercing. A credit to the school. He was going straight to Father with this report, and would lay it right under Father's nose.

Well, he *had* been industrious. He had gone over every lesson five times, and he could rattle off all the exceptions in his German grammar and all the mountains in Asia, even those with the awfully hard names.

Really, it was rather pleasant to know your lessons well and rank with the good scholars. Now he could be able to crow over Asta. She often had to sit the whole afternoon with her fingers in her ears, mumbling and studying, and even then couldn't get her lessons sometimes, and would cry; but, of course, she was only a girl.

He would take this report to Uncle Isaac of Kingthorpe, too.

*From *Johnny Blossom*. Used by permission of the publishers, The Pilgrim Press.

THROUGH FAIRY HALLS

Uncle Isaac was always questioning and probing to find out how he got on at school. Now he should see! Sharp whistling again pierced the air.

Another wonderfully interesting thing was that "Goodwill of Luckton" had arrived. He had seen it at Frosberg's wharf when he was going to school. At this thought Johnny Blossom broke into a run. Darting through the little gate to their own back yard, he burst into the entry and, in the same headlong fashion, into the dining room. The family was already at the table.

"Here is my monthly report and 'Goodwill of Luckton' has come," exclaimed Johnny.

Father and mother looked at the report. "Very good, John," said Father; and Johnny felt Mother's gentle hand stroking his hair.

"But what is it that has come?"

" 'Goodwill of Luckton', of course."

Johnny was gulping his soup with great haste.

"Express yourself clearly and eat properly."

Everything had to be so proper to suit Father.

"The apple boat, the one Mr. Lind and Mrs. Lind own, you know—that comes every autumn."

Yes, the apple boat. It was painted green as it had been last year; the sails were patched; the poorest apples lay in heaps on the deck, the medium sort were in bags, and the best apples were in baskets. In the midst of this tempting abundance Mrs. Lind, who was uncommonly stout, usually sat knitting. When her husband was up in town delivering apples Mrs. Lind took care of the boat, the apples, and Nils and everything. Nils, their son, was more to look after than all the rest put together for he was the worst scalawag to be found along the whole coast.

John kept on eating and talking. "Nils is a bad boy, Mother. When he talks to his mother, he keeps the side of his face toward her perfectly sober; but he makes faces with the side toward us. It is awfully funny and we laugh; and Mrs. Lind thinks we are laughing at her, and then she scolds, and oh! her scolding is so funny!"

Shortly after dinner Johnny Blossom was out in the wood-shed whittling a boat. How delightful and how queer that he should be "a credit to the school!" He would be awfully industrious now every single day; go over every lesson six times, at least.

This boat that he was making was going to be a fine one—Johnny Blossom held it out and peered sharply at it, first lengthwise, then sidewise—the finest boat any one had ever whittled. Every one who saw it would say, "Who made that beautiful, graceful boat?" Well, here was the boy who could do it!

One of these days he must carve a big ship about half a yard long and make it an exact copy of a real ship.

Johnny Blossom lost himself in wondering whether, when it was finished, he shouldn't take the ship to school to show to the Principal! If he did, the Principal would of course praise him very much, for it would be an extraordinarily well-shaped, handsome ship.

Yes, Johnny Blossom decided that he would take it to school for the Principal to see. It should be painted and have real sails. Oh, dear! Then he would have to ask Asta to hem the sails! Horrid tease as she was, she sewed remarkably well. Girls weren't good for much else.

How would it be to make a sloop next—one exactly like the "Goodwill of Luckton"?

At this he threw down the boat which was to be so wonderfully graceful and rushed off toward the wharf. How stupid of him to stay at home whittling when the "Goodwill of Luckton" had come!

THROUGH FAIRY HALLS

Of course there were several boys hanging around there—Aaron, Stephen, and Carl. Otherwise not even a cat was to be seen. Streets and wharf were deserted in the quiet noon hour. Mrs. Lind sat nodding upon the deck. Nils lounged on some bags at the front of the boat, amusing himself making faces. Mr. Lind was probably up in the town doing errands.

"Give us an apple," whispered Stephen to Nils. Nils did not answer, but gave Stephen a sly look and then made a hideous face.

"Throw some ashore," suggested Johnny Blossom.

"Just one apiece," whispered Carl.

"Well, don't then, you miser!" said Aaron.

Suddenly Nils, with a slyer look than usual on his sly face, went down into the cabin. A minute after he came stamping up again.

"Mother, Mother! The coffee is boiling over. Hurry!"

Mrs. Lind waddled hastily across the deck and squeezed herself down the narrow stairway.

"Come now!" called Nils guardedly to the boys on shore. "Come now! Hurry up and take some apples."

The boys on the wharf did not wait to be called again but jumped upon the deck and rushed at the bags of fruit.

"Mother, Mother!" roared Nils. "Hurry! There are thieves at the apples! Oh, hurry!"

In an incredibly short time Mrs. Lind had come upstairs, and there stood Mr. Lind also, exactly as if he had shot up out of the ground.

Nils declared loudly: "Before I knew a thing about it, these boys rushed on board and began grabbing some of the best apples."

Oh, how Mr. Lind and his wife scolded as they seized the astounded boys! Mr. Lind held two of them and Mrs. Lind two—she had a remarkably strong grip—while Nils flew after a policeman. The frightened boys cried and begged to be set free. A crowd gathered on the wharf in no time.

Soon the policeman came. "You will have to go with me to the police station," said he to the boys. They tried to explain that Nils had invited them on board, but it availed nothing. "You go with me to the police station," was the only reply the policeman made to anything they said.

Oh, but it was horrid, having to go along the streets with him! Nils should have his pay for getting them into this trouble! At the police station their names were recorded and then the boys were allowed to go. Johnny Blossom, shamefaced and troubled, ran straight home.

In the afternoon the policeman called to talk with Father. Father was very serious and Mother looked frightfully worried. Sister Asta stared with open mouth. John had a bitter time of it while the matter was being settled, and afterward Asta's teasing voice followed him everywhere as she kept calling out:

"Credit to the scho-ol! Great credit! Wonderful credit! Credit to the scho-ol!"

Oh, how horrid, how horrid everything was! Well, he wouldn't go out any more to-day, that he wouldn't; he would stay in his room with the door locked. He had been so delighted with his report, and now even that gave him no pleasure. Of course he couldn't go to Uncle Isaac with it after this disgrace.

A sudden thought struck him. He would not keep the report any longer. To have "A credit to the school" upon it was too embarrassing after what had happened.

He had *not* stolen apples, he really had not; but he had been taken to the police station and his name, John Blossom, was written on the police records. Though he had not stolen apples, he had known very well that Mr. Lind and his wife would be angry if boys went on board and helped themselves to apples, even if Nils had said they might.

Pshaw! Everything was horrid. The boys at school would soon know all about it and then they would tease just as Asta did. No, he would not keep the report; he would give it back to the Principal; that was just what he would do. So Johnny Blossom, saying nothing at home of his intention, went with determined step to the Principal's house. His cap, instead of being set jauntily far back on his head, was jammed well down over his eyes.

"Is the Principal at home?"

"Yes, come in."

The Principal was a large man with a thick, blond beard and sharp, blue eyes.

"Good day, Johnny! What did you want to see me about?"

"It is horrid, but"—great searching first in one pocket of his trousers, then in the other—"but if you will please take this report back"—

"Take it back? What do you mean, John?"

"Why, because it says here he is a credit to the school, and he isn't that—not now."

"What is that you say? Speak out, my boy."

The boy looked very little as he stood with his knees shaking before the big Principal.

"Because—because his name has been written in the police records today, and the policeman took him there, and so it was horrid that this report should say he was a credit"—

"Come, John, tell me about it from the beginning."

"Why, Nils of the 'Goodwill of Luckton' got his mother to go down-stairs and then he called us boys to come aboard and get some apples; and when we went he told his mother there were thieves on board; and he called the policeman."

"Nils asked you to come on board?"

"Oh, yes; but for all that I knew Mr. and Mrs. Lind would be angry. I knew that perfectly well. But I went, and then I wasn't a credit to the school; so if you will please take this report back"—

There was a short silence.

"I think you may keep the report," said the Principal at last. "For you will surely not do anything of the kind again, Johnny Blossom."

"No. I shan t nave to be taken up by a policeman ever any more." Johnny shook his head energetically. "And I'm going to study hard. Thank you."

At the door he repeated his "thank you" as he bowed himself out.

When he was in the street he put the precious report into his pocket, whistling joyously a beautiful tune that his mother often played. Who cared for any one's teasing now? Even the boys might try it if they liked, for he was ready for them. The Principal knew all there was to know. Awfully kind man, that Principal!

THROUGH FAIRY HALLS

A BOY'S SONG

JAMES HOGG

Where the pools are bright and deep,
Where the gray trout lies asleep,
Up the river and o'er the lea,
That's the way for Billy and me.

Where the blackbird sings the latest,
Where the hawthorn blooms the sweetest,
Where the nestlings chirp and flee,
That's the way for Billy and me.

Where the mowers mow the cleanest,
Where the hay lies thick and greenest,—
There to trace the homeward bee,
That's the way for Billy and me.

Where the hazel bank is steepest,
Where the shadow lies the deepest,
Where the clustering nuts fall free,
That's the way for Billy and me.

The Luck Boy of Toy Valley*

KATHERINE DUNLAP CATHER

In a chalet high up among the Austrian mountains, blue-eyed Franz was very unhappy because his mother and brother Johan were going to Vienna and he had to stay at home with his old grandfather. He bit his lips to keep back the tears as he watched the packing of the box that was to carry their clothing. Then his mother tried to comfort him.

"Never mind, lad," she said. "I'll send you a present from Vienna, and we'll call it a 'luck gift' and hope it will bring good luck. If it does you'll be a lucky boy."

He smiled even if he did feel sad. He had often heard of luck children, for among the Tyrolean peasants there were many stories of those who had been led by fairies to have such wonderful good fortune that ever afterward they were spoken of as the elf-aided, or "Glücks Kinder," and it was so delightful to think about being one of them that he forgot his sorrow. Of course it would be very fine to travel down to Vienna and go into the service of a rich noble there, as his mother and brother were to do, but it would be still better to be a "Glücks Kind," and such things sometimes did happen. So he did not feel sad any more, but whistled and sang and helped with the packing.

*Used by the courteous permission of David C. Cook Publishing Co. and the author.

THROUGH FAIRY HALLS

Early next morning the post chaise rattled up to the door, and Johan and the mother drove away. Franz watched them go down the winding, white road, calling after them in sweet Tyrolean words of endearment until they were out of sight. Then he went back into the hut and began to sandpaper some blocks that his grandfather needed for his work. The old man was a maker of picture frames, all carved and decorated with likenesses of mountain flowers, and these, when sent to Innsbruck and Vienna, brought the money that gave him his living. The figures were too fine and difficult for Franz to carve, but he could lend a hand at fetching blocks and sandpapering. He worked with a vim, for Tyrolean boys think it a disgrace to shirk, but all the while his thoughts were on the luck gift.

"I wonder what it will be?" he said to his grandfather. They took turns at guessing, until it was time to feed the goats and house the chickens for the night.

A week later the man who had driven Johan and his mother away came by on his return from Vienna, and Franz fairly flew out to get his gift.

"It is something very big," he called to the old frame maker as he took a bulging bag. "See, it is stuffed full!" And he expected to find something very wonderful.

But when he opened it, he thought it wasn't wonderful at all. There was a blue velvet jacket, trimmed with gold braid and fastened with glittering buttons, such as Tyrolean boys wore in those days, and in one of the pockets he found a shining knife.

"Well, of all things!" he exclaimed as he held them up for his grandfather to see. "It's a splendid jacket, and the knife is a beauty, but I don't see where the luck part comes in."

But Hals Berner was old and wise, and a knowing smile played over his wrinkled face as he spoke. "It won't be the

first time luck has hidden in a knife," he said, as he bent over his carving.

Franz did not know what he meant. He had always had a knife, for being of a carver's family he was taught to whittle when he was a very little fellow, and he had become remarkably skillful for one of his years. But no wonderful good fortune had come to him, and he was very sure that although each of the presents was nice, neither would bring luck, and he sent that word to Johan. But the brother wrote back from the city, "It will surely turn out to be a luck gift, Franz. Just wait and see." And still the boy wondered.

Winter came and icy winds blew down from the peaks. There was no word from Vienna now, for the valley was shut in by a glittering wall, and travel over the snow-drifted passes was impossible. There were other boys in the village, but each had his work indoors, and there was little time to play, so Franz had no chance for games. He helped his grandfather part of the day and sometimes whittled for his own amusement. It was a lonely life there in the hut, with just the old frame maker, who was often too busy to talk, so Franz was glad to do something to keep him busy. Now he made rings and tops and then just fantastic sticks or blocks.

One day, as he whittled, his grandfather said, "Why don't you make an animal, Franz?"

The boy looked up in surprise. "I don't think I can," he answered.

"Not unless you try," came the reply. "But if you do that you may surprise yourself."

Franz hated to have any one think he was afraid to make an attempt, so he exclaimed, "I wonder if I could make a sheep?"

"Begin and see," the old man advised.

The boy went to work. At first it was discouraging. After many minutes of whittling there was little to suggest what he had in mind. But then, with an occasional turn of the knife by the frame maker, and now and then a bit of advice, the boy began to see that a sheep would grow out of the block, and when it did he felt like a hero who had won a battle.

"It wasn't a bit hard, was it lad?" Hals Berner asked when it was finished.

And Franz agreed that it was not.

That was the beginning, and every day thereafter Franz worked at his whittling, and animal after animal grew under his knife. He was so busy he did not have time to be lonely, and had quite forgotten how sad he had felt over having to stay at home. It was such fun to see the figures come out of the wood and feel that he had made them. Of course they were crude, and not half so handsome as those his grandfather could have made; but anyone could tell what they were, and that was worth a great deal.

By spring he had a whole menagerie, and when his mother came home she found he had been a busy boy, and a happy one as well.

"All made with the luck knife," Johan said as he looked over the work.

"So grandfather says," Franz answered. "It's a splendid knife, but I don't see where the luck comes in."

And again the knowing smile went over the old man's face.

One day soon afterward his mother had word from the man who had been her employer in Vienna that his little son was not well and he was sending him to regain his health in the mountain air. A week later the child arrived with his nurse, and the first thing that attracted his attention was Franz's menagerie.

"Oh! oh!" he exclaimed, "dogs, cats, sheep, goats, lions, elephants, and all made of wood! I want them."

"He means that he wants to buy them," his nurse explained. "Will you sell them, Franz?"

For a minute the boy hesitated. That menagerie had meant many months of whittling, and he loved every animal in it, and if Johan hadn't interrupted, probably he would have refused.

"Why, Franz," the brother exclaimed, "it begins to look like a luck knife after all."

That put a thought into his mind that caused him to answer, "Yes, take them. I can make some more."

So, when the child went back to Vienna he took a wooden menagerie from the Tyrolean mountains. Other Viennese children, seeing it, wanted to possess one, and orders began to pour in to Franz, far more than he could fill. Then other villagers took up the work, until all over the valley people were making animals and toys.

The work grew to be a big industry, and toys from the Grodner Thal were sent all over Germany, and even to the lands beyond. One generation after another went on with the work, and although it is two hundred years since Franz began it, the craft continues there to this day. At Christmas time shops in every land are filled with toys from the Tyrolean mountains, and although they do not know the story, thousands of children have been happier because of a peasant boy's whittling.

So out of the bag sent back from Vienna there came in truth a luck gift, and it wasn't the fine jacket either, but the knife with which Franz whittled his first sheep. The boy had found out that luck doesn't mean something sent by fairies, but the doing a thing so well that it brings a rich reward, and although he lived to be a very old man, he never got over being grateful that his mother made him stay behind when she and Johan went to the city.

The little valley among the Austrian Alps is still called Grodner Thal on the maps, but because of the animals and toys that have come out of it, it is almost as well known by another name. If you are good guessers you can surely tell what it is, especially if you know that the peasants still speak of the lad who made the first menagerie there as the Luck Boy of Toy Valley.

The Duty That Was Not Paid*

KATHERINE DUNLAP CATHER

More than a hundred years ago a man and his two children were journeying from their home in Salzburg to Vienna. They traveled by the Danube boat, and Marianne, the sister, stood by the rail tossing pebbles into the water and watching the turbulent river swallow them up. Her dress was worn almost threadbare, but her face was so sweet and her eyes were so large and bright that she looked pretty for all her shabbiness.

Just behind her on the deck her father and brother were talking. "If we make some money in the city you'll buy sister a new dress, won't you, Father?" little Wolfgang asked.

Marianne whirled and started toward him. She knew that was sure to make her father sad, and she called, "Don't coax, Wolfgang. My dress will do very well until we can afford to buy another, and a new one will seem all the nicer because of my having worn this one so long."

Her brother turned his big, earnest eyes upon her, and said, "But, Marianne, I know you want one. I heard you wish for it by the evening star, and last night you put it in your prayer."

Father Mozart turned from them with a sad look on his face,

*Used by special arrangement with the author and the publishers, David C. Cook Publishing Co.

and walked up and down the deck, wishing very much he could do what Wolfgang asked. But he was just a poor orchestra conductor with an income so small he had to stretch it hard to provide food and shelter for his family. Marianne must wear the shabby frock until better times began, which he hoped would be soon. They were to give some concerts in the Austrian capital, and maybe in that rich, music-loving city would earn enough to make them more comfortable than they had been before. But until then they must not spend a penny save what was needed for food and shelter, because the customs fee on the harp they carried must be paid, and that would reduce their little fund to a very small amount.

Wolfgang, too, thought about it as the boat crept in and out between the hills, and wondered much if there was no way in which Marianne might have the dress before they played in Vienna. His old teacher in Salzburg had often told him that there is a way out of every difficulty if one is clever enough to think of it, and there must be out of this. His own suit was bright and new, for his birthday was just past and it had been his uncle's gift. But Marianne was a very shabby little girl, and he knew she was unhappy though she was brave and sweet about it.

They were gliding past the ruins of the castle that once, men said, had been the prison of Richard the First, England's Lion-Hearted King, when his enemies took him captive on his return from the holy wars. Often in the twilight time at Salzburg, as they waited for the father to come from his work, the mother told them his tale.

"He was very brave and wise, too," the boy thought as he looked at the crumbling pile. "He would have found a way for Marianne to have a new dress if she had been his sister."

Was it the prayer being answered, or just the fulfillment of the wish made by the evening star? For while he thought, an idea came into his head. It was a good idea, it seemed to him, so good that it made him smile. If it worked out, and he believed it would, Marianne might have the dress she wanted so much, because then his father would have more money to spend.

Just to the south they could see the great spire of St. Stephen's, a tall, gray finger against the sky, which told that Vienna was not far away. As it grew nearer and nearer, looming up bigger and plainer before them, Wolfgang thought more and more of his idea, until when they reached the mooring his eyes were dancing and his cheeks were aflame. His father believed the thought of seeing the great capital had excited him, but that was not it at all. He had a secret plan and could hardly wait until he knew whether or not it would work out.

The journey was ended and the people were going ashore. "Please loosen the cover, Father," he said as Leopold Mozart carried the harp toward the customs gate.

"Ah, you are proud of it!" the man answered with a smile.

Wolfgang did not reply, thinking what a poor guesser his father was. He watched him as he set the instrument down and undid the wrapping, bringing the polished frame and glistening strings into full view. Then he went over and took his place beside the harp as the customs officer drew near, and Marianne came and stood beside him. She had forgotten all about her dress in her eagerness to find out how much duty they would have to pay.

"What have you to declare?" the man asked.

"Only a harp," Leopold Mozart answered, as he laid his hand on their one treasure.

"It is a beautiful instrument and valuable," the official said as he looked at it, and named as the price of the duty an amount so big as to cut their little hoard almost in half.

Father Mozart's face grew very serious, and the merriment

went out of Marianne's eyes. But Wolfgang did not worry. He still had that idea in his mind, and believed it would work out.

Leopold Mozart reached into his pocket for the little sack containing his savings, but it was not necessary to open it, for just as he was about to do so, Wolfgang started to play. The customs officer turned with a start and listened, and the people, gathered there, forgot all about duty charges as they crowded around the little musician. His tiny hands swept the strings as if his fingers had some magic power, and the melody they made was sweeter than ever heard on that old wharf. For five minutes, ten, he kept at it, and there was not a whisper or a murmur, only a sort of breathless surprise that one so young could play so wonderfully.

"What!" one exclaimed as he finished, "a lad of his age to perform like that!"

"Yes," the father answered with a smile, "he does well at the harp."

"Amazing," the officer murmured, "I've heard many a good harpist in my day, but never anything sweeter than that."

Wolfgang smiled. The idea was working out, and he was very glad. Already he had visions of a happy sister in a handsome new gown, and turning again to the instrument, he played even more beautifully than before, for the gladness that crept into his heart was creeping also into the music.

For some minutes he picked the strings, while the people listened as if held in a spell, until the father said, "We must go now, for it is getting late, and we have yet to find lodgings in the city." And he handed the money to the officer.

But the man shook his head. "No," he said, and his eyes were very tender. "A boy who can give as much pleasure as that deserves something. Keep the money and buy a present for him."

As Wolfgang heard the words he gave a bound. "Father,"

he exclaimed, with sparkling eyes, "buy the dress for Marianne.
You can do it now, since you have saved the customs money."

The officer looked at him in amazement. "He is a wonderful
lad, truly," he exclaimed, "and as kind as he is wonderful!"

"Yes," came the low reply. "He has wanted nothing so
much as a new dress for his sister."

And she did get it, too, a beautiful one of soft, bright red,
all trimmed with shining buttons. Wolfgang danced with delight
when he saw it, and there was no happier child in all Vienna.

They gave many concerts there, some before the royal family;
and Maria Theresa, the empress, became greatly attached to
both brother and sister, gave them handsome clothes and beautiful gifts, and forgot all about affairs of state while Wolfgang
played. She called him the "little sorcerer," and agreed with
the customs officer that he was a wonderful child.

Then, after some weeks, they went back to the home in
Salzburg, where the boy kept on at his music, doing such marvelous things that his fame traveled far. He grew to be the
great master, Mozart, at whose glorious music the world still

wonders, and he was a generous
and sweet-souled man, just as he
was a big-hearted and thoughtful
child. Many lovely acts are told
of him, but none that shows his
kindness and tenderness in a more
delightful way than when as a
boy on the Vienna wharf he
charmed the customs officer and
all others who heard, and Marianne got the dress for which she
had wished with the duty money
that wasn't paid.

The Story of a Beaver*
WILLIAM DAVENPORT HULBERT

A broad, flat tail came down on the water with a whack that sent the echoes flying back and forth across the pond, and its owner ducked his head, arched his back, and dived to the bottom. It was a very curious tail, for besides being so oddly paddle-shaped, it was covered with what looked like scales, but were really sections of hard, horny, blackish-gray skin. Except its owner's relations, there was no one else in all the world who had one like it. But the strangest thing about it was the many different ways in which he used it. Just now it was his rudder, steering him as he swam under water—and a very good rudder, too.

In a moment his little brown head reappeared, and he and his brothers and sisters went chasing each other round and round the pond, ducking and diving and splashing, raising such a commotion that they sent the ripples washing all along the grassy shores, and having the jolliest kind of a time. It isn't the usual thing for young beavers to be out in broad daylight, but all this happened in the good old days before the railways came, when there were fewer men in northern Michigan than there are now.

When the youngsters wanted a change they climbed up onto a log, and nudged and hunched each other, poking their noses into one another's fat little sides, and each trying to shove his brother or sister back into the water. By and by they scrambled out on the bank, and then, when their fur had dripped a little, they set to work to comb it.

*From *Forest Neighbors*. Used by the permission of Doubleday, Page & Co.

Up they sat on their hind legs and tails—the tail was a stool now, you see—and scratched their heads and shoulders with the long, brown claws of their small, black, hairy hands. Then the hind feet came up one at a time and combed and stroked their sides till the moisture was gone and the fur was soft and smooth and glossy as velvet.

After that they had to have another romp. They were not half as graceful on land as they had been in the water. In fact they were not graceful at all, and the way they stood around on their hind legs, and shuffled, and pranced, and wheeled like baby hippopotami, and slapped the ground with their tails, was one of the funniest sights in the heart of the woods. And the funniest and liveliest of them all was the one who owned that tail. He was the one whom I shall call the Beaver—with a big B.

But even young beavers will sometimes grow tired of play, and at last they all lay down on the grass in the warm, quiet sunshine of the autumn afternoon. The wind had gone to sleep, the pond glittered like steel in its bed of grassy beaver-meadow, the friendly wood stood guard all around, and it was a very good time for five furry little babies to take a nap.

The city in which the Beaver was born was a very old one, and may have been the oldest in North America. Nobody knows when the beavers first began to build the dam that stretched across the stream and backed the water up until it spread out across the valley in a broad, quiet pond. It was probably centuries ago, and for all we can tell it may have been thousands of years back in the past.

Family after family of beavers had worked on that dam, building it a little higher and a little higher, a little longer and a little longer, year after year; and raising the round domes of their houses as the pond rose around them. Their city streets, like those of Venice, were mostly of water, and they themselves were navigators from their earliest youth, and took to the water as naturally as ducks or Englishmen. They were lumbermen, too, and when the timber was all out from along the shores of the pond, they dug canals across the low, level, marshy ground, back to the higher land where the birch and the poplar still grow, and floated the branches and the smaller logs down the water-ways to the pond. In this way they stored up a supply of food for winter, for the beaver's favorite meal is made of tender branches and the bark of trees.

And there were land roads, as well as canals, for here and there narrow trails crossed the swamp, showing where one family after another of busy workers had passed back and forth between the felled trees and the water's edge. Streets, canals, public works, dwellings, lumbering, rich stores laid up for the winter— what more do you want to make a city, even if the houses are few in number, and the population somewhat smaller than that of London or New York?

The first year of our Beaver's life was an easy one, especially the winter, when there was little for anyone to do except to eat, to sleep, and now and then to fish for the roots of the yellow water-lily in the soft mud at the bottom of the pond. During that season not only was he increasing in size and weight, but he was storing up strength for the work that lay before him. It would take much muscle to force those long, yellow teeth of his through the hard, tough flesh of the maple or the birch or the poplar. It would take vigor and push to roll the heavy billets of wood over the grass-tufts to the edge of the water. So it was well for the youngster that for a time he had nothing to do but grow.

But spring came at last. Though the Beaver had many and many a fine romp with his brothers and sisters, still he began to learn to be a little useful in the world, and to do the sort of things that his father and mother did.

Now, on a dark autumn night, behold the young Beaver toiling with might and main. His parents have felled a tree, and it is his business to help them cut up the best portions and carry them home. He gnaws off a small branch, seizes the butt end between his teeth, swings it over his shoulder, and makes for the water, keeping his head twisted around to the right or left so that the end of the branch may trail on the ground behind him. Sometimes he even rises on his hind legs, and walks almost upright, with his broad, strong tail for a prop to keep him from tipping over backward if his load happens to catch on something. Arrived at the canal or at the edge of the pond, he jumps in and swims for town, still carrying the branch over his shoulder, and finally leaves it on the growing pile in front of his father's lodge. Or perhaps the stick is too large and too heavy to be carried in such a way. In that case it must be cut into short billets and rolled to the water's edge. This means he must push with all his might, and there are so many, many grass-tufts and little hillocks in the way! Sometimes the billet rolls down into a hollow, and then it is very hard to get it out again. He works *like a beaver*, and pushes and shoves and toils with tremendous energy, but I am afraid that more than one choice stick never reaches the water.

THROUGH FAIRY HALLS

These were his first tasks. Later on he learned to fell trees himself. Standing up on his hind legs and tail, with his hands braced against the trunk, he would hold his head sidewise, open his mouth wide, set his teeth against the bark, and bring his jaws together with a savage nip, that left a deep gash in the side of the tree. A second nip deepened the gash, and gave it more of a downward slant, and two or three more carried it still farther into the tough wood. Then he would choose a new spot a little farther down, and start a second gash, which was made to slant up towards the first. And when he thought they were both deep enough he would set his jaw firmly in the wood between them, and pull and jerk and twist at it until he had wrenched out a chip—a chip perhaps two inches long, and from an eighth to a quarter of an inch thick. He would make bigger ones when he grew to be bigger himself, but you musn't expect too much at first.

Chip after chip was torn out in this way, and gradually he would work completely around the tree. Then the groove was made deeper, and after awhile it would have to be broadened so that he could get his head farther into it. He seemed to think it was of immense importance to get the job done as quickly as possible, for he worked away with tremendous energy as if felling that tree was the only thing in the world that was worth doing.

Once in a while he would pause for a moment to feel of it with his hands, and to glance up at the top to see whether it was getting ready to fall. Several times he stopped long enough to take a refreshing dip in the pond; but he always hurried back, and pitched in again harder than ever. In fact, he sometimes went at it so impetuously that he slipped and rolled over on his back.

Little by little he dug away the tree's flesh until there was nothing left but its heart. At last it began to sway and crash. The Beaver jumped aside to get out of the way. Hundreds and hundreds of small, tender branches, and delicious little twigs and buds came crashing down where he could cut them off and eat them or carry them away at his leisure.

And so all the beavers in the city labored, and their labor brought its rich reward; everybody was busy and contented, and life was decidedly worth living.

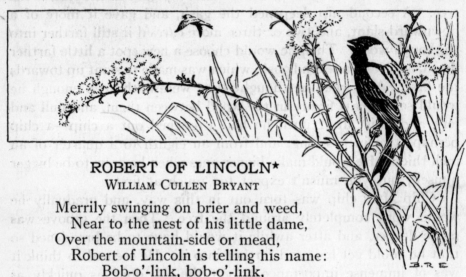

ROBERT OF LINCOLN*
WILLIAM CULLEN BRYANT

Merrily swinging on brier and weed,
    Near to the nest of his little dame,
Over the mountain-side or mead,
    Robert of Lincoln is telling his name:
        Bob-o'-link, bob-o'-link,
          Spink, spank, spink,
Snug and safe is this nest of ours,
Hidden among the summer flowers,
          Chee, chee, chee.

Robert of Lincoln is gayly drest,
    Wearing a bright, black wedding-coat;
White are his shoulders and white his crest,
    Hear him call, in his merry note,
        Bob-o'-link, bob-o'-link,
          Spink, spank, spink,
Look what a nice new coat is mine,
Sure there was never a bird so fine!
          Chee, chee, chee.

*Used by permission of the publishers, D. Appleton & Co.

Music-Loving Bears*
JOAQUIN MILLER

A bear loves music better than he loves honey, and that is saying that he loves music better than he loves his life.

We were going to mill, father and I, and Lyte Howard, in Oregon, about forty years ago, with ox-teams, a dozen or two bags of wheat, threshed with a flail and winnowed with a wagon cover, and were camped for the night by the Calipoola River; for it took two days to reach the mill. Lyte got his fiddle, keeping his gun, of course, close at hand. Pretty soon the oxen came down, came very close, so close that they almost put their cold, moist noses against the backs of our necks as we sat there on the ox-yokes or reclined in our blankets, around the crackling pine-log fire and listened to the wild, sweet strains that swept up and down and up till the very tree tops seemed to dance and quiver with delight.

Then suddenly father seemed to feel the presence of something or somebody strange, and I felt it, too. But the fiddler felt, heard, saw nothing but the divine, wild melody that made the very pine trees dance and quiver to their tips. It is strange how a man—I mean the natural man—will feel a presence long before he hears it or sees it.

*From *True Bear Stories*. Used by special arrangement with the publishers, Rand McNally & Company.

Father got up, turned about, put me behind him as an animal will its young, and peered back and down through the dense tangle of the deep river bank between two of the huge oxen which had crossed the plains with us, to the water's edge; then he reached around and drew me to him with his left hand, pointing between the oxen sharp down the bank with his right forefinger.

A bear! two bears! and another coming; one already more than half way cross the great, mossy log that lay above the deep, sweeping waters of the Calipoola; and Lyte kept on, and the wild, sweet music leaped up and swept through the delighted and dancing boughs above. Then father reached back to the fire and thrust a long, burning bough deeper into the dying embers, and the glittering sparks leaped and laughed and danced and swept out and up and up as if to companion with the stars. Then Lyte knew. He did not hear, he did not see, he only felt; but the fiddle forsook his fingers and his chin in a second, and his gun was to his face with the muzzle thrust down between the oxen. And then my father's gentle hand reached out, lay on that long, black, Kentucky rifle barrel, and it dropped down, slept once more at the fiddler's side. And again the melodies; and the very stars came down, believe me, to listen, for they never seemed as big and so close by before. The bears sat down on their haunches at last, and one of them kept opening his mouth and putting out his red tongue, as if he really wanted to taste the music. Every now and then one of them would lift up a paw and gently tap the ground, as if to keep time with the music. And both my papa and Lyte said next day that those bears really wanted to dance.

And that is all there is to say about that, except that my father was the gentlest gentleman I ever knew and his influence must have been boundless; for who ever before heard of any

hunter laying down his rifle with a family of fat black bears holding the little snow-white cross on their breasts almost within reach of its muzzle.

The moon came up by and by, and the chin of the weary fiddler sank lower and lower, till all was still. The oxen lay down and ruminated, with their noses nearly against us. Then the coal-black bears melted away before the milk-white moon, and we slept there, with the sweet breath of the cattle, like incense, upon us.

The Dance of the Forest People*

From *The Arkansas Bear*

ALBERT BIGELOW PAINE

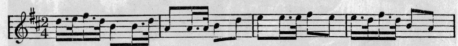

Oh, there was a little boy and his name was Bo,
Went out into the woods when the moon was low,

And he met an Old Bear who was hungry for a snack,
And the folks are still awaiting for Bosephus to come back.

For the boy became the teacher of this kind and gentle creature,
Who was faithful in his friendship and was watchful in his care.

And they traveled on forever and they'll never, never, sever,
Bosephus and the fiddle and the Old—Black—Bear.

THE camp fire had died down to a few red embers, and the big moon hanging on the tree-tops made all the world white and black, with one bright splash in the brook below.

The little boy, Bosephus, and Horatio, the old black Bear, had finished their supper.

While the Bear played on his fiddle the little boy had been watching a slim, moving shadow that seemed to have drifted out from among the heavier shadows into the half-lit open space

*Taken from *The Arkansas Bear*, copyrighted by Henry Altemus Company. Used by the kind permission of the publishers.

in front of them.   As the music ceased, it drifted back again.

"Play some more, Ratio," he whispered.

Again the Bear played and again the slim shadow appeared
in the moonlight and presently another and another.   Some of
them were slender and graceful; some of them heavier and slower
of movement.   As the music continued they swung into a half
circle and drew closer.   Now and then the boy caught a glimpse
of two shining sparks that kept time and movement with each.
He could hardly breathe in his excitement.

"Look here, Ratio," he whispered.   Horatio did not stir.

"Sh-h!" he said, softly.   "My friends—the forest people."

The Bear slackened the music a little as he spoke and the
shadows wavered and drew away.   Then he livened the strain
and they trooped forward again eagerly.   Just then the moon
swung clear of the thick trees and the dancers were in its full
flood.   The boy watched them with trembling eagerness.

A tall, cat-like creature, erect and graceful, swayed like a
phantom in and out among the others and seemed to lead.   As
it came directly in front of the musicians it turned full front
toward them.   It was an immense gray panther.

At any other time Bo would have screamed.   Now he was
only fascinated.   Its step was perfect and its long tail waved
behind it, like a silver plume, which the others followed.   Two
red foxes kept pace with it.   Two gray ones, a little to one side,
imitated their movements.   In the background a family of three
bears danced so awkwardly that Bo was inclined to laugh.

"We will teach them to do better than that," he whispered.

Horatio nodded without pausing. The dancers separated, each group to itself, the gray panther in the foreground. Spellbound, the boy watched the beautiful, swaying creature. He had been taught to fear the "painter," as it was called in Arkansaw, but he had no fear now. He almost felt that he must step out into that enchanted circle and join in the weird dance.

New arrivals stole constantly out of the darkness to mingle in the merrymaking. A little way apart a group of rabbits skipped wildly together, while near them a party of capering wolves had forgotten their taste for blood. Two plump 'coons and a heavy-bodied 'possum, after trying in vain to keep up with the others, were content to sit side by side and look on. Other friends, some of whom the boy did not know, slipped out into the magic circle, and, after watching the others for a moment, leaped madly into the revel. The instinct of the old days had claimed them when the wild beasts of the forest and the wood nymphs trod measures to the pipes of Pan. The boy leaned close to the player.

"The rest of it," he whispered. "Play the rest of it!"

"I am afraid. They have never heard it before."

"Play it! Play it!" commanded Bo, excitedly.

There was a short, sharp pause at the end of the next bar, then a sudden wild dash into the second half of the tune. The prancing animals stopped as if by magic. For an instant they stood motionless, staring with eyes like coals. Then came a great rush forward, the gray panther at the head. The boy saw them coming, but could not move.

"Sing!" shouted Horatio; "Sing!"

For a second the words refused to come. Then they flooded forth in the moonlight. Bo could sing, and he had never sung as he did now.

THROUGH FAIRY HALLS

"Oh, our singing, yes our singing, all our friends to us 'tis bringing,
For it sets the woods to ringing, and the forest people know

That we do not mean to harm them in their dancing, nor alarm them—
We are seeking but to charm them with the sounds of long ago.

At the first notes of the boy's clear voice the animals hesitated; then they crept up slowly and gathered about to listen. They did not dance to this new strain. Perhaps they wanted to learn it first. Bo sang on and on. The listening audience never moved. Then Horatio played very softly, and the singer lowered his voice until it became like a far off echo. When Bo sang like this he often closed his eyes. He did so now.

The music sank lower and lower, until it died away in a whisper. The boy ceased singing and opening his eyes gazed about him. Here and there he imagined he heard a slight rustle in the leaves, but the gray panther was gone. The frisking rabbits and the capering wolves had vanished. The red and gray foxes, the awk- ward bears and the rest of that frolicking throng had melted back into the shadows. So far as he could peer into the dim forest he was alone with his tried and faithful friend.

Little Nell and Mrs. Jarley's Wax Works*
CHARLES DICKENS

IT was not a shabby, dingy, dusty cart, but a smart little house upon wheels, with white dimity curtains festooning the windows, and window-shutters of blue picked out with panels of orange. Neither was it a gipsy caravan, for at the open door (graced with a bright brass knocker) sat a lady, stout and comfortable to look upon, her bonnet trembling with bows. And this lady's occupation was the very pleasant one of taking tea. The tea-things, including a cold knuckle of ham, were set forth upon a drum, covered with a white napkin; and there, as if at the most convenient round-table in all the world, sat this roving lady.

It happened that at that moment she had her cup to her lips, and it was not until she was in the act of setting it down, that she beheld an old man and a young child walking slowly by, and glancing at her tea things with longing eyes.

"Hey," cried the lady of the caravan shortly but kindly, "Who are you?"

The child, who was a pretty little blue eyed girl, answered in a soft voice, "My name is Nell." Then she took the hand of the old man with a tender, protecting air, as though he were the child and she his mother, "and this is my grandfather. Can you tell us how far we shall have to walk before we come to the next town?"

The stout lady answered that the town was at least eight miles off.

This information a little discouraged the child, who could scarcely keep back a tear as she glanced along the darkening road. Her grandfather made no complaint, but he sighed heavily as he leaned upon his staff, and vainly tried to see into the dusty distance.

*Arranged from *The Old Curiosity Shop*.

THROUGH FAIRY HALLS

The lady of the caravan was about to gather her tea things together and clean the table, but noting the child's anxious manner, she hesitated and stopped. The child curtsied, thanked her for her information, and had already led the old man some fifty yards or so away, when the lady of the caravan called to her to return.

"Come nearer, nearer still," said she, beckoning to her to ascend the steps. "Are you hungry, child?"

"Not very, but we are tired, and it's—it is a long way."

"Is your home in the next town?"

"No, we have no home! We are wanderers."

"Well, hungry or not, you had better have some tea. I suppose you are agreeable to that, old gentleman?"

The grandfather humbly pulled off his hat and thanked her. The lady of the caravan then bade him come up the steps likewise, but the drum proving too small a table for two, they went down again, and sat upon the grass, where she handed them the tea-tray, the bread and butter, the knuckle of ham, and in short every thing of which she had eaten herself.

"Set 'em out near the hind wheels, child, that's the best place," she said, directing the arrangements from above. "Now hand up the teapot for a little more hot water, and a pinch of fresh tea, and then both of you eat and drink as much as you can, and don't spare any thing; that's all I ask of you."

So the two made a hearty meal and enjoyed it to the utmost.

While they were thus engaged, the lady of the caravan alighted on the earth, and with her hands clasped behind her, and her large bonnet trembling excessively, walked up and down in a very stately manner, looking over the caravan from time to time with an air of calm delight, and enjoying particularly the orange panels and the brass knocker, of which she was very proud. When she had taken this gentle exercise for some time, she sat

down upon the steps and called "George"; whereupon a man
in a carter's frock, who had been hidden from sight in a hedge,
parted the twigs that concealed him and appeared in a sitting
attitude, supporting on his legs a baking-dish, and bearing in
his right hand a knife, and in his left a fork.

"Yes, Missus," said George.

"How did you find the cold pie, George?"

"It warn't amiss, mum."

"We are not a heavy load, George. Would these two travelers make much difference to the horses, if we took them with
us?" asked his mistress, pointing to Nell and the old man who
were painfully preparing to resume their journey on foot.

"They'd make a difference in course," said George doggedly.

But his mistress turned to the old man and the child and told
them they should go on to the town with her in the caravan.
Nell was overjoyed and thanked the lady earnestly.

She helped with great readiness to put away the tea-things,
and, the horses being by that time harnessed, mounted into the
vehicle, followed by her delighted grandfather. The lady then
shut the door and sat herself down by her drum at an open window. The steps were taken down by George and stowed under
the carriage. Then away they went, with a great noise of flapping and creaking and straining; and the bright brass knocker,
which nobody ever knocked at, knocking one perpetual double
knock of its own accord as they jolted along.

When they had traveled slowly forward for some short distance, Nell ventured to look round the caravan and observe it
more closely. One half of it was carpeted, and so partitioned
off at the further end as to form a sleeping-place, made after
the fashion of a berth on board ship. This was shaded, like
the little windows, with fair white curtains, and looked comfortable enough, though by what kind of gymnastic exercise the

lady of the caravan ever managed to get into it, was a mystery. The other half served for a kitchen, and was fitted up with a stove, whose small chimney passed through the roof. It held also, a closet or larder, several chests, a great pitcher of water and a few cooking-utensils. These latter necessaries hung upon the walls, which were also ornamented with a triangle and a couple of well-thumbed tambourines.

The lady of the caravan sat at one window, and little Nell and her grandfather at the other, while the caravan jogged on. At first the two travelers spoke little, and only in whispers, but as they grew more familiar with the place, they ventured to talk about the country through which they were passing, and the different objects that presented themselves, until the old man fell asleep. The lady of the caravan, seeing this, invited Nell to come and sit beside her.

"Well, child," she said, "how do you like this way of traveling?"

Nell replied that she thought it was very pleasant indeed.

Then getting up, the lady brought out from a corner a large roll of canvas about a yard in width, which she laid upon the floor and spread open with her foot, until it nearly reached from one end of the caravan to the other.

"There, child," she said proudly, "read that."

Nell walked down it, and read aloud, in enormous black letters, the inscription,

JARLEY'S WAX-WORKS

"Read it again," said the lady, enjoying the fine sounding words.

"Jarley's Wax-Works," repeated Nell.

"That's me," said the lady. "I am Mrs. Jarley."

And she unfolded another scroll, whereon was written, "ONE HUNDRED FIGURES THE FULL SIZE OF LIFE." And then another, "THE ONLY STUPENDOUS COLLEC-

TION OF REAL WAX-WORK IN THE WORLD," and then several smaller scrolls with such inscriptions as:

"I never saw any wax-work, ma'am," said Nell. "Is it funnier than Punch?"

"Funnier!" said Mrs. Jarley, in a shrill voice. "It is not funny at all. It's figures of people made out of wax, and so like life, that if wax-work only spoke and walked about, you'd hardly know the difference."

"Is it here in the cart, ma'am?" asked Nell, whose curiosity was awakened by this description.

"Is what here, child?"

"The wax-works, ma'am."

"Why bless you, child, what are you thinking of—how could such a collection be here, where you see every thing except the inside of one little cupboard and a few boxes? It's gone on in the other vans to the Assembly-rooms, and there it'll be exhibited the day after to-morrow. You are going to the same town, and you'll see it I dare say."

"I shall not be in the town, I think, ma'am," said the child.

"Not there!" cried Mrs. Jarley. "Then where will you be?"

"I — I — don't quite know. I am not certain."

"You don't mean to say that you're traveling about the country without knowing where you're going to?" said the lady of the caravan. "What curious people you are!"

"We are poor people, ma'am," returned Nell, "and are only wandering about. We have nothing to do; I wish we had."

"You amaze me more and more," said Mrs. Jarley, after remaining for some time as silent as one of her own figures.

At length she summoned the driver to come under the window at which she was seated, and held a long conversation with him in a low tone, as if she were asking his advice on an important point. Then she drew in her head again, and, seeing the grandfather had awakened, said:

"Do you want a good place for your grand-daughter to work, master? If you do, I can put her in the way of getting one."

"I can't leave her," answered the old man. "We can't separate. What would become of me without her?"

"If you want to employ yourself, too," said Mrs. Jarley, "there would be plenty for you to do in the way of helping to dust the figures, and so forth. What I want your grand-daughter for, is to point out to the company; she would soon learn who the figures are, and she has a way with her that people wouldn't think unpleasant, though she does come after me; for I've been always accustomed to go round with visitors myself. It's not a common offer, bear in mind," said the lady, rising into the grand tone in which she was accustomed to address her audiences; "it's Jarley's wax-works, remember."

As to salary she could pledge herself to no certain sum until she had seen what Nell could do, and watched her in the performance of her duties. But board and lodging, both for her and her grandfather, she bound herself to provide, and she furthermore passed her word that the board should always be good and plentiful.

Nell and her grandfather consulted together, while Mrs. Jarley, with her hands behind her, walked up and down the caravan with uncommon dignity.

"Now, child," cried Mrs. Jarley, coming to a halt as Nell turned toward her.

"We are very much obliged to you, ma'am," said Nell, "and thankfully accept your offer."

"And you'll never be sorry for it," returned Mrs. Jarley. "I'm pretty sure of that. So as that's all settled, let us have a bit of supper."

In the meanwhile, the caravan came at last upon the paved streets of a town which were clear of passengers, and quiet, for it was by this time near midnight and the townspeople were all abed. As it was too late an hour to go to the room where they were to show the wax-works, they turned aside into a piece of waste ground that lay just within the old town-gate, and drew up there for the night, near to another caravan, which was employed in carrying the wonderful figures from place to place.

This caravan being empty (for it had left the wax-works at the place of exhibition) was pointed out to the old man as his sleeping-place for the night; and within its wooden walls Nell made him up the best bed she could from the materials at hand. For herself, she was to sleep in Mrs. Jarley's own traveling-carriage, as a mark of that lady's favor and confidence.

Sleep hung upon the eyelids of the child so long, that, when she awoke, Mrs. Jarley was already decorated with her large bonnet, and actively engaged in preparing breakfast. She received Nell's apology for being so late, with perfect good-humor, and said that she would not have roused her if she had slept on until noon.

The meal finished, Nell assisted to wash the cups and saucers, and put them in their proper places. These household duties performed, Mrs. Jarley arrayed herself in an exceedingly bright shawl for the purpose of making a very grand appearance as she walked through the streets of the town.

"The van will come on after me to bring the boxes," said Mrs. Jarley, "and you had better come in it, child. I am obliged to walk, very much against my will; but the people expect it of me. They must have a look at Mrs. Jarley, owner of the one and only Jarley's Wax-Works. How do I look, child?"

Nell returned a satisfactory reply, and Mrs. Jarley, after sticking a great many pins into various parts of her figure, and trying several times to see her own back, was at last satisfied with her appearance, and went forth majestically.

The caravan followed at no great distance. As it went jolting through the street, Nell peeped from the window, curious to see in what kind of place they were. It was a pretty large town, with an open square, in the middle of which was the Town-hall, with a clock-tower and a weather-cock. There were houses

of stone, houses of red brick, houses of yellow brick, houses of plaster; and houses of wood, many of them very old, with withered faces carved upon the beams, and staring down into the street. These had very little, winking windows, and low-arched doors, and, in some of the narrower ways, quite overhung the pavement. The streets were very clean, very sunny, very empty, and very dull. Nothing seemed to be going on but the clocks, and they had such drowsy faces, such heavy, lazy hands, and such cracked voices, that they surely must have been too slow. The very dogs were asleep.

THROUGH FAIRY HALLS

Rumbling along with most unwonted noise, the caravan stopped at last at the place of exhibition, where Nell dismounted amidst an admiring group of children, who evidently supposed her to be one of the wax figures. The chests were soon taken in to be unlocked by Mrs. Jarley, who, attended by George and another man, was waiting to decorate the room with the red festoons and other ornaments that came from the chests.

As the stupendous collection was yet concealed by cloths, lest the dust should injure their complexions, Nell bestirred herself to help and her grandfather also was of great service. The two men being well used to it, did a great deal in a short time; and Mrs. Jarley served out the tin tacks from a linen pocket which she wore for the purpose.

When the festoons were all put up as tastily as they might be, the stupendous collection was uncovered. There were displayed, on a raised platform some two feet from the floor, running round the room and parted from the public by a crimson rope, a number of wax figures as big as life, singly and in groups. They were clad in glittering dresses of various climes and times, and standing more or less unsteadily upon their legs, with their eyes wide open, and all their faces expressing great surprise. All the gentlemen were very pigeon-breasted and very blue about the beards, and all the ladies and all the gentlemen were looking intensely nowhere, and staring with extraordinary earnestness at nothing.

When Nell was over her first joy at this glorious sight, Mrs. Jarley gave her a willow wand, long used by herself for pointing out the characters, and was at great pains to tell her just what she must do.

Soon Nell knew all about the fat man, and the thin man, the tall man, the short man, the wild boy of the woods, and other historical characters. And so apt was she to remember them all, that she was soon perfectly able to guide all visitors.

Mrs. Jarley then took her young friend and pupil to see the other arrangements. The passage had been changed into a grove of green cloth, hung with the inscriptions she had already seen. A highly ornamented table was placed at the upper end for Mrs. Jarley herself, where she was to sit and take the money, in company with his Majesty King George the Third, Mary

Queen of Scots, and other important personages. The preparations without doors had not been neglected either; for a beautiful nun was standing on a balcony over the door; and a brigand with the blackest possible head of hair, and the clearest possible complexion, was at that moment being taken round the town in a cart.

In the midst of the various plans for attracting visitors to the show, little Nell was not forgotten. Decorated with paper flowers, she was given a seat beside the Brigand in the cart dressed with flags and streamers, wherein he rode. In this state and ceremony, she rode slowly through the town every morning, giving out handbills from a basket, to the sound of drum and trumpet. The beauty of the child, coupled with her gentle bearing, produced quite a sensation in the little country place. Grown-up folks began to be interested in the bright-eyed girl, and some score of little boys left nuts and apples, directed to her, at the wax-works door.

All this interest in Nell was not lost upon Mrs. Jarley, who soon sent the Brigand out alone again, and kept Nell in the show-room, so that the people who were interested in her, would pay to come inside, where she described the figures every half-hour to the great satisfaction of all.

Although her duties were not easy, Nell found in the lady of the caravan a very kind and considerate person, who not only liked to be comfortable herself, but wished to make everybody about her comfortable also.

So Nell and her grandfather found a comfortable home for some time with

MRS. JARLEY'S WAX-WORKS.

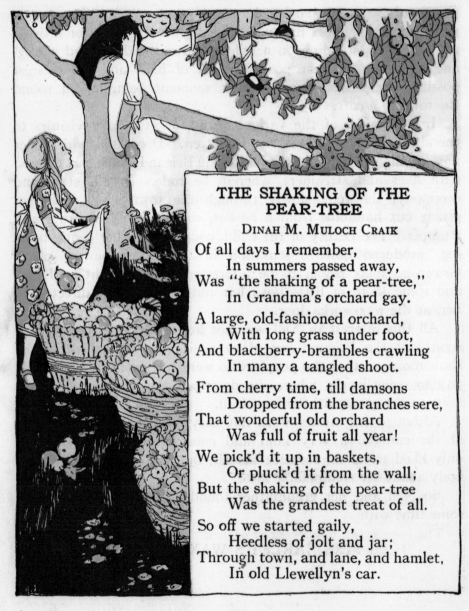

THE SHAKING OF THE PEAR-TREE

DINAH M. MULOCH CRAIK

Of all days I remember,
  In summers passed away,
Was "the shaking of a pear-tree,"
  In Grandma's orchard gay.

A large, old-fashioned orchard,
  With long grass under foot,
And blackberry-brambles crawling
  In many a tangled shoot.

From cherry time, till damsons
  Dropped from the branches sere,
That wonderful old orchard
  Was full of fruit all year!

We pick'd it up in baskets,
  Or pluck'd it from the wall;
But the shaking of the pear-tree
  Was the grandest treat of all.

So off we started gaily,
  Heedless of jolt and jar;
Through town, and lane, and hamlet,
  In old Llewellyn's car.

142

THROUGH FAIRY HALLS

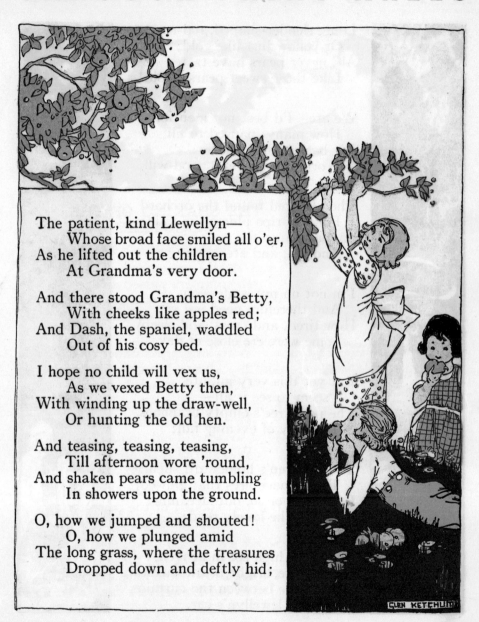

The patient, kind Llewellyn—
    Whose broad face smiled all o'er,
As he lifted out the children
    At Grandma's very door.

And there stood Grandma's Betty,
    With cheeks like apples red;
And Dash, the spaniel, waddled
    Out of his cosy bed.

I hope no child will vex us,
    As we vexed Betty then,
With winding up the draw-well,
    Or hunting the old hen.

And teasing, teasing, teasing,
    Till afternoon wore 'round,
And shaken pears came tumbling
    In showers upon the ground.

O, how we jumped and shouted!
    O, how we plunged amid
The long grass, where the treasures
    Dropped down and deftly hid;

Long, slender-shaped, red-russet,
  Or yellow just like gold;
Ah! never pears have tasted
  Like those sweet pears of old!

We ate—I'd best not mention
  How many: paused to fill
Big basket after basket;
  Working with right good-will;

Then hunted round the orchard
  For half-ripe plums—in vain;
So, back unto the pear-tree,
  And ate, and ate again.

I'm not on my confession,
  And therefore need not say
How tired, and cross, and sleepy,
  Some were ere close of day,

But yet this very minute,
  I seem to see it all—
The pear-tree's empty branches,
  The grey of evening fall;

The children's homeward silence,
  The furnace fires that glowed,
Each mile or so, out streaming
  Across the lonely road;

And high, high set in heaven,
  One large, bright, beauteous star,
That shone between the curtains
  Of old Llewellyn's car.

The Twelve Months
A Bohemian Fairy Tale

THERE was once a woman who had in her care two children. Katinka, the elder, was the woman's own daughter, and she was as ugly in face as she was in heart, but Dobrunka, the younger, who was only a foster-child, was both beautiful and good. Now the sight of Dobrunka with all her winsome ways, made Katinka appear more than ever hateful and ugly. So the mother and daughter were always in a rage with Dobrunka.

She was made to sweep, cook, wash, sew, spin, weave, cut the grass and take care of the cow, while Katinka lived like a princess. All this Dobrunka did with great good will, but that only made Katinka and her mother the more angry. The better she was, the more plainly did their own wickedness show by contrast, and as they had no wish to do away with their wickedness, they made up their minds to do away with Dobrunka.

One cold day in January, when frost castles glistened on the window panes and the earth was white with snow, Katinka took a fancy for some violets. She called Dobrunka harshly to her and said, "Go to the forest, lazy-bones, and bring me a bunch of violets, that I may put them in my bosom and enjoy their fragrance."

"O sister," answered Dobrunka gently, "I cannot find you any violets under the snow."

But Katinka snapped out angrily, "Hold your tongue and do as I bid you. Go to the forest and bring me back a bunch of violets or you'll find this door forever slammed shut in your face!"

Upon this Katinka and her mother took Dobrunka by the arm, thrust her, without wraps or warm winter clothing, out into the cold, and drew the bolt on her.

The poor girl went to the forest weeping sadly. Everything was covered with snow. There was not a foot path anywhere, and the giant pines and oaks bowed their branches low, borne down with their icy burdens. Soon in all this white and glittering wilderness, Dobrunka lost her way and wandered about, famishing with hunger and perishing with cold. Still in her heart she trusted that help would come to one who had done no harm.

All at once she saw a light in the distance, a light that glowed in the sky and quivered now and again as if from the flickering flame of some mighty fire. With her eyes fixed hopefully on that light, Dobrunka climbed toward it. Higher and higher she climbed until at last she reached the top of a giant rock, and there, about a fire, their figures bright in the light and casting long, dark shadows behind, sat twelve motionless figures on twelve great stones. Each figure was wrapped in a long, flowing mantle, his head covered with a hood which fell over his eyes. Three of these mantles were white like the snow, three were green like the grass of the meadows, three were golden like sheaves of ripe wheat, and three were purple as ripened grapes. These twelve figures, who sat there gazing at the fire in perfect silence, were the Twelve Months of the Year.

Dobrunka knew January by his long, white beard. He was the only one who had a staff in his hand. The sweet girl was confused at this sight, for she was not one to thrust herself forward with strangers. Still she spoke to them with great respect.

"My good sirs, I pray you let me warm myself by your fire; I am freezing with cold."

January nodded his head and motioned her to draw near the blaze.

"Why have you come here, my child?" he asked. "What are you looking for?"

"I am looking for violets," replied Dobrunka.

"This is not the season for violets. Dost thou expect to find violets in the time of snow?" January's voice was gruff.

"Nay," replied Dobrunka sadly, "I know this is not the season for violets, but my foster sister and mother thrust me out of doors and bade me get them. They will never let me come under the shelter of their roof again unless I obey. O my good sirs, can you not tell me where I shall find them?"

Old January rose, and turning to a mere youth in a green mantle, put his staff in his hand and said:

"Brother March, this is your business."

March rose in turn and stirred the fire with the staff, when behold! the flames rose, the snow melted, the buds began to swell on the trees, the grass turned green under the bushes, faint, faint color peeped forth through the green, and the violets opened, —it was Spring.

"Make haste, my child, and gather your violets," said March.

Dobrunka gathered a large bouquet, thanked the Twelve Months, and ran home joyously. Katinka and her mother were struck dumb with astonishment when they saw her spring lightly in with shining face at the doorway. The fragrance of the violets filled the whole house.

"Where did you find these things?" asked Katinka when she had recovered the use of her tongue.

"Up yonder, on the mountain," answered Dobrunka. "It looked like a great blue carpet under the bushes."

But Katinka only snatched away the flowers, put them in her own bosom, and never once said so much as a "Thank you!"

The next morning Katinka, as she sat idling by the stove, took a fancy for some strawberries.

"Go to the forest, good-for-nothing, and bring me some strawberries," cried she to Dobrunka.

"O sister," answered Dobrunka, "but there are no strawberries under the snow."

"Hold your tongue and do as I bid you."

And the mother and daughter took Dobrunka by the arm, thrust her out of the door and drew the bolt on her once again.

So the sweet girl returned to the forest, singing this time to keep up her courage, and looking with all her eyes for the light she had seen the day before. At length she spied it, and reached the great fire, trembling with cold, but still singing.

The Twelve Months were in their places, motionless and silent.

"My good sirs," said Dobrunka, "please to let me warm myself by your fire; I am almost frozen."

"Why have you come hither again?" asked January. "What are you looking for now?"

"I am looking for strawberries," answered she.

"This is not the season for strawberries," growled January, "there are no strawberries under the snow."

"I know it," replied Dobrunka sadly, "but alas! I may never again cross my foster mother's threshold, unless I find them."

Old January rose, and turning to a full grown man in a golden mantle, he put his staff in his hand, saying,

"Brother June, this is your business."

June rose in turn, and stirred the fire with the staff, when behold! the flames rose, the snow melted, the earth grew green, the trees were covered with leaves, the birds sang, the flowers burst into bloom—it was Summer. Thousands of little white stars dotted the green turf, then turned slowly to red strawberries, ripe and luscious in their little green cups.

"Make haste, my child, and gather your strawberries," said June.

Dobrunka filled her apron, thanked the Twelve Months and ran home joyfully. Once again Katinka and her mother were struck dumb with astonishment when they saw her spring lightly in with shining face at the doorway. The fragrance of the strawberries filled the whole house.

"Where did you find these fine things?" asked Katinka, when she had recovered the use of her tongue.

"Up yonder on the mountain," answered Dobrunka as she handed the berries to Katinka, "there were so many of them, that they looked like a crimson carpet on the ground."

Katinka and her mother devoured the strawberries and never once said so much as a "Thank you."

The third day, Katinka took a fancy for some red apples, and she thrust Dobrunka out to fetch them with the same threat she had used before. Dobrunka ran through the snow. So she came once more to the top of the great rock and the motionless figures around the fire.

"You here again, my child?" said January, as he made room for her before the fire. Dobrunka told him sadly it was rosy red apples she must bring home this time.

Old January rose as before.

"Brother September," said he to a man with an iron-gray beard who wore a purple mantle, "this is your business."

September rose and stirred the fire with the staff, when behold! the flames ascended, the snow melted, yellow and crimson leaves appeared on the trees, gently a brown leaf floated down—it was autumn. But Dobrunka saw one thing only, an apple tree with its rosy fruit.

"Make haste, my child, shake the tree," said September.

Dobrunka shook it; an apple fell; she shook it again, and down fell another.

"Now take what thou hast and hurry home!" cried September.

The good child thanked the Twelve Months and obediently ran back home. Now the astonishment of Katinka and her mother knew no bounds—

"Apples in January! Where did you get them?" asked Katinka.

"Up yonder on the mountain; there is a tree there loaded down with them."

"Why did you bring only these two? You ate the rest on the way!"

"Nay, sister, I did not touch them. I was only permitted to shake the tree twice, so only two apples fell down."

At that Katinka cried angrily, "I do not believe you. You have eaten the rest. Begone!" and she drove Dobrunka out of the room. Then she sat down and ate one of the apples while her mother ate the other. Their flavor was delicious. They had never tasted the like before.

"Mother," cried Katinka, "Give me my warm fur cloak. I must have more of these apples. I shall go to the mountain, find the tree and shake it as long as I like, whether I am permitted or not. I shall bring back for myself all the delicious fruit on the tree."

The mother tried to stop her from going forth into the wintry forest. But the spoiled child would not heed her. Wrapping herself in her warm fur coat, and pulling the hood down over her ears, she hurried away.

Everything was covered with snow, there was not even a foot path. Katinka lost her way, but, urged on by greedy desire

for the apples, she still went forward till she spied a light in the distance. Then she climbed and she climbed till at last she reached the place where the Twelve Months sat about their fire. But she knew not who they were, so she pushed rudely through their midst and up to the fire without even a "By your leave."

"Why have you come here? What do you want?" asked old January gruffly.

"What matters it to you, old man?" answered Katinka. "It is none of your business." And without another word she turned and disappeared in the forest.

January frowned till his brow was black as a storm cloud. He raised his staff above his head, and in a twinkling, the fire went out, black darkness covered the earth, the wind rose and the snow fell.

Katinka could not see the way before her. The snow beat on her face and into her eyes and loomed up, mountains high, before her. She lost herself and vainly tried to find the way home. She called her mother, she cursed her sister, she shrieked out wildly. The snow fell and the wind blew, the snow fell and the wind blew—

The mother looked for her darling ceaselessly. First from the door and then from the window, and then from the door and then from the window. The hours passed—the clock struck midnight and still Katinka did not return.

"I shall go and look for my daughter," said the mother. So she wrapped herself warmly in her great fur cloak and hood and waded off through the drifts into the forest.

Everything was covered with snow; there was not even a foot path. At each step the woman called out through the storm for her daughter. The snow fell and the wind blew, the snow fell and the wind blew—

THROUGH FAIRY HALLS

Dobrunka waited at home through the night but no one returned. In the morning she sat herself down at her spinning wheel and began to spin, but ever and again she sprang up and looked out at the window.

"What can have happened?" she said. But the only answer was the glare of the sun on the ice and the cracking of the branches beneath their heavy burdens.

Winter passed and summer came, but Katinka and her mother never returned to the little cottage beside the forest. So the house, the cow, the garden and the meadow fell to Dobrunka. In the course of time her Prince came. She married and the place resounded with laughter and joy and singing. The Spring Months called the world into bloom for her; Summer brought her flowers and sunny skies and green things growing; Autumn filled her storehouses with golden grain and ripened fruit, and Winter gave her sweet home joys with her little ones by the blazing hearth. No matter how much the North wind blew, and the house shook, and the snow fell—there was always spring and summer in Dobrunka's heart. So the roses climbed up over her cottage, the sweetest song birds sang at her door, her blossoming fruit trees perfumed the air, and the laughter of her children made music everywhere.

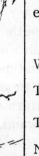

PROVIDENCE

When all thy mercies, O my God,
　My rising soul surveys,
Transported with the view, I'm lost
　In wonder, love, and praise.

Ten thousand thousand precious gifts
　My daily thanks employ;
Nor is the least a cheerful heart,
　That tastes those gifts with joy.

—*Joseph Addison.*

The Three Wishes
A Spanish Fairy Tale

One winter's night many years ago, an old man, named Pedro, and his wife, Joanna, sat by their cozy fire, talking to one another, in a little old village in Spain. Now Pedro was comfortably well off in the goods of this world, but instead of giving thanks to God for the benefits they enjoyed, he and his wife spent all their time in wishing for the good things possessed by their neighbors.

"Bah!" cried Pedro. "This wretched little hut of ours is only fit to house a donkey! I wish we had the fine house and farm of our neighbor, Diego!"

"Aye! Diego's house and farm are well enough," answered Joanna. "Still I should like a mansion such as the grandees possess—such a one as that of Don Juan de la Rosa."

"Then there's that old donkey of ours," went on Pedro sullenly. "Good for nothing—nothing at all. He cannot carry an empty sack! Would that I owned Diego's strong Andalusian mule!"

"O aye!" said Joanna. "Diego's mule is better than our donkey. Yet, for me, I should like a white horse with trappings of scarlet and gold, like Donna Isabella's. Strange how some people have only to wish in order to get a thing. I've never been in such luck. Would that we had but to speak to have our wishes come true!"

Scarcely were the words out of Joanna's mouth when lo! on the hearth before the old couple appeared a beautiful little lady. She was not more than eighteen inches high and her garments were white and filmy and full of opal tints as though made of smoke, while a smoky veil floated down from a crown of sparks on her head. In her hand she bore a little golden wand, on the end of which glowed a single spark.

"I am the Fairy Fortunata," said she. "I have heard your complaints and am come to give you what you desire. Three

wishes you shall have,—one for you, Joanna,—one for you, Pedro,
—and the third you shall agree upon between you, and I will
grant it in person when I return at this time tomorrow."

So saying, the Fairy Fortunata sprang through the flames and
disappeared. Ah! but the old couple were delighted. Three
wishes to come true! They began to think at once of what they
most desired in all the world. Wishes came swarming to them as
thick as bees to a hive. The old man would be content with such
prosperity as his neighbor, the farmer Diego, enjoyed, but the old
woman—ah! her desires flew high—a palace with domes and spires
and cupolas, and floors tiled with sapphire, and walls and ceilings
done with arabesques of crimson, blue and gold; colonnaded
courtyards with fountains playing in the centre, and gardens and
servants and what not besides! Well, so many were the desires
that came crowding to the old couple, that they could not agree
off-hand on just which three to wish for. So they determined to

put off their decision until the next day and began talking of different things altogether.

"I dropped in at Diego's this morning," said Pedro, "and they were making black puddings. Um! but they smelled good! Diego can buy the best of food. He does not have to put up with such poor stuff as we have to eat!"

"True! True!" said Joanna. "I wish I had one of Diego's puddings this minute to roast on the ashes for supper!"

The words were not out of Joanna's mouth when presto! on the hearth appeared a delicious black pudding! The woman's eyes opened wide; but Pedro jumped up in a rage.

"You greedy creature!" he cried. "You have used up one of our precious wishes! Good heavens, to wish for nothing more than one poor little pudding! It makes me wild, you goose! I wish the silly pudding were stuck fast to your nose!"

Whisk! Flop! Splotch! there flew the great black pudding and hung from Joanna's nose. The old man shrieked in surprise. Joanna gurgled with horror; but shake her head as she might, she could no more shake off the pudding than she could shake off her nose!

"See what you have done, you evil tongue!" she wailed. "If I employed my wish badly, it injured only myself, but you—you—look!"

Thereupon, the dog and cat, having sniffed the savory pudding, came leaping up, springing and pawing, to lick that luscious morsel that was now Dame Joanna's nose!

"Down! Down!" shrieked Joanna, as she wildly defended the part attacked. "I shall agree to nothing else for our third wish than that this miserable pudding be taken off my nose!"

"Wife, for heaven's sake!" cried Pedro, "don't ask that! What of the new farm I wanted?"

"I will never agree to wish for it!"

"But listen to reason! Think of the palace you desired, with domes and spires and cupolas, and walls of crimson and gold."

"It does not matter!"

"O my dear! let us wish at least for a fortune, and then you shall have a golden case set with all the jewels you please, to cover the pudding on your nose!"

"I will not hear of it!"

"Then, alas and alack, we shall be left just as we were before!"

"That is all I desire! I see now we were well enough off as we were!"

And for all the man could say, nothing could change his wife's mind. And so at last they agreed. On the following night the Fairy rose from the flames and bade them tell her their third wish, but they answered both together:

"We wish only to be as we were before."

And lo, their wish was granted.

WHITE HORSES*

HAMISH HENDRY

I saw them plunging through the foam,
    I saw them prancing up the shore—
A thousand horses, row on row,
    And then a thousand more!

In joy they leaped upon the land,
    In joy they fled before the wind,
Prancing and plunging on they raced,
    The huntsman raced behind.

When this old huntsman goes to sleep,
    The horses live beneath the waves;
They live at peace, and rest in peace,
    Deep in their sea green caves.

But when they hear the huntsman's shout
    Urging his hounds across the sea,
Out from their caves in frenzied fear
    The great white horses flee!

Today they plunged right through the foam,
    Today they pranced right up the shore,
A thousand horses, row on row,
    And then a thousand more.

*Used by permission of the publishers, G. P. Putnam's Sons.

Why the Sea is Salt*

A Norse Folk Tale

GUDRUN THORNE-THOMSEN

Once on a time, but it was a long, long time ago, there were two brothers, one rich and one poor.

Now, one Christmas eve, the poor one had not so much as a crumb in the house, either of meat or bread, so he went to his brother to ask him for something with which to keep Christmas. It was not the first time his brother had been forced to help him, and, as he was always stingy, he was not very glad to see him this time, but he said, "I'll give you a whole piece of bacon, two loaves of bread, and candles into the bargain, if you'll never bother me again—but mind you don't set foot in my house from this day on."

The poor brother said he wouldn't, thanked his brother for the help he had given him, and started on his way home.

He hadn't gone far before he met an old, old man with a white beard, who looked so thin and worn and hungry that it was pitiful to see him.

"In heaven's name give a poor man a morsel to eat," said the old man.

"Now, indeed, I have been begging myself," said the poor brother, "but I'm not so poor that I can't give you something on the blessed Christmas eve." And with that he handed the old man a candle, and a loaf of bread, and he was just going to cut off a slice of bacon, when the old man stopped him—"That is enough and to spare," said he. "And now, I'll tell you something. Not far from here is the entrance to the home of the underground folks. They have a mill there which can grind out anything they wish for except bacon; now mind you go there. When you get inside they will all want to buy your bacon, but

*From *East o' the Sun and West o' the Moon.* Used by special arrangement with the author and the publisher, Row, Peterson & Co.

don't sell it unless you get in return the mill which stands behind the door. When you come out I'll teach you how to handle the mill."

So the man with the bacon thanked the other for his good advice and followed the directions which the old man had given him, and soon he stood outside of the hillfolks' home.

When he got in, everything went just as the old man had said. All the hillfolk, great and small, came swarming up to him, like ants around an ant-hill, and each tried to outbid the other for the bacon.

"Well!" said the man, "by rights, my old dame and I ought to have this bacon for our Christmas dinner; but, since you have all set your hearts on it, I suppose I must give it up to you. Now, if I sell it at all, I'll have for it that mill behind the door yonder."

At first the hillfolk wouldn't hear of such a bargain and higgled and haggled with the man, but he stuck to what he said, and at last they gave up the mill for the bacon.

When the man got out of the cave and into the woods again, he met the same old beggar and asked him how to handle the mill. After he had learned how to use it, he thanked the old man and went off home as fast as he could; still the clock had struck twelve on Christmas eve before he reached his own door.

"Wherever in the world have you been?" said his old dame. "Here have I sat hour after hour, waiting and watching, without so much as two sticks to lay under the Christmas porridge."

"Oh!" said the man, "I could not get back before, for I had to go a long way first for one thing and then for another; but now you shall see what you shall see."

So he put the mill on the table, and bade it first of all grind lights, then a tablecloth, then meat, then ale, and so on till they had everything that was nice for Christmas fare. He had only to speak the word and the mill ground out whatever he wanted.

THROUGH FAIRY HALLS

The old dame stood by blessing her stars, and kept on asking where he had got this wonderful mill, but he wouldn't tell her.

"It's all the same where I got it. You see the mill is a good one, and the mill stream never freezes. That's enough."

So he ground meat and drink and all good things to last out the whole of Christmas holidays, and on the third day he asked all his friends and kin to his house and gave them a great feast. Now, when his rich brother saw all that was on the table and all that was in the cupboards, he grew quite wild with anger, for he could not bear that his brother should have anything.

"'Twas only on Christmas eve," he said to the rest, "he was so poorly off that he came and begged for a morsel of food, and now he gives a feast as if he were a count or a king," and he turned to his brother and said, "But where in the world did you get all this wealth?"

"From behind the door," answered the owner of the mill, for he did not care to tell his brother much about it. But later in the evening, when he had gotten a little too merry, he could keep his secret no longer, and he brought out the mill and said:

"There you see what has gotten me all this wealth," and so he made the mill grind all kinds of things.

When his brother saw it, he set his heart on having the mill, and, after some talk, it was agreed that the rich brother was to get it at hay-harvest time, when he was to pay three hundred dollars for it. Now, you may fancy the mill did not grow rusty for want of work, for while he had it the poor brother made it grind meat and drink that would last for years. When hay-harvest came, the rich brother got it, but he was in such a hurry to make it grind that he forgot to learn how to handle it.

It was evening when the rich brother got the mill home, and next morning he told his wife to go out into the hayfield and toss hay while the mowers cut the grass, and he would stay

home and get the dinner ready. So, when dinner time drew near, he put the mill on the kitchen table and said:

"Grind herrings and broth, and grind them good and fast."

And the mill began to grind herrings and broth, first of all the dishes full, then all the tubs full, and so on till the kitchen floor was quite covered. The man twisted and twirled at the mill to get it to stop, but for all his fiddling and fumbling the mill went on grinding, and in a little while the broth rose so high that the man was nearly drowning. So he threw open the kitchen door and ran into the parlor, but it was not long before the mill had ground the parlor full too, and it was only at the risk of his life that the man could get hold of the latch of the housedoor through the stream of broth. When he got the door open, he ran out and set off down the road, with the stream of herrings and broth at his heels, roaring like a waterfall over the whole farm.

Now, his old dame, who was in the field tossing hay, thought it a long time to dinner, and at last she said:

"Well! though the master doesn't call us home, we may as well go. Maybe he finds it hard work to boil the broth, and will be glad of my help."

The men were willing enough, so they sauntered homewards. But just as they had got a little way up the hill, what should they meet but herrings and broth, all running and dashing and splashing together in a stream, and the master himself running before them for his life, and as he passed them he called out: "Eat, drink! eat, drink! but take care you're not drowned in the broth."

Away he ran as fast as his legs would carry him to his brother's house, and begged him in heaven's name to take back the mill, at once, for, said he, "If it grinds only one hour more the whole parish will be swallowed up by herrings and broth."

So the poor brother took back the mill, and it wasn't long before it stopped grinding herrings and broth.

And now he set up a farmhouse far finer than the one in which his brother lived, and with the mill he ground so much gold that he covered it with plates of gold. And, as the farm lay by the seaside, the golden house gleamed and glistened far away over the sea. All who sailed by put ashore to see the rich man in the golden house, and to see the wonderful mill the fame of which spread far and wide, till there was nobody who hadn't heard of it.

So one day there came a skipper who wanted to see the mill, and the first thing he asked was if it could grind salt.

"Grind salt!" said the owner. "I should just think it could. It can grind anything."

When the skipper heard that, he said he must have the mill, for if he only had it, he thought, he need not take his long voyages across stormy seas for a lading of salt. He much preferred sitting at home with a pipe and a glass. Well, the man let him have it, but the skipper was in such a hurry to get away with it that he had no time to ask how to handle the mill. He got on board his ship as fast as he could and set sail. When he had sailed a good way off, he brought the mill on deck and said, "Grind salt, and grind both good and fast."

And the mill began to grind salt so that it poured out like water, and when the skipper had got the ship full he wished to stop the mill, but whichever way he turned it, and however much he tried, it did no good; the mill kept on grinding, the heap of salt grew higher and higher, and at last down sank the ship.

There lies the mill at the bottom of the sea, and grinds away to this very day, and that is the reason why the sea is salt— so some folks say.

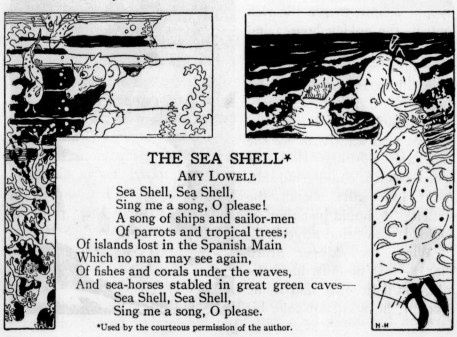

THE SEA SHELL*
AMY LOWELL
Sea Shell, Sea Shell,
Sing me a song, O please!
A song of ships and sailor-men
Of parrots and tropical trees;
Of islands lost in the Spanish Main
Which no man may see again,
Of fishes and corals under the waves,
And sea-horses stabled in great green caves—
Sea Shell, Sea Shell,
Sing me a song, O please.

*Used by the courteous permission of the author.

The Strong Boy
A Canadian Fairy Tale

Once upon a time, long, long ago, there was an Indian woman, who went on a journey with her infant son through the wild Canadian woods. As the woman trudged along with her baby slung at her back, there came out of the woods a great Grizzly Bear. When the Bear saw the woman with no companions to guard her, he growled fiercely, fell upon her, seized her in his great, shaggy arms and carried her and her son off to his cave in the mountains. There in his deep, dark den he kept them prisoners year after year. They must live on what poor scraps of food he threw them when not too ill-tempered to give them nothing at all, and the woman must dance every night to his bidding, dance and amuse him till she was quite wearied out. If ever she rebelled and refused to obey, she got a cruel scratch from his claw on her cheek or a cuff from his mighty paw. And never once could the woman or her son get one little glimpse of day-light, for the Bear had five great grizzly sons and when he was from home, his sons stood guard at the door of the cave so they could not hope to get out.

Well, of course the woman's baby didn't stay always a baby, but grew to be a fine boy. One day when he was about nine years old, he sat at the back of the den, looking into a pool, which was formed by a little stream that came bubbling into the cave. As he looked, lo! he saw a face peering up at him out of the water.

"What is the use of a boy who sits still and lets his mother be bullied?" said a voice from below the water.

"Ah," answered the Boy, "though I long ever so much to save my mother, how can a boy like me overcome a great grizzly bear and his great grizzly sons?"

"You will never overcome them if you sit still in this cave and do not even use what strength you have," said the Water Sprite. "You can only grow strong enough for such a deed by going out into the world and doing each day something stronger and greater than you did the day before."

"But how am I to get out into the world?" asked the Boy, "with the Bear's grizzly sons forever on guard at the only door."

"Ah," gurgled the Water Sprite, "don't be too sure that's the only door. Slip out of the cave as I slipped in." And with another gurgle, the face in the pool disappeared.

Then the Boy ran to his mother and told her what had occurred.

"My son," said the woman, but with sadness as of tears in her voice, "the Water Sprite is right. The time has come when you must leave me and go out into the world to grow strong."

Just as they spoke, in came the Bear, and with greater fierce-ness than ever before, he rose up on his hind feet, and bade the poor woman dance. At that the Boy could stand it no longer, but rushed upon him. The Bear was so astonished that he stood for a moment with gaping mouth and paws poised high in the air. Then he made a great lunge to catch the Boy in his arms and hug the breath out of him. No chance at all had a child against such a huge, powerful beast. But as the great bully sprang forward, he knocked the lad over into the pool before he could stop himself. The moment his paws touched the water, he let go his hold and began to howl. "Ow-wow! Ow! Ow! Stop stinging me!" For the Water Sprite was after him, so the coward jerked his paws out of the water and the little Boy was free.

The next thing the Boy knew he was gliding along comfortably under the water and the Water Sprite was beside him. Pretty soon they rose smoothly up to the surface, and there all about was the great, wide, beautiful, sunlit world. The Water Sprite guided the Boy to the shore and then he bade him farewell.

"Go now and grow strong," said he, "so you can return and rescue your mother. When you are ready to go back, come to the river and call for me."

So the boy thanked the Water Sprite, climbed out of the water and off he went on his journey. He hadn't gone far when he met a man lifting a great canoe from the water. There were rapids in the stream just ahead and the man was going to carry his canoe along the bank till he could launch it in smooth water again.

"Let me help you," said the Boy to the Man. The Man looked him over from head to foot and saw he was but a child. At that he laughed with derision and said:

"Much help you'll be, little squirrel. Take hold of that end down there, if you like. Perhaps you can lift as much as a grasshopper!"

So the Man turned the canoe upside down and put it on his shoulders; the Boy put his shoulders under one end and away they marched. The canoe seemed to the Boy very heavy at

first but as they went farther, it grew lighter and lighter, and he bore more and more of the weight with each step, till by and by the Man had shifted it all onto his shoulders and was only pretending to carry it.

"Well," said the man when they launched the canoe again in the river, "you are a strong boy. Let us journey on together." For he thought within himself that he could make good use of such a strong fellow as this.

They travelled far and they travelled long, and every day the man gave the Boy more work to do and did less and less himself, so every day the Boy grew stronger and stronger, and the Man grew weaker and weaker. One night they encamped at a place on the river where the current was swift and strong. Scarcely had the Boy gathered the firewood and lit the fires, when they saw a large canoe filled with people come madly swirling along down the stream. The people had lost their paddles, so they could not control the canoe and the current was bearing it straight for the spot where the river plunged down in a mighty fall and would dash the frail little bark into pieces. Men, women, and children were frantically waving their hands and begging some one on shore to save them. At that, there came suddenly out of the forest a great, burly man who seized a long pine pole and running it out across the river, put it under the plunging canoe. Then he raised the canoe with all the people straight up out of the water and drew it slowly toward the shore.

"There is a strong man, I'll be bound," said the Boy to himself. But just then he saw that the man's strength was giving out. He had drawn the canoe well up toward the shore, but was just about to drop it again and lose it once more in the current. So the Boy rushed out into the river, picked up the whole canoe full of people and carried it safely up onto the bank. Then said the man who had tried to save the people: "You are a strong boy—let me journey on with you."

So now there were three of them paddling off down the stream together, and every day the Men shifted more and more of the work to the Boy and every day as he worked he grew stronger and stronger while the Men grew weaker and weaker.

At last one day they went ashore and said they would build a wigwam where they could rest awhile. The Men made many motions, but the Boy did all the work, and when he had put up a comfortable lodge, the Men bade him go and hunt to provide them with food for the winter. They would stay home said the two, for some one must mind the wigwam and prepare the evening meal. Well, when the Boy was gone, the two lazy Men lolled about all day with their pipes and did no work at all; only towards evening they made ready the supper. Just as they had finished cooking it, a small boy came to the door of the wigwam, crying bitterly and begging for food. He looked very, very tiny and very, very weak and very, very poor and very, very miserable, so the Men bade him come in and help himself to a bite. But no sooner had the tiny little boy seated himself to the food, than in a twinkling he gobbled up all that had been prepared for the three strong men. At that the Men were very angry and they fell upon the little fellow to beat him. But the little fellow gripped them with hands of iron. Tiny as he was, he held those two strong men so they could not move a muscle. And he banged their heads together, and gave them such a drubbing as they had never had in all their lives before.

When the boy came home he found his two comrades sighing and groaning, and heard the tale of the terrible little imp who had stolen their supper and given them a beating. The next day the Men said it was their turn to go hunting and the Boy should stay home, for, though they had never intended to do any work at all, they much preferred going a-hunting to staying behind and running the chance of falling in once more with the imp. So off went the Men, and the Boy stayed home and worked about the wigwam and got the supper. When it was all cooked, there to the door came the tiny wee fellow, crying bitterly as before and begging for something to eat.

"Come in," said the Strong Boy. At once the imp made a rush for the food, but the Strong Boy caught him and held him fast and then there was a struggle. The imp had his strength by magic and was almost a match for the Strong Boy. They wrestled and tussled and tussled and wrestled. But at last the Strong Boy got the imp down and sat on him and then the imp began screeching and shrieking and pleading for his life.

"Let me go! Let me go!" he cried, "I never thought there was anyone in the world strong enough to beat me. Let me go and I'll show you how you can use your strength to win great treasures of blankets and wampum."

"Nay," said the Boy, "I have no wish to use my strength to win great treasures."

"For what are you going to use it then?" whined the imp.

"I am going to save my mother from the Bear!"

"Oh," begged the imp, "but let me go and I'll show you how you can conquer a chief and rule over his tribe."

"Nay," said the Boy, "I have no wish to conquer a chief and rule over his tribe. I wish to save my mother from the Bear."

So, when the imp saw that he could not turn the Boy aside from the purpose for which he had got his strength, he knew full well that he could not rule over him. So long as he did not forget that it was to save his mother he had grown strong, there was nothing that could stand against him. So the imp said:

"I yield. I am the servant of a terrible giant who has never been defeated. If you will go and overcome the giant, I will be your servant from this time on and serve you faithfully."

So the Strong Boy let the imp go free and off they went to the giant's cave in the side of the hill. When they went in, there stood the giant looming up as big and dark as the shadow of pine woods at midnight, and he sprang upon the Strong Boy with all the strength of the whirlwind. They fought for a night and a day. But at last the Strong Boy overcame the giant and made an end of him and then the little imp became his faithful servant. When he went back to the wigwam and his two comrades saw that he had conquered the imp and made him his faithful servant, and heard how he had conquered a giant, they began to think that he had grown too strong altogether, and they were afraid of him because they were now so much weaker than he. So when they set out again on the river they began to plan how they could get rid of him. At last they came to a place where the river ran into a narrow valley with great, dark cliffs towering up on either side. They wanted to land but the precipices came straight down to the water's edge and they could find no place to beach their canoe. At that the Men said:

"You stay here and we will climb up the cliff. Then we will

let down a rope and pull you up with the canoe.''

So they climbed up the cliff and let down a rope and the Strong Boy was going to tie the rope to the canoe and let them pull him up.

"Don't do that," said the imp. "Those men are afraid of you now. They know you could easily be their master and when they have you half way up the cliff they will cut the rope, so that you will come crashing down."

So the Strong Boy got a huge rock and tied it to the rope, then he called to the Men above to pull. They tugged and they tugged, but when they had the rock half way, sure enough, they let go and the rock came crashing down. Then the Boy climbed up the cliff safe and sound, and when the Men saw him they were so astonished and terrified that they ran for their lives.

When he was thus freed of his unworthy companions, the Strong Boy took the imp by the hand and flung himself into the river. As he did so, he called on the Water Sprite, for now he was ready to be taken back to the cave. The Water Sprite came at once to his aid and soon they were gliding smoothly along underneath the water. In less time than it takes to tell they came up in the Grizzly Bear's den. The Bear had just come home and he was more ugly and threatening than ever.

"Dance!" he was saying to the poor woman. "Dance, till your teeth rattle! Dance, I tell you. Dance!"

But the Strong Boy rushed out and seized him. It was a different story now from what it had been when they fought before, for in the Strong Boy's arms the wicked old fellow could not even move. In a trice the breath was crushed out of him. As to the Bear's five sons, who all rushed out to save their father, the imp finished them, and soon the Strong Boy was leading his mother out of the cave and into the great, wide, beautiful world. So he built a good wigwam for her and took care of her always, and the imp and the Water Sprite lived close by, and they all were happy ever after.

The Ogre That Played Jackstraws*

DAVID STARR JORDAN

Once there was a terrible giant ogre, and he lived in a huge castle that was built right in the middle of a valley. All men had to pass by it when they came to the king's palace on the rock at the head of the valley. And they were all terribly afraid of the ogre, and ran just as fast as they could when they went by. And when they looked back as they were running, they could see the ogre sitting on the wall of his castle. And he scowled at them so fiercely that they ran as fast as ever they could. For the ogre had a head as large as a barrel, and great black eyes sunk deep under long, bushy eyelashes. And when he opened his mouth they saw that it was full of teeth, and so they ran away faster than ever, without caring to see anything more.

And the king wanted to get rid of the ogre, and he sent his men to drive the ogre away and to tear down his castle. But the ogre scowled at them so savagely that their teeth began to fall out, and they all turned back and said they dare not fight such a horrid creature. Then Roger, the king's son, rode his black

*From *The Book of Knight and Barbara*. Used by permission of the author and the publishers, D. Appleton & Co.

horse Hurricane up against the door of the ogre's castle, and struck hard against the door with his iron glove. Then the door opened and the ogre came out and seized Roger in one hand and the great black horse in the other and rubbed their heads together, and while he did this he made them very small. Then he tumbled them over the wall into the ogre's garden. And they crawled through a hole in the garden fence and both ran home, Roger one way and Hurricane the other, and neither dared tell the king nor anyone else where he had been, nor what the ogre had done to him. But it was two or three days before they became large again.

Then the king sent out some men with a cannon to batter down the walls of the ogre's castle. But the ogre sat on the wall and caught the cannon balls in his hand and tossed them back at the cannon, so that they broke the wheels and scared away all the men. And when the cannon sounded the ogre roared so loudly that all the windows in the king's palace were broken, and the queen and all the princesses went down into the cellar and hid among the sugar barrels, and stuffed cotton in their ears till the noise should stop. And whatever the king's men tried to do the ogre made it worse and worse. And at last no one dared to go out into the valley beside the ogre's castle, and no one dared look at it from anywhere, because when the ogre scowled all who saw him dropped to the ground with fear, and their teeth began to fall out, and when the ogre roared there was no one who could bear to hear it.

So the king and all his men hid in the cellar of the castle with the queen and the princesses, and they stuffed their ears full of cotton, and the ogre scowled and roared and had his own way.

But there was one little boy named Pennyroyal, who tended the black horse Hurricane, and he was not afraid of anything because he was a little boy. And the little boy said he would go out and see the ogre and tell him to go away. And they were all so scared that they could not ask him not to go. So Pennyroyal

put on his hat, filled his pockets with marbles and took his kite under his arm, and went down the valley to the castle of the ogre. The ogre sat on the wall and looked at him, but the little boy was not afraid, and so it did the ogre no good to scowl. Then Pennyroyal knocked on the ogre's door, and the ogre opened it and looked at the little boy.

"Please, Mr. Ogre, may I come in?" said Pennyroyal; and the ogre opened the door, and the little boy began to walk around the castle looking at all the things. There was one room filled with bones, but the ogre was ashamed of it, and did not want to let the little boy see it. So when Pennyroyal was not looking the ogre just changed the room and made it small, so that instead of a room full of bones it became just a box of jackstraws. And the big elephant he had there to play with he made into a lap-elephant, and the little boy took it in his hand and stroked its tiny tusks and tied a knot in its trunk. And anything that could frighten the little boy the ogre made small and pretty, so that they had great times together.

And by and by the ogre grew smaller and smaller, and took off his ugly old face with the long teeth and bushy eyebrows and dropped them on the floor and covered them with a wolf-skin. Then he sat down on the wolf-skin and the little boy sat down on the floor beside him, and they began to play jackstraws with the box of jackstraws that had been a room full of bones. The ogre had never been a boy himself, so jackstraws was the only game he knew how to play. Then the elephant he had made small snuggled down between them on the floor. And as they played with each other, the castle itself grew small, and shrank away until there was just room enough for them and for their game.

Up in the palace, when the ogre stopped roaring, the king's men looked out and saw that the ogre's castle was gone. Then Roger, the king's son, called for Pennyroyal. But when he could not find the boy, he saddled the black horse Hurricane himself and rode down the valley to where the ogre's castle had been. When he came back he told the king that the ogre and his castle were all gone. Where the castle stood there was nothing left but a board tent under the oak tree, and in the tent there were just two little boys playing jackstraws, and between them on the ground lay a candy elephant.

That was all. For the terrible ogre was one of that kind of ogres that will do to folks just what folks do to them. There isn't any other kind of ogre.

A SONG FROM "THE FLOWER OF OLD JAPAN"*

ALFRED NOYES

There when the sunset colours the streets
    Everyone buys at wonderful stalls
Toys and chocolates, guns and sweets,
    Ivory pistols, and Persian shawls;
Everyone's pockets are crammed with gold;
    Nobody ever grows tired and old,
    And nobody calls you "Baby" there.

There with a hat like a round, white dish
    Upside down on each pig-tailed head,
Jugglers offer you snakes and fish,
    Dreams and dragons and gingerbread;
Beautiful books with marvellous pictures,
    Painted pirates and streaming gore,
And everyone reads, without any strictures,
    Tales he remembers for evermore.

*From *Collected Poems*. Reprinted by permission of Frederick A. Stokes Company.

The Moon-Maiden

A Japanese Fairy Tale

There dwelt once on the edge of the forest at the foot of Fujiyama, a bamboo-cutter and his wife. They were honest, industrious people who loved each other dearly, but no children had come to bless them, and therefore they were not happy.

"Ah, husband," mourned the wife, "more welcome to me than cherry blossoms in springtime would be a little child of my own."

One evening she stood on the porch of her flimsy bamboo cottage and lifted her eyes toward the everlasting snows on the top of Fujiyama. Then, with swelling breast, she bowed herself to the ground and cried out to the Honorable Mountain:

"Fuji no yama, I am sad because no little head lies on my breast, no childish laughter gladdens our home. Send me, I pray thee, from thine eternal purity, a little one to comfort me."

As she spoke, lo! from the top of the Honorable Mountain

there suddenly sparkled a gleam of light as when the face of a child is lit by a beaming smile.

"Husband, husband, come quickly," cried the good woman. "See there on the heights of Fujiyama a child is beaming upon me."

"It is but your fancy," said the bamboo-cutter and yet he added, "I will climb up and see what is there."

So he followed the trail of silvery light through the forest, and up the steep slope where Fujiyama towered white and still above him. At last he stopped below a tall bamboo by the bank of a mountain stream, from whence the glow seemed to come. There, cradled in the branches of the tree, he found a tiny moon-child, fragile, dainty, radiant, clad in flimsy, filmy moon-shine, more beautiful than anything he had ever seen before.

"Ah, little shining creature, who are you?" he cried.

"I am the Princess Moonbeam," answered the child. "The Moon Lady is my mother, but she has sent me to earth to comfort the sad heart of your wife."

"Then, little Princess," said the Woodman eagerly, "I will take you home to be our child."

So the woodman bore her carefully down the mountain side.

"See, wife," he called, "what the Moon Lady has sent you."

Then was the good woman overjoyed. She took the little moon-child and held her close, and the moon-child's little arms went twining about her neck, as she nestled snug against her breast. So was the good wife's longing satisfied at last.

As the years passed by, Princess Moonbeam brought nothing but joy to the woodman and his wife. Lovelier and lovelier she grew. Fair was her face and radiant, her eyes were shining stars, and her hair had the gleam of a misty silver halo. About her, too, there was a strange, unearthly charm that made all who saw her love her.

One day there came riding by in state the Mikado himself.

THROUGH FAIRY HALLS

He saw how the Princess Moonbeam lit up the humble cottage, and he loved her. Then the Mikado would have taken her back with him to court, but no!—the longing of the earthly father and mother for a little child had been fulfilled, the Princess Moonbeam had stayed with them till she was a maiden grown, and now the time had come when she must go back to her sky mother, the Lady in the Moon.

"Stay, stay with me on earth!" cried the Mikado.

"Stay, stay with us on earth!" cried the bamboo-cutter and his wife. Then the Mikado got two thousand archers and set them on guard close about the house and even on the roof, that none might get through to take her. But when the moon rose white and full, a line of light like a silver bridge sprung arching down from heaven to earth and floating along that gleaming path came the Lady from the Moon. The Mikado's soldiers stood as though turned to stone. Straight through their midst the Moon Lady passed and bent caressingly down for her long-absent child. She wrapped her close in a garment of silver mist. Then she caught her tenderly in her arms, and led her gently back to the sky. The Princess Moonbeam was glad to go back home, yet as she went, she wept silvery tears for those she was leaving behind. And lo! her bright, shining tears took wings and floated away to carry a message of love, that should comfort the Mikado, and her earthly father and mother.

To this very day the gleaming tears of the little Princess Moonbeam are seen to float hither and yon about the marshes and groves of Japan. The children chase them with happy cries and say, "See the fire-flies! How beautiful they are!" Then their mothers, in the shadow of Fujiyama, tell the children this legend— how the fire-flies are shining love messages of the little Princess Moonbeam, flitting down to bring comfort to earth from her far-off home in the silver moon.

DONN P. CRANE

THE VILLAGE FAIR*

NICHOLAS NEKRASSOV

(Translated from the Russian by Juliet M. Soskice)

Our peasants determine
To see the shop windows,
The handkerchiefs, ribbons,
And stuffs of bright color;
And near to the boot-shop
Is fresh cause for laughter;
For here an old peasant
Most eagerly bargains
For small boots of goat-skin
To give to his grandchild.
He asks the price five times;
Again and again
He has turned them all over;
He finds they are faultless.

"Well, Uncle, pay up now,
Or else be off quickly."
The seller says sharply.

*Used by the courteous permission of The Oxford University Press.

THROUGH FAIRY HALLS

But wait! the old fellow
  Still gazes, and fondles
The tiny boots softly,
  And then speaks in this wise:
"My daughter won't scold me,
  My wife—let her grumble—
My poor little grandchild
  She clung to my neck,
And she said, 'Little Grandfather,
  Buy me a present.'

"Her soft little ringlets
  Were tickling my cheek,
And she kissed the old Grand-dad.
  You wait, little bare-foot,
Wee spinning-top, wait then,
  Some boots I will buy you,
Some boots made of goat-skin."
  And then must old Vavil
Begin to boast grandly,
  To promise a present
To old and to young.
  But now his last farthing
Is swallowed. . . .

Then came forward
  Pavloosha Varenko;
He now rescued Vavil,
  And bought him the boots
To take home to his grand-child.
The old man fled blindly,
  But clasping them tightly,
Forgetting to thank him,
  Bewildered with joy.
The crowd was as pleased, too,
  As if had been given
To each one a rouble—

The Good Comrades of The Flying Ship

A Russian Tale

THERE lived once upon a time in Russia a peasant and his wife, and they had three sons; two were clever, but the third was thought a fool. The elder brothers were forever telling him he had no wits, and he found himself always treated as of no use whatsoever. One day they all heard that a writing had come from the Tsar which said:

"Whoever builds a ship that can fly, to him will I give my daughter, the Tsarevna, to wife."

The elder brothers resolved to go and seek their fortune, and they begged a blessing of their parents. The mother got ready their things for the journey, and gave them the best she had in the house to eat on the way. Then the fool began to beg them to send him off too. His mother told him he should not go.

"Why shouldst thou go?" said his mother. "Dost thou think thou canst do what wiser men cannot?"

But the fool was always singing the same refrain, "I think I can! I want to go!"

At length his mother saw she could do nothing with him, so she gave him a poor crust of black bread and sent him out. The fool went and went, and at last he met an old man. They greeted each other, and the old man asked, "Where art thou going?"

"Look now," said the fool, "the Tsar has promised to give his daughter to him who shall make a flying ship!"

"And canst thou make such a ship?"

"No, I cannot, but I'll get it made for me somewhere."

"And where is that somewhere?"

"God only knows."

"Well, in that case, sit down here, rest and eat a bit. Share with me what thou hast in thy knapsack."

"Nay, it is such stuff that I am ashamed to share it with thee."

"Nonsense! Take it out! What God has given is quite good enough to be eaten."

The fool undid his knapsack and could hardly believe his eyes. There, instead of the dry crust of brown bread, lay white rolls and divers savory meats, and he gave of it to the old man. So they ate together and the old man said to the fool:

"Go into the wood, straight up to the first tree. Strike the trunk with thine axe, then fall with thy face to the ground and wait till thou art aroused. Thou wilt see before thee a ship quite ready. Sit in it and fly, and whomsoever thou dost meet on the road, gather him up and give him a lift on his journey."

So our fool blessed the old man, took leave of him, and went into the wood. He went up to the first tree and did exactly as he had been commanded. He struck the trunk with his axe, fell with his face to the ground and went to sleep. In a little while, something or other awoke him. The fool rose up and saw the ship quite ready beside him. Without loss of time, he got into it, and the ship flew up into the air. It flew and flew and look!—there on the road below a man was lying with his ear to the earth.

"Good day, uncle!" cried the fool.

"Good day!"

"What art thou doing?"

"I am listening to what is going on in the world."

"Art thou traveling?"

"Yea."

"Then take a seat in the ship beside me. I'll give thee a lift on thy journey."

So the man got into the ship and they flew on further. They flew and flew and look!—a man was coming along hopping on one leg, with the other leg tied tightly to his ear.

"Good day, uncle! Why art thou hopping on one leg?"

"Why, if I were to untie the other, I should stride around half the world at a single stride, so long are my steps!"

"Then take a seat in the ship beside me."

So the man got into the ship and they flew on further. They flew and flew and look!—a man was standing with a gun and taking aim, but at what they could not see.

"Good day, uncle, at what art thou aiming?"

"Oh, I'm aiming at a mark the size of a pea at a distance of one hundred leagues. That's what I call shooting!"

"Art thou traveling?"

"Yea!"

"Then take a seat in the ship beside me. I'll give thee a lift on thy journey."

So the man sat down and they flew on. They flew and flew and look!—a man was walking in the forest, and on his shoulders was a bundle of wood.

"Good day, uncle, why art thou dragging wood about?"

"Oh, but this is not common wood!"

"Of what sort is it, then?"

"It is of such a sort that if it be scattered, a whole army will spring up."

"Take a seat with us, then. I'll give thee a lift on thy journey."

So he also sat down with them and they flew on further. They flew and flew and look!—a man was carrying a sack of straw.

"Good day, uncle, whither art thou carrying that straw?"

"To the village."

"Is there little straw in the village, then?"

"Nay, but this straw is of such a kind that if it be scattered on the hottest summer day, cold will at once set in, with snow and frost."

"Take a seat with us then. I'll give thee a lift on thy journey."

So they flew and flew and soon they flew into the Tsar's court-yard. The Tsar was sitting at table when he saw the flying ship drop from the sky just outside his window. In great sur-prise, he sent his servant to ask who it was that had accomplished the task.

The servant went to the ship and looked and brought back word to the Tsar that it was but a miserable little peasant who was flying the ship. The Tsar fell a-thinking. He did not wish to give his daughter to a simple peasant, so he began to consider how he could rid himself of such a son-in-law.

"I will set him a task he can never perform," thought he.

Immediately he called his servant and bade him say to the fool: "Thou shalt get thy master, the Tsar, some of the living

and singing water from the other end of the world. And mind that thou bringest it here before the end of the meal which he is even now eating. Shouldst thou fail to do this, thou shalt pay for it with thy life."

Now at the very time when the Tsar was giving this command to his servant, the first comrade whom the fool had taken into the ship (that is to say Sharp-ear) heard what the Tsar said and told it to the fool.

"What shall I do now?" said the fool. "If I travel for my whole life I shall never get to the other end of the world, let alone bringing the water here before the imperial meal is over."

"Never fear," said Swift-of-foot, "I'll manage it for thee."

The servant came and made known the Tsar's commands.

"Say I'll fetch it," replied the fool, and Swift-of-foot untied his leg from his ear, ran off and in a twinkling was at the other end of the earth. There he got the living and singing water.

"I must make haste and return presently," said he, "but I've plenty of time for a nap first." And he sat down under a water-mill and went to sleep.

The Tsar's dinner was drawing to a close. He was eating dessert and was just putting his last sweetmeat to his lips, still Swift-of-foot did not turn up, so it appeared that all hope was lost for the fool. But Sharp-ear bent down to the earth and listened.

"Oh ho!" he cried, "Swift-of-foot has fallen asleep beneath the mill. I can hear him snoring."

Then Hit-the-mark seized his gun and fired a shot into the mill just above the sleeper's head. The noise awoke Swift-of-foot, who took one great stride and there he was back at the ship with the water. The Tsar was just ready to rise from the table, when the fool laid the water at his feet.

At this the Tsar was astounded. He saw he must think of

some other way to get rid of the fool, so he sent his servant to him and bade him prepare for his wedding.

"First go to the bath-room assigned thee, and have a good wash," he ordered.

Now this bath-room was made of cast-iron, and the Tsar commanded that it should be heated hotter than hot. So they heated the bath red hot. The fool went to wash himself, but when he drew near and felt the waves of heat that came forth from the door, he summoned the comrade with the straw.

"I must strew the floor," said the comrade. So both were locked into the bath-room, the comrade scattered the straw, the room at once became icy cold, and the water in the bath froze, so the fool could scarcely wash himself properly. He crept up onto the stove and there he passed the whole night.

In the morning servants opened the door of the bath and they found the fool alive and well, lying on the stove, and singing songs.

They brought word thereof to the Tsar. The Tsar was now sore troubled. He did not know how to get rid of the fool. He thought and thought, and at length he commanded the fool to produce a whole army of his own.

"How will a simple peasant be able to gather an army?" thought he, "he will surely fail this time."

The servant came to the fool and said: "If thou wilt have the Tsarevna, thou must, before morning, put a whole army on foot."

As soon as the fool heard this, he said:

"You have delivered me from my straits more than once, my friends, but it is plain that nothing can be done now."

"Thou art a pretty fellow," said the man with the bundle of wood. "Why, thou hast clean forgotten me!"

So the fool took courage again and sent this word to the Tsar: "I agree; I shall raise up the army our master, the Tsar, demands of me. But tell him that should he again refuse to keep his word with me, with the very army he bids me raise, I shall conquer his whole kingdom."

At night the fool's companion went out into the fields, took his bundle of wood, and began scattering the fagots in different directions. Immediately a countless army sprang up, both horse and foot. In the morning the Tsar saw it, a multitude in arms, swarming over his whole country side, and then at last he cried:

"I am forced to yield; such an army as this could conquer my whole kingdom!"

So he sent in all haste to the fool with gifts of precious ornaments and raiment, and bade him come to be welcomed at court and married to the Tsarevna.

The fool attired himself in these costly garments. Then he richly repaid the friends who had proven such good comrades and was off to the Tsar. That same day he wedded the Tsarevna and lived henceforth with her at court. It now appeared that he was no fool at all, as men had thought him, but in truth a wise and clever young man. So the Tsar and Tsarevna grew very fond of him and it was soon his wisdom that was governing the kingdom.

Pigling and Her Proud Sister*
A Korean Cinderella Tale
WILLIAM ELLIOT GRIFFIS

Pear Blossom had been the name of a little Korean maid who was suddenly left motherless. When her father, Kang Wa, who was a magistrate high in office, married again, he took for his wife a proud widow whose daughter, born to Kang Wa, was named Violet. Mother and daughter hated housework and made Pear Blossom clean the rice, cook the food and attend the fire in the kitchen. They were hateful in their treatment of Pear Blossom, and, besides never speaking a kind word, called her Pigling, or Little Pig, which made the girl weep often.

*Taken from *Unmannerly Tiger and Other Korean Tales* published by Thomas Y. Crowell Company.

It did no good to complain to her father, for he was always busy. He smoked his yard-long pipe and played checkers hour by hour, apparently caring more about having his great white coat properly starched and lustred than for his daughter to be happy. His linen had to be beaten with a laundry club until it glistened like hoar frost.

Poor Pigling had to perform this task of washing, starching and glossing, in addition to the kitchen work, and the rat-tat-tat of her laundry stick was often heard in the outer room till after midnight, when the heartless mother and daughter had long been asleep.

There was to be a great festival in the city and for many days preparations were made in the house to get the father ready in his best robe and hat, and the women in their finery, to go out and see the king and the royal procession.

Poor Pigling wanted very much to have a look at the pageant but the mother, setting before her a huge straw bag of unhulled rice and a big cracked water jar, told her she must husk all the rice, draw water from the well, and fill the crock to the brim before she dared to go out on the street.

What a task to hull with her fingers three bushels of rice and fill up a leaky vessel! Pigling wept bitterly.

While she was brooding thus and opening the straw bag to begin spreading the rice out on mats, she heard a whir and rush of wings and down came a flock of pigeons. They first lighted on her head and shoulders, and then hopping to the floor began diligently to work with beak and claw, and in a few minutes the rice lay in a heap, clean, white and glistening, while with their pink toes they pulled away the hulls and put these in a separate pile. Then, after a great chattering and cooing, the flock was off and away.

Pigling was so amazed at this wonderful work of the birds

that she scarcely knew how to be thankful enough. But, alas, there was still the cracked crock to be filled. Just as she took hold of the bucket to begin, there crawled out of the fire hole a sooty, black imp, named Tokgabi.

"Don't cry," he squeaked out. "I'll mend the broken part and fill the big jar for you." Forthwith, he stopped up the crack with clay, and pouring a dozen buckets of water from the well into the crock, filled it to brimming so the water spilled over on all sides. Then Tokgabi bowed and crawled into the flues again, before the astonished girl could thank her helper.

So Pigling had time to dress in her plain but clean clothes. She went off and saw the royal banners and the king's grand procession of thousands of loyal men.

The next time, Violet and her mother planned a picnic on the mountain. So the refreshments were prepared and Pigling had to work hard in starching the dresses to be worn—jackets, long skirts, belts, sashes, and what not, until she nearly dropped with fatigue. Yet instead of thanking and cheering her, the heart-

less woman told Pigling she must not go out until she had hoed all the weeds in the garden and pulled up all the grass between the stones of the walk.

Again the poor girl's face was wet with tears. She was left at home alone, while the others went off in fine clothes, with plenty to eat and drink, for a day of merrymaking.

While she wept thus, a huge, black cow came along and out of its great, liquid eyes seemed to beam compassion upon the kitchen slave. Then, in ten mouthfuls, the animal ate up the weeds, and, between its hoof and lips, soon made an end of the grass in the stone pathway.

With her tears dried, Pigling followed this wonderful brute out over the meadows into the woods, where she found the most delicious fruit her eyes ever rested upon. She tasted and enjoyed, feasting to the full and then returned home.

When Violet heard of the astonishing doings of the black cow, she determined to enjoy a feast in the forest also. So on the next gala-day she stayed home and let the kitchen drudge go to see the royal parade. Pigling could not understand why she was excused, even for a few hours, from the pots and kettles, but she was still more surprised by the gift from her stepmother of a rope of cash to spend for dainties. Gratefully thanking the woman, she put on her best clothes and was soon on the main street of the city enjoying the gay sights and looking at the happy people. There were tight rope dancing, music with drum and flute by bands of strolling players, tricks by conjurers and mountebanks, with mimicking and castanets, posturing by the singing girls and fun of all sorts. Boys peddling honey candy, barley sugar and sweetmeats were out by the dozen. At the eating-house, Pigling had a good dinner of fried fish, boiled rice with red peppers, turnips, dried persimmons, roasted chestnuts and candied orange, and felt as happy as a queen.

The selfish Violet had stayed home, not to relieve Pigling of work, but to see the wonderful cow. So, when the black animal appeared and found its friend gone, it went off into the forest. Violet at once followed in the tracks of the cow that took it into its head to go very fast, and into unpleasant places. Soon the girl found herself in a swamp, wet, miry and full of brambles. Still hoping for wonderful fruit, she kept on until she was tired out and the cow was no longer to be seen. Then, muddy and bedraggled, she tried to go back, but the thorny bushes tore her clothes, spoiled her hands and so scratched her face that when at last, she got home, she was in rags and her beauty gone.

But Pigling, rosy and round, looked so lovely that a young man from the south, who saw her that day, was struck by her beauty. As he wanted a wife, he immediately sought to find out where she lived. Then he secured a go-between who visited both families and made all arrangements for the betrothal and marriage.

Grand was the wedding. The groom, Su-Wen, was dressed in white and black silk robes, with a rich horsehair cap and head-dress denoting his rank as a gentleman.

Charming, indeed, looked Pear Blossom, in her robe of brocade. Dainty were her red kid shoes curved upward at the toes.

So with her original name now restored, and henceforth called Ewa, or Pear Blossom, the daughter of Kang Wa was to be Mrs. Su-Wen.

Leaving her home in a palanquin borne by four lusty bearers, Pear Blossom went forth to live amid rich rice fields of a southern province. Her home was with a father and mother-in-law, who, having no other children but their one son, became very fond of their new daughter. Summer after summer the pear trees bloomed and Ewa, the Pear Blossom, lived ever happily.

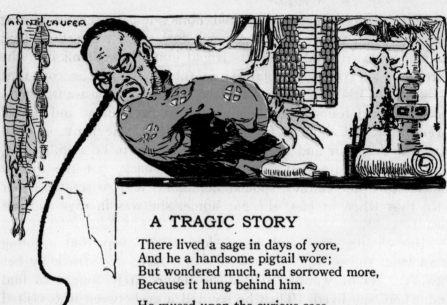

A TRAGIC STORY

There lived a sage in days of yore,
And he a handsome pigtail wore;
But wondered much, and sorrowed more,
Because it hung behind him.

He mused upon the curious case,
And swore he'd change the pigtail's place,
And have it hanging at his face,
Not dangling there behind him.

Says he, "The mystery I've found—
I'll turn me round,"—he turned him round;
But still it hung behind him.

Then round and round, and out and in,
All day the puzzled sage did spin;
In vain—it mattered not a pin,
The pigtail hung behind him.

And right, and left, and round about,
And up, and down, and in, and out
He turned; but still the pigtail stout
Hung steadily behind him.

And though his efforts never slack,
And though he twist, and twirl, and tack,
Alas! still faithful to his back,
The pigtail hangs behind him.

—*Albert von Chamisso.*

(*Translated by William Makepeace Thackeray.*)

Aruman, a Hero of Java

On the island of Java, that rises like a garden a-bloom from the blue Indian Ocean, there lived once in the long, long ago, a boy called Aruman. Now Aruman's mother was dead. It was his good old baboo or nurse, named Sumarr, who had brought him up. When he was a baby, Sumarr carried him close against her breast in the sash that hung from her shoulders. She wreathed his little brown body with garlands of jessamine flowers; she made him toy umbrellas of white tanjong blossoms; she played with him and loved him as tenderly as a mother. And when evening came, she crooned him to sleep with a queer, little, one-toned song like the rustling of reeds in the wind. Then she spread out her small strip of matting on the floor, and lay down to sleep beside his bed, like some faithful dog guarding its master.

So, though Aruman had no mother, his childhood was happy. But one day, while he was still a young lad, there was much noise of many people stirring about in his father's house, and towards evening a grand procession came up to the door. There were men on hobby horses beating strange musical instruments; an orchestra of bells, drums, kettles and viols; wooden figures of a giant and giantess, carried by men and seeming to walk of themselves; women with paper birds, flowers, and tall fans of peacock feathers. Then, borne high on the shoulders of four men, a great litter, in which rode three flower-wreathed maidens, and behind all, on horseback—Drahman, Aruman's father.

"It is a wedding procession, Sumarr! What does it mean?" asked Aruman.

"Ah, little cricket," answered the good baboo, "it means that thy father has brought thee home a new mother. Up there she sits in the litter with her maids. Ma Qualoan is her name."

Now Ma Qualoan had not long taken her place in Drahman's household before she began to show a great dislike for Aruman. Her heart was hard and she could not bear that Aruman should have any share in his father's love.

" 'Tis a lazy lad of thine," she would say to Drahman, "lazy and gluttonous. All day long he does nothing but eat and sleep. Fie for shame! He has no knowledge of the sacred writings. He will not study and he knows not right from wrong!"

So Ma Qualoan went on till Aruman was shut out of his father's heart altogether. Aruman must live with the servants, Aruman must eat scraps from his father's table, Aruman should have less of the light of his father's eyes than Drahman's pet cock! And when Aruman did at last make his way to Drahman, throw himself at his feet and beg that his love should return, Drahman drove the boy with harsh words out of his presence.

In great distress Aruman fled to Sumarr, and on her faithful bosom, poured forth all his grief. Sumarr soothed him as best she could and went herself to Drahman to plead for the child, but her words, too, were in vain.

"Thou hast brought up a son who is a disgrace to me," cried Drahman. "Get thee out of my sight!"

At last, from all Ma Qualoan told him, Drahman grew fearful lest Aruman should do some deed so wicked as to bring shame upon him, so he determined to rid himself of the child.

It happened that Aruman wandered one day alone into the forest. A fragrant shower of white blossoms floated down from the tanjong branches about him; red and orange flowers dropped from the flame-of-the-forest and lay like red embers on his path, but Aruman, who loved the flowers so well, had no eyes for them today. He was thinking only how he had been shut out from his father's heart. So he sat himself down sadly beneath the spreading branches of a giant waringen tree near a stream and wept. Soon, as he sat there, lo! he saw his father come toward him. Aruman rose in respectful greeting, but Drahman stood sternly still, pointing one finger toward the mass of small trunks that formed the giant trunk of the waringen tree.

"Like the waringen tree, I hoped my sons would be," said Drahman, "countless in number, sturdy, upright and all joined as one to mine honor. But lo! I have only thee who disgrace me." So saying, he seized the child, bound him with ropes, and cast him into the river, crying, "Begone forever."

"Father, Father," shrieked the boy, but the stream bore him on and away, on, on and away.

Presently, as he floated along, he came upon an alligator and a fish who were lurking in the river.

"Ah," he cried to the two, "swallow me up, for who is there left in the world to care?"

But the alligator and the fish, after a single glance at the lad, cried, as with one voice:

"Swallow such a one as you? Nay! that will we never do! You are destined to do great deeds in the world, and we will not swallow, but help you." So they guided him in safety to the bank of the stream and there loosed him from the cords by which he was bound.

"Stay a moment," said the alligator as he disappeared in a deep part of the water. "I have that in my keeping which has long waited for just such a lad as you." And he soon reappeared bearing a pair of tumpak cunchang—that is to say, floating shoes.

"With these," said he, as Aruman bound them on his feet, "you can walk upon the waves of the broadest rivers and the deepest ocean as easily as though you were on dry land."

"In that case," said Aruman, "I will make good use of the shoes."

So Aruman thanked the alligator and the fish for their kindness, and stepped out boldly and confidently upon the water.

He found it to be quite true, as the alligator had said, that he could walk easily on the waves, so he made his way down the river as far as the ocean. And when he saw the boundless blue of the sea stretching off before him, nothing would do but he must venture even out onto that. As he wandered along at a great distance from land, enjoying his new accomplishment, he presently caught sight of a vessel coming toward him. At the same moment he himself was observed by the Nakoda, or captain, who seeing a small boy walking on the surface of the water, could scarcely believe his eyes. As Aruman drew nearer, however, Nakoda invited the lad aboard and ordered him to be served with the sailors' usual repast, namely, rice and salt fish.

During the meal, of which the child partook plentifully, he recounted his adventures and sorrows to the captain and the crew, his story calling forth the sympathy and interest of all who heard.

THROUGH FAIRY HALLS

In the meantime the eye of the Nakoda had discovered the tumpak cunchang which Aruman wore, and he at once began to think how he could contrive to obtain them.

"What use are those shoes to you, boy?" said he. "Mark my words, some day when you feel the safest, you'll sink. Give them to me and I will let you have in exchange my flying cloak. Wrapped in that, you can fly in safety over land and sea; you can skim over the water like a swallow or soar up into the very clouds like a strong-winged kite."

"Very well," said the boy, "give me the cloak and here are my shoes."

So the bargain was struck and the exchange made. Now the cloak had indeed been given to the captain long ago as a flying cloak, but, though he had often wrapped it about him and tried timidly and cautiously to fly, he had never been able to lift himself off the ground. So he had concluded the garment was useless and was more than willing to trade it. Yet the moment that Aruman stepped confidently forth in it, with never a doubt that he could do what the captain said, he darted up through the air like a bird, and soared like a strong-winged kite.

"Now who would have thought it?" mumbled Nakoda, as he watched the boy. Then he started out in the shoes. He had gone uncertainly some little distance, when, in a sudden panic of fear, he began to sink. The shoes would bear him up no longer the moment he was afraid. Down sank Nakoda beneath the waves, and only because he was an expert swimmer, was he ever able to regain his boat, where his crew pulled him, exhausted, up onto the deck.

Aruman, who had hovered about above and perceived the captain's sad plight, approached the vessel and looked down in friendly compassion, but Nakoda, vexed beyond words at all that had happened, began to cry out:

"Cheat! rogue! you have robbed me of my wonderful cloak! Your shoes are worthless!"

Aruman laughed good-naturedly at this unmerited chiding but the captain steered his vessel close to land, and, getting into a small boat, made the shore, where he loudly challenged the boy to meet him in single combat. At this Aruman descended to the ground, still without anger, and spoke courteously, hoping to appease the wrath of the captain without fighting. But Nakoda was by this time so beside himself that he would not listen to reason.

"Come on! Come on!" he cried, "I'll soon do for you, little wretch!" And he drew his kriss, flourishing it in great style, and rushing furiously upon the lad, never dreaming of any difficulty in a duel with such a youngster. But he was mistaken. Aruman, though young, could not be roused to anger. He managed his weapon with such coolness and courage that he soon had the wrathful captain entirely at his mercy. When the man had been brought to his knees and forced to acknowledge that he alone was to blame for the bargain he had made, Aruman left him and flew off in the direction of his father's dwelling.

He passed over valleys and forests, till he came at last into a strange and gloomy country, where, under the sombre branches of giant trees, numberless caverns yawned before him. Wondering what could be within such bottomless pits he descended and looked into one. The mouth of it was so black that it seemed to be the entrance into a region of endless night. But while he stood, gazing into it, a figure suddenly appeared, lighting up the recess with a weird, red light. As it left the cavern and drew near him, the figure seemed to be that of a wrinkled old woman, bearing a queer, ill-favored, black bird in one bony hand. She held the bird over her head for a moment, then, mumbling some strange words, she opened her hand and the creature flew away, making circles in the air as it mounted, and ever and anon taking the form of a man on whose face was the expression of one in deep sorrow and regret for some evil deed he had done.

Before these strange apparitions, the boy stood his ground as firmly and confidently as he had before the captain. Then the weird woman began throwing pebbles on the ground that turned into little headless dwarfs to dance and swarm about him, but Aruman extended his arm with a gesture of command and lo! all the grotesque phantoms vanished. Then there appeared in their place a beautiful vision—a maiden lovely as the dawn wreathed in flowers and smiling on him. Her Aruman would gladly have kept before his eyes, but in another moment she, too, had faded away and he was left alone.

Slowly he turned to grope his way out of the darkness. His foot slipped on the marshy ground, he became entangled in thorn bushes, he stumbled over rocks and stones. But, though he knew it not, the woman whom he had thought a witch, was a good fairy, watching over him unseen. Having satisfied herself that he was a brave and dauntless boy, she despatched two tigers to walk on either side of him, and by the light of their eyes, which shone like lamps, he was guided out of the jungles.

Aruman now made straight for his father's home, and when he was come as far as the great waringen tree, whence his father had cast him into the stream, he saw Drahman himself standing on the spot where he had committed his wicked deed. For the first

time anger surged up in Aruman's heart. He seized his father roughly by the shoulder and drew his kriss, but as his father turned his face toward him, lo! there was in his features the same expression of sorrow and regret for what he had done, that the strange, black bird had revealed to Aruman in the land of phantoms. Slowly Aruman released the wretched man.

"Ah," he cried, "if that is how thou art punished in thine own heart, then go and wash thy heart clean in the waters of Zem-Zem. Aruman forgives thee."

"I go, my son!" cried Drahman, and fled from Aruman's presence.

Aruman then went on to his old home, where he found Ma Qualoan sitting in the portico, counting over the jewelled ornaments which Drahman had showered upon her. At sight of her, thus employed, the boy was tempted, as he had been in the case of his father, to fall upon her with his kriss, but, recalling once again the strange vision of the bird, he restrained himself, and did no more than suddenly show himself before her.

Seeing him, whom she had wronged, thus so unexpectedly returned, Ma Qualoan fell prostrate before him. He passed her by without a word and went on to find the good Sumarr.

THROUGH FAIRY HALLS

In the night that followed, some unseen force carried Ma Qualoan into the forest. There she was chained with invisible chains to a great rock overlooking a pool wherein she saw clearly reflected all her own wicked deeds.

For some time Aruman lived on quietly in his home attended by the faithful Sumarr. But the news of his exploits and his sorrows at length reached the ears of the King of Java, who invited the daring boy—now grown a fine youth—to live in his palace. There, to his great astonishment, Aruman again beheld the lovely maiden of his vision in the forest. She was the daughter of the King and in time she became his bride. Then his good old baboo, Sumarr, went to live with him at the palace. Some years later, Aruman himself became King of Java. He was a wise and just King and reigned long and happily with his beautiful Queen. To this day he is a favorite hero with the people of Java and his adventures are often acted by them in plays or recounted in puppet shows with little puppets of gilded leather.

A MALAYAN MONKEY SONG*
(Kra is the monkey)

He runs along the branches, Kra!
Carrying off fruit with him, Kra!
Over the seraya trees, Kra!
Over the rambutan trees, Kra!
Over the live bamboos, Kra!
Peering forward, Kra!
And dangling downward, Kra!
He runs along the branches and hoots, Kra!
Peering forward, Kra!
Among the young fruit trees, Kra!
And showing his grinning teeth, Kra!

—*Translated from the Semang (Malay Peninsula) by Skeat and Blagden.*

*Reprinted through the courtesy of The Macmillan Company.

The Fisherman Who Caught the Sun
A Hawaiian Legend

FAR across the blue Pacific Ocean, on the mountainous little island of Hawaii, a brown Hawaiian mother sat before a tiny straw-thatched hut, and told her little brown children stories. Before her the great round sun was sinking toward the ocean. Out on the water were big brown boys in their queer shaped canoes; others were swimming about, and some were riding the waves, standing up straight and balancing in a wonderful fashion on narrow boards that were carried landwards, rocking, and rolling, on the curling crests of the waves.

The younger children were all at home and grouped about their mother. They had decked themselves out gaily with garlands of flowers and long strings of colored seeds as they dearly loved to do, and, while they watched the setting sun, their mother told them, in the soft, musical Hawaiian tongue, an old Hawaiian tale:

"Many, many years ago, the Sun used to burst forth from the ocean at dawn and race so swiftly across the sky, that he would fling himself over the top of the great fire mountain and sink down again into the ocean before half a day's work was done. Sunset followed so quickly on sunrise that men began to complain:

" 'Alas! The Sun, in his headlong haste, is cheating us of our due. We have not daylight enough to finish our hunting and fishing, to build our canoes, and gather our yams and bananas and cocoanuts. Night comes on and finds our work but half done.'

"Then there rose up a brave Fisherman and he said: 'I shall go to the Sun and teach him to make his journey as he should. He shall no more bolt across the sky at any pace he may choose.'

"The Fisherman's friends began to wail, and bid him remember what it meant to face such a powerful foe as the Sun. But the Fisherman never once stopped plaiting long ropes to make a snare, and he said: 'I do not fear the Sun.   In this snare I shall catch him.'

"So when the Sun had run his mad race for the day and left the world to night, the Fisherman got into his canoe and sailed out into the Eastern ocean.   Far he sailed and farther through the shadows, down the silvery path that the moon lit up across the dark waste of the waters.   Thus he came to the very edge of the earth, to the spot where the Sun would soon burst forth when he rose from under the ocean.   And there he set his snare, gripping tight in his hands the ends of the rope from which he had made it.

"Soon the moon set and the world was wrapped in darkness. Then the Fisherman sat in his rocking canoe on the edge of the world and waited.   At last the darkness faded into gray; bright jewels of light flashed now and again from the ocean.   Purple and rose appeared in the sky and lo! a small rim of the sun peeped up to touch the white crests of the waves into fire and set all the ocean aflame.

"Still the Fisherman sat in his rocking canoe on the edge of the world and waited.   In another moment a flood of gold streamed over the earth and the whole great Sun burst forth to begin his wild race across the sky. But ah! he had bolted straight into the snare and was tangled close in its meshes.   Then the Fisherman rose in his canoe, and pulled tight the ropes in his hand.   The great Sun raged!   He flared and flamed, but the Fisherman held on fast.

" 'Sun,' he cried, undaunted, 'from this day forth, you shall travel at proper speed.   You shall no more do as you please and race at your own headlong pace across the sky.   You shall give man a day that is long enough so he may finish his hunting and fishing, build his canoes and gather his yams and bananas and cocoanuts.'

"The rage of the Sun grew scorching, withering, blasting.   He struggled with all his might to be free. But the Fisherman braced his feet, balanced his rocking canoe on the waves, and held to the ropes with a grip that would never, never yield. At last the Sun saw he had met his master. Then he slowly softened his glare and stood still.

" 'I promise,' he said, 'I will race no more at my own headlong pace, but will travel at proper speed, slowly, steadily, over the sky.'

"When he had promised thus, the Fisherman set him free, but he did not remove from him all of the ropes. Some he left fastened securely at the edge of the world in order to bind him to keep his promise.

" 'You shall never again be free to have your own will,' he said.

"Then the Fisherman went back home and his people hailed him with music and singing, as one who had been their savior, for ever thereafter the Sun kept his word and the days were sufficiently long for all the work that had need to be done.

"But to this very day when the Sun rises or when he sets, you may still see the ropes hanging down. Look now, as he sinks toward the ocean! You say he is drawing water, but I tell you those brilliant rays that seem to anchor him to the sea, are in truth the meshes of that snare by which the Fisherman bound him."

DONN P. CRANE

THROUGH FAIRY HALLS

A TROPICAL MORNING AT SEA*
EDWARD ROWLAND SILL

Crests that touch and tilt each other
   Jostling as they comb;
Delicate crash of tinkling water,
   Broken in pearling foam.

Off to the East the steady sun-track
   Golden meshes fill—
Webs of fire, that lace and tangle,
   Never a moment still.

Sea depths, blue as the blue of violets—
   Blue as a summer sky,
When you blink at its arch sprung over
   Where in the grass you lie.

Thinned to amber, rimmed with silver,
   Clouds in the distance dwell,
Clouds that are cool, for all their color,
   Pure as a rose-lipped shell.

*Taken from *Hermitage and Later Poems*. Used by permission of, and special arrangement with, Houghton Mifflin Co., the publishers.

MY NICARAGUA*
Salomon de la Selva

When the Winter comes, I will take you to Nicaragua,
You will love it there!
You will love my home, my house in Nicaragua,
So large and queenly looking, with a haughty air
That seems to tell the mountains, the mountains of Nicaragua,
"You may roar and you may tremble, for all I care!"

It is shadowy and cool;
Has a garden in the middle where fruit-trees grow,
And poppies, like a little army, row on row,
And jasmine bushes that will make you think of snow,
They are so white and light, so perfect and so frail,
And when the wind is blowing they fly and flutter so!

The bath is in the garden, like a sort of pool,
With walls of honey-suckle and orchids all around.
The humming-bird is always making a sleepy sound.
In the night there's the Aztec nightingale.

But when the moon is up, in Nicaragua,
The moon of Nicaragua and the million stars,
It's the human heart that sings, and the heart of Nicaragua,
To the pleading, plaintive music of guitars.

*From *Tropical Town and other Poems.* Copyright 1918, by John Lane Company.

210

How Night Came*

A Brazilian Fairy Tale

ELSIE SPICER EELS

It is late afternoon in my Brazilian garden. The dazzling blue of sea and sky which characterizes a tropical noonday has become subdued and already roseate tints are beginning to prepare the glory of the sunset hour. A lizard crawls lazily up the whitewashed wall. The song of the *sabiá*, that wonderful Brazilian thrush, sounds from the royal palm tree. The air is heavy with the perfume of the orange blossom. There is no long twilight in the tropics. Night will leap down suddenly upon my Brazilian garden from out the glory of the sunset sky.

Theresa, the *ama*, stands before us on the terrace under the mango trees, and we know that the story hour has come. Theresa, daughter of the mud huts under the palm trees, is a royal queen of story land. For her the beasts break silence and talk like humans. For her all the magic wonders of her tales stand forth in living truth. Her lithe body sways backwards and forwards to the rhythm of her words as she unfolds her tales to us. She is a picture to remember as she stands under the mango trees on our terrace. Her spotless white "*camiza*" is decorated with beautiful pillow lace, her own handiwork. Her skirt of stiffly starched cotton is red and purple in color. A crimson flowered, folded shawl hangs over her right shoulder,

*Taken from *Fairy Tales from Brazil*. Copyright, 1917, by Dodd, Mead & Company, Inc.

and great strings of beads ornament the ebony of her neck and arms. To sit at the feet of Theresa, the *ama*, is to enter the gate of story land.

"Years and years ago at the very beginning of time, when the world had just been made, there was no night. It was day all the time. No one had ever heard of sunrise or sunset, starlight or moonbeams. There were no night birds, nor night beasts, nor night flowers. There were no lengthening shadows, nor soft night air, heavy with perfume.

"In these days the daughter of the *Great Sea Serpent*, who dwelt in the depths of the seas, married one of the sons of the great race known as Man. She left her home among the shades of the deep seas and came to dwell with her husband in the land of daylight. Her eyes grew weary of the bright sunlight and her beauty faded. Her husband watched her with sad eyes, but he did not know what to do to help her.

" 'O, if night would only come,' she moaned as she tossed about wearily on her couch. 'Here it is always day, but in my father's kingdom there are many shadows. O, for a little of the darkness of night!'

"Her husband listened to her moanings. 'What is night?' he asked her. 'Tell me about it and perhaps I can get a little of it for you.'

" 'Night,' said the daughter of the *Great Sea Serpent*, 'is the name we give to the heavy shadows which darken my father's kingdom in the depths of the seas. I love the sunlight of your earth land, but I grow very weary of it. If we could have only a little of the darkness of my father's kingdom to rest us part of the time!'

"Her husband at once called his three most faithful slaves. 'I am about to send you on a journey,' he told them. 'You are to go to the kingdom of the *Great Sea Serpent*, who dwells in the depths of the seas, and ask him to give you some of the darkness of night, that his daughter may find rest here amid the sunlight of our earth land.'

"The three slaves set forth for the kingdom of the *Great Sea Serpent*. After a long, dangerous journey they arrived at his home in the depths of the seas and asked him to give them some of the shadows of night to carry back to the earth land. The *Great Sea Serpent* gave them a big bagful at once. It was securely fastened and the *Great Sea Serpent* warned them not to open it until they were once more in the presence of his daughter, their mistress.

"The three slaves started out, bearing the big bag full of night upon their heads. Soon they heard strange sounds within the bag. It was the sound of the voices of all the night beasts, all the night birds, and all the night insects. If you have ever heard the night chorus from the jungles on the banks of the rivers you will know how it sounded. The three slaves had never heard sounds like those in all their lives. They were frightened.

" 'Let us drop the bag full of night right here where we are and run away as fast as we can,' said the first slave.

" 'We shall perish. We shall perish, anyway, whatever we do,' cried the second slave.

" 'Whether we perish or not, I am going to open the bag and see what makes all those sounds,' said the third slave.

"Accordingly, they laid the bag on the ground and opened it. Out rushed all the night beasts and all the night birds and all the night insects and out rushed the great black cloud of night. The slaves were more frightened than ever and escaped to the jungle.

"The daughter of the *Great Sea Serpent* was waiting anxiously for the return of the slaves with the bag full of night. Ever since they had started out on her journey she had looked for

their return, shading her eyes with her hand and gazing away off at the horizon, hoping with all her heart that they would hasten to bring the night. In that position she was standing under a royal palm tree, when the three slaves opened the bag and let night escape. 'Night comes. Night comes at last,' she cried, as she saw the clouds of night upon the horizon. Then she closed her eyes and went to sleep there under the royal palm tree.

"When she awoke she felt greatly refreshed. She was once more the happy princess who had left her father's kingdom in the depths of the great seas to come to the earth land. She was now ready to see the day again. She looked up at the bright star shining above the royal palm tree and said, 'O, bright, beautiful star, henceforth you shall be called the morning star and you shall herald the approach of day. You shall reign queen of the sky at this hour.'

"Then she called all the birds about her and said to them, 'O, wonderful, sweet singing birds, henceforth I command you to sing your sweetest songs at this hour to herald the approach of day.' The cock was standing by her side. 'You,' she said to him, 'shall be appointed the watchman of the night. Your voice shall mark the watches of the night and shall warn the others that the *madrugada* comes.' To this very day in Brazil we call the early morning the *madrugada*. The cock announces its approach to the waiting birds. The birds sing their sweetest songs at that hour and the morning star reigns in the sky as queen of the *madrugada*.

"When it was daylight again the three slaves crept home through the forests and jungles with their empty bag.

"'O, faithless slaves,' said their master, 'why did you not obey the voice of the *Great Sea Serpent* and open the bag only in the presence of his daughter, your mistress? Because of your disobedience I shall change you into monkeys. Henceforth you shall live in the trees. Your lips shall bear the mark of the sealing wax which sealed the bag full of night.'

"To this very day one sees the mark upon the monkey's lips, and in Brazil night leaps out quickly upon the earth just as it leaped quickly out of the bag in those days at the beginning of time. And all the night beasts and night birds and night insects give a sunset chorus in the jungles at nightfall."

THE TWILIGHT*
MADISON CAWEIN

In her wimple of wind and her slippers of sleep,
The twilight comes like a little goose-girl,
Herding her owls with many "Tu-whoos,"
Her little brown owls in the woodland deep,
Where dimly she walks in her whispering shoes,
And gown of shimmering pearl.

*Used by permission of Madison Cawein, son of the author, and the publishers, The Macmillan Company.

The Man Who Loved Hai Quai
An Indian Tale of Mt. Tacoma

WHERE the pines loom dark against the sky, beneath the glistening snow peak of the great white Mt. Tacoma, there dwelt once a hunter. In the fragrant pine woods he followed the game; he fished in the rivers and in the placid lake where Tacoma stands upside down in the water. But more than all else he loved hai quai—glittering strings of shells—shell money—treasure, treasure, treasure. There came a time when he thought of nothing but hai quai. He would steal the lip-jewels of women, he would snatch little strings from the children's necks, and he longed to learn of some magic, by which he could heap up still more of the treasure. Ah, then the evil one came and dwelt in his heart and whispered to him always, "Hai quai! More hai quai!"

One day the hunter stood on the shore of the lake dreaming of shell money, when there came to him out of the forest, Moos-Moos, the great Elk, his *tahmahnawis* who watched over him.

"You want hai quai," said Moos-Moos. "Hearken, I know where you will find it, find it in great heaps, more than any red man has in all your lodges."

The hunter listened eagerly.

"Go to the very top of the mountain," said Moos-Moos. "Amid the snow on its peak you will find a valley cleft out of the rocks, and there lies a lake of black, black water. On the shores of this lake rise three giant rocks. One is like a salmon, one like the kamas root, and one like me, an Elk. Beneath the Elk's head, dig. There you will find hai quai, great shining strings of hai quai. And when you have it, show your thanks to the Great Spirit and to me by placing one string on each of the rocks."

"I will be rich! Men shall call me Great Chief!" cried the

hunter, and he bade farewell to the Elk and went back to his lodge. "I go away on a long hunt," he said to his squaw. Then he seized his elk-horn pick and set forth.

Through the dense forests he climbed, by the side of rushing mountain brooks, over flowery upland meadows, among mighty rocks, where the snow began, past gnarled and twisted trees that grew on the edge of the timber, and so on up into the everlasting snows. Then darkness overtook him. It was bitter cold. He rolled himself in his blanket and lay down to sleep. In his sleep he dreamed. He had strings and strings of hai quai hanging about his neck. Tighter they grew and tighter, tighter and tighter. Ah! they were choking him. With a wild cry, he awoke. It was only a dream, and still he wanted hai quai.

Before the sun, he was up and on his way once more. Just as dawn glowed rosy over the snow, he reached the mountain top. There before him, as Moos-Moos had said, was the lake of black water and, rising from it, the giant rocks of the salmon, the kamas root, and the Elk. Seizing his pick, he began at once to dig at the foot of the rock that was shaped like the Elk. All day long he worked, digging, eagerly digging, and twelve great otters rose up out of the strange, dark waters to watch him.

Just as the sun was sinking he came upon the treasure, great heaps of glittering hai quai. His eyes glowed like fire; from his lips came weird sounds like the laughter of a loon; deep down into the shining shells he dug his hands. He slipped the strings over his neck, his arms, he clutched them tight to his bosom. He held them up to the light to catch the last gleam of the setting sun. He thought not of Moos-Moos, nor of the Great Spirit, to offer thanks. He hung no strings on the rocks, but clutching them tighter and tighter, he started off down the mountain.

Then the otters uttered a strange, sad cry and dove down into the waters, and Tootah, the thunder, in answer, went crashing across the sky. The wind began to howl and shriek, snow came swirling fiercely down. And still the hunter clutched his treasure tight and struggled on and on.

The storm increased, the wind roared, Tootah, the thunder, seemed rending the very heavens. Then the hunter took one single string of shells and cast it grudgingly to the winds. "For the Great Spirit," he said. But as he hugged his treasure the storm burst more furiously on him. The night and the mountain found voices and on every side they shrieked in his ear, "Hai quai! Hai quai! Hai quai!"

One by one, he cast his precious strings away, and he groaned as he did so, as though he gave up a part of himself. At last they were gone, those shining strands—he flung the last one from him. Then he fell to the ground, exhausted, and his eyelids closed in sleep.

When he awoke the sun was shining and in his heart was a wonderful peace. He found himself at the foot of a tall fir tree, the same beneath which he had dropped the night before, and, above, the great white mountain smiled graciously upon him. He was hungry but as he started to rise, he found his limbs were stiff, his clothing was in rags and from his head hung hair as white as the snow on Tacoma. Astonished, he looked about him. All was the same as it had been the night before, and yet somehow it was different. He dug some roots to eat and then started slowly down the mountain.

He thought now no more of hai quai. In his ears was the song of birds, in his eyes the golden glow of the sun through the soft smoky haze of Indian summer, and in his heart calmness, utter peace, like the calmness of the mountain, majestic and serene.

At length he came to a lodge before which sat a squaw. She was old and her hair was white. He knew her not and passed her by, yet no! She called him back. Her voice was glad and sweet, and lo! it was his own wife and his own lodge! Not two

short nights, but years and years had passed since he left her.

"How many moons you have been gone!" she cried. "I have traded much since you went and made much hai quai. I will give it all to you."

"Nay," said the old man. "Give me a seat by the lodge fire and a welcome. I care not for hai quai, I care only for peace!"

Then the good squaw was astonished.

Henceforth the old man sat at his lodge door, pondered much, and gave friendly greeting to all who passed him by. To those in need he gave hai quai, to those in trouble he gave good counsel, and to old and young who sought his advice, his answer was always skokum (good).

So he was much beloved, and there dwelt, evermore undisturbed in his heart, the wisdom, peace and quiet that he learned from the great white Tacoma.

The Adventures of Yehl and
The Beaming Maiden

An Alaskan Legend

ALL Alaska was once in a dim, gray twilight. There was neither sun, moon, nor stars in the sky. In those days there lived in Alaska a proud and powerful chief, named Chet'l. On the totem pole before his lodge was carved the figure of the raven, on his deerhorn spoons was carved the raven, into his blankets was woven the raven, on his canoes was painted the raven.

"Chet'l is of the raven clan. Raven keeps guard over Chet'l," said the Chief. But Chet'l was of a dark and stormy mood, dark as the midnight sky. Near him lived Nuschagak, his sister, and often she suffered beneath his anger. Before her lodge, too, rose the totem pole of the raven.

"Raven keeps guard over quiet one," said Nuschagak, "not over stormy one that always shrieks I! I! I!"

Now Chet'l would have none of Nuschagak in his lodge, and so there dwelt there no woman. One dim, gray day up rose Chet'l and went far, far into the Northland. There in the midst of the ice and snow, he saw a maiden of dazzling beauty, more beautiful than anything man had ever beheld before. When she smiled her face beamed and light streamed forth on all about.

"Maiden go back with Chet'l to his lodge!" cried the Chief. So the Maiden gave him her hand and glided along by his side. When they were come to his home, Chet'l gave her rich furs to lie on and many precious blankets. He never asked her to make the fire or do the work of woman. But, though he loaded her with gifts, he wished to keep her all to himself.

"Keep your smiles alone for Chet'l!" he cried.

"Nay," replied the maiden, "I was not made to make happy one only. I smile on all alike. I give my love to all."

Then was Chet'l as the storm cloud.

"Smile on any other," he roared, "and Chet'l buries you deep, where none shall have joy of your beaming!"

"Ah," the maiden made answer, "bury me as deep as you like. You will only shut yourself out from my smile. You can never quench my beaming. I shall go on smiling forever."

Then went Chet'l and fetched eight small redbirds. He whispered to them, "Stand guard over this rebellious maid while Chet'l goes out hunting. See that she smiles on no one. Thus bids thee the great Chet'l." And he fastened the door of his lodge from without and strode away into the forest.

No sooner was he gone than the maiden rose and went to the door. Lo! as she beamed on the solid wood, a little opening appeared; she leaned her head through the opening and smiled on all who passed. And all on whom she smiled felt warmed and cheered and strengthened.

"We bloom as the young grass," they cried, "as the grass when the snow is gone."

Then the little redbirds made great noise and clamor. Out they flew by the hole in the roof, through which the smoke escaped from the hearth—off and away to tell Chet'l.

Thundering with anger, his eyes flashing lightnings, back came Chet'l. He seized the beautiful maiden and thrust her into a great wooden chest. Then he forced down the lid, made fast the lock, and carried the chest away to a dark little inner room that no one was ever permitted to enter.

"There," said he, "now that smile is hid where Chet'l shares it with no man."

Ah, but the world was dark, and in it was no joy at all for Chet'l. All the people began to wail and lament. Never before was such darkness.

"Give her back to us, the Maiden-that-beams!" they cried, yet Chet'l would not relent and restore to them the maiden.

Then came to Chet'l Nuschagak, his sister.

"Set her free—the Maiden," said Nuschagak. "On your totem pole the raven frowns—frowns at the deed that Chet'l has done."

Up rose Chet'l like a whirlwind! He fell on his sister's lodge and razed it to the ground. The totem pole before her door he hacked to bits and cast the raven to the winds.

"Chet'l cares not for the raven," he cried. "Chet'l does as he pleases. And you, little snarling fox, forth with you into the forests, and come no more back to Chet'l, lest he serve you as he did the maiden."

In grief and sorrow, Nuschagak wandered down to the sea. As she stood there, weeping, lo! a raven appeared before her.

"Be not sad, good daughter," said the Raven. "You shall have a child that will be greater than Chet'l. Train him up to be a man and he will yet save you and the Maid."

So Nuschagak went away, built a rude lodge in the forest and set up before it the totem pole of the raven. Soon there came to her a son. The child was beautiful and wonderful. In ten days he had grown to the height of a man and mastered all the knowledge that belongs to manhood. Then the mother knew that there had come to her Yehl—Yehl, the ever-living one, who always was and always will be, who appears to men in whatsoever form is suited best to the need of the time.

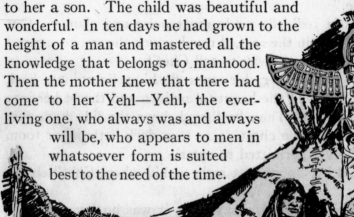

THROUGH FAIRY HALLS

When Yehl had made Nuschagak a comfortable lodge and gathered for her a goodly store of food, she sent him forth to face Chet'l. Straight to the great chief's lodge went Yehl.

"I am your sister's son," said he. Then Chet'l saw that he was a goodly youth and dared not do less than bid him welcome, but in his heart he said, "He knows the secret of the Maid. I shall soon find means to be rid of him."

When there came the dim gray dawn that was all there was to the next day's light, he took Yehl in his canoe and paddled out to sea—"to fish for great fish," said Chet'l. Far, far out he went till the shore had long faded from sight, and the waters lay black, of boundless depth, beneath their rocking keel. Then Chet'l overturned the canoe and plunged Yehl into the deep.

"Let him find a lodge with the whales," cried he. "He is not welcome to Chet'l!" and he righted his canoe and made his way back to shore.

But Yehl dropped quietly to the bottom of the sea, walked safely over the smooth, hard sand and appeared at evening in the door of his uncle's lodge!

"Hah!" muttered Chet'l. "Some whale must have borne him back to shore. Mayhap the whale is his totem! But there be other means to put him out of my way."

The next day he took Yehl out into the forest. There in the midst of a deep dark grove of cypress, spruce and hemlock, set up high upon poles, was a great canoe that Chet'l had been building. It was hewn of a solid log, and had been burned with fire to hollow out the center.

"Step into the canoe, Son-of-my-sister," said Chet'l, "and chip off the burnt wood about the sides to make the inside smooth."

Yehl did as his uncle bade him, but while he was bent over at work, Chet'l sent a great log crashing down and pinned him in where he sat.

"If whale be your totem," he jeered, "what can save you now?"

No sooner was he gone, than Yehl stretched out his arms. At that, the canoe fell to pieces and Yehl stepped forth from under the log. Then he picked up the different parts of the craft, put them together again, and finished it, complete. That evening he appeared at the door of Chet'l's lodge bearing the great canoe on his shoulder.

Then Chet'l's tongue was dumb. But when the night was come, he crept up to the couch of skins whereon his nephew slumbered. "I shall have you yet!" cried he. Just as his hand was at the youth's throat, Yehl turned himself into a raven, slipped out of his grasp and flew up into the sky.

"Ah, he is the Raven, the Raven himself!" cried Chet'l, and he minded how he had cried out that he cared not for the Raven, but would do what pleased himself. "No use to contend with the Raven!" And he plunged off into the forest.

Then came Yehl back to the lodge and found his way to the

darkened chamber. He groped about in the gloom till he came upon a chest.

"Now," said he, "at last I shall set free the Maid." Up came the lid beneath his grasp, but out of the chest rose no Maid. Instead, there flew forth a glistening flock of tiny white birds that darted up into the sky and lo! they became the stars.

Then Yehl groped about again till he once more fell upon something. He pulled up the lid of a second chest. But still no maiden appeared. One great silver bird with pale, gleaming wings soared up into the sky and lo! it became the moon.

"Yehl will not rest till he finds her!" cried the youth, and he searched again till he found a third and last chest. Heavy was its lid—far heavier than the others. He forced it up but a little way and a light shone forth through the crack, like the first faint rose of dawn. As he pulled it higher and higher, the light became dazzling gold, streamed forth in boundless splendor and flooded all the room. Then up rose the smiling Maiden.

"Well done, Yehl," said she. And she floated in shimmering glory up to the sky. Behold! She was the Sun.

Then Yehl rejoiced and Nuschagak rejoiced and all the people on earth rejoiced.

"It is gone—the cold and dark!" they cried. "Light and warmth are come! Behold we bloom again like grass when the snow is melted!"

As to Chet'l, when he saw the shining Maid in the sky smiling on all the world, he went off and hid himself in a dark cave on Mt. Edgecomb. There he became the Thunder-bird. He is still trying to shut up the Sun and keep her from beaming. When he comes forth, the flapping of his great wings makes the thunder and the flash of his eyes the lightning, but no matter what walls of clouds he builds up to shut in the Sun, her smile always finds a way through them, and to this very day, from her place in the sky, she beams in gentle radiance on everyone alike.

AFAR IN THE DESERT

(South Africa)

THOMAS PRINGLE

Afar in the desert I love to ride,
With the silent Bush-boy alone by my side.
Away—away from the dwellings of men,
By the wild deer's haunt, by the buffalo's glen;

By valleys remote where the oribi plays,
Where the gnu, the gazelle, and the hartêbeest graze,
And the kudu and eland unhunted recline
By the skirts of gray forest o'erhung with wild vine;

Where the elephant browses at peace in his wood,
And the river-horse gambols unscared in the flood,
And the mighty rhinoceros wallows at will
In the fen where the wild ass is drinking his fill.

THROUGH FAIRY HALLS

Afar in the desert I love to ride,
With the silent Bush-boy alone by my side.
O'er the brown karroo, where the bleating cry
Of the springbok's fawn sounds plaintively;

And the timorous quagga's shrill whistling neigh
Is heard by the fountain at twilight gray;
Where the zebra wantonly tosses his mane,
With wild hoof scouring the desolate plain;

And the fleet-footed ostrich over the waste
Speeds like a horseman who travels in haste,
Hieing away to the home of her rest,
Where she and her mate have scooped their nest,
Far hid from the pitiless plunderer's view
In the pathless depths of the parched karroo.

Afar in the desert I love to ride,
With the silent Bush-boy alone by my side.
Away—away—in the wilderness vast
Where the white man's foot hath never passed,
And the quivered Coranna or Bechuan
Hath rarely crossed with his roving clan.

The Lost Spear
A South African Tale

Once upon a time, when the fairies were still in this land, and the black man had not been driven inland away from the seashore, a mighty King called all his chiefs together to witness a contest between the four strongest, bravest, and handsomest young men in his kingdom. The prize was the King's youngest daughter—the black-eyed Lala—and that one of the four who should throw the assegai the farthest was to win her for his bride.

Three of these young men were sons of great chieftains, but the fourth was only a poor herdsman. Yet the Princess Lala, who stood at her father's hut, thought him the best of them all. A sandy plain that stretched between the mountains was chosen, and the four champions stood in a row ready to throw. The first threw his assegai so well it fell upright into an ant-hill far, far away. The second assegai stood quivering in the bark of a young fir tree many paces beyond the ant hill. The spear of the third pierced the breast of a gold and green sugar-bird that was fluttering over a tall aloe blossom still further away. But the herdsman, who was fourth, threw his assegai so vigorously that it flew like a flash of lightning up into the heavens, and struck a hawk that was soaring there in search of prey.

Loud were the acclamations of the people, and they adjudged the fourth the winner. The Princess wept for joy, but the King, who did not wish his daughter to wed a humble herdsman, said,—

"Let them throw again with spears that I shall give them. This man's weapon was surely bewitched."

So on the morrow the King sent for fresh spears of gold. And to the princes were given splendid, equally-balanced ones; but the herdsman's was clumsy and untrue. Again they threw, and again the herdsman's assegai out-distanced those of the others. This time it flew into the clouds, and was lost to sight.

But the King was unjust, and said: "Not till you have found the spear, and bring it to my feet, shall you win my daughter, the beautiful Lala. Go!"

The Princess clung to her father and wept, saying she loved this gallant herdsman; but the King took her arms from round his neck, and bade her go. To disobey the King meant death, and the girl went.

Thus Zandilli, the herdsman, set out in search of the Royal assegai. He wandered some days among the mountains, for it was in the wind-clouds on their brows the spear had disappeared. It was on the fourth day of his wanderings that, whilst he was gazing down into the depths of a brown pool, a "butcher-bird" fell at his feet, clutching in his talons a tiny green frog. The frog cried for help, and Zandilli saved it from the bird.

The frog expressed its gratitude, and said: "If ever you are in trouble, and think I can help you, close your eyes and call to mind this brown pool, and I shall come to your assistance."

Zandilli thanked the frog, who then disappeared in the water.

A little further on he saw a large black and yellow butterfly impaled upon a thorn of prickly-pear. He released it, and the butterfly said,—

"I was thrust upon that thorn by a pair of tiny brown hands belonging to a little maid with large black eyes. She was cruel but you are kind, and I am grateful. If ever you are in difficulty or danger call me, and I shall be at your service."

Then the glorious insect spread its wings, and flew away to play with its mates among the crimson orchids.

Night was approaching on the fifth day, and still the lost spear had not been found. It was a warm summer's night, and the moon rose, a great ball of crimson fire, from out the fog in the east. Zandilli was anxious to find some shelter for the night, and to that end entered a narrow gorge, through which trickled a tiny stream. It was very dark in this ravine. Its walls were high, he fell in deep water-holes, and stumbled over slippery boulders; but Zandilli persevered, knowing how often small caves are found in these ravines. And such a cave at last he came upon. The moon, now clear of the fog, had floated up into the heavens, and shone into the gorge, lighting up its western wall. Into a large cavity her light fell in a broad pathway of silver.

Zandilli entered boldly; he, who had lived among the mountains all his life, knew no fear. The light of the moon did not enter very far into the cave, and he was too tired to explore the darkness beyond, so he lay down to rest, with his spear close at hand.

He awoke to find the cave in total darkness, and a strange, soft music greeted his ears. It was music sweeter than that of the turtle-dove calling to her mate, softer than the murmur of the wind among the grass-bells. Its sound thrilled the listener's heart, and made him long to look upon the being whose voice could discourse such sweet music. Zandilli arose, and crept with steps as noiseless as the leopard's towards the place whence the music came.

As he advanced the cave grew broader and higher, and a pale light seemed to flood the walls. Louder grew the music at each step, loftier the walls, and more brilliant the light, until suddenly such a sight burst upon his astonished eyes as never mortal had seen before.

A large lake spread its sapphire waters before him. The roof of the cave shone as the sun, and great pillars, which sparkled with the glitter of countless diamonds, raised themselves from the waters and were lost in the blazing glory of the dome. In the very center of the lake a magnificent flight of glittering golden steps led to a throne, which sent forth flashes of green fire— being fashioned of a single emerald beautifully carved. The lake seemed boundless, for its shores were lost in darkness.

From out of the shadow from all directions countless large rose-colored lilies came floating, each bearing towards the throne a fairy. It was from these lilies the lovely music floated, for each fairy sat singing as she combed her long golden hair. Never had Zandilli seen such beautiful forms. More delicate-looking were they than the soft wind-flowers that crown the precipices; more beautiful than the crimson orchids. Their hair that spread behind them was not less brilliant than the fiery tail of the great star which comes to warn the black man of approaching drought and famine; and it gleamed against their snowy breasts as does the golden tongue of the arum. Their forms were as graceful as that of the slender antelope; their arms were whiter than the spray which tips the waves. Their brows were crowned with white star-blossoms, and their voices excelled anything Zandilli had ever heard. The lily-boats floated from all sides, and seemed

to be guided by some unseen power. As they touched the golden
steps the fays stepped from the pink petals, and shaking their
golden hair around their shoulders as a mantle, they joined
throngs of others as fair as themselves around the throne.

All this Zandilli gazed upon with eyes large with wonder.
Only who it was that sat upon the throne he could not see, for
a brilliancy of flashing lights clothed the occupant as in a veil.
The empty boats dotted the lake, as do the blue water-lilies the
quiet reaches of the rivers, floating lazily backwards and forwards.

Suddenly the music ceased—his presence seemed to have
become known to these strange people. There was much whispering among the throngs upon the steps of the throne. Then a
broad pathway was opened among them, a Being, clothed in
light, stepped from the throne to the water's edge and a silvery
voice spoke,—

"Mortal, you are not unexpected. You are Zandilli, the
herdsman. Your quest is not unknown to us. You seek a Royal
spear, and dare to aspire to win a Royal bride. The moon has
risen five times since you vanquished the three princes in throwing the spear. When she shall have shone yet twice upon land
and sea, your bride, unless you save her, will have wed another.
Yet have no fear, brave Zandilli, the spear is within your reach."

The silvery tones ceased; Zandilli fell upon his face, and said,—

"Oh, great Being! whose light is as the sun's, help your servant to find that spear which you say is within his reach!"

A strange-shaped canoe of gold shot from the steps of the
throne and rested at Zandilli's feet. He entered it fearlessly,
and as quick as light he was carried across to the golden steps.
The dazzling Being who stood there reached a hand to him as
he stepped from the canoe. He raised his eyes, and saw before
him a woman lovely as the morning. Countless rays of light
streamed from a girdle and breast-plate of diamonds, and from

the flowing robes of silver tissue that clothed her, leaving only the lily-white arms and throat bare. Her golden hair fell to her feet, and was crowned with a wreath of star-flowers.

"Welcome to the land of the Moon-Fairies!" she cried, as she took his hand and led him to a seat beside herself upon the throne. The crowd upon the steps bowed humbly before them as they passed through its midst.

Then Zandilli spoke: "Oh, great Queen! whiter than the wind-clouds, fairer than the dawn, tell your servant how best he can serve you and win the spear!"

She bent her eyes, blue as the lake, upon him, and said: "Would that I could say it is yours now—yours to take away; but there is an ancient law amongst us that forbids even the Queen to take from our treasure-trove anything. And the golden spear which fell at the mouth of this cavern, has been given a place among our treasures.

"It was prophesied in years remote that a Mortal would come amongst us in quest of a weapon that would give the possessor great joy. When he should appear two tasks were to be set him. If he performed them the object of his search should be given him. You, Zandilli, the herdsman, are that Mortal, for do you not seek a spear that will give you a lovely bride? We will deliberate upon the tasks to be set you. Meanwhile you will be shown the beauties of our home by my maidens."

With these words the Queen rose and descended to the lily-boat, which bore her quickly away. Now three of the loveliest of the fairies stepped with Zandilli into the golden canoe—wonder after wonder unfolded itself to his astonished gaze. All was glitter and light. But there was one dark cavern, whose walls were lusterless and black as night. Now Zandilli was impatient to win the spear, especially as the Queen had spoken of another who was to win the Princess Lala ere two moons had risen.

He therefore begged to be taken back to the Queen, who sat again upon her throne. She greeted him with a smile, and laid her lily-white hand upon his bronze arm. "We have decided," she said, "upon your first task. My councilors have made it no easy one. You have seen the black chamber? It is the one blot upon our home. If you can make it as beautiful as each of the others half your task will be fulfilled. Before the moon has risen again this must be performed, or death will be your doom."

Zandilli was taken to the black chamber; and there he was left alone in the golden canoe, with despair at his heart, for he had no means of beautifying those hideous walls. He thought of the foam-flecked sea, which he should never see again; of the shy maiden who was to have been his bride. He thought of the flowers, the birds, the butterflies. At the thought that then came, he laughed. The butterfly he had saved! Could it help him? It seemed hopeless.

Zandilli sighed, and, overcome by fatigue, laid himself to sleep. But the butterfly heard its savior's scarce-formed cry for help. At break of day it called together its brethren and its cousins, the fire-flies. Then they all flew into the dark cavern. The sound of their fluttering wings awoke Zandilli. Great was his surprise to find the dull walls transformed into a fairy palace of gorgeous wings and tender, pale-green gems. The butter-flies and fire-flies had spread themselves over the entire walls.

When the Queen and her followers came to see if the task had been performed, great surprise and joy did they express at the wonderful transformation the Mortal had worked. With one voice they cried,—"He has won! He has won!"

All that day was spent in revelry; but the Queen was absent. She was with her wise men, discussing the second task.

At the close of the day, the Queen spoke thus to Zandilli:

"You have completed your first task, and the spear is partly won. It has therefore been placed here upon the steps before my throne. See! This is to be your second task—my maidens' robes are woven from the wings of flies. Our looms are idle, for our store-rooms are empty. To you is given the task of filling a hundred of our boats with the wings of flies." Then the Queen disappeared.

Zandilli lay down in the canoe, and gave way to despair. This task seemed far more hopeless even than the first. Never more should he see the sun; never should he hunt the leopard again. Never should he see the tumbling streams and cool brown pools, nor see the great black eyes of his Princess smile upon him. He fell asleep at last with these sad thoughts upon him. But the frog heard his saviour's sigh for a sight of the brown

pool, and called his brethren and his friends the lizards. Each came with his burden of flies, and soon filled the boats.

Their busy croaking awoke Zandilli, who found his task performed; and when the Queen and her followers came again, they cried,—"He has won! The spear is his!"

Then Zandilli ascended the golden steps to take his well-earned prize. Impatiently he seized the golden spear, and jumping into the canoe, propelled it with the spear to the edge of the lake, where he bounded ashore. In a few hours he was back at the hut of the King and had claimed his bride, the beautiful black-eyed Lala.

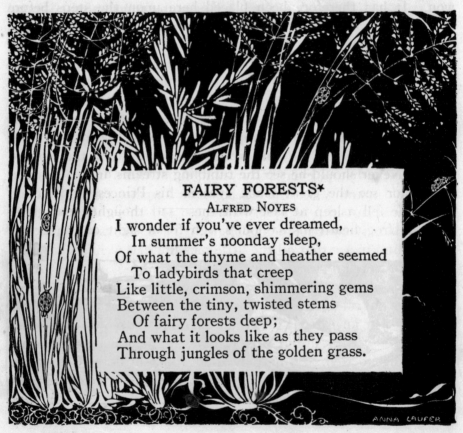

FAIRY FORESTS*
ALFRED NOYES

I wonder if you've ever dreamed,
  In summer's noonday sleep,
Of what the thyme and heather seemed
  To ladybirds that creep
Like little, crimson, shimmering gems
Between the tiny, twisted stems
  Of fairy forests deep;
And what it looks like as they pass
Through jungles of the golden grass.

*From *Collected Poems*, published by Frederick A. Stokes Company.

How Brer Rabbit Met Brer Tar-Baby

Way down south in the land o' cotton, when the moon hung in the sky like a great, big, round persimmon, and the mocking bird was singing in the trees, the negroes used to gather all together before their cabins, sing queer, sweet old melodies, dance strange dances, and tell stories in the moonlight. Sometimes a little white boy or girl would slip away of an evening from the great house with the big white pillars where the owner of the plantation lived, and go down among the little pickaninnies to hear the tales and join in the fun.

All of a sudden, the banjos and the fiddles, the singing and dancing would stop, everybody would squat down in a circle, and a little old mammy with a red bandana kerchief round her head would burst out in a high, shrill laugh, "Hi, yi, yi, yi!" her teeth shining like ivory in the moonlight. Then she would roll her eyes around to see that all the little pickaninnies were still as mice and begin to tell a story.

" 'Twa'n't my time an' 'twa'n't you' time, but 'twas a berry good time dat all de beastises got togeder—Brer Fox an' Brer Wolf an' Brer Bear an' Brer 'Possum an' all de rest, an' dey say, 'We's gwine dig a well!' All but Brer Rabbit, an' he 'low he ain't gwine wuk to dig no well. So he play roun' 'bout in de bushes an' he play roun' an' he play roun' an' he play roun'. An' de udder beastises dey say to him, 'Brer Rabbit, if you don' dig no well, wot you gwine do w'en you wants wateh?' Den Brer Rabbit he say, 'Oh, I'se gwine get it an' drink it!'

"De udder beastises dey all say, 'We's gwine plough de field an' plant co'n.' So dey all plough de field an' plant co'n. But Brer Rabbit he 'low he ain't gwine wuk to plant no co'n. So he play roun' an' he play roun' an' he play roun'. Den de udder beastises dey say to him, 'Brer Rabbit, if you don' plant no co'n, wot you gwine do w'en you wants food?' An' Brer Rabbit he say, 'Oh, I'se gwine get it an' eat it!'

"But w'en Brer Fox an' Brer Wolf an' Brer Bear an' Brer 'Possum an' all de rest, had dug de field, an' planted it, an' cut it, den Brer Rabbit he come 'long an' help hisself to de co'n. An' w'en Brer Fox an' Brer Wolf an' Brer Bear an' Brer 'Possum an' all de rest had dug de well, den Brer Rabbit he come 'long an' help hisself to de wateh.

"Den Brer Wolf an' Brer Fox an' Brer Bear an' Brer 'Possum an' all de rest, dey make up de minds to cotch Brer Rabbit, so's he cyan't drink dere wateh an' eat dere co'n no mo'! But Brer Rabbit he am too wise. He don' come to de well twice at de same time. He jes' slip in w'en nobody ain't lookin' an' help hisself to de wateh an' de co'n, an' slip away again. So nobody cyan't cotch him.

"But Brer Wolf he say, 'By jing! I'se gwine cotch him yet!' An' he take some straw an' make it into a baby wid haid, body, ahms, laigs; an' he smear it wid tar—soft, sticky black tar, till dat dar baby's black, black, black as any you little pickaninnies! Den he set Tar-Baby up right dar 'side de well an' go 'way.

"Bimeby de moon come out, de whip-poor-will begin to w'istle in de swamps, an' ain't nobody awake anyw'ere at all, 'ceppin' Uncle Rastus' yaller dog a way off summ'ers howlin' at de moon. Den 'long come ole Brer Rabbit, mighty keerful-like, lookin' here an' lookin' dere, a-listenin' fur ev'ry sound an' duckin' down behin' a stone w'en de wind go, 'Zoo-oo!' through de trees. Purty soon he come to de well an' den, wot he see in de moonshine, but Tar-Baby settin' dar in his way, big an' black as a live pickaninny!

"Fust he gwine fur ter run, but he want to get some wateh mighty bad, so he sets up an' he puts on his best comp'ny man-nehs an' he say, 'Good ebenin', suh! Fine weatheh, suh!'

"But Tar-Baby ain't say nothin'.

" 'How's you' mudder, suh, an' you' grandmudder, suh, an' de chilluns, an' all de rest ob de fambly?' Brer Rabbit say, an' he creep up a leetle nearer.

"But Tar-Baby ain't say nothin'.

"Den Brer Rabbit he get mighty brave w'en he see Tar-Baby don' move, an' he drop his comp'ny mannehs right flat, an' he say, 'Look yere,' says'e, 'Get out o' my way!'

"But Tar-Baby ain't move an' ain't say nothin'.

" 'Look yere,' says Brer Rabbit again, says'e, 'You see dis yere paw,' an' he hol' up his right fo' paw, 'If you don' get out o' my way, I'se gwine hit you wid dis paw an' knock de stuffin' out o' you!'

"But Tar-Baby ain't move and ain't say nothin'! So Brer Rabbit he take his paw and blimp! he hit Tar-Baby a crack fur to knock de stuffin' out o' him, but Brer Rabbit's paw is jes' stick fast in de tar an' he cyan't pull it loose. Den Brer Rabbit begin fur to holler, 'Le' me go! Le' me go, you black rascal!' But Tar-Baby don' le' go! Den Brer Rabbit he hol' up his lef' fo' paw an' he say, 'You see dis yere paw. If you don' le' go, I'se gwine hit you wid dis paw an' knock de daylights out o' you!' But Tar-Baby don' le' go! So Brer Rabbit he take his paw an' blimp! he hit Tar-Baby anudder crack an' t'udder paw stick fast in de tar!

"Den Brer Rabbit begin fur to holler wuss'n ever, an' he say, 'Le' go! Le' go, you black rascal! Le' go! Le' go! You see dis yere foot! If you don' le' go, I'se gwine kick you wid dis foot an' knock you sky high!' But Tar-Baby don' le' go. So Brer Rabbit he take his right foot an' blimp! he hit Tar-Baby anudder crack, an' his right foot stick fast in de tar. Den Brer Rabbit begin fur to holler like a screech owl, an' he lift up his left foot an' he say, 'Le' go! Le' go, you black rascal! Le' go! Le' go! You see dis yere foot? If you don' le' go, I'se gwine kick you wid dis foot an' sen' you sailin' up to de moon!' But Tar-Baby don' le' go! So Brer Rabbit he take his left foot an' blimp! he hit Tar-Baby anudder crack, an' his left foot stick fast in de tar!

"Den Brer Rabbit he get madder'n a hornet an' he say, 'Le' go! Le' go, you black rascal! Le' go! Le' go! If you don' I'se gwine butt you wid my haid an' knock you all to pieces!' But Tar-Baby don' le' go. So Brer Rabbit he butt Tar-Baby wid his haid an' his haid stick tight in de tar.

"Den Brer Rabbit he holler an' he screech an' he howl! But he cyan't get loose, an' dar he have to stay till de mawnin'.

" 'Bout sun-up 'long come Brer Wolf fur to see wot's happen, an' dar he see Brer Rabbit stuck to Tar-Baby tighter'n a burr. Den Brer Wolf he open his mouf an' laugh an' show all his toofs, an' he say, sweet as honey, 'Good mawnin', Brer Rabbit. How is you dis fine mawnin'?'

"Now Brer Rabbit ain't say nothin', but he begin to shake in de knees, kase he know wot's comin' to 'im. An' Brer Wolf he say, 'Wot for you don' speak to me, Brer Rabbit? 'Pears like you is a little *stuck up* dis mawnin'!' An' he laugh fit to split, 'Hi, yi, yi, yi! I hear you is lookin' fur a drop o' wateh, so I'se jes' gwine take you an' frow you in de well!' An' he cotch hol' o' Brer Rabbit by de hind laig. Now Brer Rabbit he's got de shakes all ober! 'Pears like he's gwine ter en' up in de well. But he been a thinkin' an' he say, 'O Brer Wolf, please do frow me into de well! Dat'll gi'e me de bes' drink ob water I'se ebber had. Dat's jes' w'ere I wants to be—in de well. But, whatebber you do, don', don', don', please don' frow me in de brier-patch!'

"Now Brer Wolf he's mighty s'prised w'en he hear Brer Rabbit say he wants to get frowed in de well, an' so he say, 'Well den, I jes' ain't gwine frow you in de well. I'se gwine build a fire fer ter roast some o' dat co'n you'se a-hankerin' atter, an' I'se gwine frow you in de fire!'

" 'O Brer Wolf! Brer Wolf!' says Brer Rabbit (but he's shakin' like a leaf w'en he say it). 'Please do frow me in de fire. Den I'll eat all dat co'n I'se hankerin' atter. In de fire's jes' w'ere I wants to be. But, whatebber you do, don', don', don', please don' frow me in de brier-patch!'

"Den Brer Wolf he scratch his haid an' he say, 'You wants me to frow you in de well, you wants me to frow you in de fire; well den, you rascal dat plays roun', an' plays roun', an' plays roun', an' don' do no wuk, an' eats co'n udder folks plants, an' takes wateh out a well udder folks digged, I'se gwine do de wustest thing you don' want me to,—*I'se gwine frow you straight in de brier-patch!*'

"An' he yank Brer Rabbit loose from Tar-Baby an' frow him straight into de brier-patch. 'Dar now,' he say, 'de briers 'll scratch 'im, an' poke 'im, an' jab 'im! I done finish Brer Rabbit!'

"But jes' den he hear Brer Rabbit laughin' an' see him goin' lippity clippity through de briers, an' Brer Rabbit call out to him, 'Thank you, Brer Wolf, kind Brer Wolf! Thank you fur sendin' me straight back home! I an' all my fambly was bo'n an' raised in de brier-patch. Hi, yi, yi, yi!' "

Melilot*

IT had been raining for ten months, and everybody felt as if it had been raining for ten years. There was a breath of wet on everything in-doors, and a flood of wet on everything out of doors, and over the great waste of bog between the two lakes in the valley, thick mist brooded and the rain fell with never-ending splash.

Melilot was wet through as she made her way slowly down toward the valley. A pretty little girl of twelve was Melilot, and she lived in a cottage way up the mountains. She had been the only child of hard-working parents who taught her all that was good. But now both her father and mother were dead and she was left quite alone to care for herself. For days she had had little or nothing to eat and that morning the rain had beaten a hole through the roof of her hut, so the water came pouring in and drenched everything through and through. Faint with hunger and weeping with grief, Melilot went down into the valley to ask for human help. The waterfall that broke into foam on the rocky basin near her cottage door, dashed with a mighty roar over a precipice into the swollen stream that carried its flood to one of the lakes, and it was by this steep and rocky path the road down into the valley ran. Melilot's nearest neighbors lived in a wretched hovel on the oozing marsh and Melilot knew that her father had always avoided these people, and forbidden her to go near them. But to what others could she turn in her loneliness and great need? Shivering and weeping, she crept along through the mist and fog, and knocked at the cottage door.

"Who's there?" asked a hoarse voice inside.

"It's Melilot, from up above us," answered a hoarser voice.

"Come in, little Melilot," said the hoarsest voice of all.

At sound of those harsh voices the child flinched, but at last she summoned all her courage and opened the door. There she

*Retold from the story in *Oberon's Horn* by Henry Morley.

stopped short on the threshold. Before her was a muddy puddle and in it three men sat squatted like frogs. They had broad noses and spotted faces and the brightest of eyes all fixed upon her.

"We are glad to see you, Melilot," said the one who sat in the middle, holding out a hand that had all of its fingers webbed together. He was the one who had the hoarsest voice. "My friend on the right is Dock, Dodder sits on the left, and I am Squill. Come in and shut the door behind you."

Melilot hesitated for just an instant—they certainly were ugly enough to look at—but at length she went bravely in and shut the door behind her.

"A long time ago your father came here, but he went out as soon as he saw us," said Dock. "You are wiser than he, little girl."

"My father, O my dear father!" mourned Melilot, weeping.

"She is very sad and hungry," said Dodder, "and we have nothing to offer her but tadpoles, which she cannot eat."

"Dear neighbors," sobbed the child, "the rain has beaten a hole through the roof of my cottage. I am there all alone and in

very great need. Will you come up the mountain and help me?"

"She asks us to her house," said Dock.

"We may go," said Dodder, "if we are invited."

"Little Melilot," said Squill in his hoarsest tone, "we will all follow you to the mountain hut." Then the three ugly creatures splashed out of their pool and moved with ungainly hopping toward her. But Melilot looked frankly into their faces and saw that their eyes, though bright, were neither hard nor cruel. Arm in arm behind her, they hopped along up the mountain. Rain still poured from the sky, runlets flooded their path and the great cataract roared by their side. Once Melilot, faint and weary, lost her footing and fell, but her three neighbors lifted her gently to her feet and helped her tenderly on. At last, after toilsome climbing, they reached the hut. Dock, Dodder and Squill at once bestirred themselves to mend the great hole in the roof. Late into the night they worked and when they had finished their task, the half famished child raked the embers of the fire and put on fresh wood till a blaze leaped up. Then she bade the three ugly monsters sit down in the warmth and rest.

"I am sorry, dear neighbors," she said, bravely pressing back the tears, "that I have no supper to offer you who have been so kind to me."

"Ah, but you have supper," said Dock.

In astonishment the child followed the glance of his eyes, and lo! on the round table near the fire, where she and her parents used to eat, there stood a loaf of bread and a cup of milk, just as if her dear father and mother themselves had provided them.

"Oh, I am thankful," cried Melilot, and she broke the loaf into three pieces and gave a piece to each of her guests, saving nothing at all for herself.

"She is starving," whispered Dodder, "yet she gives us all the food."

THROUGH FAIRY HALLS

"We must eat it all," said Squill. "You know the reason why."

So they ate every crumb and Melilot smiled as they basked in the firelight, her heart brimming over with joy that she had this bread to give. Never once did she think that nothing was left for herself. But no sooner had the three neighbors eaten, than lo! there appeared on the table another loaf of bread and another and larger cup of milk.

"That must be supper for the good little daughter Melilot and no one else," said Squill.

Warmed through and through as if by her mother's very presence, Melilot gratefully ate. But she did not eat all that was set before her. No, for she thought to ask her kind friends to stay with her through the night, so she saved enough from her sore-needed supper to provide for their breakfast next morning. It was long since the sun had set, reddening the mists of the plain and now the mountain path beside the torrent was dark and difficult to follow. So when Melilot asked the monsters to sleep in the hut, they assented eagerly. There were but two beds in the cottage, a poor little straw pallet and the large and comfortable one where Melilot's father and mother had slept. With simple hospitality Melilot gave up to her guests the larger bed, reserving the poor one for herself. After looking at her gratefully, the three monsters lay down and went to sleep with their arms twined about each other. The child looked down on them clinging together in their sleep, and noted many a kindly line and many a line of sorrow in their half frog-like faces. If one stirred in his sleep it was to nestle closer to the other two.

"How strange," she said to herself, "that I should at first have thought them ugly." Then she knelt in prayer by her little nest of straw, and did not forget them in her prayers. There was a blessing on them in her heart as she settled down to sleep. But as she lay there, the rushing noise of the torrent fixed her attention and drew her towards the window from which she looked out into the night. There was a short lull in the rain, though the wind still howled around the mountain, and through a chance break in the scurrying clouds the full moon now and then flashed. It lit the lakes in the valley far below, and caused the torrent outside the window to gleam like silver through the shadows. Thence came to the ear of the lonely child—hark! it seemed low and wondrous music. Could it be the song of busy fairies at work in the waterfall?

Up to the moon and cut down that ray!
In and out the foam-wreaths plaiting:
Spin the froth and weave the spray!
Melilot is watching! Melilot is waiting!
Pick the moonbeam into shreds,
Twist it, twist it into threads!
Threads of the moonlight, yarn of the bubble,
Weave into muslin, double and double!
Fold all and carry it, tarry ye not,
To the chamber of gentle and true Melilot.

Almost at the same moment the door of the hut opened and on the threshold two beautiful youths appeared, bright as the silver moonlight. At the feet of the gentle little maid they laid a bale of fairy muslin, woven from the spray of the waterfall. Then they turned into gleaming fire-flies and flitted out of the room.

"Ah," said the child to herself as she looked once again at the monsters cuddled together on the bed. "The fairies have brought me this that I might not have to send my kind helpers away without a gift. I will make them three dresses before they wake that they may see I am glad to work for them as they have worked for me."

Very carefully, so as not to awaken them, she began measuring her neighbors with the string of her poor little apron; then she retired with her scissors and thread and the fairy muslin into the

farthest corner of the hut, and set to work by the fitful light of a
pine stick. All through the night the little maid stitched, but
all night long as she patiently worked, the fairies sang outside,
and a wonder it was that her needle never once needed threading.
Keeping time to the low, sweet music, her fingers flew with a
marvelous speed. One needleful of thread made all the three
coats and still the thread was as long as before. When the first
faint gray of dawn came creeping into the hut, the dresses were
ready, and all the muslin had been used except a small litter of
pieces. Melilot daintily folded the coats with that corner upper-
most in which she had embroidered the owner's name—Dock
in one, Dodder in another, and Squill in the corner of a third.
Then she laid them by the bed of her guests and, weary with toil,
lay down for a little sleep.

Dock, Dodder and Squill awakened before Melilot and the
moment they opened their eyes, the very first thing each saw by
the bed was his dainty new garment. In a twinkling they all
dressed themselves, and the very moment they stood arrayed in
the white muslin coats, lo! they turned into three fairy youths
of bright and wonderful beauty. Then they went, hand in hand,

and stood with joyful tears by the bed of the good little maid.

"She has set us free, the dear child," said Dock.

"With all the muslin she had, she has saved nothing for herself," said Squill. "Did not the child once wish to wear muslin in place of those rags? I kiss them, brothers, for her sake." But Squill's kiss on the girl's ragged frock changed it into a splendid satin gown embroidered with jewels.

"And I kiss the walls that sheltered us," said Dodder. But Dodder's kiss on the wretched walls changed them into a network of fragrant blossoms.

"And I kiss the lips that bade us come hither," Dock said. At his kiss the child smiled and opened her eyes. But she did not yet know the three handsome youths for her ugly guests. She thought them the Fairies who had brought her the muslin.

"Ah, Fairies," she cried, "those are the dresses I made for my three kind neighbors. I beg you do not take back your gift. It made me so happy to think I might do something for them. It is true I have done nothing of myself. The muslin is yours and the thread too, and it was you who made the needle run, yet I beg you let me have the coats to give to them."

"Ah, dear little Melilot," said the Fairies, speaking in softest unison, "you say you have done nothing of yourself, yet the kindness in your heart has done more for us than all our love and service will repay, for tonight it has changed us from the ugly monsters who were your neighbors into our rightful forms again."

"Then you are my dear neighbors," said the child springing up. "And all is changed in the cottage. Why are the walls covered with flowers and my dress with jewels?"

"It is the kindness in your heart has done it all," said the Fairies again. And lo! little Melilot saw that the rain no longer fell. The sun had driven away the clouds, and the bright morning beams played in the spray of the cataract. Joyously she ran out of doors and the Fairies after her. But they had no sooner reached the open than Dock peered up at the sky.

"Do you see anything between us and the sun?" cried he.

"A speck," said Dodder.

"The wicked Frogbit herself," said Squill, and they all hurried into the cottage again taking Melilot with them. There Squill, as if preparing to meet some evil, began shaping into a net the left-over shreds of Fairy muslin. Soon there came an icy wind striking a chill through the flowery cottage.

"It seems to me," said Melilot, peering out at the windows, "that this wind comes from that great black raven that has just lit on our roof."

"Ah, Frogbit," cried Squill, "come on! We are ready for you."

At that the ugly bird let out a shrill croak as if in defiance and began to beat a way through the roof. At her touch the leaves of the bower withered and the blossoms shrivelled up. But just as Frogbit dropped in triumph through the hole, Squill leapt up and caught her fast in his net. Then, beat her wings as she would, she could not break through the Fairy muslin.

"Well done," cried Dock and Dodder, but Melilot said, pityingly, "Poor bird! Why do you treat her so?"

"Waste no pity on her. She came on a bad errand," said Dock.

But Melilot, who loved man, bird and beast, bent over the

249

fluttering raven, and though it struck at her fiercely with its bill, she took it net and all, to her bosom.

"How can a poor raven be your enemy?" said the child.

"Their enemy and yours," shrieked the raven.

"Mine," cried Melilot in surprise. "How can you be my enemy? I would do you no hurt for I love you." And she stooped to kiss the raven's head through the thin muslin, but the bird struggled to escape from the kiss with an agony of terror.

"Nay," said the gentle child, "no evil can come of a true kiss." And she firmly and tenderly pressed her lips to its head. But lo! at the touch of her kiss, the wicked Frogbit changed from a raven into naught but a black, shapeless lump of earth.

"What have I done?" the child cried, weeping.

But the three Fairies joyously threw the lump of earth into the waterfall and told her just what she had done. Of old they had lived happily with their brothers in the torrent and in the valley below till the wicked Frogbit came with her own evil race and drove the good Fairies out of the valley. Dock, Dodder and Squill, Frogbit had taken prisoner. Then she had turned the land below into a marshy wilderness and brought down never ending rain. The three Fairies of the bright, running water she condemned to sit in a stagnant puddle, having their own bright natures hidden from view in outward forms the most detestable.

"Live here," she had said, "till a little child can look at you without being afraid; can believe in you entirely, invite you to her house, give up to you her own supper, and of her own free thought make white muslin dresses for your filthy shapes."

"And you, dear Melilot," said the Fairies, "have done all this."

"Then I have really been a friend to you," cried the child.

"Aye, and to Frogbit, too," they replied. "An innocent kiss is the charm that breaks all evil spells. You have broken the spell that raised her from a clod of earth into a creature of mischief.

THROUGH FAIRY HALLS

We of the torrent will direct the waters that they wash away the clod. Purified now of evil, it shall yield beautiful flowers of which good Fairies shall be born."

So the three Fairies returned to their race, but Melilot grew to womanhood their friend and the favorite of all the Fairies of the waterfall. Her rich and splendid dress she laid away and never wore, for she was arrayed by the Fairies in simple garments of their own shining muslin, woven from the white sheets of the torrent's foam, a dress so pure it would take no speck of soil. And still all the bread and milk she needed appeared on the table each morning and evening, and in her heart was a sense of satisfied love as though her dear parents were ever with her. As to the marsh, the bad fairies over whom Frogbit ruled must have left it, for the mists and brooding fog vanished; it dried up and became a plain where men tilled the soil and reaped bounteous harvests.

THE FOG*

CARL SANDBURG

The fog comes
on little cat feet.
It sits looking
over harbor and city
on silent haunches
and then moves on.

The Ragged Pedlar*
AUNT NAOMI

At the foot of a big, bleak mountain stood a small town in which all the people were grumblers. They were never satisfied with anything and they were always unhappy.

"Ours is only a very small town," said the tradesmen. "Visitors never come to us, merchants never tarry with their caravans."

"We have no beautiful buildings, no fine squares and streets," said others, "and the mountain which frowns on us is bare of vegetation and always looks gloomy and even threatening."

"We have no rich inhabitants," said those who were lazy. "We have all to work, work continually for a bare subsistence."

Even the children were discontented, and lay idly on the ground at the street corners when the day was hot. Nobody seemed to notice that the fields at the foot of the mountain were bright and fresh and beautifully green for several months in

*From *Jewish Fairy Tales*. Used by permission of the publishers, Bloch Publishing Co.

the year, and that when the snow covered the mountain it glistened and shone dazzlingly white in the sunshine and glowed rosy pink in the sunset.

It was true that nothing seemed to happen in the town, but if there were no wealthy dwellers, there were also very few poor people. Nobody had much to give away, and so everybody was compelled to work to earn his living. But people who grumble do not notice these things.

One day when the weather had been very hot and the people lazier than ever, a strange visitor came into town just before the sun began to set. The heat was passing, a little breeze was beginning to spring up, and even the barren mountain began to look a little beautiful under the rosy glow of the sky. Some of the huge, frowning boulders and great stones began to reflect the setting sun until they shone like gold.

Perhaps the strange visitor noticed this, if the inhabitants did not, and he called out, in a loud, musical voice—

"Come hither, ye dwellers of this beautiful city of the setting sun. Yon mountain shines like burnished gold, your hundreds of roofs and minarets and domes and spires reflect the rosy hue of the sky. Yet ye are not happy. Come to me and I will sell you happiness."

The people all laughed loudly.

"What manner of fool are you?" they said to the visitor, "and where did you get those strange clothes?"

"Yes, and what did you pay for them?" asked the children.

"I paid naught for this magnificent traveling outfit," replied the stranger.

Everybody roared with laughter when he said this, because the man was dressed in rags! Except for a huge basket slung from his shoulders and a long rope wound round his body, he wore almost nothing. The rest was made up of a few patches of different colours. In his quaint cap were many holes through which his unkempt hair wound itself in fantastic fashion.

"It must take you an hour to remove your hat," said one.

"Oh, no," answered the pedlar, and he took it off with a flourish and put it back again, and every hair found its way through its old hole as if by magic!

"Thou art no ordinary pedlar, sir stranger," said Ahmed, the fishmonger, to him.

"Have I not said so?" replied the pedlar. "I sell happiness."

"If thou but sellest cheaply," returned Ahmed, "thou shouldst do well here. Set down thy basket."

The big basket jumped from the man's shoulders by itself and stood itself upside down in the midst of the crowd that had gathered. The people stared in great wonderment.

"There can be nothing in it," they said.

Immediately the basket of its own accord turned a somersault and stood the other way up. It was empty.

"The man must be mad," cried Ahmed.

"And the basket bewitched," added Mustapha Ben, the tailor.

The pedlar said nothing, but handed the end of the rope which was round his waist to one of the children. The child took it and began to pull. The pedlar spun round and round like a top until the people could hardly see him, and the rope that unwound itself seemed endless. It lay coil upon coil upon the ground until it made a pile as high as the basket. Then the man stopped spinning. He took one end of the rope and threw it up in the air. Away it spun, uncoiling itself right to the other end of the street where it caught itself neatly on a post. There was a post a few yards away from where the pedlar was standing, and he threw the loose end of the rope towards that. Again it caught, and the people then noticed that the rope was just the length of the distance between the two posts.

"A funny performance," they all said. "What does it mean, sir pedlar?"

"My store is open; I am ready to begin business," he replied.

"But where are your wares?"

"You will supply those," was the answer, as the man took up his basket.

"Now then," he cried, "all you who are unhappy bring here your miseries, your discontentments. I will exchange them for happiness."

Everybody found that each could bring his own unhappiness and they rushed forward eagerly to put it into the basket. Soon it seemed quite full. There was not a man or woman in the town that did not bring something. Even many of the children had some thing to put into the basket.

"Observe now," said the pedlar, and he took the basket and lifted it on to the rope. It stood there, balancing itself like a tight-rope walker.

"Do your duty," commanded the pedlar, and the basket began to roll over and over along the rope. All along it tumbled merrily, dropping the troubles as it went until everyone of them hung nicely across the rope. There was Ahmed's lame leg, Mustapha Ben's red hair, Granny Yochki's crutch, Suliman's empty pockets, and lots of other queer things. Every cause of unhappiness and discontent in the town was hung upon the line.

"Hearken now unto me, ye good people of the city of the setting sun," cried the pedlar, in his loud, musical voice. "The day is waning fast, and I cannot stay with you. I promised to barter all your miseries for happiness. It is a simple task. Take each of you from the line the smallest trouble that you can see."

At once there was a big rush forward and a general scramble to snatch the smallest thing from the line. Everybody to his surprise, as he looked over other peoples' troubles, found that his own was the smallest. In a few seconds the line was quite empty.

"Have each of you taken the smallest trouble?" asked the pedlar.

"Yes," answered Mustapha Ben, fixing on his red hair again.

"Yes," cried the others in chorus.

"Then rest ye content, good people of the city of the setting sun," answered the pedlar, in his strong, musical voice. "Come, my faithful basket and rope," and the basket jumped on to his shoulder and the rope wound itself rapidly round his body.

"Farewell, be contented," he sang out in a cheerful voice, and the people saw him ascend the barren mountain still glowing like gold in the setting sun. When he got to the top, he waved his hand and disappeared.

And ever after the people ceased to grumble.

THE PEDLAR'S SONG

WILLIAM SHAKESPEARE

Will you buy any tape,
Or lace for your cape,
My dainty duck, my dear-O?
Any silk, any thread,
Any toys for your head,
Of the newest and finest wear-O?

—*From "A Winter's Tale."*

David and Goliath
I Samuel; 17.

Now the Philistines gathered together their armies to battle. And Saul and the men of Israel were gathered together, and pitched by the valley of Elah, and set the battle in array against the Philistines. And the Philistines stood on the one side, and Israel stood on a mountain on the other side, and there was a valley between them.

And there went out a champion out of the camp of the Philistines, named Goliath, of Gath, whose height was six cubits and a span. And he had an helmet of brass upon his head, and he was armed with a coat of mail; and the weight of the coat was five thousand shekels of brass. And he had greaves of brass upon his legs, and a target of brass between his shoulders. And the staff of his spear was like a weaver's beam; and his spear's head weighed six hundred shekels of iron; and one bearing a shield went before him.

And he stood and cried unto the armies of Israel, and said unto them, "Why are ye come out to set your battle in array? Am not I a Philistine, and ye servants to Saul? Choose you a man for you, and let him come down to me. If he be able to fight with me, and to kill me, then will we be your servants; but if I prevail against him, and kill him, then shall ye be our servants, and serve us. I defy the armies of Israel this day; give me a man, that we may fight together."

When Saul and all Israel heard these words of the Philistine, they were dismayed, and greatly afraid.

Now David was the son of that Ephrathite of Bethlehem-judah, whose name was Jesse; and he had eight sons. And the three eldest sons of Jesse went and followed Saul to the battle. And David was the youngest. But David went and returned from Saul to feed his father's sheep at Bethlehem.

And the Philistine drew near morning and evening, and presented himself forty days.

And Jesse said unto David, his son, "Take now for thy brethren an ephah of this parched corn, and these ten loaves, and run to the camp; and carry these ten cheeses unto the captain of their thousand, and look how thy brethren fare, and take their pledge."

Now Saul, and they, and all the men of Israel, were in the valley of Elah, fighting with the Philistines. And David rose up early in the morning, and left the sheep with a keeper, and took, and went, as Jesse had commanded him; and he came to the trench as the host was going forth to the fight, and shouted for the battle.

And David left his carriage in the hand of the keeper of the carriage, and ran into the army, and came and saluted his brethren. And as he talked with them, behold, there came up the champion, the Philistine of Gath, Goliath by name, out of the armies of the Philistines, and spake according to the same words; and David heard them.

And all the men of Israel, when they saw the man, fled from him, and were sore afraid. And the men of Israel said, "Have ye seen this man that is come up? Surely to defy Israel is he come up: and it shall be, that the man who killeth him, the king will enrich him with great riches, and will give him his daughter, and make his father's house free in Israel."

And David spake to the men that stood by him, saying, "What shall be done to the man that killeth this Philistine, and taketh away the reproach from Israel? For who is this uncircumcised Philistine, that he should defy the armies of the living God?"

And the people answered him after this manner, saying, "So shall it be done to the man that killeth him."

And Eliab his eldest brother heard when he spake unto the men; and Eliab's anger was kindled against David, and he said, "Why camest thou down hither? And with whom hast thou left those few sheep in the wilderness? I know thy pride, and the naughtiness of thine heart; for thou art come down that thou mightest see the battle."

And David said, "What have I now done? Is there not a cause?" And he turned from him toward another, and spake after the same manner: and the people answered him again after the former manner. And when the words were heard which David spake, they rehearsed them before Saul: and he sent for him.

And David said to Saul, "Let no man's heart fail because of him; thy servant will go and fight with this Philistine." And Saul said to David, "Thou art not able to go against this Philistine to fight with him: for thou art but a youth, and he a man of war from his youth."

And David said unto Saul, "Thy servant kept his father's sheep, and there came a lion, and a bear, and took a lamb out of the flock: and I went out after him, and smote him, and delivered it out of his mouth: and when he arose against me, I caught him by his beard, and smote him, and slew him. Thy servant slew both the lion and the bear: and this uncircumcised Philistine shall be as one of them, seeing he hath defied the armies of the living God. The Lord that delivered me out of the paw of the lion, and out of the paw of the bear, he will deliver me out of the hand of this Philistine."

And Saul said unto David, "Go, and the Lord be with thee."

And Saul armed David with his armour, and he put an helmet of brass upon his head; also he armed him with a coat of mail. And David girded his sword upon his armour, and he essayed to go;

DONN P. CRANE

but he had not proved the King's armour or his weapons. And David said unto Saul, "I cannot go with these; for I have not proved them." And David put them off him. And he took his staff in his hand, and chose him five smooth stones out of the brook, and put them in a shepherd's bag which he had, even in a scrip; his sling was in his hand, and he drew near to the Philistine.

And the Philistine came on and drew near unto David; and the man that bare the shield went before him. And when the Philistine looked about, and saw David, he disdained him: for he was but a youth, and ruddy, and of a fair countenance. And the Philistine said unto David, "Am I a dog, that thou comest to me with staves?" And the Philistine cursed David by his gods. And the Philistine said to David, "Come to me, and I will give thy flesh unto the fowls of the air, and to the beasts of the field."

Then said David to the Philistine, "Thou comest to me with a sword, and with a spear, and with a shield; but I come to thee in the name of the Lord of hosts, the God of the armies of Israel, whom thou hast defied. This day will the Lord deliver thee into mine hand; and I will smite thee, and I will give the carcasses of the host of the Philistines this day unto the fowls of the air, and to the wild beasts of the earth; that all the earth may know that there is a God in Israel. And all this assembly shall know that the Lord saveth not with sword and spear: for the battle is the Lord's, and he will give you into our hands."

And it came to pass, when the Philistine arose, and came and drew nigh to David, that David hasted, and ran toward the army to meet the Philistine. And David put his hand in his bag, and took thence a stone, and slang it, and smote the Philistine in his forehead, that the stone sunk into his forehead; and he fell upon his face to the earth.

So David prevailed over the Philistine with a sling and with a stone, and smote the Philistine, and slew him; but there was no sword in the hand of David. And when the Philistines saw their champion was dead, they fled.

And the men of Israel and of Judah arose, and shouted, and pursued the Philistines.

Rhodopis and her Gilded Sandals

The First Cinderella Story*

A Folk Tale of Ancient Egypt

HEAR, O youth! Rho-do'pis, the rosy cheeked, came down through the palm groves to bathe in the river Nile. Beautiful was Rhodopis, lovely as the day-dawn; rosy as clouds of the morning. Her mouth was pure of evil-speaking; her hands were pure of evil doing; her eyes were clearer than stars. On the brink of the river Rhodopis left her garments and a pair of small gilded sandals. Then she flung herself lightly on the sacred waves of the Nile. But as she disported herself, lo, there came flying toward her a wide-winged, royal eagle. Hovering above the waters, he spied a sudden glistening amid the papyrus reeds. Down to the earth he swooped. He seized one gilded sandal, one beautiful jewelled sandal, and soared again to the heavens. Rhodopis cried aloud. She stretched forth her arms, entreating; but already the eagle was lost to sight in the bright beams of Ra, the sun.

Now it chanced at that very hour, that there sat in the great square of Memphis, before the Temple of Ptah, the King administering justice and wearing upon his head the crowns of Upper and Lower Egypt. Before him one came dragging a husbandman bound in chains.

"This fellow refuseth his tax!" the tax-collector cried. "He refuseth the tenth of his harvest to thy granaries and to thee!"

The husbandman fell on his face, prostrate before the King.

*The Cinderella story, of which nearly every race has some version, is one of the oldest in the world, and unites human nature of all times and climes in the common love of a beautiful fancy. This legend woven about Queen Nitokris, called in the Greek Rhodopis (the rosy cheeked), is probably the oldest. It was told to little children several thousand years before Christ, and is to this very day a favorite fairy tale in Egypt.

"Hail unto thee," he cried, "great Lord of Truth and Justice! Worms destroyed half my wheat; rats laid waste my fields; little birds came and pilfered; hippopotami ate the rest! And when I had naught wherewith to pay thy tax collector, the keepers of the doors of thy granary came and beat me with cudgels. They bound me hand and foot. My wife they cast into chains! My children they left to hunger. Justice, O great King! Justice!"

Then rose up the King, furious like a panther, glowing as the sun-god. And he cried to the tax-collector:

"My Majesty causes no child of tender age to mourn! My Majesty spoils no woman! Thou shalt serve me no more. Begone!"

And he bade those who held the husbandman to loose him and let him go with a gift to his wife and children.

But he sighed within his breast and unto his own heart he whispered:

"The man is poor and oppressed, yet hath he, in his poverty, that which My Majesty lacks, even a wife and children to bring him delight of love." For Pharaoh had found no woman yet worthy to share his throne, worthy to wear on her brow the royal asp of Egypt.

But even as he sighed, there suddenly soared above the square, sweeping in mighty circles, a wide-winged, royal eagle. The eagle hung for a moment poised on the air above, then, lo, from his beak there fell directly into the great king's lap a tiny gilded sandal, a maiden's small jewelled sandal. His majesty was astounded. He held the trinket forth in the palm of his powerful hand.

"In the name of Isis," he cried, "What maid could wear such footgear, such small and dainty footgear?"

And as he saw in the sandal the marks of the little foot, there rose in his mind a vision of what she must be like who once had worn that sandal,—a tiny, well-made, lovely maid, a lithe and

graceful and willowy maid, a little one like a swift-coursing doe, that bounded over the desert.

"Today My Majesty heareth no more complaints," he cried. Back to the Great House, the Per-o, he went, borne in the royal litter. And he called to his servants and said:

"Haste and bring before me the Chief of the Royal Scribes."

And straightway they brought the Scribe.

And the King said unto the Scribe:

"Thou shalt write me a proclamation."

And the Chief of the Scribes obeyed. And these were the words of the King.

"Let every maid in Egypt try her foot to this sandal; for My Majesty makes decree that she whose foot it fits shall be My Majesty's queen."

Then the Scribe went forth to the city and a servant bore the sandal on a splendid cushion before him. In squares and public places the Scribe read the King's proclamation, and straightway the ladies came flocking before the throne of the King in the square of the Temple of Ptah, to try on the little sandal. They came in goodly array, high-born maidens and low-born maids, daughters of nobles and daughters of blacksmiths, daughters of glass-blowers, daughters of goldsmiths, daughters of armorers, daughters of potters, daughters of generals, daughters of princes, virgins from Upper Egypt, the Land-of-the-Serpent-goddess, and virgins from Lower Egypt, the realm of Nekhbet, the vulture, but never a one among them, never a single maid in all that vast array, could squeeze her foot into the sandal.

Days passed and days and days. The King was in despair.
His heart grew weary with longing, his heart that was stout as
a lion's. Again and again he beheld the boat of the sun slowly
rising, mounting the River of Heaven and creeping across the
sky, as with the pace of a snail, and yet the maiden came not.
Nowhere could she be found. He dreamt of her sleeping and
waking,—a tiny, well-made, lovely maid, a lithe and graceful and
willowy maid, a little one like a swift-coursing doe, that bounded
over the desert.

Then came to the King's Chief Scribe even that very same
husbandman to whom the King had of late forgiven the royal
tax. And the husbandman said to the Scribe:

"Go to the great Sphinx by the pyramids in the desert. There
cometh each day at daybreak to greet the rising sun, a maid as
lovely as day-dawn, as rosy as clouds of the morning."

The Scribe bore the news to the King and the heart of the
King leapt within him.

"My Majesty goes tomorrow," he said, "to the great Sphinx
of the desert."

In the grayness of early morn, the King and the Scribe set
forth while the first faint beams of Ra crept over the green Nile
valley to the sandy edge of the desert. So they drew near the
Sphinx, where it rose in solemn grandeur out of the yellow sands.
Slowly the red ball of Ra pushed up its topmost rim and a voice
broke out on the stillness, lovely and clear as a bird-song,
greeting the rising sun:—

> *"Thy appearing is beautiful in the horizon of heaven;*
> *Thou fillest all lands with thy beauty.*
> *The birds fly in their haunts,*
> *Their wings adoring thee!"*

And Ra burst forth all at once, flooding the earth with glory,
and touching with sudden light the figure of her who was sing-

ing,—Rhodopis, lovely as daylight, rosy as clouds of the morning. The heart of the King leapt within him. He took from the Scribe the sandal and crossed to the maiden's side, saying:

"Little one, daughter of morning, pray try thy foot to this sandal."

But the maiden bounded away, shy as a doe of the desert, startled as game in the marshes. Twenty paces she ran, then slowly she halted and turned, coming back, half reluctant, half willing. One slender bare foot she put forth while the Great King knelt before her and slipped on the little sandal. And the Great King said to the maiden:

"My Majesty sees in thee the beauty of day at its dawning, the freshness of lotus lilies opening their buds on the water. Thou art as a garden of flowers in the coolness of early breezes. For all the days of my life I would delight in thee. Be thou my wife and my queen."

The maiden's eyes opened wide. She fluttered again as a game-bird. Then sudden her heart was smitten for him who stood there before her, him who was radiant with courage, whose heart was stout as a lion's, who fed upon Truth and Justice.

Shyly she pulled from her girdle the mate to the little sandal and put it upon her foot. Then she placed her hand in the hand of the King saying:

"Thine will I be, great Lord, thou who shinest with strength, whose heart is stout like the lion's! The paths where we walk shall be beautiful because we walk together."

And the King gently kissed her lips and they crossed the desert, hand in hand, unto the city of Memphis, unto the Great House, the Per-o.

Thenceforward by the side of the just and merciful King Rhodopis reigned over Egypt, Rhodopis, lovely as day-dawn, who wore the small gilded sandals.

Phaeton
A Greek Myth

There dwelt once in Greece the nymph Clymene and her son, Phaeton, a bold and headstrong youth. Among his schoolfellows Phaeton once boasted that his father was no common mortal like theirs, but Phoebus Apollo, the mighty Lord of the Sun, who drove across the blue dome of heaven the flaming chariot of day.

"Ho!" laughed his schoolfellows, "words come easy." And they mocked him and scoffed at his boast. "Phoebus seems in no such haste to call thee son as thou art to call him father. For any notice he has ever taken of thee, thou mightest be son of a swineherd."

Then was Phaeton wrathful and stormed back home to his mother.

"These fellows will not believe," he said, "that I am son of Apollo. I shall go to my father and demand that he give me some sign to show them I speak the truth."

"Go, my son," said Clymene. "Thy father will bid thee welcome. But ask of him a modest and moderate sign becoming thy youthful years. Remember he is Lord of the Sun and thou art but a youth."

Phaeton paid little heed to her words. He flung himself out of her presence and was off on his journey. Toward India he travelled, the region of the Sunrise. At length far, far to eastward he came upon the Palace of the Sun. Reared high on splendid columns it stood, ablaze with gold and jewels. Nothing abashed by all its splendor, Phaeton toiled up the steep ascent and entered the halls of the palace. Boldly he pushed on into the very presence of Apollo. But there he was forced to stop for so bright were the rays streaming from that august head that Phaeton was dazzled by them.

Arrayed in purple robes, Phoebus sat on a throne that glistened as with diamonds. On his right hand and his left stood the Day, the Month and the Year, while ranged about were the Hours. Behind him stood Spring with garlands of flowers, Summer crowned with ripened grain, Autumn wreathed with purple grapes, and icy Winter coated with frost. Surrounded by these attendants, Apollo beheld the youth and mildly asked him his errand.

"O light of the boundless world!" cried Phaeton. "Phoebus, my father—if thou dost permit me to use that name—I come to be-

DONN P. CRANE

seech thee, if I am indeed thy son, give me some proof by which I may be known to the world."

When he ceased speaking, his father laid aside the beams that blinded the boy, held out his arms and bade him approach. Then he held him in a close embrace.

"Thou art indeed my son," said he. "Ask what thou wilt as proof, I solemnly vow to grant thy request."

Phaeton's eyes gleamed. He sprang from his father's arms and flung back his head.

"Grant me that I may drive for one day across the heavens thy mighty chariot of the Sun."

Then was the father alarmed at such a foolhardy request and repented his rash promise.

"Nay, my Phaeton," he said. "This request only do not make. I beg thee withdraw it. It is not a boon that is safe for thee nor suited at all to thy youth and strength. In thine ignorance thou dost think to attempt what I only am able to do. None but myself may drive the flaming car of day."

"I will have no other boon," cried Phaeton.

"But my son, the first part of the way is so steep my horses, when fresh in the morning, can hardly make the climb. The middle is so high up in the heavens that I myself can scarcely look down without alarm and behold the earth and sea stretched beneath me. The last part of the road descends at a giddy pace so one must know just how to drive to keep from plunging head-long."

Still the obstinate boy insisted.

"Perhaps thou dost think there are splendid palaces and temples to be seen on the way, but ah! on the contrary, the road lies through the midst of frightful monsters—constellations of stars they are called on Earth. Thou must pass by the horns of the Bull, and the gaping jaws of the Lion, between the claws of the Scorpion and the Crab. Nor wilt thou find it easy to guide those fire-breathing horses. I can scarcely hold them myself if they chance to grow unruly. I beg thee to choose more wisely."

"I will have naught but to drive thy car," cried Phaeton.

So at last all unwillingly, Phoebus led the way to where stood the lofty chariot. It was of gold, the pole and wheels of gold, the spokes of silver. Along the seat were rows of chrysolites and diamonds which reflected all around the brightness of the sun. While the wilful youth gazed in admiration, the Dawn threw open the purple doors of the East, and showed the pathway strewn with roses. Slowly the stars withdrew, led by the Day-star. When he saw the East beginning to glow and the Moon preparing to retire, Phoebus ordered the Hours to harness up the horses. Forth from the lofty stalls they led the steeds, full fed with ambrosia, and attached the jewelled reins. Then the father reluctantly set the crown of brilliant rays on his son's head and said with a sad farewell sigh:

"Ah, my son, in this at least heed my advice, spare the whip and hold tight the reins. Thou wilt see the marks of the wheels on the road and they will serve to guide thee."

The agile youth sprang into the chariot, stood erect and grasped the reins with reckless delight.

Meanwhile the horses fill the air with their snortings and fiery breath and stamp the ground, impatient. Now the bars are let down and the boundless plain of the universe lies open before them. They dart forward, cleave a way through the clouds, and outrun the morning breezes.

The steeds soon feel that the load they draw is lighter than usual. And now they refuse to obey the reins and turn from the travelled road. Phaeton is alarmed. He knows not how to guide them. He plies them madly with his whip. Forward they race at breakneck speed.

Phaeton looks down—far down to the earth. His knees shake. In spite of the glare all around him, the sight of his eyes grows dim. He wishes he had never touched his father's horses, never prevailed in his request. He is borne along like a vessel that flies before a tempest, when the pilot can do no more. Much of the heavenly road is left behind but more remains before. He rolls his eyes from the goal whence he began his course to the realms of sunset which he will never reach. He loses his self-command and knows not what to do—whether to draw tight the reins or throw them loose; he forgets the names of the horses. He sees with terror the monstrous forms scattered over the surface of heaven. Here the Scorpion stretches his great arms with his tail and crooked claws over two signs of the Zodiac. When the boy beholds him, his courage fails, and he drops the reins from his hands. Now altogether unrestrained, the horses plunge headlong. In among the stars they dash hurling the chariot over pathless places, now up in high heaven, now down almost to the earth.

The clouds begin to smoke and the mountain tops take fire, the fields are parched with heat, the plants wither, the trees with their leafy branches shiver, the harvest is ablaze. Great cities burn with their walls and towers.

So Phaeton beholds the world on fire, and feels the heat unbearable. The air he breathes is like a furnace. He dashes forward—he knows not whither. Then it is believed the people of Ethiopia were scorched black and the Libyan desert dried up to a waste of burning sand. The Nymphs who dwelt in the fountains mourned the loss of their waters, nor were the rivers safe beneath their banks. The earth cracked open, the sea shrank up. Where before was water, it became a dry plain. The fishes sought the lowest depths and the dolphins no longer dared sport as before on the waves. Even Nereus, the old man of the Ocean, and his wife Doris, with the Nereides, their daughters, sought refuge in the deepest caves. Earth, screening her face with her hand, cried out with a husky voice on Jupiter, King of the Heavens, to save her.

Then Jupiter, all powerful, perceiving the ruin wrought by this mad race, mounted the lofty tower whence he sends clouds over the earth and hurls the forked lightnings. Thence he launched a thunderbolt and struck Phaeton from his seat. Headlong, like a shooting star, plunged the youth, his hair ablaze, down, down into the depths of the river Eridanus. And so the earth was saved; showers refreshed her, and she burst again into bloom.

THE CLOUD

PERCY BYSSHE SHELLEY

I bring fresh showers for the thirsting flowers,
 From the seas and the streams;
I bear light shade for the leaves when laid
 In their noonday dreams.
From my wings are shaken the dews that waken
 The sweet buds every one,
When rocked to rest on their mother's breast,
 As she dances about the sun.
I wield the flail of the lashing hail,
 And whiten the green plains under;
And then again I dissolve it in rain,
 And laugh as I pass in thunder.

The Golden Touch
NATHANIEL HAWTHORNE

Once upon a time, there lived a very rich man, and a king besides, whose name was Midas; and he had a little daughter, whom nobody but myself ever heard of, and whose name I either never knew, or have entirely forgotten. So, because I love odd names for little girls, I choose to call her Marygold.

This King Midas was fonder of gold than anything else in the world. If he loved anything better, or half so well, it was the one little maiden who played so merrily around her father's footstool. But the more Midas loved his daughter, the more did he desire and seek wealth. He thought, foolish man! that the best thing he could possibly do for this dear child would be to bequeath her the immensest pile of yellow, glistening coin, that had ever been heaped together since the world was made. Thus, he gave all his thoughts and time to this one purpose.

And yet, in his earlier days, before he was so entirely possessed of this insane desire for riches, King Midas had shown a great taste for flowers. He planted a garden, in which grew the biggest and beautifullest and sweetest roses that any mortal ever saw or smelt. But now, if he looked at them at all, it was only to calculate how much the garden would be worth if each of the innumerable rose petals were a thin plate of gold.

At length (as people always grow more and more foolish, unless they take care to grow wiser and wiser), Midas had got to be so exceedingly unreasonable that he could scarcely bear to see or touch any object that was not gold. He made it his custom, therefore, to pass large portions of every day in a dark and dreary apartment, under ground, at the basement of his palace. It was here that he kept his wealth. Here, after carefully locking the door, he would take a bag of gold coin, or a gold cup as big as a washbowl, or a heavy golden bar, or a peck measure of gold dust, and bring them from the obscure corners of the room into the one bright and narrow sunbeam that fell from the dungeon-like window. He valued the sunbeam for no other reason but that his treasure would not shine without its help. And then would he reckon over the coins in the bag; toss up the bar, and catch it as it came down; sift the gold-dust through his fingers; look at the funny image of his own face, as reflected in the burnished circumference of the cup, and whisper to himself, "O Midas, rich King Midas, what a happy man art thou!" But it was laughable to see how the image of his face kept grinning at him, out of the polished surface of the cup. It seemed to be aware of his foolish behavior, and to have a naughty inclination to make fun of him.

Midas called himself a happy man, but felt that he was not yet quite so happy as he might be. The very tiptop of enjoyment would never be reached, unless the whole world were to become his treasure-room, and be filled with yellow metal which should be all his own.

Midas was enjoying himself in his treasure-room, one day, as usual, when he perceived a shadow fall over the heaps of gold; and, looking suddenly up, what should he behold but the figure of a stranger, standing in the bright and narrow sunbeam! It was a young man, with a cheerful and ruddy face. Whether it was that the imagination of King Midas threw a yellow tinge over everything, or whatever the cause might be, he could not help fancying that the smile with which the stranger regarded him had a kind of golden radiance in it. Certainly, although his figure intercepted the sunshine, there was now a brighter gleam upon all the piled-up treasure than before. Even the remotest corners had their share of it, and were lighted up, when the stranger smiled, as with tips of flame and sparkles of fire.

As Midas knew that he had carefully turned the key in the lock, and that no mortal strength could possibly break into this treasure-room, he, of course, concluded that his visitor must be something more than mortal. Midas had met such beings before now, and was not sorry to meet one of them again. The stranger's aspect, indeed, was so good humoured and kindly, if not beneficent, that it would have been unreasonable to suspect him of intending any mischief. It was far more probable that he came to do Midas a favour. And what could that favour be, unless to multiply his heaps of treasure?

The stranger gazed about the room; and when his lustrous smile had glistened upon all the golden objects that were there he turned again to Midas.

"You are a wealthy man, friend Midas!" he observed. "I doubt whether any other four walls on earth, contain so much gold as you have contrived to pile up in this room."

"I have done pretty well—pretty well," answered Midas, in a discontented tone. "But, after all, it is but a trifle, when you consider that it has taken me my whole life to get it together."

"What!" exclaimed the stranger. "Then you are not satisfied?"

Midas shook his head.

"And pray what would satisfy you?" asked the stranger.

Midas paused and meditated. He felt a presentiment that this stranger, with such a golden luster in his good-humoured smile, had come hither with both the power and the purpose of gratifying his utmost wishes. Now, therefore, was the fortunate moment, when he had but to speak, and obtain whatever it might come into his head to ask. So he thought, and thought, and thought, and heaped up one golden mountain upon another, in his imagination, without being able to imagine them big enough. At last, a bright idea occurred to King Midas. "I am weary of collecting my treasures with so much trouble," said he. "I wish everything that I touch to be changed to gold!"

The stranger's smile grew so very broad, that it seemed to fill the room like an outburst of the sun.

"The Golden Touch!" exclaimed he. "You certainly deserve credit, friend Midas, for striking out so brilliant a conception. But are you quite sure that this will satisfy you?"

"How could it fail?" said Midas.

"And will you never regret the possession of it?"

"I ask nothing else, to render me perfectly happy."

"Be it as you wish, then," replied the stranger, waving his hand in token of farewell. "Tomorrow, at sunrise, you will find yourself gifted with the Golden Touch."

The figure of the stranger then became exceedingly bright, and Midas involuntarily closed his eyes. On opening them again, he beheld only one yellow sunbeam in the room, and, all around him, the glistening of the metal which he had spent his life in hoarding up.

Whether Midas slept as usual that night, the story does not say. Asleep or awake, however, his mind was probably

in the state of a child's, to whom a beautiful new plaything has been promised in the morning. At any rate, day had hardly peeped over the hills, when King Midas was broad awake, and, stretching his arms out of bed, began to touch the objects that were within reach, but was grievously disappointed to perceive that they remained of exactly the same substance as before. Indeed, he felt very much afraid that he had only dreamed about the lustrous stranger, or else that the latter had been making game of him.

All this while, it was only the gray of the morning, with but a streak of brightness along the edge of the sky, where Midas could not see it. He lay in a very disconsolate mood, regretting the downfall of his hopes, until the earliest sunbeam shone through the window, and gilded the ceiling over his head. It seemed to Midas that this bright yellow sunbeam was reflected in rather a singular way on the white covering of the bed. Looking more closely, what was his astonishment and delight, when he found that this linen fabric had been transmuted to what seemed a woven texture of the purest and brightest gold! The Golden Touch had come to him with the first sunbeam!

Midas started up, in a kind of joyful frenzy, and ran about the room, grasping at everything that happened to be in his way. He seized one of the bedposts, and it became immediately a fluted golden pillar. He pulled aside a window-curtain, in order to admit a clear spectacle of the wonders which he was performing; and the tassel grew heavy in his hand,—a mass of gold. He took up a book from the table. At his first touch it assumed the appearance of such a splendidly bound and gilt-edged volume as one often meets with nowadays; but, on running his fingers through the leaves, behold! it was a bundle of thin golden plates, in which all the wisdom of the book had grown illegible. He hurriedly put on his clothes, and was enraptured to see himself in a magnificent suit of gold cloth, which retained its flexibility and softness, although it burdened him a little with its weight. He drew out his handkerchief, which little Marygold had hemmed for him. That was likewise gold, with the dear child's neat and pretty stitches running all along the border, in gold thread! Somehow or other, this last transformation did not quite please King Midas. He would rather that his little daughter's handiwork should have remained just the same as when she climbed his knee and put it into his hand.

But it was not worth while to vex himself about a trifle. Midas now took his spectacles from his pocket, and put them on his nose. To his great perplexity, however, he discovered that he could not possibly see through them. On taking them off, the transparent crystals turned out to be plates of yellow metal, and of course, were worthless as spectacles, though valuable as gold. It struck Midas as rather inconvenient that, with all his wealth, he could never again be rich enough to own a pair of serviceable spectacles.

"It is no great matter, nevertheless," said he to himself. "We cannot expect any great good, without its being accompanied with some small inconvenience. The Golden Touch is worth the sacrifice of a pair of spectacles, at least. My own eyes will serve for ordinary purposes, and little Marygold will soon be old enough to read to me."

Wise King Midas was so exalted by his good fortune, that the palace seemed not sufficiently spacious to contain him. He therefore went downstairs, and smiled, on observing that the balustrade of the staircase became a bar of burnished gold, as his hand passed over it, in his descent. He lifted the door-latch (it was brass only a moment ago, but golden when his fingers quitted it), and emerged into the garden. Here, as it happened, he found a great number of beautiful roses in bloom, and others

in all the stages of lovely bud and blossom. Very delicious was their fragrance in the morning breeze. Their delicate blush was one of the fairest sights in the world.

But Midas knew a way to make them far more precious, according to his way of thinking, than roses had ever been before. So he took great pains in going from bush to bush, and exercised his magic touch until every individual flower and bud, and—even the worms at the heart of some of them, were changed to gold. By the time this good work was completed, King Midas was summoned to breakfast; and as the morning air had given him an excellent appetite he made haste back to the palace.

On this particular morning, the breakfast consisted of hot cakes, some nice little brook trout, roasted potatoes, fresh boiled eggs, and coffee, for King Midas himself, and a bowl of bread and milk for his daughter Marygold.

Little Marygold had not yet made her appearance. Her father ordered her to be called, and, seating himself at table, awaited the child's coming, in order to begin his own breakfast. To do Midas justice, he really loved his daughter. It was not a great while before he heard her coming along the passageway crying bitterly. This circumstance surprised him, because Marygold was one of the cheerfullest little people whom you would see in a summer's day, and hardly shed a thimbleful of tears in a twelvemonth. When Midas heard her sobs, he determined to put little Marygold into better spirits, by an agreeable surprise; so, leaning across the table, he touched his daughter's bowl (which was a china one, with pretty figures all around it), and transmuted it to gleaming gold. Meanwhile, Marygold slowly opened the door, and showed herself with her apron at her eyes, still sobbing as if her heart would break.

"How now, my little lady!" cried Midas. "Pray what is the matter with you, this bright morning?"

Marygold, without taking the apron from her eyes, held out her hand, in which was one of the roses which Midas had so recently transmuted.

"Beautiful!" exclaimed her father. "And what is there in this magnificent golden rose to make you cry?"

"Ah, dear father!" answered the child, as well as her sobs would let her; "it is not beautiful but the ugliest flower that ever grew! As soon as I was dressed I ran into the garden to gather some roses for you. But, oh dear, dear me! What do you think has happened? All the beautiful roses, that smelled so sweetly and had so many lovely blushes, are blighted and spoilt! They are grown quite yellow, as you see this one, and have no longer any fragrance! What can have been the matter?"

"Poh, my dear little girl—pray don't cry about it!" said Midas, who was ashamed to confess that he himself had wrought the change which so greatly afflicted her. "Sit down and eat your bread and milk! You will find it easy enough to exchange a golden rose like that (which will last hundreds of years) for an ordinary one which would wither in a day."

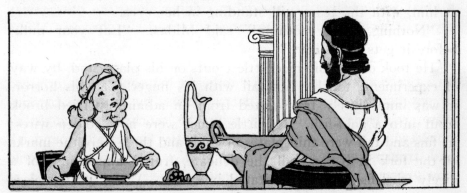

"I don't care for such roses as this!" cried Marygold tossing it contemptuously away. "It has no smell, and the hard petals prick my nose!"

The child now sat down to table, but so occupied with her grief for the blighted roses that she did not even notice the wonderful transmutation of her china bowl. Perhaps this was all the better; for Marygold was accustomed to take pleasure in looking at the queer figures, and strange trees and houses, that were painted on the circumference of the bowl; and these ornaments were now entirely lost in the yellow hue of the metal.

Midas, meanwhile, had poured out a cup of coffee, and, as a matter of course, the coffee-pot, whatever metal it may have been when he took it up, was gold when he set it down. He thought to himself that it was rather an extravagant style of splendor in a king of his simple habits, to breakfast off a service of gold, and began to be puzzled with the difficulty of keeping his treasures safe. Amid these thoughts, he lifted a spoonful of coffee to his lips, and sipping it, was astonished to perceive that, the instant his lips touched the liquid, it became molten gold, and the next moment, hardened into a lump!

"Ha!" exclaimed Midas, rather aghast.

"What is the matter, father?" asked little Marygold, gazing at him, with the tears still standing in her eyes.

"Nothing, child, nothing!" said Midas. "Eat your milk, before it gets quite cold."

He took one of the nice little trouts on his plate, and, by way of experiment, touched its tail with his finger. To his horror, it was immediately transmuted from an admirably fried brook trout into a gold-fish. Its little bones were now golden wires; its fins and tail were thin plates of gold; and there were the marks of the fork in it, and all the delicate, frothy appearance of a nicely fried fish, exactly imitated in metal. A very pretty piece of work, as you may suppose; only King Midas, just at that moment, would much rather have had a real trout in his dish than this elaborate and valuable imitation of one.

"I don't quite see," thought he to himself, "how I am to get any breakfast!"

He took one of the smoking-hot cakes, and had scarcely broken it, when, to his cruel mortification, though a moment before it had been of the whitest wheat, it assumed the yellow hue of Indian meal. Almost in despair, he helped himself to a boiled egg, which immediately underwent a change similar to those of the trout and the cake.

"Well, this is a quandary!" thought he, leaning back in his chair, and looking quite enviously at little Marygold, who was now eating her bread and milk with great satisfaction. "Such a costly breakfast before me, and nothing that can be eaten!"

Hoping that, by dint of great dispatch, he might avoid what he now felt to be a considerable inconvenience, King Midas next snatched a hot potato, and attempted to cram it into his mouth, and swallow it in a hurry. But the Golden Touch was too nimble for him. He found his mouth full, not of mealy potato, but of solid metal, which so burnt his tongue that he roared aloud, and, jumping up from the table, began to dance and stamp about the room, both with pain and affright.

"Father, dear father!" cried little Marygold, who was a very affectionate child, "pray what is the matter?"

"Ah, dear child," groaned Midas, dolefully, "I don't know what is to become of your poor father!"

Here was literally the richest breakfast that could be set before a king, and its very richness made it absolutely good for nothing. The poorest laborer, sitting down to his crust of bread and cup of water, was far better off than King Midas. And what was to be done? Already, at breakfast, Midas was excessively hungry. Would he be less so by dinnertime? And how ravenous would be his appetite for supper, which must undoubt-edly consist of the same sort of indigestible dishes as those now before him! How many days, think you, would he survive a continuance of this rich fare?

These reflections so troubled wise King Midas, that he began to doubt whether, after all, riches are the one desirable thing in the world, or even the most desirable. But this was only a passing thought. So fascinated was Midas with the glitter of the yellow metal, that he would still have refused to give up the Golden Touch for so paltry a consideration as breakfast.

Nevertheless, so great was his hunger, and the perplexity of his situation, he again groaned aloud, and very grievously too. Our pretty Marygold could endure it no longer. She sat, a moment, gazing at her father, and trying, with all the might of her little wits, to find out what was the matter with him. Then, with a sweet and sorrowful impulse to comfort him, she started from her chair, and running to Midas, threw her arms affection-ately about his knees. He bent down and kissed her. He felt that his little daughter's love was worth a thousand times more than he had gained by the Golden Touch.

"My precious, precious Marygold!" cried he.

But Marygold made no answer.

Alas, what had he done. How fatal was the gift which the stranger bestowed! The moment the lips of Midas touched Marygold's forehead, a change had taken place. Her sweet, rosy face, so full of affection as it had been, assumed a glittering yellow color, with yellow tear-drops congealing on her cheeks. Her beautiful brown ringlets took the same tint. Her soft and tender little form grew hard and inflexible within her father's encircling arms. Little Marygold was a human child no longer, but a golden statue!

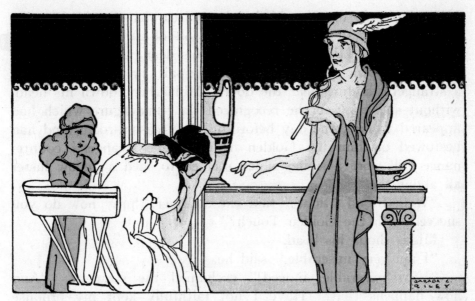

Yes, there she was, with the questioning look of love, grief, and pity, hardened into her face. It was the prettiest and most woeful sight that ever mortal saw. All the features and tokens of Marygold were there; even the beloved little dimple remained in her golden chin. But, the more perfect was the resemblance, the greater was the father's agony at beholding this golden image, which was all that was left him of a daughter. Now, at last, when it was too late, he felt how infinitely a warm and tender heart that loved him, exceeded in value all the wealth that could be piled up betwixt the earth and sky!

It would be too sad a story, if I were to tell you how Midas, in the fulness of all his gratified desires, began to wring his hands and bemoan himself; and how he could neither bear to look at Marygold, nor yet to look away from her. There was the precious little figure, with a yellow tear-drop on its yellow cheek, and a look so piteous and tender, that it seemed as if that very expression must needs soften the gold, and make it flesh again.

Midas had only to wring his hands, and to wish that he were the poorest man in the wide world, if the loss of all his wealth might bring back the faintest rose-color to his dear child's face.

While he was in this tumult of despair, he suddenly beheld a stranger standing near the door. Midas bent down his head, without speaking; for he recognized the same figure which had appeared to him, the day before, in the treasure-room, and had bestowed on him the Golden Touch. The stranger's countenance still wore a smile, which seemed to shed a yellow luster all about the room.

"Well, friend Midas," said the stranger, "pray how do you succeed with the Golden Touch?"

Midas shook his head.

"I am very miserable," said he.

"Very miserable, indeed!" exclaimed the stranger. "And how happens that? Have I not faithfully kept my promise with you? Have you not everything that your heart desired?"

"Gold is not everything," answered Midas. "And I have lost all that my heart really cared for."

"Ah! So you have made a discovery, since yesterday?" observed the stranger. "Let us see, then. Which of these two things do you think is really worth the most—the gift of the Golden Touch, or one cup of clear, cold water?"

"Oh blessed water!" exclaimed Midas. "I will never moisten my parched throat again!"

"The Golden Touch," continued the stranger, "or a crust of bread?"

"A piece of bread," answered Midas, "is worth all the gold on earth!"

"The Golden Touch," asked the stranger, "or your own little Marygold, warm, soft, and loving as she was an hour ago?"

"O my child, my dear child!" cried poor Midas, wringing

his hands. "I would not have given that one small dimple in her chin for the power of changing this whole big earth into a solid lump of gold!"

"You are wiser than you were, King Midas!" said the stranger, looking seriously at him. "Your own heart, I perceive, has not been entirely changed from flesh to gold. You appear to be still capable of understanding that the commonest things, such as lie within everybody's grasp, are more valuable than the riches which so many mortals sigh and struggle after. Tell me, now, do you sincerely desire to rid yourself of this Golden Touch?"

"It is hateful to me!" replied Midas.

A fly settled on his nose, but immediately fell to the floor, for it, too, had become gold. Midas shuddered.

"Go then," said the stranger, "plunge into the river that glides past the bottom of your garden. Take likewise a vase of the same water, and sprinkle it over any object that you may desire to change back again from gold into its former substance. If you do this in earnestness and sincerity, it may possibly repair the mischief which your avarice has occasioned."

King Midas bowed low; and when he lifted his head, the lustrous stranger had vanished.

You will easily believe that Midas lost no time in snatching up a great earthen pitcher (but, alas me! it was no longer earthen after he touched it), and hastening to the riverside. As he scampered along, and forced his way through the shrubbery, it was positively marvellous to see how the foliage turned yellow behind him, as if the autumn had been there, and nowhere else. On reaching the river's brink, he plunged headlong in, without waiting so much as to pull off his shoes.

"Poof! poof! poof!" snorted King Midas, as his head emerged out of the water. "Well; this is really a refreshing bath, and

I think it must have quite washed away the Golden Touch. And now for filling my pitcher!"

As he dipped the pitcher into the water, it gladdened his very heart to see it change from gold into the same good, honest earthen vessel which it had been before he touched it. He was conscious, also, of a change within himself. A cold, hard, and heavy weight seemed to have gone out of his bosom. No doubt, his heart had been gradually losing its human substance, and transmuting itself into insensible metal, but had now softened back again into flesh. Perceiving a violet that grew on the bank of the river, Midas touched it with his finger, and was overjoyed to find that the delicate flower retained its purple hue, instead of undergoing a yellow blight. The curse of the Golden Touch had, therefore, really been removed from him.

King Midas hastened back to the palace. The first thing he did, as you need hardly be told, was to sprinkle it by handfuls over the golden figure of little Marygold.

No sooner did it fall on her than you would have laughed to see how she began to sneeze and sputter!—and how astonished she was to find herself dripping wet, and her father still throwing more water over her.

"Pray do not, dear father," cried she. "See how you have wet my nice frock, which I put on only this morning!"

For Marygold did not know that she had been a little golden statue; nor could she remember anything that had happened since the moment when she ran with out-stretched arms to comfort poor King Midas.

Her father did not think it necessary to tell his beloved child how very foolish he had been, but contented himself with showing how much wiser he had now grown. For this purpose he led little Marygold into the garden, where he sprinkled all the remainder of the water over the rose bushes, and with such good effect that above five thousand roses recovered their beautiful bloom. There were two circumstances, however, which as long as he lived, used to put King Midas in mind of the Golden Touch. One was, that the sands of the river sparkled like gold; the other, that little Marygold's hair had now a golden tinge, which he had never observed in it before she had been transmuted by the effect of his kiss.

When King Midas had grown quite an old man, and used to trot Marygold's children on his knee, he was fond of telling them this marvellous story. And then would he stroke their glossy ringlets, and tell them that their hair, likewise, had a rich shade of gold.

"And to tell you the truth, my precious little folks," quoth King Midas, diligently trotting the children all the while, "ever since that morning, I have hated the very sight of all other gold, save this!"

THE HUMMING BIRD*
EDWIN MARKHAM

Tell me, O Rose, what thing it is
That now appears, now vanishes?
Surely it took its fire-green hue
From daybreaks that it glittered through;
Quick, for this sparkle of the dawn
Glints through the garden and is gone!
What was the message, Rose, what word:
Delight foretold, or hope deferred?

*Reprinted with the permission of the Author and the Publishers, Doubleday, Page & Co.

THE ACORN AND THE PUMPKIN
LA FONTAINE

God's works are good.   To prove this truth
I need not search the world, forsooth!
I do it by the nearest Pumpkin!

"Fie! fruit so large on vine so small!"
Exclaimed one day a wise young bumpkin!
"What could He mean who made us all?
This Pumpkin here is out of place.

If I had ordered in this case,
Upon that oak it should have hung—
A noble fruit as ever swung
To grace a tree so firm and strong.

290

Indeed there's been a great mistake!
Had my opinion but been sought,
When God set out the world to make,
All things had then been as they ought!
All things had then in order come!
This Acorn for example,
No bigger than my thumb,
Had not disgraced a tree so ample.

The more I think, the more I wonder!
The Pumpkin on the oak should grow,
The Acorn on the vine below;
God surely made an awful blunder!"

With such reflections proudly fraught,
Our Sage grew tired of mighty thought,
And threw himself on Nature's lap,
Beneath an oak, to take a nap.

It chanced that during his repose,
An Acorn fell plump on his nose!
He wakened with a mighty start;
He shrieked and seized the injured part!

"Oh! Oh! alas! I bleed! I bleed!
This Acorn 'twas that did the deed!
I see that God had reasons good,
And all His works were understood,
For, truly, what had been my woes,
Had, then, a Pumpkin whacked my nose!"
Thus home he went in humbler mood!

The Golden Bird

A German Fairy Tale

IN the olden time there was a king, who had behind his palace a beautiful pleasure garden in which there was a tree that bore golden apples. One day when the apples were getting ripe, they were counted, but on the very next morning one was missing. This was told to the King and he ordered that a watch should be kept every night beneath the tree.

The King had three sons, the eldest of whom he sent as soon as night came on, into the garden; but when it was about midnight he could not keep himself from sleeping, and next morning again an apple was gone.

The following night the second son had to keep watch. It fared no better with him; as soon as twelve o'clock had struck he fell asleep, and in the morning an apple was gone.

Now it came to the turn of the third son to watch; and he was quite ready. The King had not much trust in him and thought that he would be of less use even than his brothers, but at last he let him go. The youth lay down beneath the tree, but kept awake and did not let sleep master him. When it struck twelve, he was still at his post watching. Then something rustled through the air, and in the moonlight he saw a bird coming whose feathers were all shining with gold. The bird alighted on the tree, and had just plucked off an apple, when the youth shot an arrow at him. The bird flew off, but the arrow had struck his plumage and one of his golden feathers fell down. The youth picked it up and the next morning took it to the King and told him what he had seen in the night. The King declared at once:

"The rascal that carries off my apples is none other than the beautiful Golden Bird that was stolen long ago from my garden. He must be found and restored to me."

THROUGH FAIRY HALLS

So the eldest son set out. He trusted to his own cleverness and thought he would easily find the Golden Bird. When he had gone some distance he saw a Fox sitting at the edge of a wood. So he cocked his gun and took aim at him.

"Do not shoot me," cried the Fox, "and in return I will give you some good counsel. You are on the way to find the Golden Bird; this evening you will come to a village in which stand two inns opposite to one another. One of them is lighted up brightly and all goes on merrily within, but do not go into it; go rather into the other, even though it seems a very plain one."

"How should such a silly beast give advice to a wise fellow like me?" thought the King's son, and he pulled the trigger. But he missed the Fox, who stretched out his tail and ran quickly into the wood.

So the King's son pursued his way, and by evening came to the village where the two inns were; in one all the lights were lit, and there was singing and dancing, but the other had a poor, plain, dingy look.

"I should be a fool indeed," he thought, "if I were to go into the shabby tavern and pass by the good one." So he went into the cheerful inn, lived there in pleasure and revelling and forgot the bird and his father and all good counsel.

When some months had passed and the eldest did not come back home, the second son set out to find the Golden Bird. The Fox met him as he had met the eldest and gave him the same good advice. But the second brother likewise paid no heed to his counsel. He came to the two inns; and his brother was standing at the window of the one from which came the music, and called out to him. He could not resist, but went inside, lived only for pleasure and forgot the bird and all good counsel.

Again months passed and then the King's youngest son wanted to set off to find the bird. For some time his father would not

allow it. "How should such a young know-nothing find the bird when his elder brothers have failed?" said he. But at last, as the lad gave him no peace, he let him go. Again the Fox was sitting outside the wood and offered his advice. Now the youngest son was good natured and modest, and willing to take good counsel, so he said to the Fox:

"Be easy, little Fox, I will do you no harm, but will follow your advice."

"You shall not repent it," answered the Fox. "And that you may get on more quickly, get up behind on my tail." Scarcely had the King's son seated himself when the Fox began to run, and away he went over stock and stone till his hair whistled in the wind. When they came to the village the youth got off. He followed the good advice, and without looking around turned into the little inn, where he spent the night quietly.

The next morning, as soon as he got into the open country, there sat the Fox already and said, "I will tell you further what you have to do. Go on straight ahead and at last you will come to the castle where lives the King who has your father's bird. In front of the castle lies a whole regiment of soldiers but do not trouble yourself about them, for they will all be asleep and snoring. Go straight through the midst of them into the castle, and go through all the rooms till at last you will come to a chamber where the Golden Bird hangs in a plain wooden cage. Close by, there stands an empty gold cage which is very splendid. But that cage is all for show. Beware of taking the bird out of the plain cage and putting it into the fine one or it may go badly with you." With these words, the Fox again stretched out his tail, the King's son seated himself upon it and away and away he went over stock and stone till his hair whistled in the wind.

When he came to the castle, he found everything as the Fox had said. Through the midst of the snoring soldiers he made his way, and so on into the chamber where stood the Golden Bird. He was shut up in a wooden cage with the golden apples lying near. Hard by, stood the splendid golden cage, and as the King's son looked at it, he thought:

"It would be absurd if I were to leave the beautiful bird in the common and ugly cage." So he opened the door, laid hold of the bird and put it into the golden cage. At the same moment the bird uttered a shrill cry, the soldiers awoke, rushed in and dragged the youth off to prison. The next morning he was taken before a court of justice and sentenced to death.

The King of the country, however, said that he would grant him his life on one condition—namely, if he brought him the Golden Horse which ran faster than the wind. And in that case he should receive, over and above, as a reward, the Golden Bird.

The King's son set off but he sighed and was very sorrowful, for how was he ever to find the Golden Horse? All at once, he saw his old friend, the Fox, sitting in the middle of the road.

"Look you," said the Fox, "this has happened because you did not give heed to me, but be of good courage, I will give you my help again, and tell you how to get to the Golden Horse.

At this, the King's son rejoiced and promised once more to obey him.

"You must go straight on," said the Fox, "and you will come to a castle where in the stable, stands the horse. The grooms will be lying in front of the stable but they will be asleep and snoring, and you can quietly lead out the Golden Horse. Of one thing only you must take heed; put on him the common saddle of wood and leather, and not the golden one, which hangs close by, else it will go ill with you."

Then the Fox stretched out his tail, the King's son seated himself upon it and away he went over stock and stone till his hair whistled in the wind.

Everything happened just as the Fox had said; the prince came to the stable in which the Golden Horse was standing, but just as he was going to put the plain saddle upon him, he thought: "It will be a shame to such a beautiful beast, if I do not give him the splendid saddle which belongs to him by right." So he flung the golden saddle over the horse's back. Scarcely had he done so when the horse began to neigh loudly. The grooms awoke, seized the youth and threw him into prison. The next morning he was sentenced by the court to death, but the King promised to grant him his life and the Golden Horse as well, if he would bring back the Beautiful Princess from the Golden Castle.

"The Beautiful Princess," he said, "is my promised bride, but her guardian keeps her forcibly from me."

With a heavy heart the youth set out, yet soon he found the trusty Fox.

"I ought only to leave you to the consequences of your own disobedience," said the Fox, "but I pity you and will help you once more out of your trouble. This road takes you straight to the Golden Castle. You will reach it by eventide; and at night when everything is quiet, the Beautiful Princess goes from the castle to the bathing house in the castle yard. When she enters it run up to her and give her a kiss, then she will wish to follow you and you can take her away with you. Only remember this, do not allow her to take leave of anyone in the castle."

Then the Fox stretched out his tail, the King's son seated himself upon it and away the Fox went over stock and stone till his hair whistled in the wind.

When he reached the Golden Castle, it was just as the Fox had said. He waited until midnight when everything lay in deep sleep, and the Beautiful Princess was going to the bathing house. Then he sprang out and gave her a kiss. She said at once that she would like to go with him, but she asked him pitifully and with tears to allow her to take leave of the King, her guardian. At first he withstood her request, but when she begged more and more earnestly and fell at his feet, he at last gave in. No sooner had the maiden reached the bedside of the King, than he and all the rest of the castle awoke, and the youth was laid hold of and cast into prison.

"You may only have the Beautiful Princess if you take away the hill which shuts off the view from my windows," said the King, "and you must finish your work within eight days."

The King's son began and dug and shovelled without leaving off, but after seven days he saw how little he had done, so he fell into great sorrow and gave up all hope. On the evening of the seventh day, however, the Fox appeared and said:

"You do not deserve that I should take any more trouble about you, nevertheless you have faithfully tried to fulfill your task, so lie down to sleep, I will finish it for you."

The next morning when the King's son awoke and looked out of the window the hill was gone. Full of joy, he ran to the King and told him the task was performed, and whether he liked it or not, the King had to keep his promise and give up the Princess.

So the King's son and the Princess set forth together, and it was not long before the trusty Fox came up with them. Then the King's son told the Princess how he was taking her to be the bride of the King who had the Golden Horse. But the Beautiful Princess wept and said it was not true she was promised to him and she did not wish to be his bride. All she wanted was to go home with the King's son. Besides, the Golden Horse did not belong to the wicked old King at all. It was her own and he had stolen it from her. So the good Fox said to the King's son:

"If the Beautiful Princess chooses you, yours she must be. Go now and recover for her her Golden Horse."

"But how may I get the Horse and keep the Princess if I go, one man as I am, to that rascally King who has a castle full of soldiers?" asked the King's son.

"That I will tell you," answered the Fox. "First take the beautiful Maiden to the King. Thinking he has her at last in his power, he will rejoice and gladly have her Golden Horse led forth to exchange. Mount it as soon as possible, then take the Princess by the hand, swing her up on to the horse before you and gallop swiftly away. No one will be able to bring you back."

All was brought to pass successfully, and the King's son in spite of all the soldiers about, carried off the Beautiful Princess on the Golden Horse.

The Fox did not remain behind and he said to the youth, "Now I will help you to recover your father's Golden Bird. When you come near the castle where the Golden Bird is to be found, let the Maiden down and I will take her into my care. Then ride with the Golden Horse boldly into the castle yard. When the Golden Bird is brought forth, seize the cage in your hand and gallop away to us like the wind."

Well, this plan succeeded, too, and the King's son was about to ride home with all his wonderful treasures, when the Fox said:

"Now you are returning home with good success, yet before
I leave you, I will give you still one more piece of advice. Be
careful about two things. Do not beg off any thief or other
malefactor from his punishment and do not sit at the edge of
any well." And then he ran off into the wood.

So the Prince rode on with the beautiful maiden and his road took him again through the village in which his two brothers had remained. There was a great stir and noise there and when he asked what was going on, he was told that two men were going to be hanged for their many evil deeds. As he came nearer to the place he saw that the two men were his two brothers, who had been playing all kinds of wicked pranks in the neighborhood. At once he began to think that he should like to get his brothers off from their punishment, and he inquired whether there was any way by which he could set them free. "If you will pay for them they may go free," answered the people. "But why should you waste your money on setting free wicked men when they have by no means repented the evil they have done?" But the King's son did not think twice about it. He paid for his brothers and when they were set free, they all went on their way together. Soon they came to the wood where the Fox had first met them. The sun shone hotly outside, but within the wood it was cool and pleasant, so the two brothers said:

"Let us rest a little here by the well and eat and drink." The Prince agreed and forgetting once more the Fox's counsel, he sat down upon the edge of the well. At once the two brothers threw him backward into the well. Then they took the maiden, the horse, and the bird, and went home to their father.

"Here we bring you not only the Golden Bird," said they, "we have won the Golden Horse also, and the maiden from the Golden Castle." And they threatened the Princess with death if she told the truth. So the King believed their tale and rejoiced greatly, but the horse would not eat, the bird would not sing, and the Maiden sat and wept.

Meantime it happened that the well into which they had cast the younger brother was dry and he fell upon soft moss without being hurt at all, but he could not get out again. Now even in this strait the faithful Fox did not leave him. It came bounding along, leapt straight down to him in the pit, and said:

"Once again by your disobedience you have forfeited all right to my help, yet I cannot leave you altogether. I will give you one more chance to follow my advice and even at this late day if you are obedient, you may still be happy. Your brothers have surrounded the wood with watchers who are to kill you if you are ever able to get out of this well. So you must change clothes with the man who is cutting wood up above by the roadside, then none will recognize you and you will pass safely by the man your brothers have set to catch you. But mind you wear the poor clothes you will get from the woodcutter, and do not exchange them for fine ones till you are safe in your father's presence."

Then the Fox bade the Prince grasp his tail and keep tight hold of it, and so he pulled him up out of the well. There the youth exchanged his good clothes for the ragged ones of the woodcutter and in this way he arrived safely at his father's castle. Now he would have liked to exchange his poor clothes for fine ones before he came into the presence of his father and the beautiful Maiden, but this time he remembered the Fox's wise counsel and obeyed him. Thus no man knew who he was and the elder brothers never even dreamed that he was in the castle, but all of a sudden the bird began to sing, the horse began to eat and the beautiful Maiden left off weeping.

"I am so happy," she said, "I feel as if my true bridegroom had come." And she grew so full of courage, withal, that she told the King the whole story of what the elder brothers had done.

At once the King commanded that all people who were in his castle should be brought before him, and amongst them came the youth in his ragged clothes. But the Maiden knew him at once and fell upon his neck. So the wicked brothers were beaten out of the Kingdom, but the Prince married the Princess, the Fox was ever their friend, and nothing was wanting to their happiness.

THE BELLS

EDGAR ALLAN POE

Hear the sledges with the bells—
Silver bells!
What a world of merriment their melody foretells!
How they tinkle, tinkle, tinkle,
In the icy air of night!
While the stars, that oversprinkle
All the heavens, seem to twinkle
With a crystalline delight;
Keeping time, time, time,
In a sort of Runic rhyme,
To the tin-tin-nab-u-la-tion that so musically wells
From the bells, bells, bells, bells,
Bells, bells, bells—
From the jingling and the tinkling of the bells.

THROUGH FAIRY HALLS

The Snow Queen

HANS CHRISTIAN ANDERSEN

ONCE upon a time there was a wicked, mischievous Hobgoblin. One day he was in a very good humor because he had made a mirror with the power of causing all that was good and beautiful, when it was reflected therein, to look poor and mean; while that which was good for nothing and ugly, stood out and looked worse than ever. In this mirror the most beautiful landscapes looked like boiled spinach, and the best persons were turned into frights, or appeared to stand on their heads. "That's glorious fun!" said the Hobgoblin.

All the little Hobgoblins told each other that now only would it be possible to see how the world really looked. They ran about with the mirror; and at last there was not a land or a person who was not represented there twisted all out of shape. So then they thought they would fly up to the sky, and have a joke there. The higher they flew with the mirror, the more terribly it grinned; they could hardly hold it fast. Suddenly the mirror shook so terribly with grinning, that it flew out of their hands and fell to the earth, where it was dashed in a hundred million pieces. And now it worked much more evil than before; for some of these pieces were hardly so large as a grain of sand, and they flew about in the wide world, and when they got into people's eyes there they stayed; and then people saw everything perverted, or only had an eye for that which was evil. Some persons even got a splinter in their heart, and then their heart became a lump of ice. Then the wicked Hobgoblin laughed till he almost choked, for all this tickled his fancy. The fine splinters still flew about in the air; and now we shall hear what happened.

I

In a large town, where there are so many houses and so many people that there is no room left for everybody to have a garden, there lived two little children. They were not brother and sister, but they loved each other just as much as if they were. Their parents lived opposite each other in two attic rooms. The roof of one house just touched the roof of the other with only a rain water gutter between them. They each had a little dormer window so one had only to step over the gutter to get from one window to the other. Out on the leads the parents had placed two wooden boxes, in which grew pea vines, vegetables, and some little rose trees. In summer the children were allowed to take their little stools and sit out on the roof among the roses, where they could play delightfully. In winter there was an end of this pleasure. The windows were often frozen over; but then they heated copper pennies on the stove, and laid the hot pennies on the window-pane. Thus they made capital peepholes through which to look out at each other. The boy's name was Kay, the girl's was Gerda. In summer, with one jump, they could get to each other; but in winter they were obliged first to go down the long stairs, and then up the long stairs again, and out-of-doors there was quite a snow-storm.

"It is the white bees that are swarming," said Kay's old grandmother.

"Do the white bees choose a queen?" asked the little boy; for he knew that the honey-bees always have one.

"Yes," said the grandmother, "she flies where the swarm hangs in the thickest clusters. She is the largest of all; and she never stays quietly on the earth, but flies up again into the black clouds. Many a winter's night she flits through the streets of the town, and peeps in at the windows; and then they freeze in wonderful patterns that look like flowers."

"Yes, I have seen it," said both the children.

In the evening, when little Kay was home, and half undressed, he climbed up on the chair by the window, and peeped
out of the little hole. A few snow-flakes were falling, and one,
the largest of all, remained lying on the edge of the flower-pot.
The flake of snow grew larger and larger and at last it was like
a beautiful maiden, dressed in the finest white gauze, made of
a million little flakes, like stars. She was so lovely and delicate,
but she was of ice; of dazzling, sparkling ice; her eyes glittered
like two stars; but there was neither rest nor peace in them.
She nodded toward the window, and beckoned with her hand.
The little boy was frightened, and jumped down from the chair.
Then he fancied that a great white bird flew away.

The next day was sharp and frosty, and then the spring came; the sun shone, green leaves appeared, swallows built their nests, windows were opened, and the little children again sat in their pretty garden, high up on the leads at the top of the house.

That summer the roses flowered in unwonted beauty. The little girl had learned a hymn, in which there was something about roses, and she sang it to the little boy, who then sang it with her:—

> "The rose in the valley is blooming so sweet,
> The Child Jesus is there the children to greet."

And the children held each other by the hand, kissed the roses, and rejoiced in God's bright sunshine. What lovely summer days those were! How delightful to be out in the air, near the fresh rose-bushes, that seemed as if they would never finish blooming!

One day Kay and Gerda were looking at a picture-book— the clock in the church-tower was just striking five—when Kay cried "O! Something struck me sharply in the heart; and now something has got into my eye!"

The little girl threw her arms around his neck. He winked his eyes; no, she could see nothing in them.

"I think it is out now," said he; but it was not. It was one of those pieces of glass that had got into his eye—a splinter from the magic mirror that made everything great and good look mean and ugly; and poor Kay had got another piece right in his heart, which began to turn into a lump of ice.

"Why are you crying?" asked he. "It makes you look so ugly! There's nothing the matter with me. Ah," said he at once, "that rose is worm-eaten, and look, this one is quite stunted! What ugly roses they are!" and he gave the box a kick and broke off both the roses.

"What are you doing?" cried the little girl. As he saw her

alarm, he pulled up another rose, ran in at his own window, and left dear little Gerda alone.

When she next brought out her picture book, he said it was only fit for babies, and if his grandmother told him stories, he always interrupted her; besides, if he could manage it, he would get behind her, put on her spectacles, and imitate her way of speaking. He was soon able to imitate the gait and manner of every one in the street. Everything that was peculiar and displeasing in them,—that Kay made fun of. It was the glass he had got in his eye, the glass that was sticking in his heart, which made him tease even Gerda, whose whole soul was devoted to him.

His games now were quite different from what they had been. One winter's day, when the snow was falling, he spread out his coat, and caught the snow. Then he took a magnifying glass. "Look through this glass, Gerda," said he. Every flake seemed larger, and appeared like a lovely flower, or a sharply-pointed star: it was splendid to look at! "That's much more interesting than real flowers!" said Kay. "They are all made exactly by rule; there is no fault in them. If only they did not melt!"

Shortly after this, Kay appeared one day with his warm gloves on, and his little sledge at his back. He bawled right into Gerda's ears, "I'm going out into the square to play with the other boys," and away he went.

There, in the market-place, the boldest boys used to hitch their sledges to the carts as they passed, and so they got a good ride. It was such fun! Just as they were in the very height of their amusement, a large sledge appeared in the square; it was painted white, and there was some one in it who wore a white fur coat and a white fur cap. The sledge drove round the square twice. Kay tied his little sledge to it, and off he drove. On they went quicker and quicker into the next street; the person who drove turned round to Kay, and nodded to him in a friendly

manner, just as if they knew each other. Every time he was
going to untie his sledge the driver nodded to him, and then
Kay sat still once more. So on they went till they came outside the gates of the town. Then the snow began to fall so
thickly, that the little boy could not see an arm's length before
him, but still on he went; suddenly he let go the string he held
in his hand in order to get loose from the big sledge, but it was
of no use; his little sledge hung fast and on he went like the
wind. He cried out, but no one heard him. The snow drifted
and the sledge flew on. Sometimes it gave a jerk as though
they were driving over hedges and ditches. He was quite frightened, and he tried to repeat the Lord's Prayer; but he was only
able to remember the multiplication table.

The snow-flakes grew larger and larger, till they looked like
great white birds. Suddenly the large sledge stopped, and the
person who drove rose up. It was a lady, tall, slim and glittering, her cloak and cap of snow. It was the Snow-Queen.

"We have travelled fast," said she. "It is freezingly cold;
creep in under my coat." And she put him in the sledge beside

her, and wrapped the fur round him. He felt as though he were sinking into a snow-drift.

"Are you still cold?" she asked, and kissed his forehead. Ah! the kiss was cold as ice; it went to his very heart, which was already almost a frozen lump; but a moment more and he grew to like it. He no longer felt the cold that was around him.

"My sledge! Don't forget my sledge!" It was the first thing he thought of, and there it was, tied to one of the white birds, who flew along behind with it on his back. The Snow-Queen kissed Kay once more, and then he forgot little Gerda, grandmother, and all whom he had left at his home.

Kay looked at her. She was very beautiful; a more clever or a more lovely face he could not fancy to himself; and she no longer appeared of ice as before, when she sat outside the window, and beckoned to him; in his eyes she was perfect. He did not fear her at all, and told her that he could do arithmetic sums in his head, and with fractions even; that he knew the number of square miles there were in the different countries, and how many inhabitants they contained; and she smiled while he spoke. On she flew with him; high over the black clouds while the storm moaned and whistled. On they flew over woods and lakes, over seas and many lands. Beneath them, the wolves howled, the snow crackled; above flew large, screaming crows, and higher still the moon shone, large and bright.

II

But what became of little Gerda when Kay did not return? Where could he be? Nobody knew. All the other boys could tell was that they had seen him tie his sledge to another large

and splendid one, which drove down the street and out of the town. Little Gerda wept long and bitterly.

At last spring came with its warm sunshine.

"I'll put on my red shoes," said she. "Kay has never seen them; then I'll go down to the river and ask if he has fallen in."

So she kissed her grandmother, who was still asleep, put on her red shoes, and went alone to the river.

"Is it true that you have taken my little playfellow?" she asked. "I will make you a present of my red shoes, if you will give him back to me."

The blue waves nodded in a strange manner, it seemed to her, so she took off her red shoes, the most precious things she possessed, and threw them both into the river. But they fell close to the bank, and the little waves bore them immediately back to her. Gerda thought she had not thrown them out far enough, so she clambered into a boat which lay among the rushes, went to the farthest end, and threw out the shoes again. The boat was not fastened, and her movements made it drift from the shore. She felt it moving and tried to get out; but already it was more than a yard from the land, and gliding quickly onward.

Little Gerda began to cry; but no one heard her except the Sparrows. So she sat quite still with only her stockings on. Her little red shoes swam behind, but they could not catch the boat, it went so much faster than they.

The banks on both sides were beautiful, with lovely flowers, fine old trees, and slopes dotted with sheep and cows, but not a human being anywhere to be seen.

"Perhaps the river will carry me to little Kay," said she; and then she grew less sad. Presently she sailed by a large cherry-orchard, where stood a little cottage with curious red and blue windows; it was thatched, and before it two wooden soldiers stood sentry, presenting arms when any one went past.

Gerda called to them, for she thought they were alive; but they, of course, did not answer. As the stream drove the boat quite near the land, she called out louder still and then an old woman came out of the cottage, leaning upon a crooked stick. She wore a large broad-brimmed hat which was painted with the most beautiful flowers.

"Poor little child!" said the old Woman; then she went into the water, caught hold of the boat with her crooked stick, drew it to the bank, and lifted little Gerda out. "Come and tell me who you are, and how you came here."

When Gerda had told her everything, and asked her if she had seen little Kay, the Woman answered that he had not passed there yet, but he no doubt would come. She told her not to be sad, but to taste her cherries, and look at her flowers. Then she took Gerda by the hand, led her into the little cottage, and locked the door.

The windows were very high up; the glass was red, blue, and green, and the sunlight shone through quite wondrously in all sorts of colors. On the table stood the most delicious cherries, and the old Woman let Gerda eat as many as she chose, while she combed her hair with a golden comb so it curled and shone like gold round that sweet little face that was so like a rose.

"I have often longed for such a dear little girl," said the old Woman. "Now you shall see how happy we shall be together." And while she combed little Gerda's hair, the child forgot her foster-brother Kay more and more, for the old Woman understood magic, and she wanted very much to keep little Gerda. She therefore went out into the garden, and stretched out her crooked stick towards the rose-bushes. Beautifully as they were blooming, they all sank into the earth, and no one could tell where they had stood. She feared that if Gerda saw the roses, she would remember Kay and run away to seek him.

She now led Gerda into the garden. O, what fragrance and what loveliness was there! Every flower that one could think of, and of every season, stood there in fullest bloom. Gerda jumped for joy, and played till the sun set behind the cherry-trees. Then she was put into a pretty bed, with a red silken coverlet filled with violets. There she slept and had pleasant dreams.

The next morning she played again with the flowers in the warm sunshine, and so many days passed by. Gerda knew every flower; but however many they were, it still seemed to her that one was missing, though she did not know which. One day, while she was looking at the old Woman's hat that was painted with flowers, the most beautiful of them all seemed to her to be a rose. The old Woman had forgotten to take the rose from her hat when she made the others vanish in the earth. "What!" said Gerda; "are there no roses here?" and she ran about amongst the flower-beds, and looked, and looked, but there was not one to be found. Then she sat down and wept; but her hot tears fell just where a rose-bush had sunk; and when they watered the ground, the tree shot up suddenly fresh and blooming. Gerda kissed the roses, and thought at once of little Kay.

"O how long I have stayed! I intended to look for Kay!" And off ran Gerda to the further end of the garden.

The gate was locked, but she shook the rusted bolt till it was loosened, and the gate opened; out she ran with her little bare feet and no one followed her. At last she could run no longer so she sat down on a large stone. Then she saw that summer had passed; it was late autumn, though no one would ever have known it in the beautiful garden she had left where there were always flowers and sunshine the whole year round.

"Dear me, how long I have stayed!" said Gerda. "I must not rest any longer." And she sprang up to run on.

III

At length Gerda had to rest herself again, and there came hopping towards her over the snow a large raven. He had long been looking at Gerda and shaking his head; and now he said, "Caw! caw! Good day! Good day!" And he asked her where she was going all alone. So Gerda told him her whole story, and asked if he had seen Kay.

The Raven nodded very gravely, and said, "It may be—it may be!"

"What! do you really think so?" cried the little girl; and she nearly smothered the Raven with kisses.

"Gently, gently," said the Raven. "I think I know; I think that it may be little Kay. But now he has forgotten you for the Princess."

"Does he live with a princess?" asked Gerda.

"Yes," said the Raven.

"O, won't you take me to the palace?" said Gerda. "When Kay

313

hears that I am here, he will come out directly to fetch me."

So the Raven led Gerda into a garden, where one leaf was falling after the other; and when the lights in the palace had all gradually disappeared, he took her to the back-door, which stood half open.

O how Gerda's heart beat with anxiety and longing! She wanted so to know if little Kay was there. They were now on the stairs where a single lamp was burning. Then they entered the first apartment which was of rose-colored satin, with arti-ficial flowers on the wall. Each hall was more magnificent than the other. At last they came into a room where the ceiling was made of great leaves of glass; from this were hung by golden ropes two beds, each shaped like a lily. One was white, and in this lay the Princess; the other was red, and it was here that Gerda hoped to find little Kay. She bent back one of the red leaves, and saw a brown neck—O, that was Kay! She called him quite loudly by name, and held the lamp toward him—he awoke, turned his head, and—it was not little Kay at all!

The Prince was only like him about the neck. Then out of the white lily leaves the Princess peeped too, and asked what was the matter. Little Gerda cried and told them her story.

"Poor little thing!" said the Prince and the Princess, and they put Gerda to bed. "How good men and animals are to me," thought the child as she fell asleep.

The next day she was dressed from head to foot in silk and velvet. They offered to let her stay at the palace, and lead a happy life; but she would not. She begged to have a little carriage with a horse in front, and a small pair of shoes, so that she might go forth in the wide world and look for Kay.

Shoes and a muff were given her; and when she was about to set off, a new carriage drew up before the door. It was of pure gold, and the arms of the Prince and Princess shone like a star upon it; inside, it was lined with sugar plums and in the seats were fruits and gingerbread. The coachman, the footmen, and the outriders all wore golden crowns. The Prince and the Princess assisted Gerda into the carriage themselves, and wished her all success, while the Raven accompanied her for the first three miles. Then the Raven bade her farewell, flew into a tree, and beat his wings as long as he could see the carriage.

IV

They drove through the dark wood; but the carriage shone like a torch, and caught the eyes of robbers.

"It's gold! It's gold!" cried they; and they rushed forward, seized the horses, knocked down the postilion, the coachman, and servants, and pulled little Gerda out of the carriage.

"How plump, how beautiful she is! She looks good enough to eat," said the old Robber-woman, who had a long, scrubby beard, and bushy eyebrows that hung down over her eyes. Then she drew out a knife, the blade of which shone and glittered.

"Ah," cried her little daughter who was very spoiled and very headstrong, "but you shall not touch her. She shall give me her muff, and her pretty frock! She shall play with me and sleep in my bed!"

The little Robber-maiden was as tall as Gerda, but stronger, broader-shouldered, and of dark complexion. Her eyes were quite black; they looked almost sad. She threw her arms around Gerda and said, "They shall not hurt you as long as I am not displeased with you. You are a princess, aren't you?"

"No," said little Gerda; and she then told all that had happened to her, and how much she loved little Kay.

The Robber-maiden looked at her with a serious air, and nodded her head slightly, then she dried Gerda's eyes, and put both her hands in the handsome muff which was so soft and warm.

"If you are naughty," said she, "no one else shall kill you! I'll do it myself!" And she led Gerda off to the courtyard of the robber's castle. It was full of cracks from top to bottom, and out of the holes ravens and crows were flying; great bulldogs, each of which looked as if he could swallow a man, jumped up, but they did not bark, for that was forbidden. In the midst of the large, old, smoky hall burnt a great fire on the stone floor. The smoke all went up to the ceiling where it had to find a way.

"You shall sleep with me to-night, with all my animals," said the little Robber-maiden. They had something to eat and drink; and then went into a corner, where straw and carpets were lying. Beside them, on laths and perches, sat nearly a hundred pigeons. All seemed to be asleep, yet they moved a little when the Robber-maiden came. "They are all mine," said she. At the same time she seized one by the legs and shook it so that its wings fluttered. "Kiss it!" she cried, and flung it in Gerda's face. "And here is my dear old Bac." She dragged out by the horns a reindeer, that was tied up there. "We are obliged to lock this fellow in, or he would make his escape. Every evening I tickle his neck with my sharp knife; it makes him jump about so!" and the little girl drew forth a long knife from a crack in the wall, and let it glide over the reindeer's neck. The poor animal kicked; the girl laughed, and pulled Gerda into bed with her.

"Do you intend to keep your knife while you sleep?" asked Gerda, looking sidewise at the knife.

"I always sleep with the knife," said the little Robber-maiden; "there is no knowing what may happen. But tell me now, once more, all about little Kay, and why you have started off into the wide world alone." So Gerda related all, from the very beginning; the Wood-pigeons cooed above in their cage, and the others slept. Then the little Robber-maiden wound her arm round Gerda's neck, held the knife in the other hand, and began to snore so loudly that everybody could hear her. But Gerda could not close her eyes. The Robbers sat round the fire, sang and drank; and the old Robber-woman jumped about so, that it was outlandish to see her.

Then the Wood-pigeons said, "Coo! coo! we have seen little Kay! A white bird carried his sledge! He sat by the side of the Snow-Queen. They floated low down over the trees, as we lay in our nest. Coo! coo!"

"Where did the Snow-Queen go?" cried Gerda. "Do you know anything about it?"

"She is no doubt gone to Lapland where there is always snow and ice. Ask the reindeer who is tied up here."

"Aye, ice and snow indeed! There it is glorious and beautiful!" said the Reindeer. "You can run and jump about as

HILDA BANNM

you like on those big glittering plains. The Snow-Queen has her summer-tent there; but her fixed home is high up towards the North Pole, on the island called Spitzbergen."

"O Kay! poor little Kay!" sighed Gerda.

"Do you choose to be quiet?" said the Robber-maiden.

In the morning Gerda told her all that the Wood-pigeons had said. "Do you know where Lapland is?" asked she of the Reindeer.

"Who should know better than I?" said the animal with sparkling eyes. "I was born and bred there on the snow-fields."

"Listen," said the Robber-girl to Gerda, "you see that all the robbers are gone. Only my mother is left and she will soon fall asleep. Then I shall do something for you."

When the Robber-woman was having a nap, the little Robber-maiden went to the Reindeer and said, "I should like to give you still many a tickling with the sharp knife, for then you are so amusing; however, I will untie you so that you may go to Lapland. But you must go quickly, and take this little girl to the Snow-Queen, where her playfellow is."

The Reindeer leaped for joy. The Robber-maiden lifted up little Gerda, and took care to bind her fast on the Reindeer's back; she even gave her a small cushion to sit on. "Here are your worsted leggins, for it will be cold," she said, "the muff I shall keep for myself,—for it is so very pretty. But here are my mother's great fur gloves. They will come up to your elbows. Creep into them."

Gerda wept for joy.

"Don't make such faces!" said the little Robber-maiden. "This is just the time when you ought to look pleased. Here are two loaves and a ham for you." The bread and the meat were fastened to the Reindeer's back; the little maiden opened the door, called in all the dogs, and then with her knife cut the rope that fastened the animal. "Now off with you," she cried, "but take good care of the little girl!"

Gerda stretched out her hands with the large fur gloves towards the Robber-maiden, and said, "Farewell!" Then the Reindeer flew on over bush and bramble, through the great wood, over swamps and plains. The wolves howled, the ravens screamed, and the red lights quivered up in the sky.

"Those are my dear old northern lights," said the Reindeer; "look how they gleam!" And on he sped faster still,—day and night on he went. The loaves were eaten, and the ham too, and now they were in Lapland.

V

Suddenly they stopped before a little house, which looked very miserable; the roof reached to the ground and the door was so low that the people had to creep on their hands and knees when they went in or out. Nobody was at home except an old Lapp woman, who was dressing fish by the light of an oil lamp. And the Reindeer told her the whole of Gerda's story.

"Poor thing," said the Lapp woman, "you have far to run still. You have more than a hundred miles to go before you get to Finland; there the Snow-Queen has her country-house, and burns blue lights every evening. I will give you a few words from me, written on a dried fish skin, for paper I have none. This you can take with you to the Finn woman, and she will be able to give you more information than I."

When Gerda had warmed herself, and had eaten and drunk, the Lapp woman wrote a few words on a dried fish, begged Gerda to take care of them, put her on the Reindeer, bound her fast, and away sprang the animal. Flicker, flicker blazed the beautiful northern lights, and at last they came to Finland. They knocked at the chimney of the Finn woman, for door she had none.

There was such a heat inside that the Finn woman herself

wore very few clothes. She immediately loosened Gerda's clothes, and pulled off her gloves and boots, for otherwise the heat would have been too great. Then she read and re-read what was written on the fish-skin.

The Reindeer told her Gerda's story, at which the Finn woman winked her eyes, but said nothing.

"You are so clever," said the Reindeer; "you can, I know, twist all the winds of the world together in a knot. Will you give the little maiden a drink that she may possess the strength of twelve men, and overcome the Snow-Queen?"

"The strength of twelve men!" said the Finn woman; "much good that would do her! 'Tis true little Kay is at the Snow-Queen's and finds everything there to his taste; he thinks it the best place in the world, but the reason of that is, he has a splinter of glass in his eye and in his heart. These must be got out first; otherwise, he will never go back to mankind, and the Snow-Queen will keep her power over him."

"But can you give little Gerda nothing to take which will give her power to conquer all this?"

"I can give her no more power than she has already. Don't you see how great is her power? Don't you see how men and animals are forced to serve her; how well she gets through the world, barefooted? That power lies in her heart, because she is a sweet and innocent child! If she cannot get to the Snow-Queen by herself, and rid little Kay of the glass, we cannot help her. Two miles from here the garden of the Snow-Queen begins; there you may carry the little girl. Set her down by the large bush with red berries, standing in the snow. Don't stay talking, but hasten back as fast as possible." And now the Finn woman placed little Gerda on the Reindeer's back, and off he ran with all imaginable speed.

"O! I have not got my boots, nor my gloves!" cried little Gerda. She missed them in the piercing cold, but the Reindeer dared not stand still. On he ran till he came to the great bush with the red berries; there he set Gerda down, and kissed her mouth, while bright tears flowed from his eyes. Then back he ran. There stood Gerda now, without shoes or gloves, in the very middle of freezing, icy Finland.

She ran on as fast as she could. A whole regiment of snow-flakes rushed against her. They did not fall from the sky, for it was quite clear, with the northern lights shining brightly. These flakes ran along the ground, and the nearer they came the larger and more terrific they grew. They were the advance guard of the Snow-Queen. Some looked like large, ugly porcupines; others like knots of snakes, and others like bears, with hair on end! All were of dazzling whiteness—all were alive.

Little Gerda repeated the Lord's Prayer. The cold was so great that her breath froze as it came out of her mouth and she could see it like a cloud of smoke in front of her. It grew thicker and thicker, till it formed itself into bright little angels, that grew bigger and bigger when they touched the earth. All had helmets on their heads and spears and shields in their hands; more and more of them appeared, and when Gerda had finished the Lord's Prayer, she was surrounded by a whole legion. They pierced the snow-flakes with their spears, and shivered them into a thousand pieces; so little Gerda walked on bravely and in safety through them. The angels patted her hands and feet; and then she hardly felt how cold it was, but went on quickly towards the palace of the Snow-Queen.

Now we shall see what Kay was doing. He was not thinking of Gerda, least of all that she stood before the palace.

VI

The walls of the palace were of driven snow; and the doors and windows of piercing winds. There were more than a hundred halls there, shaped just as the snow had drifted. The largest one stretched for many miles; and all were lit up by the cold, precise northern lights. All were so large, so empty, so icy, and so glittering! Mirth never reigned there; there was never even a little bear-ball, with the storm of music, while the polar bears went on their hind-legs and showed off their steps; there was never a little tea-party of white young lady foxes! In the middle of the empty, endless hall of snow was a frozen lake cracked in a thousand pieces, each piece just like the other, and in the middle of this lake sat the Snow-Queen when she was at home. Then she said she was sitting on the Mirror of Reason, and that this was the best and only thing in the world to rest on.

Little Kay was quite blue with cold; but he did not know it, for the Snow-Queen had kissed away his feelings, and his heart was a lump of ice. He was pulling about some sharp, flat pieces of ice, which he laid together in all possible ways, puzzling out how to make something with them. He fitted them into a great many shapes, and shapes the most complicated, for they were the "Ice Puzzles of Reason." In his eyes the figures he made were exceedingly beautiful, and of the utmost importance; but this was because of the bit of glass which was still in his eye. Moreover, no matter how many wonderful words he could shape

322

the ice into, the word he wanted most of all he could never make them spell—that word was "Eternity." The Snow-Queen had said, "If you can shape out that word, you shall be your own master, and I will give you the whole world and a pair of new skates besides." But he could not puzzle it out.

"I am going now to the warm lands," said the Snow-Queen. "I must powder my black kettles." (This was what she called the volcanoes, Vesuvius and Etna.) "It does the lemons and grapes good." Then away she flew, and Kay sat alone in the empty halls trying to solve his ice puzzle. There he sat so stiff and immovable one might have thought him frozen.

Suddenly little Gerda stepped through the great portal of cutting winds into the palace. She repeated her evening prayer, and the winds dropped as if lulled to sleep. Then she entered the vast, empty, cold halls. There she beheld Kay, and knew him at once. She flung her arms around his neck, held him fast and cried, "Kay, sweet little Kay! Have I found you at last?"

But he sat quite still, stiff and cold. Then little Gerda wept hot tears which fell on his breast, and they thawed his heart and melted away the bit of the mirror there. He looked at her, and she sang:

> "The rose in the valley is blooming so sweet,
> The Child Jesus is there the children to greet."

At the sound of the song, Kay burst into tears; he wept so

much that the last glass splinter was washed from his eye. Then
he knew Gerda, and cried, "Gerda, sweet little Gerda! where
have you been so long? And where have I been?" He looked
around him. "How cold it is here!" said he. "How empty
and cold!" And he clung fast to Gerda, who laughed and wept
for joy. It was such a happy time as Kay warmed into life
again, that even the bits of ice danced about for joy, and when
they laid themselves down lo! they formed exactly the letters
the Snow-Queen had told Kay he must find out if he was to
become his own master, and have the whole world and a pair
of new skates.

Gerda kissed his cheeks, and they grew rosy; she kissed his
eyes, and they shone like her own; she kissed his hands and
feet, and he was once more merry and strong. The Snow-Queen
might come back as soon as she liked; there stood his order of
release—the word "Eternity" written in letters of ice.

Kay and Gerda took each other's hands, and wandered out
of the great hall, talking of their grandmother, and of the roses
on the roof. Wherever they went, the winds were hushed, and
the sun burst forth. When they reached the bush with the
red berries, they found the Reindeer waiting. He carried them
first to the Finn woman; she warmed them in her hot room,
and told them what they were to do on their journey home;
and then to the Lapp woman, who made some new clothes for
them and lent them her sledge.

When they reached the country where the first green growing things peeped forth, they took leave of the Reindeer. "Farewell! farewell!" said they all. Soon they heard the first little
birds twittering and there came out of the wood toward them,
riding on a beautiful horse which Gerda knew had once drawn
her golden chariot, a young damsel in a bright red cap with pis-
tols at her belt. This was the little Robber-maiden who was

tired of being at home and had set out into the world. She and Gerda knew each other at once. It was a joyful meeting.

"You are a nice fellow!" said she to Kay; "I should like to know if you deserve to be run after to the end of the world!"

But Gerda patted her cheeks, and told her their story.

"Schnipp-schnapp-schnurre, it's all right at last," said the Robber-maiden; and she took the hands of each, and promised that if she should ever pass through the town where they lived, she would come and visit them. Then away she rode off into the wide world.

Kay and Gerda walked on hand in hand. It was lovely spring weather, with flowers and greenery everywhere. Soon they recognized the big town where they lived with its tall towers in which the bells still rang their merry peals. They went straight on and hastened up to their grandmother's room, where everything was standing just as they had left it. The clock said "Tick! tack!" and the hands moved round. But as they entered, they remarked that they were now grown up. The roses hung blooming in at the open window; there stood the little children's chairs, and Kay and Gerda sat down on them, still holding each other by the hand. All the cold, empty splendor of the Snow-Queen's palace had passed from their memory like a bad dream. Grandmother sat in the bright sunshine, and read aloud from the Bible: "Unless ye become as little children, ye cannot enter the kingdom of heaven."

And Kay and Gerda looked in each other's eyes, and all at once they understood the old hymn:—

"The rose in the valley is blooming so sweet,
The Child Jesus is there the children to greet."

There sat the two grown-up people; grown-up, and yet children —children in heart. And it was summer-time, glorious summer!

Prince Cherry

From the French of
MADAME LA PRINCESSE DE BEAUMONT

ONCE upon a time there was a King who led so gracious and praiseworthy a life that his subjects called him the Good King. One day as he was out hunting, a little white rabbit, closely pursued by the hounds, threw itself into his arms. The King at once began to pet and stroke the little creature, and he said:

"Since you have come to me for protection, I shall see that you are well cared for."

He then carried the rabbit home to his palace, ordered a pretty little house to be made for it, and gave it abundance of fresh green things such as rabbits love to eat.

That very same night, when he had retired alone to his chamber, there suddenly appeared to him a beautiful lady. She was dressed in neither gold nor silver, but her flowing robes were as white as snow, and on her head she wore a crown of white roses. The Good King was greatly astonished to behold such a sight, for his door was locked and he did not see how anyone could have found entrance. But the lady in white explained.

"I am the Fairy Candide," she said. "I have heard much of your goodness, and as I chanced to be passing through the wood while you were hunting, I felt a great desire to know if you were truly as good as men say you are. To discover this, I took the form of a rabbit and sought protection in your arms, for I was sure that he who would be merciful to a dumb beast, would be at least as merciful to his fellow men. Had you refused me your protection, I should have concluded that you were wicked in your heart, in spite of all your show of goodness. But you deserve the name by which you are called; you are the Good King. I thank you for your kindness and assure you that I will always be your

friend. You have only to ask what you most desire and I promise you if it be within my power, your wish shall be granted."

"Madame," said the Good King, "I have one well-beloved
and only son, Prince Cherry. If you have any kindly feeling
for me, I pray you become, for my sake, the friend and pro-
tectress of my son."

"Willingly," said the Fairy. "I can make your son the
Handsomest, the Richest or the most Powerful Prince in the
world. Which of these gifts do you choose for him?"

"I choose none of them," answered the Good King. "I choose
to have you make him the Best of all Princes. Of what use
would Riches or Beauty or Power be to him if he were wicked
in his heart? You know very well, madame, that it is Goodness alone which can make him happy."

"You have spoken well," said the Fairy Candide, "but, much
as I might wish to do so, it is not in my power to make Prince
Cherry a good man. That is something each one must do for
himself. All I can promise you is to give him good advice. I
can point out his faults to him and punish him if he will not
repent of his wickedness and correct it."

The Good King was well content with this promise, and
shortly afterwards he died, leaving his throne to his dearly beloved son. Two days after this, Prince Cherry was resting in
his chamber when the Fairy Candide appeared to him just as
she had to his father.

"I promised your father," said she to him, "to be your friend,
and in order to keep my word to him, I am come to make you
a present." She placed on Cherry's hand a little gold ring, and
continued, "Take great care of this ring; it is not much to look
at, but it is in truth more precious than diamonds. Whenever
you are about to do something wrong, it will prick your finger.
In this way you will always know when you are doing evil,

but if, in spite of the warning, you still continue in the error of your ways, then you will lose my friendship altogether."

As she finished speaking, she disappeared, leaving Cherry so greatly amazed that he almost thought himself dreaming. But there in truth was the ring on his finger. For some time he was so wise and good that it did not prick him at all. But one day he was out hunting and it chanced that he found no game whatever. This put him into an ill humor, and he began to show his vexation in his face and manner. At that his ring grew tight and uncomfortable, but it did not prick him, so he paid no further heed to it. He was returning to his chamber when his little dog, Bibi, ran as usual to meet him, and leaped up and down before him, licking his hand and inviting caresses. But the Prince cried out impatiently;

"Out of my way sir! I'm in no humor to play with you!"

The poor little dog who had been accustomed to nothing but petting and did not understand a word that his master said, kept on leaping before him and began to tug at his clothes to win at least his attention. This made Cherry so angry that he altogether lost his temper and gave his poor little pet a kick that sent him across the room. Instantly the ring pricked him as sharply as though it had been a pin.

"What!" he cried. "My ring pricking me for this! The Fairy must be making game of me! Is it a crime to kick an animal that was teasing me? Why am I ruler over a mighty empire if I may not even kick my own dog?"

"Nay!" said a voice in answer, "the master of a mighty empire has the right to do good but not evil. If it were permitted for the great to ill treat those beneath them, I could at this very moment beat you, since a fairy is far more powerful than a man. But I shall not beat you; I prefer to leave you to mend your ways. You have been guilty of three bad faults today, bad

328

temper, anger, cruelty. See that
you do better tomorrow."

The Prince, humbled and
ashamed, promised to correct
his faults and for some time
kept his word. Still, he had
always believed that a King
could do anything he chose,
and when he found that he, the
King, had to give up his own
will, had to learn to govern his
anger and his temper like the
meanest churl in his kingdom,
it made him both vexed and angry. Thus he began to do many
a wayward, wilful thing. His companions, however, and especially a wicked foster-brother were forever praising him and
telling him a king could do no wrong. Only old Suliman, his
tutor, who loved him like a son, dared still tell him of his faults
and urge him to correct them.

Soon his ring was pricking him very often. Sometimes he
stopped at its warning, but more often he did not. He insisted
more and more on having his own way and cared not how cruelly
or unjustly he treated those beneath him. One day, angered
at Suliman's gentle but firm remonstrances, he sent the good
old man into exile, far away from court. After that, the ring
annoyed him continually. Then he lost all patience with its
friendly warnings, and wishing to be entirely free to do as he
chose, he flung it with all his strength onto the dust heap. Now
he thought he should be the happiest and freest of men. So
every day he did exactly as he chose and every day he grew more
and more miserable.

One day as Cherry was walking in the fields, he saw a young

girl watching her sheep and twining garlands by a brook, and she was so extremely beautiful, that he resolved at once to make her his wife. Being always accustomed to have everything he wanted, and thinking that any girl would esteem herself happy to be his Queen, he at once told her what he purposed. But to his astonishment, Zelia—for that was the maiden's name—replied:

"Sire, I am only a shepherdess, still I will not marry you."

"What! Is my appearance then displeasing to you?" asked the Prince, astounded that any one should refuse him.

"Not at all," answered Zelia. "On the contrary, you are handsome. But of what use to me would be all your beauty, and the riches you might give me? Every day you give way to bad temper, and force all about you to do whatever you will. With you I should be miserable and so I will not marry you."

At this, Prince Cherry fell into violent anger, and bade his guards carry Zelia forcibly off to his palace. He then took counsel with his foster-brother as to how he should treat the girl. At first he confided to him that he had half resolved to correct his faults, conquer his wilfulness and try to grow virtuous to please Zelia, but this wicked companion answered:

"What! bow down to the wishes of a little shepherdess! If I were in your place, I should compel the girl to obey me. Feed her on bread and water until she comes to her senses, and if she still holds out, throw her into a dungeon as a warning to your other subjects what shall happen to them if they dare disobey you. You would be forever disgraced if you let a simple little shepherdess conquer you!"

"But," said Prince Cherry, "shall I not be disgraced if I harm an innocent person? After all, Zelia has committed no crime."

"It is a crime not to yield to your wishes," replied the foster-brother. "Rather be unjust, than let anyone suppose he can safely go against your will."

THROUGH FAIRY HALLS

What the man said touched Cherry on his weakest point, and his good impulses faded. He resolved to go at once to the room where Zelia was confined, ask her once more to be his wife, and if she still refused, to cast her into a miserable dungeon.

But on entering the room of the shepherdess, Cherry was astounded to find it empty! She was gone! How could she have gotten away? He had the key to the room in his pocket! Who could have helped her escape? At last the foster-brother and others of Prince Cherry's friends came and told him that Suliman had come back to court and been overheard to boast that he would set Zelia free. These men still feared the tutor's good influence over Cherry, and planned in this way to be rid of him forever. In a fury, Prince Cherry ordered his old friend to be loaded with irons and cast into prison. Then he shut himself up in his chamber and raged like a lion. Suddenly, there was a sound like thunder, and there stood Candide before him.

"Prince," said she sternly, "I promised your father to give you good advice and to see that you were punished if you did not heed me. My counsel you have despised, my ring you have cast away. You still keep the outward appearance of a man,

but in your heart you are no better than the beasts you chase—a lion in fury, a serpent in vengefulness, a bull in stubborn wilfulness, a wolf in ferocity. Bear henceforth in your outward form the likeness of all these animals."

Scarcely had Candide spoken when Prince Cherry, to his horror, found himself transformed into the monster the fairy had decreed. He had a lion's head, a bull's body and horns, a wolf's feet and a serpent's tail. At the same time, he felt himself carried away, and behold! he stood in the midst of a grove on the banks of a stream, and before him he saw in the water his own ugly form reflected. Then he heard a voice saying:

"Look at thyself and know that the ugliness of thy body but expresses the ugliness of thy soul."

Hoping to be rid of the sight of himself, Cherry dashed away into the depths of the forest. But scarcely had he gone twenty paces when he fell into a pit that had been dug to catch bears. In an instant the trappers who had hidden in a tree hard by, were upon him. Only too pleased to have found such a strange-appearing monster, they loaded him with chains, put him into a cage, and dragged him along to the capital of his own kingdom.

As he drew near the city, he perceived that some great merry-making was afoot. The trappers asked what was the cause of it all and were informed that the people were rejoicing because Prince Cherry, their tyrannical ruler, had been struck by a thunderbolt. "His wickedness could no longer be endured," they said, "so heaven has rid the earth of the monster." Four of his courtiers, who had been his chosen companions in evil, had wished to divide his kingdom between them, but the people had risen up and given the crown to the good old tutor, Suliman.

All this the monster heard and he groaned with rage, for his own subjects whom he had ruled with an iron hand so short a time before, stood about, gaped into the cage and made sport of him. When he was dragged into the great square before his own palace, he saw Suliman on a splendid throne and heard all the people bless him and pray that he might make good the injustice they had suffered under Cherry. But the good Suliman answered the people that he would only wear the crown as a viceroy. He knew that Prince Cherry was not really dead, but would some day return, to rule over them, when he was become in truth the good man of whom his early years had given such rich promise.

Suliman's words touched the poor beast deeply. He now felt how true had been the old man's love for him, and he ceased to beat himself against the iron bars of the cage in which the hunters were carrying him about. Quiet as a lamb, he allowed himself to be carried to a menagerie, and chained up among the other wild beasts. Little had he thought when he visited this very place as a boy that he would some day be shut up there!

The time had come at length, when he was ready to admit that he had deserved all that had come upon him, and he resolved to begin at once to amend his ways by being obedient to the keeper who cared for him. This was no easy task, for the man often treated the animals cruelly. One day while the keeper was sleeping, a tiger broke loose from his cage and sprang upon him. At first Cherry felt a thrill of pleasure at the thought of getting even with the man, but almost instantly he refused such a thought, and wished earnestly that he were free to help him.

No sooner had he become conscious of this good wish, than presto! the doors of his cage swung open and he rushed to the assistance of the keeper. The man had been almost overcome, but Cherry leaped upon the tiger and struggled until he had killed the beast. Then he flung himself at the feet of the man he had saved, longing to be petted. The keeper, in gratitude, lifted his hand to stroke him, but as he did so, a voice was heard saying, "Good actions are never unrewarded," and there stood before him, not a frightful monster, but a pretty little dog.

Cherry, delighted to find himself so changed, leaped up and

licked the keeper's hand. Won by his caresses, the man took him up into his arms. Soon after this, the keeper carried him off to the King of a neighboring kingdom with whom he had certain dealings. To him he related the wonderful story of the little creature and the Queen at once expressed the wish to have the dog for her own. With her he was lodged so elegantly and treated so kindly that he would have been well content, could he have forgotten Zelia and the fact that he was once a man.

One day he took the piece of bread which had been given him for his breakfast, and being seized with the fancy to eat it in the palace garden, went off toward the banks of a stream where he often drank. But when he reached the spot, instead of the stream, he saw rising up a splendid palace glittering with gold and precious gems. Fine as this palace appeared, there wandered before it a young woman who seemed to be half famished. She was looking about the lovely garden and vainly trying to find amidst all its flowery grandeur something that she could eat.

"Poor thing," said Cherry to himself, "she is far more in need of food than I. I must help her."

So the little dog ran up to her and dropped his bread at her feet. The young woman picked up the bread and ate it gratefully. Soon she looked quite herself again, and then Cherry saw to his great amazement that she was no other than his beloved Zelia. But no sooner had he recognized this amazing fact, than four ruffians rushed out of the woods, seized her and dragged her off forcibly toward the palace.

Alas! what could a little dog do to defend his loved one. Oh, how he wished himself a monster again that he might have power to save her. He ran forward and barked at the men and bit their heels, but they chased him away with heavy blows and dragged Zelia into the palace. Then Cherry lay down sadly in front of the door to keep watch.

"What!" thought he, "I can see the wickedness of these

men who have carried Zelia away. And yet did I not do the same thing myself? Did I not think to cast her into prison? Who knows how much more wickedness I might have done to her and to others if heaven's justice had not stopped me in time."

At that moment he heard the voice in the air repeat again: "Good actions are never unrewarded," and Cherry found himself changed into a beautiful little white pigeon.

The first use he made of his wings was to fly up to the palace windows in search of Zelia. He found one window open, entered, and flew through the whole rich palace, but nowhere did he see a single sign of his loved one. She had disappeared entirely. Then he made his way out again, full of sorrow, and resolved to fly over the whole wide world, if need be, till he found her.

He flew and he flew. Over many countries he flew, and at last he came to the waste and barren desert. Here in a cave, sharing with an old hermit his frugal breakfast, he found the lovely Zelia. Transported with joy, he flew to her, perched on

her shoulder, and expressed by every means in his power the joy he felt in seeing her. Zelia, charmed by the gentleness of the little bird, and seeing that he was trying to say he devoted himself to her, softly stroked him with her hand.

"Hast thou come to stay with me?" she cried. "Then will I love thee always."

"What hast thou done, Zelia?" cried the hermit, for even as she spoke these words the white pigeon vanished, and there in its place, in his true form once more, appeared Prince Cherry.

Moreover, the form of the hermit began to change. His soiled garments became of dazzling whiteness and his long beard and withered countenance grew into the shining hair and lovely face of the Fairy Candide.

"Prince," said she, "you regained your true form when you lost the last of the traits that made you beastlike and so won Zelia to pledge you her faith. She has always loved your true nature and now that it is no more hidden by faults, you shall always live happily together."

Then Cherry and Zelia, grasping each other by the hand, threw themselves at the Fairy's feet.

"Rise, my children," said Candide, "I shall now transport you to your kingdom and restore to Cherry the crown of which he is at last worthy."

She had scarcely spoken the words, when they found themselves in the chamber of Suliman. The old man was delighted to find his beloved pupil now a worthy son of the Good King. He willingly gave back to him his throne and became the most faithful of his subjects. So King Cherry and Queen Zelia reigned together many years and the Fairy Candide restored to Cherry the valuable ring which he had cast away. But it is said that henceforth he governed himself so well, that he was able to govern others justly, and the ring never had to prick him severely again.

Gigi and The Magic Ring*

An Italian Fairy Tale

ANNE MACDONELL

"I'll make you rich and happy yet," said Gigi (Jeejee) to his mother. "But first I must go out into the world. Maria, my sister, will take care of you while I am gone; and remember if you hear nothing of me for a time, no news is good news."

So off he went; and soon he had to pass through a town. Do you think he lost sight of poor folks there? Not a bit of it! The very first person he set eyes on was an old woman bending under the weight of a heavy oil jar she was carrying. "I wouldn't let my old grandmother carry that," said Gigi. "Here!" he cried, "give it to me." And he took the jar from her, swung it upon his shoulder, and bore it up the steep street at the top of which she lived, and set it down in her kitchen.

"Thank you, my fine young man," said the old woman, "and may good luck go with you! Will you sit down and rest a while? My place is poor, but you are right welcome."

"I have a long way before me," replied Gigi, "but a seat in your chimney corner for a minute or two I will not refuse." And he sat down and played with the dog and cat that lay before the fire.

"And where are you going, my fine young man?"

"Into the world," he answered.

"A place full of wonders, to be sure, but the road will be a bit lonesome for you. Have you no friend to go along with you?"

"No," replied Gigi.

"Then what do you say to taking my dog and cat? They are wiser than their kind, and their company might hearten you on the road."

*From *The Italian Fairy Book*, published by Frederick A. Stokes Company.

337

"That would it now," said the young man. "Fine company they would be! Thank you, good mistress."

"Three mouths to feed instead of one, 'tis true," she went on; "and sometimes the tables of the world are poorly spread. But should that happen, I have something here will help you." She went to a cupboard and brought out a ring.

"Take this," she said, "and when you want anything very much, wear it on your finger and turn it about. Then you'll see what you'll see! Never lose it or give it away, or let it be stolen or changed. For then you will be worse off than ever, and the ring might get into bad hands."

"It is too much," said Gigi politely. He knew nothing at all about jewelry and thought it was probably a poor kind of thing; but to accept it seemed like robbing a poor old woman. However, she insisted, and when he bade her good-bye the ring was in his pocket. Soon he had forgotten all about it. The dog and the cat were running along or capering about him in wild glee. When they had left the town miles behind them, the night clouds began to gather, and Gigi looked out for a place to sleep. There were no houses in sight, but there was thick wood.

"We can enter here without rapping at any man's door," said Gigi. So they made the wood their inn and all three snuggled down together and tried to go to sleep. But sleep was impossible to Gigi. He was too hungry.

"This would be the best place in all the world," he said, "if only there was something to eat. I wish—oh, I wish a table could be set before me now, with a fine supper on it." His fingers had been playing with the ring in his pocket. Now he put it on, and he was twisting and turning it about, when all at once his wish came true! It was not too dark but that he could see close by him a table spread with a fine cloth, with dishes, forks, knives and spoons, and hot, smoking roast duck on it, and delicious fruit, and more things than he had ever had for supper before.

"Oh-h-h!" he said. The dog and the cat sat up, their noses in the air. It wasn't real, of course. It couldn't be. He touched it. It was real. He smelt it. The dog and cat sniffed too and grew excited. He tasted. Oh, now there was no doubt about it! Everything was real—and so good! He ate and he drank, and the dog and cat ate along with him; and they were all three as merry as possible over their banquet in the woods.

"The old woman must have been a fairy," he said to himself. That was a ring indeed she had given him. What should he wish for next? He thought of hundreds of things—gold and silver, fine clothes for himself and his mother and Maria, horses and carriages, guns and swords; but the wishes came tumbling on top of each other, head over heels and all fell in a jumbled heap.

"How stupid I am," said Gigi, "I can't imagine what I wish for most. Well, I've often heard that people lose their heads when good luck comes their way; but I'd like to keep mine on my shoulders." Then he lay down again on the bed of leaves, without wishing for anything, and the dog was at his head and the cat at his feet; and they all fell fast asleep.

He woke next morning early, and was up and astir, with the dog and the cat at his heels; and everything about him shone and sang. There was nothing so fine in all the world as stepping out into the fresh morning world. Was he wishing for horses and carriages? He laughed at the idea. Two good legs and a sapling from the wood where he had slept, were better than the King's state coach. Up hill and down dale, through wood and field, by stream and meadow he went, easily, cheerily, and his two good friends were the best of company.

At last he came to a fine palace built on the roadside; and out of an upper window looked a beautiful maiden, and she smiled as Gigi passed below.

"Oh, I could look at her all day long!" he said. "But she would never speak to a poor boy like me," he sighed. "Oh, I wish—;" and as he said the word, he remembered he could have whatever he wanted in the world. The ring was on his finger on the instant; and he turned it about as he said, "I want a fine mansion, but much finer it must be than the one that lovely girl is looking out of. And I want it just opposite hers."

In a twinkling he stood, no longer in the open road, but in a great palace, more splendid than any he had ever seen; and when he looked out at the window, there was a maiden at the window opposite, and smiling, quite plainly smiling at him. Yet he was still Gigi, in his old clothes with the dust of the road on them; and his dog and his cat were there at his heels. Well, decidedly it was a ring worth having! He wished for fine clothes. They were on his back. For servants. They came at his call. For meat and drink. He did not know the names of all the fine things that were set before him.

"Perhaps she would speak to me now," he said. There was no doubt about that. The very next morning her father and mother came and called on him, and said they wished to make the acquaintance of their new neighbor, who was evidently an eminent gentleman. They could hardly take their eyes off his fine furniture, his fine clothes, and the gold chain he wore about his neck. They flattered him a great deal; and Gigi thought they were very amiable people indeed.

Next day he returned their call, and received a cordial welcome. He was presented to their only daughter, Maliarda, and the two young people quickly made friends. Before the day was over Gigi had asked her hand in marriage, and her parents, who thought he must be at least a great prince, or favored by an enchanter, were only too glad to consent. They thought Gigi would be very useful to them.

Now, on the eve of the wedding-day they all paid a visit to Gigi, and while they talked together, Maliarda asked him to tell her how it came about that his splendid house had sprung up so suddenly. He was the simplest, truthfullest lad in the world; and so he told her all about his journeying into the world, his meeting with the old woman, her present of the ring, and everything that followed. "And do you keep that precious ring always on your finger?" she asked. "Always!" he replied. "Night and day, waking and sleeping."

She whispered the secret to her mother. When they were having supper, the mother poured something from a phial into Gigi's wine while his back was turned, and into the plates of his dog and cat under the table. It was a sleep-drink she had given them; and soon after Gigi's eyes began to close, and the cat and dog slept and snored.

"Your lord is weary after hunting," said the father to the servant who was waiting. "Carry him to that couch; and we will take our leave." Then he called all the servants together and said, "Come to my house. I have your master's orders to instruct you in your duties tomorrow." And they followed him out of the palace. But Maliarda stayed behind a moment; going up to Gigi, as he lay in a deep sleep, she took the ring from his finger and fled. His dog and cat were too drowsy to warn him.

Once out of the house, she put the ring on her finger, and as she turned it, she said, "I wish that lord Gigi's palace be moved to the highest, steepest, snowiest peak of yonder mountain range!" And on the instant the palace was removed to where she had decreed. Maliarda ran back to her parents' house and told what had happened. They feigned surprise, and turning to the servants, informed them of the vanishing of their master's house, and said, "Your master must have been an evil magician. He has played a cruel trick on you. What an escape our daughter has had!" Then they gave the servants money and dismissed them.

When Gigi awoke next morning he was shivering and shaking. Where was he? In his own palace, though evidently he had not gone to bed. And there were his two friends the dog and the cat. But why was he so cold? He got up, walked to the window, and looked out, expecting to see the palace of his neighbors, and perhaps thinking to catch a glimpse of Maliarda. This was his wedding day! But all familiar things had vanished, and he saw only mountain peaks and snow and sky. What did it mean? He rang the bell violently. No one answered. He called for his valet, for his butler, for his cook, for his coachman. Nobody came. The house was quite still. He searched upstairs and downstairs, and found he was alone in his palace save for the dog and cat, and on the top of the highest mountain peak. Beneath him could be seen only ice, snow, and terrible precipices!

"Who has done this to me?" he cried. "Have I an enemy? Well, what does it matter? I have only to wish myself down and turn my ring." But his ring was gone! Who was the thief? He tried to recall what had happened. He had been very sleepy at supper time. He did not remember getting up from the table or bidding his guests good-night. And only one person knew the value of the ring—! Oh, could his beautiful Maliarda be a traitor?

Impossible to get down the mountain. There was no path; and if he tried to make one, he would perish in the snow, or roll over into some terrible precipice. And there was not two days' food in all the palace!

Now the dog and the cat were sorely troubled at their master's sadness, and soon they found out the reason of it. "Have patience, dear master," they said. "Where a man dare not walk, we can. Give us a day, and see if we do not get back your ring."

"You are my only hope," answered Gigi. He fed them well, and then opened the door for them. So the dog and cat set off, and they slipped, and slid, and crawled, and hung on, and climbed and sprang, and helped each other, and never stopped till they were down on the green plain. There they came to a river. The cat sat on the dog's back, and the dog swam across.

At last they came to the palace of the faithless Maliarda. By this time it was night, and the household were all in bed and asleep. Of course all doors and windows were barred; but in the back door was a little cat-hole; and they squeezed through one after the other. Then said the cat to the dog, "Stay you here and keep guard. I will go upstairs and see what can be done." She slipped up and went to the door of Maliarda's room. But the door was shut, and there was no little hole to

creep through. The cat sat down and thought and thought; and as she sat there thinking, a little mouse ran across the floor. The cat smelt her in the dark, put out a paw and caught her. What a delicious mouthful she would be! But the mouse squeaked out piteously, and begged that her life might be saved. "Very well," said the cat; "but in return you must promise to gnaw a hole in that door opposite, for I have business inside."

The mouse began to gnaw; and she gnawed as hard as she could. She gnawed and she gnawed till all her teeth were broken; and still the hole was so little she couldn't get in herself, let alone the cat.

"Have you any young ones?" said the cat to the mouse.

"Oh yes, I have seven or eight, the finest little family ever you saw."

"Bring me the littlest, then." And the mouse ran away, and came back with a tiny mite of a mousikin.

Then said the cat to the little mousikin, "Now be quick and clever and you'll save your mother's life. Get in through that hole; creep into the lady's bed, and take off the ring from her finger. If you can't get it, bite her finger softly, and she'll take off the ring herself without waking. Then bring it to me."

Mousikin ran in, but in a minute she was back again.

"The lady has no ring on her finger," she cheeped.

"Then it is in her mouth. Go again; creep into her bed; hit her nose with your tail. She will open her mouth and the ring will drop out. Bring it here to me, and you'll have saved your mother's life."

Off ran mousikin, and in another minute she was back with the ring. The mice scurried back to their holes. The cat slipped down the stairs, made a sign to the dog, and they both crept out through the hole in the back door.

"Oh, how pleased our master will be," said the cat.

But the dog was not in a good humor. He was the bigger, and he would have liked to have found the ring and carried it back to Gigi himself. So when they came once more to the river, he said, "If you give me the ring, I'll carry you across." But the cat refused. They quarrelled, and the ring fell into the river. On the instant a fish snapped at it as if it had been a pretty fly. But the dog jumped in, and dived for the fish, caught it and got the ring from its mouth. Then he said to the cat in a grand manner, "Jump on my back, pussy, and I will carry you across." The cat obeyed, but very sulkily; and soon they were on the other side. Not a word did they say to each other that was not angry and quarrelsome all the way up the mountain. The sun had risen by the time they reached the top; and there was their master waiting for them at the palace door.

"Have you the ring?" he cried. And the dog dropped it at his feet.

"But 'twas I got it back. By my cleverness, all alone, I got it back," cried the cat.

"How could you ever have reached the place at all had I not carried you over the river?" roared the dog.

"But 'twas I caught the mouse that gnawed the hole—!"

And the dog broke in growling, "It was the least you could do after the trouble I took."

"Dear friends! dear friends!" said Gigi, "do not quarrel! You have both been brave and clever and faithful. You have saved my life between you. I love one as much as the other." And with one hand he caressed the dog, and with the other the cat, and took them into the palace and fed them both. Then they were both the best of friends again, and told their master all their adventures by the way. "Now," said Gigi, "we'll say good-bye to this mountain." He put the ring on his finger, turned it and said, "I wish my palace to descend to the plain and the palace of the faithless Maliarda and her parents to be up here among the ice and snow!"

Next moment both wishes were fulfilled. He was down in the green and flowering plain; and the wicked three in their palace were up on the freezing mountain-top.

Did they ever get down any more? Well, I have heard that Gigi had a little mercy on them after some days of anger. He turned his ring, and wished the faithless three half-way down, whence they could scramble to the level, where trees grew and where there were some scattered huts. But their palace was left up on the top; and much good did it do them there! He never saw them again.

As for Gigi, he soon tired of his fine palace; and when a year and a day had passed from the time he left home, he said to his trusty companions,

"Come, my friends, we'll take to the road again. I have a longing to see my mother and my sister Maria." So he turned back to his own village. On his way he passed through the town where he had met the old woman who had given him the ring, but he could not find her nor hear any news of her. So he hurried on home.

His mother and sister hardly knew him again. That fine young man with the grand clothes their Gigi! Not possible!

"Have you found fortune already, my son?"

"I carry it on my finger." He laughed, and held out the ring.

"Very pretty," said his mother. "But instead of chattering here I should be getting ready your dinner. And nothing you like in the house! Make haste, Maria!"

"Don't trouble," said Gigi. "See what a fine cook I have become!" And there in the middle of the kitchen stood a table loaded with good things to eat—macaroni and roast goose, and grapes and oranges and wine.

"Oh-h-h-h!" cried the two women.

"Sit down and eat," said the young man, "and I'll tell you all my adventures."

They sat down; he loaded their plates; but they could hardly swallow a mouthful for their wonder at all Gigi told them. When he came to the tale of Maliarda's deceit, they wept and said he was much better at home with them.

"So I think," replied Gigi; "and I am not sure if the old woman's best gift to me be not my good friends here under the table."

"To be sure!" said his mother. "What should a strong hearty young fellow like you do with an enchanted ring? Fine mischief it has got you into already! Give it to me, and I'll hide it away in my wedding-chest among the best sheets and the winter coverlets. With the money you have on you, you can set up for yourself."

"That is so," he replied, "And if the old wife were to pass by one day, who knows but I might give her the ring back again."

Is the ring still in the wedding-chest? Does Gigi ever take it out, put it on his finger and wish? I do not know. When I have passed his way I have seem him ploughing with a fine team of fat oxen, and singing the while, or in the woods with his good friends the cat and dog, for they are still alive and hearty. He has not yet gone back to live in a palace; but all the neighbors envy his mother her good son Gigi.

THE BALLAD OF EAST AND WEST

RUDYARD KIPLING

*Oh, East is East, and West is West, and
never the twain shall meet,
Till Earth and Sky stand presently at
God's great Judgment Seat;
But there is neither East nor West, Border, nor Breed, nor Birth,
When two strong men stand face to face,
though they come from the ends of
the earth!*

Ka'mal is out with twenty men to raise the Border side,
And he has lifted the Colonel's mare that is the Colonel's pride.
He has lifted her out of the stable-door between the dawn and
the day,
And turned the calkins upon her feet, and ridden her far away.
Then up and spoke the Colonel's son that led a troop of the Guides:
"Is there never a man of all my men can say where Ka'mal hides?"
Then up and spoke Mo-ham'med Khan, the son of the Res'sal-dar':
"If ye know the track of the morning-mist, ye know where his
pickets are.
"At dusk he harries the Ab'a-zai'—at dawn he is into Bo-nair',

Kamal, the outlawed mountaineer, from the East Indian Border-land, has ridden out with twenty men and stolen
the English Colonel's mare that is the Colonel's pride.

"But he must go by Fort Buk-loh' to
   his own place to fare.
"So if ye gallop to Fort Buk-loh' as fast
   as a bird can fly,
"By the favour of God ye may cut him
   off ere he win to the Tongue of Ja-gai'.
"But if he be past the Tongue of
   Ja-gai', right swiftly turn ye then,
"For the length and the breadth of
   that grisly plain is sown with
   Ka'mal's men.

In the Plain of Jagai lie Kamal's men and
the bolts of their rifles snick.

"There is rock to the left, and rock to the right, and low lean thorn
   between,
"And ye may hear a breech-bolt snick where never a man is seen."
The Colonel's son has taken a horse, and a raw rough dun was he,
With the mouth of a bell and the heart of Hell and the head of a
   gallows-tree.
The Colonel's son to the Fort has won, they bid him stay to eat—
Who rides at the tail of a Border thief, he sits not long at his meat.
He's up and away from Fort Buk-loh' as fast as he can fly,
Till he was aware of his father's mare in the gut of the Tongue
   of Ja-gai',
Till he was aware of his father's mare with Ka'mal upon her back,
And when he could spy the white of her eye, he made the pistol
   crack.
He has fired once, he has fired twice, but the whistling ball went wide.
"Ye shoot like a soldier," Ka'mal said.   "Show now if ye can ride!"

It's up and over the Tongue of Ja-gai', as blown dust-devils go,
The dun he fled like a stag of ten, but the mare like a barren doe.
The dun he leaned against the bit and slugged his head above,
But the red mare played with the snaffle-bars, as a maiden plays
    with a glove.
There was rock to the left and rock to the right, and low lean
    thorn between,
And thrice he heard a breech-bolt snick tho' never a man was seen.
They have ridden the low moon out of the sky, their hoofs drum
    up the dawn,
The dun he went like a wounded bull, but the mare like a new-
    roused fawn.
The dun he fell at a water-course—in a woeful heap fell he,
And Ka'mal has turned the red mare back, and pulled the rider
    free.
He has knocked the pistol out of his hand—small room was there
    to strive,

Kamal spares the Colonel's son. "If I had raised my
hand," said he, "my men would have shot you dead to
feed the jackals and kites."

"'Twas only by favour of mine,"
    quoth he, "ye rode so long
    alive:
"There was not a rock for twenty
    mile, there was not a clump
    of tree,
"But covered a man of my own
    men with his rifle cocked on
    his knee.
"If I had raised my bridle-hand,
    as I have held it low,
"The little jackals that flee so
    fast were feasting all in a row.
"If I had bowed my head on my
    breast, as I have held it high,
"The kite that whistles above
    us now were gorged till she
    could not fly."
Lightly answered the Colonel's
    son: "Do good to bird and
    beast,

"But count who come for the broken meats before thou makest a feast.

"If there should follow a thousand swords to carry my bones away,

"Belike the price of a jackal's meal were more than a thief could pay.

"They will feed their horse on the standing crop, their men on the garnered grain,

"The thatch of the byres will serve their fires when all the cattle are slain.

"But if thou thinkest the price be fair,—thy brethren wait to sup,

Lightly answered the Colonel's son: "Do good to bird and beast. Feed me to jackals and kites; but first remember who will come to pick up the bits from the feast! Remember a thousand English swords will come to pick up my bones. They will slay your cattle and trample your crops, they will seize your grain and burn your barns! Can a thief pay such a price as that just to give the jackals a feast? Howl if you think the price fair, you dog, and call in your brothers, the jackals."

"The hound is kin to the jackal-spawn,—howl, dog, and call them up!

"And if thou thinkest the price be high, in steer and gear and stack,

"Give me my father's mare again, and I'll fight my own way back!"

Ka'mal has gripped him by the hand and set him upon his feet.

"No talk shall be of dogs," said he, "when wolf and grey wolf meet.

"May I eat dirt if thou has hurt of me in deed or breath;

"What dam of lances brought thee forth to jest at the dawn with Death?"

Lightly answered the Colonel's son: "I hold by the blood of my clan:

"Take up the mare for my father's gift—by God, she has carried a man!"

The red mare ran to the Colonel's son, and muzzled against his breast;

"We be two strong men," said Ka'mal then, "but she loveth the younger best.

"So she shall go with a lifter's dower, my turquoise-studded rein,

"My broidered saddle and saddle-cloth, and silver stirrups twain."

Kamal loves the Colonel's son for the courage he has shown. He gives him freely his father's horse with his own trappings and jewelled reins. Then the Colonel's son loves Kamal for the largeness of his heart; he gives him his second pistol and they vow to be brothers and friends. So is there neither East nor West when two strong men have met.

The Colonel's son a pistol drew, and held it muzzle-end,
"Ye have taken the one from a foe," said he; "will ye take the mate from a friend?"
"A gift for a gift," said Ka'mal straight; "a limb for the risk of a limb.
"Thy father has sent his son to me, I'll send my son to him!"
With that he whistled his only son, that dropped from a mountain-crest—
He trod the ling like a buck in spring, and he looked like a lance in rest.
"Now here is thy master," Ka'mal said, "who leads a troop of the Guides,
"And thou must ride at his left side as shield on shoulder rides.
"Till Death or I cut loose the tie, at camp and board and bed,
"Thy life is his—thy fate it is to guard him with thy head.
"So, thou must eat the White Queen's meat, and all her foes are thine,
"And thou must harry thy father's hold for the peace of the Border-line.
"And thou must make a trooper tough and hack thy way to power—
"Belike they will raise thee to Res'sal-dar' when I am hanged in Pe-shawur'."
They have looked each other between the eyes, and there they found no fault,
They have taken the Oath of the Brother-in-Blood on leavened bread and salt:
They have taken the Oath of the Brother-in-Blood on fire and fresh-cut sod,
On the hilt and the haft of the Khyber knife, and the Wondrous Names of God.

THROUGH FAIRY HALLS

Kamal's son goes with the Colonel's son back to Fort Bukloh, sent as a gift from Kamal to serve the White Queen of England, to be no more an outlaw but perhaps to become a Ressaldar, Indian Captain of Indian troops in the British Indian army.

The Colonel's son he rides the mare and Ka'mal's boy the dun,
And two have come back to Fort Buk-loh' where there went forth but one.
And when they drew to the Quarter-Guard, full twenty swords flew clear—
There was not a man but carried his feud with the blood of the mountaineer.
"Ha' done! ha' done!" said the Colonel's son. "Put up the steel at your sides!
"Last night ye had struck at a Border thief—to-night 'tis a man of the Guides!"

Oh, East is East, and West is West, and never the twain shall meet,
Till Earth and Sky stand presently at God's great Judgment Seat;
But there is neither East nor West, Border, nor Breed, nor Birth,
When two strong men stand face to face, though they come from the ends of the earth!

Columbine and Her Playfellows of The Italian Pantomime

Heigho!   Heigho for the holiday time,
And the merry freaks of the pantomime!

From the very earliest days one of the favorite forms of entertainment in many countries of the world has been the pantomime or dumb show. In it the actors bring out the action of the play by means of their motions only, without speaking any words. This dumb show is accompanied by music, dancing, and singing, and at holiday times particularly it has always drawn a merry throng, to add to the joy of the season. In Italy certain characters became regular parts of every pantomime and from Italy they spread to England, France and the rest of the world. Though the old Mother Goose Rhymes and Fairy Tales were often the subjects of the pantomimes, interwoven with all these and dancing through them all, Columbine, Pierrot and Harlequin gaily chased each other. The stories about these merrymakers are somewhat different in each play that is given, but in general their characters remain very much the same.

Once upon a time there stood on one corner of the market place in a little village of Italy, a small pink stucco house, on the lower floor of which was a shop, bursting over with fruit and fresh vegetables. Here lived an old merchant named Pantaloon and his beautiful daughter, Columbine. Columbine was a merry creature, always dancing, always skipping, her little toes twinkling, her gauzy skirts rippling! For sheer joy she danced, like a sunbeam, here, there and everywhere.

Haste thee, Nymph and bring with thee, *
Jest and youthful Jollity.
Come and trip it, as you go,
On the light fantastic toe

*From Milton's *L'Allegro.

354

THROUGH FAIRY HALLS

But Pantaloon was grave and sober as an owl. Day after day he sat in a room filled with books, directly over the shop, and pored over some monstrous volume, while Columbine served their customers.

Dismal, doleful Pantaloon,
Downcast eyes and shuffle-shoon,
Up to ears in volumes old,
Buried deep in must and mould.

Whenever he saw Columbine dancing, he shook his great cane at her, and bade her be prim and sedate. But Columbine did not like to stay always close to the shop and sell cabbages and turnips, onions and garlic. Sometimes she tripped out into the sunny meadows to go a-maying among kindly shepherd folk who tended their snow white sheep.

*While the ploughman, near at hand**
Whistles o'er the furrowed land,
And the milkmaid singeth blithe,
And the mower whets his scythe,
And every shepherd tells his tale
Under the hawthorn in the dale.

Columbine returned blithely from such hey-days in the meadows, her arms filled with flowers, but always Pantaloon

*From Milton's *L'Allegro*.

greeted her angrily, tossed her flowers out of the window, threatened her with his cane and set her to work again. For her entertainment when work was over, he sent his servant to bring her upstairs, then he set her down primly before him and preached to her with a huge opened book on his knees.

Now Pantaloon's servant was the Clown.

Simple Simon, silly goose,
Blockhead, booby, most obtuse!

Whatever Pantaloon did, the Clown would mimic. While Pantaloon preached to Columbine, the Clown sat humped over a monstrous book and preached to a little white pig.

One day Pantaloon, quite beside himself with Columbine's frisking, sent the Clown to their young neighbor, Pierrot, to bid him come and mind Columbine, while Columbine minded the shop.

To bottle up her spirits,
Put snuffers on her joy,
To bridle, bit, and curb her,
Bring here that pensive boy.

So the Clown hitched his pig to a little cart and went riding off to fetch Pierrot.

Now Pierrot was a lovable fellow who had often brought nosegays to Columbine, and he was overjoyed to come and be her companion at Pantaloon's request. But he was quiet and thoughtful, and his garments were white with spots of black, like the moonlight gleam among shadows. Columbine had been longing for a gay play-fellow, but Pierrot sang to her, to the accompaniment of his lute, of the soft, tender beauty of moonlight, of the restful peace of cool shadows, the quiet calm of still waters, and the song of the nightingale.

*Sweet bird, that shunn'st the noise of folly,**
Most musical, most melancholy!

Now Columbine would have nothing to do with shadows or

*From Milton's *Il Penseroso*.

quiet. She would twinkle and beam like the sunbeam and dance everywhere. So Columbine teased poor Pierrot and he found no way to please her.

One day while they tended the shop, and Pantaloon sat in

the room above with his nose in some musty old tome, Columbine hid from Pierrot. He chased her here and there, in and out, in and out, just as the shadows of leaves play hide-and-seek with the sunbeams. Then she slipped away altogether, left him alone to sell onions and whisked away to the woodland.

As she wandered through a beautiful grove of beech trees, she threw back her head and lifted her arms and cried out for a play-fellow. Suddenly the wind came frolicking by, flipped her gauze skirts, tweaked her hair, and snatched off a rose from her bosom. Then it ducked away, swirled around a great tree and bang! there bounced out on the other side a jolly gay fellow in scarlet and yellow, who leaped up high in the air, turned hand-springs, and bounced like a rubber ball. For a moment Columbine held back and knew not what to think, but Harlequin seized her by the hand and then heigho! for a frolic!

> *Quips and Cranks and wanton Wiles,* *
> *Nods and Becks and wreathèd Smiles,*
> *Sport that wrinkled Care derides,*
> *And Laughter, holding both his sides!*

As Columbine frolicked with Harlequin, the Clown came through the woods, sent out by the angry Pantaloon, to look for the missing Columbine. Master Clown looked in the most impossible places, he bent from his hips with his knees very stiff, and peeped under tiny flowers where not even a grasshopper could have hid, he stretched up his neck like a giraffe's, to look into birds' nests in the trees, and twisted himself into bowknots as he peered everywhere about. What with looking where they could not have been, and never

*From Milton's *L'Allegro.*

where they might have been, he backed into Columbine and Harlequin and stumbled straight over them. Then he stood on his head, shook his feet in their faces, and went running off on his hands to tell his tale to his master.

Soon, sputtering and angry, shaking his head and his fists, and threatening with his cane, along through the woods came Pantaloon. Leading the way before him, importantly swaggered the Clown.

Columbine and Harlequin were still dancing, laughing, chasing, but they spied the two coming a long way off, and hid behind a tree. When Pantaloon and the Clown were almost upon them, booh! out popped Harlequin, over bowled the two in astonishment, and off danced Harlequin and Columbine. Pantaloon and the Clown picked themselves up and gave chase, but just as they were hot on the heels of the pair, the Clown tripped over a straw and fell, while his master went sprawling on top of him. The chase was long and merry. Pantaloon and the Clown caught a straying donkey and flung themselves both on his back, but the donkey balked, pitched Pantaloon into a rain-barrel and the Clown into a tub of whitewash. So Harlequin and Columbine soon out-distanced their pursuers.

Meantime, Pierrot, left alone, set out sorrowfully to find his beloved Columbine, and he sang sad songs, as he went, to his lute. At last he came to a country fair, where the shepherd folk were gathered with their sheep. Some had joined in quaint folk dances, while others crowded about the place where tumblers were giving a show.

> —*many a youth and many a maid**
> *Dancing in the chequered shade,*
> *And young and old come forth to play*
> *On a sunshine holiday.*

In the midst of the crowd, Pierrot spied Columbine and Harlequin. From a shepherd he purchased a tiny white lamb, with a silver bell on a little blue ribbon about its neck.

*From Milton's *L'Allegro*.

Humbly he offered the gift to Columbine. Columbine took it and kissed it, but Harlequin began at once to play mischievous pranks on Pierrot. He flipped his clothes, he tweaked off his cap, he pulled his hair, he startled him with strange and sudden dartings. And Columbine joined in all the laughter at Pierrot's expense. She put the little lamb down on the ground as she watched and let it wander away. At last, seeing how much she seemed to prefer the madcap Harlequin, Pierrot sadly left her.

That evening Columbine came back to Pantaloon's shop, but as days went by, she had less and less time for Pierrot. Harlequin was always popping in at the window, Crash bang! and leading her off for a frolic. So there came a day when Pierrot could endure it no more. He packed all his belongings into a bundle, tied the bundle to the end of a stick, sang one last farewell song to his lute, below Columbine's empty balcony, and set out into the world alone, with the stick slung over his shoulder.

At first, when Columbine found he was gone, she tossed her head and pretended that she did not care at all. She still raced off with Harlequin, while Pantaloon and the Clown gave chase and were outwitted at every turn by the waggish tricks of Harlequin. But at last, as month after month passed by, Columbine began to miss Pierrot sadly. She grew tired of always frolicking. Without the thoughtful quiet of Pierrot to rest in, she could not enjoy the bounding merriment of Harlequin. In the cool and peaceful shadows, by still waters, in the tender moonlight, she thought of the comrade who was gone and longed to call him home. Even Harlequin could not now make her glad. Her feet began to stop twinkling and she left off skipping and dancing. Then Pantaloon nodded his head, well content. He thought he had quenched the bubbling spring of her joy and frozen her up at last into the stiff little creature he wanted.

Gradually there came to the village the fame of a certain poet, who wrote most beautiful ballads and plays, and of whom all Italy spoke. One market day, when the village square was filled with peasant folk, a stage was set up in one corner of the market place. A play by the famous poet was to be given there. Harlequin came and begged Columbine to go. To please him, she left the shop and sadly joined the crowd.

The curtains parted and the play began. There appeared on the stage—how strange! a maiden who was the image of Columbine, and a youth like Harlequin. Then, yes!—there was a Pierrot too. And the play told how Pierrot had loved Columbine, and Columbine had deserted him, to play all day with Harlequin. The Columbine and Harlequin were only an actor and actress, but when Pierrot began to sing—ah! Columbine knew that was

Pierrot himself. And he sang of the loneliness of the world and the sadness ever in his heart, and the longing, longing for Columbine—sang till Columbine began to weep and the shepherds about were moved to tears. Pierrot himself had written the play. Pierrot himself was the poet.

When it was over and all the people applauded, she held out her hands to Pierrot. Pierrot had seen her from the first and he sprang down at once to her side. Then Columbine asked his forgiveness. In her joy at seeing him again, she forgot all about Harlequin and, hand in hand with Pierrot, wandered off into the meadows. For a moment Harlequin hung his head and collapsed like a sail when the wind dies down, but in another instant, he had flipped the skirts of a shepherd maid and was off at his boisterous pranks as before.

At evening Pierrot and Columbine came back to Pantaloon's shop with their arms full of flowers. They turned out all the onions and cabbages, turnips and garlic, and changed the place into a flower shop. Pantaloon shook his head—he could not understand such doings—but when he knew that Columbine had chosen Pierrot to be her companion forever, he was well content. Up in his room, buried deep in books, he preached no more to Columbine, but to the clown and his little white pig. So Columbine kept the shop while Pierrot wrote his poems, and every day her bubbling brightness seemed more joyous still for the quiet and calm repose of Pierrot. As to Harlequin, he often popped in at the window Crash bang! to lead them away for a frolic. And then—

With a hey, and a ho, and a hey nony no,
Racing and chasing, away they go!

THROUGH FAIRY HALLS

The Six Swans

A German Fairy Tale

Once upon a time a King went a-hunting in a great wood, and he pursued a wild boar so eagerly that none of his people could follow him. Never once did he stop to look about him until nightfall, and then he found he had quite lost his way. As he was searching for a path, he suddenly saw before him an ugly old woman, and she was a witch, though the King did not know it.

"Good dame," said the King, "can you show me the way out of the wood?"

"Oh, yes, my lord King," she answered, "but on one condition, and if you do not fulfill it, you shall never get home again."

"What is the condition?" asked the King.

"I have a daughter," said the old dame, "as fair as any in the world, and if you will promise to make her your Queen, then and then only will I lead you safely out of the forest."

Well, the King was in such a fix, he knew not what else to do, so he consented, and the old witch led him straight off to her hut. There sat her daughter by the fire, but though she was very beautiful, she did not please the King. He could not even look at her without an inward shudder. Nevertheless, as he had promised, he took her before him on his horse, the old woman showed him the way, and soon he was safely back in his castle.

Now the King had been married before and already had seven beautiful children whom he loved better than all the world, but he knew well enough that this strange new Queen would be only too likely to do them some mischief; so he took them secretly and hid them away in a lonely castle deep in the midst of a wood. The road to this place was so hard to find, that the King himself would never have found it, had it not been for a certain clew of yarn that unrolled itself when he threw it down before him and showed him the way through the forest.

Now the King went so often to see his dear children that the Queen was displeased at his absence. She grew curious and wanted to know why he so often went out alone. So she gave herself no rest until she discovered the secret of the clew. Then she made some little white shirts and sewed in each one a charm she had learned from her mother, and when the King next rode a-hunting, she took the little shirts and the ball of yarn and went off into the wood. Sure enough, the yarn showed her the way, and there she came to the hidden castle. When the children saw some one in the distance coming toward them, they thought it was their dear father and ran, jumping for joy, to meet him. But the wicked witch threw over each as he drew near, one of the little shirts, and immediately they were no longer youths, but changed into swans, that mounted up into the air and flew, soaring over the tree-tops. Then the Queen went home laughing hideously to think she was rid of the troublesome children.

But it happened that the little maid had not run out with her brothers, so the Queen knew nothing at all about her. She had seen what had happened from the window, and all day long she went sorrowfully about, picking up the feathers that had dropped from her brothers' wings in the courtyard. But when night came on, she said to herself, "I must stay here no longer. I shall go and seek for my brothers."

So she fled away farther still into the wood. She went on all that night and the next day until she could go no longer for weariness. At last she saw a rude hut before her. In she went and found there a room with six little beds, and six chairs, and six plates and knives on the table. So she guessed that this might be the place where her brothers were staying, and she crept under one of the beds to wait and see what would happen.

When it was near the time of sun-setting, she heard a rustling sound and behold! six handsome white swans came flying in at

the window. They alighted on the ground and blew at one
another until they had blown all their feathers off; then they
stripped off their swan-skins as though they had been shirts.
The maiden knew them at once for her brothers and crept gladly
from under the bed. The brothers, too, were overjoyed to see
their sister, but even as they embraced her, they cried:

"Alas! we can only stay with you one little quarter of an hour.
For that length of time every evening we keep our human shapes,
but after that we are changed again into swans."

"Can nothing be done to free you?" cried their sister, weeping.

"Oh, no!" they replied. "The work would be too hard for
you. For six whole years you would be obliged never to speak
or laugh, and you would have, during that time, to spin, weave

and make six shirts out of aster-down. If you were to let fall a single word before the work was ended, all would be lost."

Just as the brothers finished speaking, the quarter of an hour came to an end, they changed into swans and flew out of the window. At this, the maiden made up her mind on the spot to set her brothers free, no matter what it might cost her. So she went out into the wood and began gathering down from the asters. Every day she spent in the house of her brothers; she kept the beds white and clean; she fetched the wood and the vegetables; she watched the pot on the fire and always had supper ready when they came home. For a quarter of an hour each evening they would be her brothers, then off they must fly again as white swans. But, though she made them so comfortable, the Princess never spoke a word to them or laughed one little laugh. By moonlight and starlight she was always out gathering down. No matter how lonely seemed the dark forest, nor how black the shadows, she was always gathering down.

When she had been going on like this for a long, long time, it happened that the King of that country went a-hunting in the wood. He got separated from his companions and was wandering about at nightfall all alone, when whom should he see sitting up in a tree and carding her down, but a beautiful maiden.

"Who art thou?" asked the King, struck with her loveliness

She answered him not a word.

"What art thou doing up in that tree?"

She answered him not a word. He spoke to her in all the languages he knew, but still she answered him never a word. The King, however, felt a very great love for her rise in his breast, so he climbed the tree, brought her down, cast his mantel about her, set her up on the horse before him, and started off toward the castle. But the maiden wrung her hands and pointed back to her bags full of aster-down. So the King, seeing she wished to have them with her, returned and got them, put them also up on his horse and galloped away once more.

When they reached the castle, the King caused the maiden to be clad in rich garments, and her beauty shone as bright as the morning, but still not a single word would she utter. Her modesty and gentleness so pleased the King that he chose her for his wife and would have no other in all the world. Accordingly, they were married. But it happened that there dwelt with the King as head of his household, a wicked old dame, who wanted no handsome new queen in the castle to take the management out of her hands, so she began at once to speak ill of her.

"Who knows where the maid can have come from?" she said, "and dumb as a door-post, too! She is probably some beggar maid who has stolen the heart of the King!"

To all this evil-speaking the Queen made no answer whatever. No matter how cruel or untrue the words of the old woman were, she never once opened her lips. Sometimes the King begged her to speak with loving words and endearments, but, though her heart longed to reply, she answered never a word. Always she was spinning and weaving her aster-down, cutting and making her shirts.

Year after year went by, till at last the old woman began to whisper and tell abroad that the sweet young queen was a witch who had cast a spell over the King. Now the people could not understand the silent Queen who was always at work and would speak no word, nor stop to join in their festivities, so at last, aroused by the wicked old dame, they went to the King in a mass, proclaimed her a witch and demanded that she be burnt at the stake. Then the King was so sad that there was no end to his sadness, for he still loved his wife very dearly, but the Queen never spoke a word to save herself, so the people seized her out of the castle and dragged her off to the stake.

Now when all this happened, it was the very last day of the six years during which she had neither spoken nor laughed in order to free her brothers. The six shirts were ready, all except one that wanted a sleeve. When she was dragged to the stake, the Queen carried the six shirts on her arm, but just as she mounted the pile of fagots, and the fire was about to be kindled, she cried out aloud, for there, through the air flying toward her, came six beautiful snow-white swans. With rushing wings they flew and dropped in a circle about her. Quickly she threw the shirts over their heads. Then off dropped their swan skins and her brothers stood safe and sound before her. Only, as one shirt wanted the left sleeve, her youngest brother had a swan's wing instead of a left arm. While the King looked on in astonishment, the brothers and sister embraced and kissed each other. Then the Queen went up to the King and said:

"Dearest husband, now I may dare to speak and tell you I am innocent!" So she told all her tale and the King was over-joyed, while the people fell at her feet and begged her forgiveness. As to the old dame, when the Queen sent for her dearly loved father to visit her at her court, it soon appeared that she was the very same wicked old witch who had forced the Queen's father to marry her daughter, and taught the daughter the charm by means of which she had turned the young princes into swans, so she and her daughter were both cast on the fire and that was the end of the witches. But the King and Queen lived many years in great peace and joy with their father and six good brothers.

DONN P. CRANE

The Two Bad Bargains
A Servian Tale

In days gone by there lived a couple who had one only son, named Vladimir. Now Vladimir was a lad both strong and of good courage, yet of so compassionate a heart that if he saw but a dog in trouble, nothing would do but he must stop and help it. After his schooling was finished, Vladimir's father gave him a ship freighted with various sorts of merchandise and bade him go trading about the world and grow rich. Vladimir put to sea at once, in high spirits and good hope, his head full of visions of mighty fortunes to win; but he was not gone many days from port when he met a vessel swarming with savage Turks, from whence he heard noise of much weeping and wailing. Boldly Vladimir drew alongside the Turkish vessel and demanded, "Why comes there such noise of weeping from out your hold?"

The Turkish sailors made answer with ugly grins, "We have captured a ship load of slaves to sell in the great slave market of Stamboul. It is those who are chained that are weeping."

Then Vladimir must needs cry out, "How much are they worth—your ship load of slaves?" and the Captain of the slave ship answered, "As much as the value of all your lading!"

Now Vladimir saw trembling before him all his visions of fortune, if he traded his cargo to good advantage, yet the weeping of those unhappy slaves went tugging at his heart strings, and tugging, and tugging, till at last he cried out, "I will trade all my merchandise for those poor creatures."

The Captain agreed, you may be sure, and the exchange was made on the spot. Vladimir gave up all his cargo and took the slaves instead. As they came aboard and passed him by, he asked each one whence he came and told him he was free to go home. One and all, they fell with great joy at his feet. Only at the very last, there came before him an old woman who held close to her side a pale and beautiful maiden. This old woman still continued to weep.

"For," said she, "our home is so far and so far away that we can never get back again. This maid is sole daughter to a mighty king, and I am her nurse. One day we wandered in the garden too far from the palace, and the Turks fell upon us and dragged us off prisoners. Since then we have sailed both weeks and months. We shall never find our way back. Pray let us remain with you."

So Vladimir set the other slaves ashore, but he felt great pity for the beautiful maiden, and seeing she had no place whatever to go, he married her and set off for home. When he arrived with an empty vessel and naught but a penniless maid and a poor old woman to show for his cargo, his father was furiously angry.

"My foolish son!" he cried. "What have you done? Made away with a rich and valuable cargo and brought home two empty mouths to feed!" Then he closed to him the door of his house, bade him take his young bride and go about his business.

So Vladimir and Helena and the good nurse lived in great poverty, but the two young people so dearly loved each other, that even in their poor little hut with naught but hard work and the coarsest of food to eat, they were happy. Only Vladimir felt some blot on his joy because of his father's anger. At last, after some time, the father's heart softened; he took pity on his son and received him again to his house with his wife and her nurse. Then he gave him another vessel and said:

"Now, my son, you have seen the consequences of your last foolish bargain. Do not repeat your folly. Trade this merchandise to your own advantage and come back rich!"

So Vladimir was full of gratitude and joy, and leaving Helena in his father's care, he set out with more alluring visions of fortune even than those he had had before. But when he put into the very first port, what should he see coming toward him but a miserable procession of prisoners, with a white haired old man at the head, being driven harshly along by soldiers.

"Where are you driving these poor prisoners?" cried Vladimir.

"They cannot pay the King's taxes," cried the soldiers. "They shall rot in dungeons until they do!"

Now, Vladimir, remembering his father's words, tried to turn away from the pitiful sight and set about selling his cargo with great exercise of worldly wisdom, but the look of those poor prisoners and the sound of their cries were ever in his heart. For the life of him, he could not hold back. He went straight to the chief magistrate of the city and gave him all his

DONN P. CRANE

merchandise to pay up their debts and set them free. Then he returned home with an empty vessel and not a single copper to show. Falling at his father's feet, he told him what he had done and begged his forgiveness, but this time the father drove him still more sternly out of his presence.

Long were the days when Vladimir and his bride were forbidden the father's home, but fathers are fathers, and I doubt not the mother was ever pleading for her son, for, however that may be, the father yielded again at last, took his son to his heart and prepared a vessel for him still finer than the other two.

"Behold," said he, "your last chance to win fortune."

Now ere Vladimir departed, he had the portrait of his wife's old nurse painted on the stern of his ship and on the prow the face of Helena herself, beautiful as the sunrise making rosy the

snow-capped Carpathians, beautiful as the moonlight gleaming across the Danube. Then once more he took leave of his loved ones and made off.

He sailed both weeks and months, and at last he dropped anchor in the bay of a great city where dwelt a mighty king. All the citizens came swarming to the anchorage to examine this strange ship and in the afternoon the King himself proceeded thither in state to ask who the captain was and what was his business there. But no sooner had the King come close to the ship than he saw on the prow

the portrait of that wondrously beautiful maiden. Scarcely
could he believe his eyes. Instantly he ordered that the captain
be brought before him.

"Stranger-from-no-one-knows-where," he cried, "why have
you painted on the prow the face of that beautiful maid?"

Then Vladimir told him all his tale, but no sooner had he
finished than the King held out his arms with tears in his eyes,
and held him in a close embrace.

"That girl is my only child!" he cried, "stolen from me these
many years!" And when he had made an end to weeping for
joy, he took Vladimir to the palace and told the good news to
the Queen and the Court. Then was Vladimir proclaimed heir
to the King and great was the rejoicing and festivity everywhere.
Only the King's Chief Minister was silent and sullen, for to him
the hand of the Princess had been promised when she was but a
child and he had no mind to lose her now. The King soon gave
Vladimir splendid gifts for his own mother and father and a much
finer ship than his own, then he bade him go home at once to
bring Helena and all his family back to court.

"Your father shall be my brother, your mother my sister,"
he said.

Now Vladimir was overjoyed to obey, only he begged the
King to send with him one of his Ministers that his father might
not disbelieve the strange tale he should have to tell. So whom
should the King give Vladimir for companion, but that same
Minister who wanted the Princess himself. All through the
voyage, the Minister wore a fair face and made pretence to be
Vladimir's friend, but his heart was dark, and he said to himself, "When once the girl is safe in my power, I'll make an end
of this troublesome fellow."

They arrived safely in port and Vladimir's father was surprised
to see his son return in such splendid state. "It must be you

have learned at last to make a shrewd bargain!" he cried, but Vladimir answered smiling, "Nay, nay, 'tis to my first bad bargain my fortune is due." And he told his father all his tale. Then was the father astounded, but as the Chief Minister was there to bear witness to the truth of the matter, no one could doubt it. The Princess was overjoyed to think of seeing her father and mother again, and the good nurse likewise, so they all set out for that distant kingdom.

Now the Chief Minister had found Helena ten times more beautiful even than he remembered, and so he was more determined than ever to be rid of her young husband. When they had sailed a long distance and the night was dark, he summoned Vladimir to a lonely spot on the deck. The young man came with no thought of evil, but as he drew near, the Chief Minister seized him and hurled him overboard. The next morning, finding that he had disappeared, Helena and his mother and father began to lament. "Alas and alack! He has fallen overboard and been lost," the false Minister said, pretending great grief, and then he devoted himself to comforting the Princess.

Meantime, Vladimir was carried along by the waves and dashed upon a huge, barren rock. When morning came, he saw nothing about him but a dreary waste of waters, and there he must sit, scorched by the sun, with no shelter whatever and nothing at all to eat but a kind of moss that grew there. For fifteen days and fifteen nights there he sat, and how was he ever to be got off? At last and at last he saw a small boat coming toward him. He rose and made frantic signals, but little he knew whether the man in the boat would come to his aid or not, for the rock was jagged and dangerous and the waves came beating fiercely upon it, so landing was well nigh impossible. But as the man drew near enough to see Vladimir's face, lo! he stood up in the boat and in his features shone a light that was brighter than the sun. Straight he made toward the dangerous shore, for the man was none other than the white haired old fellow who had marched at the head of the prisoners Vladimir had saved from the dungeons. And let the waves beat how they would, he steered his boat up to the rocks and took Vladimir safely off. Then he bore him to the very village where the poor prisoners still were dwelling. One and all, they crowded to help him. They gave him food and new clothing and cheered him off on his way.

For thirty days more, Vladimir wandered, till his clothes were ragged as before and his face scarce to be recognized for the tan and long-grown beard. In this fashion he arrived at the palace of the King. He knocked for admittance at the garden gate, but the gardener, not knowing him at all, drove him away. Soon there came by the King with Vladimir's mother, the Queen with Vladimir's father, and Helena herself, conversing with the Minister. At sight of her, apparently so forgetful of him, Vladimir bowed his head and covered his face with his hands. Nevertheless, as his wife passed him by, she saw the wedding ring on his finger and stopped in great agitation to ask him where he got it.

"Nay, how can you speak to that dirty beggar?" asked the Minister, dragging her off. But Helena was greatly troubled, and as soon as she reached the palace, she told the King, her father, how she had recognized her husband's ring and urged him to send for the beggar and ask him how he came by it. So the King sent his servants to fetch the beggar, and as soon as Helena looked full in his face she knew him. Then she cast herself into his arms and there was great rejoicing. As to the Minister, when the Great King heard of his treachery, he was publicly disgraced and banished forever from the land. And when they were all once more united and happy, a little bird came and whispered into the ear of Vladimir's father:

"After all, is it so fruitless—your son's kind of bargaining?"

How the Waterfall Came To the
Thirsting Mountain

A Roumanian Fairy Tale

HIGH up among the wild Carpathians there was once a mountain that was dry and barren and rocky. Only a few poor trees grew on its rugged slopes, and here and there a clump of dwarfed and straggling bushes. Now the Old Man of the Mountain longed to have his mountain fresh and green, and covered with trees and flowers, so he called aloud to the Fairy who dwelt in the smiling meadows below:

"O Fairy of the Meadows, quench my thirst, I pray you, with a gift of living waters! Surely you at whose smile the meadows burst into bloom, have power to make me merry too, with the laughter of leaping waterfalls and the springing of trees and flowers."

The Fairy of the Meadows looked up at the barren mountain side; she listened to the parched, cracked voice of the Old Man of the Mountain and longed with all her heart to bring him life and bloom.

"O Man of the Mountain," she cried, "I know not at this moment how to make you a waterfall, but never again shall I be content till your slopes are as green as my meadows. I shall go out into the world and search, and you shall not see my face again till I have found you a gushing stream to leap down your barren sides and make them burst into bloom!"

So saying, the Fairy bade farewell to the Old Man of the Mountain and set out on her journey. She rode a faithful horse as she left the meadows, but she had gone only a short distance when she stopped beside a rosebush, made herself as small as a bumble bee and turned her steed into a butterfly. Then she hitched her butterfly to the rosebush and sat down inside one of the blossoms to think what she should do. She was longing, longing to be wise enough to know where to find a waterfall, when suddenly she heard the sound of voices near her. Peeping out from her safe retreat in the rose, she saw not far away a beautiful Princess kneeling at the feet of an ugly Wizard. And lo! the maiden's glorious hair swept down her back like a water-fall and gleamed like a shining stream.

"O Wizard," the maiden was crying, "take my long hair if you will, but set free my father and give him back to me."

Then the Wizard seized the maiden's locks.

"Aye! I will have your hair," he snarled.

The heart of the Fairy was touched at once with pity, so she sprang on her butterfly and flew like a flash to the Princess. Close to her ear she darted, all unseen by the Wizard, and she whispered:

"Have courage, my maid. Give not your hair to the Wizard. He has no mind to give you back your father. Whatever your trouble, trust in me!"

On hearing these words, the Princess took heart. She sprang to her feet and though the Wizard still tried to hold her locks fast, they flowed through his fingers like water and slipped, rippling, out of his reach.

"Nay, false one!" cried the maiden. "I will keep my hair and still set my father free! Begone from my sight!"

At that, the Wizard, snarling once more, vanished in a mist.

"Now," said the Fairy to the Princess, "tell me your trouble."

So the Princess took the Fairy in the palm of her hand and, between much weeping, this is the tale she told:

"My father is Michael, a great lord and hospodar of this land. Some years ago he learned that Dracul, the Wizard, who lived amid the barren crags and the thirsty crags, had in his keeping a wonderful sword that sprang from its sheath whenever

there was need of defending the pure and the good. Having need of such help to keep the peace in his kingdom, he besought the Wizard to lend him the sword. Now Dracul seemed all too willing to get the sword out of his way, so he gave it into my father's keeping, but he made him promise, under penalty of the direst punishment, that I should never touch it, nay, nor so much as mention it to anyone. The sword did many a noble deed and for a long time I obeyed Dracul's command. But one day my father chanced to leave it near me as I sat weaving. Scarcely were we alone when I heard an imploring voice. 'Save me, O maiden!' it cried, 'save me! Let but the hem of your gown touch me. I am a knight and boyar whom the Wizard imprisoned in the sword! He feared lest I should find the secret that would destroy his power to weave wicked spells. Ah, maiden, touch me but once and I shall be free!'

"The knight's voice moved me deeply. Kneeling beside the sword, I gently touched it. Then behold, O fairy! The sword was shattered. From its flashing pieces there sprang a fine young boyar in steel and silver. He knelt and kissed the hem of my gown.

" 'O maiden,' he cried, 'to you the deep thanks of my heart are due. I go forth into the world to search for the secret that will destroy Dracul's evil power. Farewell till we meet again.' And he sped over the terrace and out through the palace gates.

"Scarcely had he gone, when my maidens came rushing to tell me that at that very moment, my father had suddenly disappeared, and I knew that the Wizard had punished my deed by spiriting him away. By sunlight and starlight I traveled, by moonlight and dreary dark, and threw myself at Dracul's feet, but alas! Dracul has ever coveted my hair and you yourself know that he will not restore my father, save at the price of my locks."

Thus the Princess finished her tale.

"Trust me," said the Fairy, "we will yet learn the way to save your father." So she changed her butterfly into a horse again, bade the Princess mount the steed before her, and together they galloped away, over hill, over dale, toward the Wizard's castle.

As they went, the Fairy noticed how the Princess's beautiful hair waved and sparkled in the sunlight, and when the wind blew a single thread away, it fell on the grass by the wayside and turned into a strand of glistening dew drops.

"Ah," thought the Fairy joyously, "if one thread of her hair makes a strand of dew drops, might not all of it make a waterfall?" In her heart she was sure that she knew the reason why Dracul of the barren crags and the thirsty crags was so determined to get those shining locks, and she believed that in serving the

maiden, she could also accomplish the purpose for which she had left her green meadows and the parched Old Man of the Mountain.

They were just about to mount the hill toward the Wizard's castle, when who should come dashing across their path and draw rein before them but that fine young boyar, the Knight of the Sword himself.

"Fair maiden," he cried, "I have heard but now how you and your father have been punished because you set me free. Be at rest. I have learned what the magic power is that will destroy Dracul's evil spells."

"Ah," said the Fairy, "I too am seeking to save the Princess and her father. Tell me the charm."

So the Knight leaned over and whispered the secret into the Fairy's ear. At his words a great light shone in her face. Then she bade the Princess spring down from the horse, and the young Boyar gallantly offered to guard her well, while the Fairy went on to the castle. Up to the great gate she rode and she blew three blasts on a silver horn that hung by the great portcullis. In answer to her summons out came Dracul himself.

"I crave," said she, "a room in your castle in which to rest, and, above all, a goblet of cool, fresh water."

Now Dracul had no water to give, as the Fairy knew full well, for all his wells and springs were as parched and dried up as his wicked heart. But this was a powerful Fairy whom the Wizard did not wish to offend, so he pretended to receive her graciously and bade her rest in a splendid chamber while he went to fetch her the drink. Then he hurried off to the dungeon where he kept Michael, the hospodar.

"Aha, great hospodar, that rulest over rats and dungeon vermin," he mocked, "I have stolen your lovely daughter and taken her away to a far off land. Never shall you see her more."

The words were false, but the Wizard knew that they would

bring tears to Michael's eyes. And while the poor father wept, Dracul caught the tears in a golden goblet and carried them off to serve to the Fairy.

"Here," said he, "is your cool, fresh water." The Fairy, however, knew what was in the goblet, and when the Wizard had left her alone, she waved her wand and caused a beautiful maiden to spring up from the tears.

"Fair creature," said she, "you are all goodness, tenderness and beauty, for you are the child of loving tears. When the Wizard sees you, the evil will die in his heart."

"Ah," said the Tear-Maiden gently, "whoever looks deep into my eyes is melted at once with compassion."

Soon, back came Dracul blustering into the Fairy's chamber. Suddenly he saw, tall and beautiful before him, her eyes beaming with sorrowful gentleness and tenderness, a mild light glowing about her—the Tear-Maiden.

"Whence came you?" he cried in a fright and clapped his hands over his eyes. "Away! Away! Away!" But no one made answer. Only the Tear-Maiden continued to beam on him gently, softly, sorrowfully. And Dracul felt the light of her gaze go deep down into his heart. Slowly he dropped his fingers from his face and looked long and full into her eyes. Then his head fell on his breast, his shoulders drooped, his lips began to quiver, his chest heaved and he burst into tears of repentance.

"Ah," said the Fairy, "this maiden will stay forever by your side. If you would be able to look into her eyes and smile instead of weeping, there is but one thing to do—bring me Michael, the hospodar, free!"

Without a word, Dracul turned away and hurried off to fetch Michael. Then the Fairy ran to the window and joyously waved her kerchief to the Princess and the Boyar. The Boyar took the Princess up onto the horse before him, and off they dashed to

the castle. When they entered the Fairy's chamber, there stood
Michael himself with the Wizard, and the Princess threw herself
joyously into her father's arms.

As to Dracul, amid all the rejoicing, he stood humbly before
the Tear-Maiden and looked again deep into her eyes.

"Ah," said the Fairy to the Boyar, "his power to work evil
spells is gone forever. Your charm worked well."

Then the Princess knelt in gratitude before the Fairy and cried:

"O you, who have brought us such joy—what may I do for
you? My dearest possession I would gladly give to show you
how deep is my gratitude."

"Then," said the Fairy, "give me your hair."

So the Maiden, of her own free wish and desire, gave the
Fairy the locks that all the power of the Wizard could never get
from her.

Back to the Old Man of the Mountain went the Fairy. And
she hung that gleaming strand from the highest crag on the
mountain top. Then suddenly, lo! it began to ripple and wave,
and in another moment, down it gushed in a torrent, leaping

from rock to rock, laughing, roaring, tumbling, flinging forth sheets of shining spray. And wherever it went, there the mountain burst into splendid bloom.

"This for my thanks," said the Old Man of the Mountain, in a voice now firm and full, and he flung down into the Fairy's lap a carpet of brilliant flowers.

"It was worth searching for—that waterfall," said the Fairy of the Meadows.

THE CATARACT OF LODORE
ROBERT SOUTHEY

"How does the water come down at Lodore?"
My little boy asked me.

Advancing and prancing and glancing
    and dancing,
Recoiling, turmoiling, and toiling
    and boiling,
And gleaming and streaming and steaming
    and beaming,
And rushing and flushing and brushing
    and gushing,
And flapping and rapping and clapping
    and slapping,
And curling and whirling and purling
    and twirling,
And thumping and plumping and bumping
    and jumping,
And dashing and flashing and splashing
    and clashing,
And so never ending, but always descending,
Sounds and motions forever and ever are
    blending,
All at once and all o'er, with a mighty uproar,
And this way the Water comes down at Lodore.

383

Through The Mouse Hole
A Czech Fairy Tale

Before times long past, there reigned a King somewhere and he had three sons. One day when they were grown up and had been trained as befits princes, they came to their father and said:

"Kindly father, permit us to visit strange lands. It is well for us to know more of the world."

Now the King thought it good for his sons to ride abroad and match their strength and wits with the world, but he made this one condition: "Ye are all of an age when most young men seek the partners of their lives. So far as I know, ye will do likewise. I have no wish to tell you what princesses to choose, but this command I lay upon you—return before a year and a day and bring me some gift from your loved ones, that I may know what sort of maidens have pleased you."

The princes were astonished that their father had guessed their thoughts so well, and they agreed at once to his command. Each one said that he would shoot an arrow into the air and start out on his adventures in whatever direction the arrow fell. So they took their crossbows and set off for the open field. The eldest son let the bow-string go, and his arrow flew to the East. The second let the string go, and his arrow flew to the West.

THROUGH FAIRY HALLS

"And where am I to aim?" cried the youngest whose name was Yarmil. Just at that moment a mouse ran past him and into its hole. He let the string go, and his arrow flew after the mouse.

"Oho!" cried the brothers. "See where you must go, Yarmil! Into a mousehole!" And they thought it a matter for jesting. But Yarmil, nothing daunted, prepared for the road.

"Through a mousehole I shall find fortune, as well as by another way," cried he, and when the eldest son rode down the broad and pleasant highway to the East, and the second son down the broad and pleasant highway to the West, Yarmil made straight for the mousehole. He approached it boldly on his horse and at the very moment he came full upon it, the small entrance grew suddenly large, so he rode in quite easily without even slackening speed. Sooner than he could think, he found himself in an open country in the midst of which stood a white marble castle. Nowhere did he see a living soul, but scarcely had he entered the gate, when a lady came forth to meet him. She wore long, flowing robes of white and her face, hair, eyes, all were white as the new-fallen snow. By the bridle she held a spirited, snow-white steed and she silently beckoned to Yarmil to descend from his horse and mount the one she was holding. Scarcely had he done so, when the creature rose with him through the air, and regardless of bit, flew on and on, till it brought him to earth before a splendid castle. Round about, wherever the eye could see, was a beautiful garden abloom with flowers, wherein birds of all sorts were singing.

Yarmil dismounted in great amazement, but as he took his steed by the bridle to lead him into the courtyard, it broke suddenly from his hand, rose lightly into the air and disappeared like a great white bird in the clouds. Then Yarmil advanced and rapped on the door of the castle. No one appeared to answer his summons, but the door itself swung open. Up a flight of

broad marble steps he climbed to the door of the first chamber. Again he rapped. No answer, but this door like the first, swung open. Then Yarmil entered the most magnificent room he had ever seen, a hall ablaze with gold and jewels. Beyond this, he passed through a succession of chambers, each one more splendid than the last, and so on till he came to the eleventh. Here he paused a moment, for, in this room he saw a great crystal tub, bound about with golden hoops, and into this tub through a golden pipe, clear, fresh water was pouring. The twelfth and last chamber unlike all the others was small and bare, and, strange to relate, in the center stood a pan, made solidly of diamonds.

Advancing swiftly to the pan, Yarmil stooped to examine it, and at once he saw written upon it these strange words: "Carry me near your heart and bathe me each day, so you will set free one who is bound."

Still more astonished, Yarmil lifted from the pan a diamond cover. Below that, he found a golden cover, and last of all one of silver. As he dragged up the last cover with great difficulty, he suddenly saw at the bottom of the pan, what but an ugly toad! On first thought, he turned to run away, but no! in spite of himself

he lifted the toad from the pan and put it in his bosom. At first the touch of it chilled him through and through, but the next moment he felt himself strangely happy.

Straightway he went to the eleventh chamber, took out the toad and washed it carefully in the crystal tub with the clear, pure water that flowed from the golden pipes. But for all he bathed the creature, it still remained a toad. Carefully he put it back in its place near his heart and went out into the garden.

Here the sight of the trees, the odor of the flowers and the songs of the birds cheered him till midday. Then he went back to the castle and to his great surprise, saw in the first chamber a table spread with the daintiest dishes. Here, as he sat and ate, he was served by unseen hands. After dinner he looked more carefully about the room, and now the splendor did not charm him so much as at first. Instead, he rejoiced in the musical instruments, writing materials and books which were everywhere about. With these he made bold to busy himself, and so he did, day after day, but always his first thought was the care of the toad. The lonely life troubled him somewhat at first, for never once did a human being appear, but he mastered this feeling soon, and then one thing only grieved him—the more he washed the toad, the uglier it seemed to grow. Still he carried it always next his heart, and never failed to bathe it.

At length it was nearing the end of the year when he must return to his father and carry him a present. Yarmil knew not what to do. How could he leave the toad? What could he take to the King as a gift? Such thoughts as these made him sad and anxious. When the very last day of the year came, he was quite beside himself, but, as he was passing through his room, he suddenly saw on his writing table a sheet of paper. Seizing it quickly he read:

"Dear Yarmil,—Be patient as I am patient. A gift for thy father thou wilt find in the pan. Give it to him, but tarry not long at home. Put me back in the pan."

Hastening with joy to the twelfth chamber, Yarmil found in the pan a splendid casket. He knew not what was in it, but he took it obediently, removed the toad from his bosom, and put it carefully back in the pan. Then he hastened from the castle. In the courtyard he found the snow-white steed in waiting. At once he threw himself on its back, it rose with him into the air, and flew on and on, regardless of bit, till it dropped to earth before the white castle. The white lady appeared again, gave Yarmil his own horse and took the white one from him.

When he had passed through the gate of the castle and turned to look back, lo! there was naught behind but a mousehole. He rushed on at a gallop and arrived at his father's castle almost at the same moment as his brothers, so that all three were able to appear together before their father, and say: "Here we are, according to thy command."

"But have ye brought gifts from your princesses?" asked the king.

"Of course," cried the elder brothers, proudly. Yarmil

answered, as it were timidly, with a nod; for he knew not what was in that casket taken from the pan.

The King had invited a great number of guests to look at the gifts. All were in the banqueting-hall. The King led his sons thither, and when the feast was ended, he said to the eldest: "Now give me the gift from thy princess."

"My love is the daughter of a great king. With her I have spent the year in feasting and tourneys and tilts at arms," said the Prince proudly, and he gave his father a splendid casket.

The King took out therefrom a small mirror, about the size of an aspen leaf, and as he looked in it, he wondered not a little that he saw his whole person in such small compass. Then he said: "Well, it is not a bad gift."

The second son also said proudly that his love was the daughter of a great king and from his princess he presented his father with a mirror even smaller. Still the King only said: "It is not a bad gift," and he turned to Yarmil. "But what has thy princess sent me?" In silence and humbly, Yarmil gave him the casket. The King barely looked in it when he cried out in amazement, for therein was a mirror no bigger than one's little thumb nail, in which the King could see not only his own person, but the whole great hall, the gleaming tapers on the wall, and all the guests besides.

"Now," cried the king, "here is a Princess who knows what is what," and embracing Yarmil, he added with tenderness: "Thou hast brought me true joy, my son."

Yarmil called to mind the ugly toad, and had no regret now that he had spent a whole year in nursing it; but his brothers were enraged that he had found such a thing through a mousehole.

When the feast was over and the princes were parting with their father, he said: "Go now with rejoicing, but return in a year and a day, and bring me portraits of your princesses."

The elder brothers promised with joy, but Yarmil barely nodded, for he feared what his father would say should he bring the toad's portrait. Still he went with his brothers beyond the town, where he parted with them, and galloped on to the mouse-hole. At the white castle the white lady took his horse and gave him the white steed, which rose through the air, and regardless of bit, flew on till it reached the golden castle, where it disappeared like a dove in the clouds.

In the castle nothing was changed. Yarmil hurried to the twelfth chamber and there stood the diamond pan as before. Hastily he removed the three covers, carefully took out the toad, and placed it tenderly in his bosom. Now he bathed it twice each day, but to his grief it grew uglier. How could he take back home the portrait of such a princess?

At last the day was near in which he must return. He looked continually on his writing table till he saw to his great joy a sheet of paper on which was written in silver letters—

"Dear Yarmil,—Be patient, as I am patient. Thou hast my portrait in the pan; give it to thy father, but tarry not long. Put me back in the pan."

Yarmil hastened to the twelfth chamber, and found in the pan a casket still richer than the first. He took it quickly, and put the toad in its place. Then he hurried forth, and sat on the white steed, which brought him to the white castle, where the white lady gave him his own horse. He galloped on and arrived at the gate of his father's castle at the same time with his brothers. They stood before their father and said: "Here we are, as thou hast commanded."

"Do ye bring me portraits of your princesses?" asked the king.

"Yea!" exclaimed the two elder brothers, full of pride. But Yarmil only answered with a nod, for he knew not what portrait the casket contained.

THROUGH FAIRY HALLS

The King led them to the banqueting-hall, where the guests were assembled. When the banquet was over, he said to the eldest: "Now show me the portrait of thy princess."

The eldest brother gave a rich casket to his father. He opened it, took out a portrait, and looking at it from every side said at last: "That is a beautiful lady, she pleases me. Still there are fairer than she in the world." Then he said to his second son: "And the portrait of thy princess?"

The second son gave him promptly a richer casket, and smiled with happiness. He thought that his father could never have seen a lovelier princess, but the king only said: "A beautiful lady too, still there are more beautiful in the world."

Then he nodded to Yarmil, who gave with trembling hands his diamond casket. The King opened it and looked fixedly at what lay within, unable to utter a word. Yarmil could but hold his breath. Was it the portrait of a toad that lay there? "Ah,"

391

cried the King at last. "I had not believed in all the world such a lady was to be found."

The guests crowded around the portrait, and in one voice agreed with the King. At last Yarmil drew near and looked on the face of his princess. Such loveliness was unbelievable! Now he regretted no whit that he had spent two years in lone life caring patiently for a toad.

Next day the princes were taking farewell, and the king said to them: "After this time I will not let you go again. In a year and a day I wish to see your princesses; then we will celebrate the weddings."

Full of hope they all set out and in good time Yarmil came to the castle. He hastened at once to the twelfth chamber, eagerly hoping to find there his wondrous fair princess; but no—he found in the pan the same ugly toad as before. He was disappointed, you may be sure, but he put the little creature in his bosom, and now washed it three times each day. In vain seemed all his labor, for the more he bathed, the uglier grew the toad. When the end of the year drew near it is a wonder that he did not despair; for the toad had become so hideous that he shivered whenever he looked at it. And now he must bring this to his father as his chosen one.

Still he stuck to his task and would not give up his hope. On the very last day he reached to his bosom to look once more at the toad. At sight of it he hoped he might find some comfort; but a new surprise awaited him—the toad was gone. Now he began to lament, for after all, he loved the creature. He ran through the whole castle, and searched every room. He searched every tree and bush in the garden but no trace of the toad did he find.

At last he remembered the dish in the twelfth chamber. Thither he ran, but on the threshold he stopped as if thunderstruck: That poor chamber had become a real paradise, and in the middle of it stood a lady as beautiful, ah! more beautiful still than the portrait which he had carried to his father. In speechless amazement he looked at her, and who knows how long he might have stood there had she not turned to him sweetly and said:

"My dear, know that I am the daughter of a mighty King. Me and all my people a wicked wizard turned into toads because I refused to marry him. Thou hast endured much and patiently, but now at last thy faithful devotion has set me free from the spell. Come, let us be off at once, so as to come to thy father's in time."

Then she took him by the hand, and led him down the stairs. In front of the castle a carriage, with four white horses, was waiting. When they entered, the horses rushed off with such speed that soon they passed the white castle where the white fairy, who had kept guard over the Princess, waved them a friendly greeting. Out through the gate they went and behind them was naught but a mouse-hole. So they arrived at the King's castle just in the same moment with the two elder brothers. There were the Princesses they had brought, decked out in their gaudiest finery. But, alas! no one ever once looked at them. On Yarmil's wonderful bride was every eye fixed. Never had there been seen in the kingdom so beautiful a creature.

The King was rejoiced most of all. He conducted the bride to the banqueting-hall, where there was a multitude of guests, and with tears of delight he exalted the happiness of his youngest son.

On the following day came the weddings of the three princes; and when the feasting was over, Yarmil set out with his wife on the journey to their kingdom. They found the mouse-hole no longer a mouse-hole, but a magnificent gate leading to a great city, in the middle of which stood a golden castle. Here there were multitudes of people everywhere, and in the castle throngs of courtiers and servants, who greeted with mighty applause their master and mistress, thanking Yarmil at the same time for their liberation. The royal pair were goodness itself. and so they all lived henceforth, happily beyond measure.

APRIL*

John Galsworthy

Starry-eyed in April morn,
Rain bells glitter on the thorn.
Birds are tuning down the lane
Patter song of fallen rain.
Spring can grieve, but Spring can be
Very life of minstrelsy!

Gorse has lit his lanterns all,
Cob-webbed thrift's a fairy ball,
Earth it smells as good as new,
Winds are merry, sky is blue.

*From *Moods, Songs and Doggerels.* Reprinted by permission of the publishers, Charles Scribner's Sons.

Tudur ap Einion

A Welsh Fairy Tale

Far up among the mountains, there lies a little hollow called The Elves' Dell. Once upon a time there was a young man named Tudur ap Einion, who used to pasture his master's sheep there.

One summer night Tudur was about to return to the lowlands with his flock, when he began to loiter along and grumble to himself that it was stupid business tending sheep, and he wished a gay lad like himself might have a little fun now and then. Suddenly he saw, perched on a stone near him, a little man in moss breeches with a fiddle under his arm. He was the tiniest wee creature imaginable. His coat was made of birch leaves; he wore a gorse flower for a cap, and his feet were shod with beetles' wings.

As Tudur stared, open mouthed, at the little man, the latter took up his fiddle which was nothing more than a stringed wooden spoon and ran his fingers across it.

"Nos dawch! Nos dawch!" said the little man, which means in English, "Good Evening to you! Good Evening to you!"

"Ac i chwithan!" replied Tudur, which is, being interpreted, "The same to you!"

"You are fond of dancing, Tudur," went on the little man, "Why do anything so stupid as to tend sheep? Tarry here awhile, and you shall see some of the best dancers in Wales. I"—he swelled out his chest as he spoke, "I am their musician."

"But if you are a musician, where is your harp?" asked Tudur, loitering still more slowly. "Welshmen cannot dance without a harp."

395

"Harp!" cried the wee creature scornfully. "I can play better music for dancing upon my fiddle."

"Is that a fiddle," asked Tudur in great curiosity, "that stringed wooden spoon you have in your hand?"

For answer the little man nodded his head.

And now through the dusky twilight, Tudur saw hundreds of pretty little sprites come tripping from all parts of the mountain toward the spot where he stood. Some were dressed in white, some in blue, and some in pink, and some carried glow-worms in their hands as torches.

So lightly did they step that not a blade of grass nor any flower was crushed beneath their weight, and all made a curtsy or a bow to Tudur as they passed. Tudur responded at once to their advances by doffing his cap and bowing to each in return.

Presently the little minstrel drew his bow across the strings of his instrument, and the music he produced seemed to Tudur so enchanting, that he turned farther and farther away from his sheep and listened, open-mouthed.

At sound of the sweet melody, the fairies (if fairies they were) ranged themselves in groups and began to dance. Round and round they went as the bow of the little minstrel flew. All the dancing Tudur had ever seen could not compare with this. His feet began to keep time to the music. He longed to step into the magic circle. Yet there was something in his breast that warned him away from it, and he heard his sheep calling him to his duties down the mountain.

"Come, Tudur, join in the dance, and make merry," the little man cried.

Tudur's feet beat a faster tattoo, yet he still gave ear to the call of his sheep.

"Nay, nay," he said, "dance on, my little beauties! I take my sheep down the mountain."

THROUGH FAIRY HALLS

Nevertheless he did not go, he did not even turn away. He lingered and yielded himself more and more to the entertainment before him. The music became faster and the dance wilder.

"Come, Tudur, join in the dance and make merry," the little man cried again. Tudur began to sway with his whole body in time to the rhythm. The bleating of his sheep sounded more and more faintly in the distance.

"Come, Tudur, join in the dance and make merry," the little man cried a third time, with a sweep of his bow across the strings that seemed to the shepherd sweeter than anything he had ever heard in all his life before.

Then Tudur flung all thought of his sheep to the winds. With a bound he threw himself into the midst of the circle. Hurling his cap in the air, he cried, "Now for it! Play away, fiddler! Play away!" And he gave himself wholly up to the dance.

But what a change! No sooner was he within the ring that had seemed so pleasant when he stood looking on from without, than in a twinkling all was altered. The gorse blossom cap vanished from the minstrel's head, a pair of goat's horns branched out instead, and his face became as black as soot. The creatures that a moment before he had thought so beautiful, now became ugly goats and dogs, while some took the shape of foxes and cats. And in the midst of these Tudur went dancing on! At length the motion grew so furious that Tudur could not make out the forms of the dancers at all. They whirled round and round him so rapidly that they looked like a wheel of fire. And still he flung himself about and waved his arms in time to their music. How gladly he would have torn himself away, but it seemed to him that he could not. In the midst of the ugly company he had chosen, he was forced to dance on and on and on.

Next morning, Tudur's master went up the mountain to see what had become of his sheep, and his shepherd. He found the

flock safe and sound half way down to the valley, but was astonished to see Tudur spinning around like mad in the midst of
the hollow, all by himself.

"What in the world is the silly lad doing?" he cried.

"O, Master, Master, stop me!" shouted Tudur.

"Stop yourself!" replied the master. "In the name of heaven,
stop yourself!"

At these words Tudur suddenly stopped and blinked his
eyes. There was no ugly circle about him. There was only
the morning sunlight, the rocky crags above, and the sheep
awaiting his tendance on the green, flower-sprinkled mountain
pastures.

"Tudur ap Einion, let me not find you deserting your sheep
again!" cried his master.

Tudur hung his head and went foolishly back to his charges.

East O' the Sun and West O' the Moon
A Norse Folk Tale

Once on a time there lived a poor husbandman who had so many children that none had food or clothing enough. Pretty children they were, but the prettiest was the youngest daughter, who was so very lovely that there was no end to her loveliness.

'Twas on a Thursday evening late in the fall of the year. The weather was wild outside; rain fell and the wind blew till the walls of the cottage shook. There they all sat around the fire, busy with this thing and that. But all at once, something gave three taps on the window-pane,—tap! tap! tap! The father went out to see what it was, and, when he got out of doors, what should he see but a big, White Bear.

"Good evening to you," said the Bear.

"The same to you," said the man.

"Will you give me your youngest daughter?" said the Bear. "If you will, I'll make you as rich as you are poor tonight."

Well, the man would be glad to be rich, but give up his daughter, no, that he wouldn't, he said. But the White Bear said, "Think it over; next Thursday night I'll come back and then you can give me your answer."

So the father went into the house and told them all that had happened. Now when the lassie heard how she could lighten the poverty of her parents and brothers and sisters, she said at once she would go. Let her family beg never so hard, go she would, she said. I can't say her packing gave her much trouble. She washed and mended her rags and made herself ready to start.

Next Thursday evening the White Bear came. She got on his back with her bundle and off they went through the woods.

"Are you afraid?" said the Bear.

"No, not at all," said the lassie.

So she rode a long, long way till they came to a great steep hill. The White Bear knocked on the face of the hill, a little door opened and they entered a castle, with rooms all lit up and gleaming, splendid with silver and gold. There, too, was a table laid. It was all as grand as could be. Then the White Bear gave the lassie a bell and told her to ring when she wanted anything.

Well, after she had eaten, she thought she would go to bed, and scarcely had she lifted the bell when she found herself in a room with a bed as fair and white as any one could wish to sleep in. But when she had put out her light she heard someone enter the room next hers, and there someone stayed until dawn. Night after night the same thing occurred. Not a single human being did the lassie see through the day but when all the lights were out, someone would enter the room next hers and sleep there

until the dawn. But always before the daylight appeared whoever it was, was up and off, so as never to be seen.

Things went on well for a while, but all day long the lassie
had not a soul to talk to except for the White Bear and she knew
not whether it was man or beast who slept in the next room at
night. So at last she grew silent and sorrowful. Then the White
Bear came and said, "What troubles you, my lassie? Here you
have everything heart can wish. You have only to ring the bell
and whatever you want is brought you."

"Nay then," said the lassie, "I am lonely. Who is it that
sleeps in the room next mine?" At that the Bear begged her to
ask no such questions. "Trust me," he said. "Don't try to find
out and in due time you will know." Now the lassie was grateful to the Bear and fond of him, but in spite of what he said, she
grew more and more sorrowful and more and more lonely. Who
was it that shared the castle with her? Who was it? Who was
it? Who was it? She was forever thinking of that one thing alone.
All day long and all night long she wondered and fretted. Still
for a long, long time she obeyed the Bear and did not try to find
out. But at last she could stand it no longer. In the dead of
night she got up, lit a candle and slipped softly into the next
room. There asleep on a bed she saw the loveliest Prince one
ever set eyes on. Slowly she crept up to him, bent over and
kissed him. But as she did so, three drops of hot tallow fell
from her candle onto his shirt and awoke him.

"Alas! What have you done?" he cried. "Now you have
spoiled all that was gained by the months you were faithful to
me. Had you held out only this one year, you would have set me
free. For a witch has cast a spell upon me, so that I am a white
bear by day and a man only at night. A year of good faith and
you would have saved me, but now all is over between us. Back
I must go to the castle *East o' the Sun and West o' the Moon.*

There I must marry the witch with a nose three ells long. She must now be the wife for me."

The lassie wept but there was no help for it. Go he must, he said. Then she asked if she mightn't go with him.

No, she mightn't, he said.

"Tell me the way there, then," said she, "and I'll search you out over all the world, no matter how hard is the journey."

"But there is no way to that place," cried the Prince. "It lies *East o' the Sun and West o' the Moon*, that is all I can tell you."

Next morning when the lassie awoke, both Prince and castle were gone. There she lay on a little green patch in the midst of the gloomy, thick wood, and by her side lay the same bundle of rags which she had brought with her from home.

When she had rubbed the sleep out of her eyes and wept at her loss of the Prince, she set out on her journey and walked for many days, until she came to a lofty crag under which an old woman sat tossing a golden apple. Her the lassie asked if she knew the way to the castle that lay *East o' the Sun and West o' the Moon*. But the old woman answered:

"All I know about it is that it lies *East o' the Sun and West o' the Moon* and thither you'll come late or never. But go on to my next neighbor. Maybe she will be able to tell you more." Then she gave the lassie her golden apple. "It might prove useful," she said.

So the lassie went on a long, long time till she came to another crag, under which sat another old woman with a golden carding-comb. Her the lassie asked if she knew the way to the castle that lay *East o' the Sun and West o' the Moon*, but this old woman likewise knew nothing about the matter.

"Go on to my next neighbor," she said. "Maybe she can tell you." And she gave the lassie the carding-comb and bade her take it with her.

So the lassie went on and on, a far, far way and a weary,

weary time till at last she came to another crag under which sat another old woman spinning with a golden spinning wheel. Her too she asked if she knew the way to the castle that lay *East o' the Sun and West o' the Moon*. It was the same thing over again. She knew nothing, but this old woman said:

"Go to the East Wind and ask him. Maybe he knows those parts and can blow you thither." Then she gave the lassie her golden spinning wheel, and bade her take it with her.

So the lassie toiled on many days before she got to the East Wind's house, but at last she did get there, and then she asked the East Wind if he could tell her the way to the Prince who dwelt *East o' the Sun and West o' the Moon*. Yes, the East Wind had often heard tell of the Prince and the castle, but he didn't know the way, for he had never blown so far.

"If you will," he said, "I'll take you to my brother, the West Wind. Maybe he knows, for he's much stronger than I. Just get up on my back and I'll carry you thither."

Yes, she got on his back, and I should just think they went briskly along till they came to the West Wind's house. Then the lassie asked the West Wind if he knew how to get to the castle *East o' the Sun and West o' the Moon*.

"Nay," said the West Wind, "so far I've never blown, but if you'll get on my back, I'll carry you to our brother the South Wind. He has flapped his wings far and wide. Maybe he can tell you."

So she got on his back and travelled to the South Wind, and wasn't long on the way. And the lassie asked the South Wind if he knew the way to the castle *East o' the Sun and West o' the Moon*.

"Well, I've blustered about in most places in my time," answered the South Wind, "but so far I've never blown. Just get up on my back, and I'll carry you to my brother, the North Wind. He is the strongest of all of us, and if he doesn't know where it is, you'll never find anyone to tell you."

So she got on his back, and away he went.

When they got to the North Wind's house, he was so wild and cross that they felt his cold icy puffs when they were a long way off. "What do you want?" he roared in a voice that made them shiver. Then the lassie asked the North Wind if he knew the way to the castle *East o' the Sun and West o' the Moon*.

"Yes!" roared the North Wind. "I know well enough! Once in my life I blew an aspen leaf thither, but I was so tired I couldn't blow a puff for ever so many days after. If you really wish to go so far and aren't afraid to come along, I'll take you on my back and see if I can blow you thither."

Yes, with all her heart! She must and would get there if she could possibly do it. And as for fear, no matter how madly he went, she wouldn't be afraid at all.

Early next morning they started. The North Wind puffed himself up, and made himself so stout, 'twas gruesome to look upon him. Off they went through the air, as if they would never stop till they got to the end of the world. Down below a storm raged.

They tore on and on—no one can believe how far they went— and all the time they still went over the sea. The North Wind got more and more weary, and so out of breath he could scarcely puff; his wings drooped and drooped, till he sunk so low that the crests of the waves went dashing over his heels.

"Are you afraid?" asked the North Wind.

No, she wasn't afraid.

But they weren't very far from the land, and the North Wind still had strength enough to throw her up on the shore. Now at last she was under the windows of the castle which lay *East o' the Sun and West o' the Moon.*

All through the day the lassie saw no one, but toward night she began to play with her golden apple, tossing it into the air. At that, out came Long-nose, who was going to marry the Prince.

"What do you want for your apple?" she asked.

"It's not for sale," answered the lassie. "But if I may get

to the Prince, I will give it to you for nothing."

That she might, said Long-nose, and snatch! she seized the apple. But before Long-nose let the lassie in, she gave the Prince a drink that put him fast asleep, so though the lassie called him and shook him, she could not wake him up. Then along came Long-nose and drove her out again.

Next day the same thing happened. So long as it was light the gloomy old castle was still as death and no one even looked out of it. But at nightfall signs of life awoke, and when the lassie began to card with the golden carding-comb, out came Long-nose to buy it.

"It's not for sale for gold or money," answered the lassie. "But if I may get to the Prince, you shall have it." Now when the lassie went up this time she found the Prince fast asleep as before, and all she called, and all she shook, she couldn't wake him up. Then along came Long-nose and chased her out again.

So the next night the lassie sat down under the castle window and began to spin with her golden spinning wheel. Long-nose must have the spinning wheel too; so in went the lassie once more. But this time, the Prince's servants had told him how a beautiful lassie had come and wept over him and called him two nights running. So, when Long-nose gave him his night drink, he poured it out secretly on the floor, and the lassie found, to her joy, that his eyes were wide open. Then she told him the whole long story of how she had made the far, far journey and the Prince wept and smiled and had great joy of her coming.

"You've got here just in the nick of time," cried he, "for to-morrow's to be my wedding. Be waiting at the gate and you'll see what you will see."

Well, the wedding was to be the next night in the dark, for witches and trolls can never endure the daylight. But when the time came, the Prince announced:

"Ere I marry, I'll see what my bride can do. Here is my wedding shirt, but on it are three spots of tallow. I'll have no other for a bride save her who can wash it clean."

"No great thing to do," said Long-nose. So when the moon stood high, shining over the tree tops, she hung a caldron of boiling lye in a clearing in the woods. Thither came running, tumbling, scolding, a whole pack of trolls and witches, long-nosed, red-eyed, ugly, a hideous sight to see. First Long-nose began to wash. She washed as hard as she could, but the more she rubbed and scrubbed the bigger grew the spots. "Oh, you can't wash! Let me try!" another troll woman cried, and wash, wash, wash,—every one in turn scrubbed away on that shirt. But the more they washed, the blacker and uglier grew the shirt, till at last it was black all over as if it had been up the chimney.

"Ah!" cried the Prince, "you're none of you worth a straw.

I'll have none of you for my bride. Why! look, outside the gate there sits a beggar lass. I'll be bound she knows how to wash better than your whole pack. Come in, lassie!" he shouted.

So in came the lassie, and almost before she had taken the shirt and dipped it in the water, it was white as the driven snow.

"You are the lassie for me!" cried the Prince. Then the witches and trolls rushed raging upon him, but ah! while they had been washing, the night had slowly waned. Just then the sun came up. The moment it pierced the mist and gloom and shone directly on Long-nose, she burst, like an empty bubble. The whole pack of trolls uttered horrid shrieks and hurried away toward the castle, but it was no use at all. The instant the sun struck them squarely, they every one of them vanished.

As for the Prince and Princess, they took hold of hands and flitted away as far as they could from the castle that lay *East o' the Sun and West o' the Moon.*

The Boy
and The Elf*

SELMA LAGERLOF

Once there was a boy. He was, let us say, something like fourteen years old; long and loose jointed and tow headed. He wasn't good for much, that boy. His chief delight was to eat and sleep, and after that he liked best to make mischief.

It was a Sunday morning and the boy's parents were getting ready for church. The boy, in his shirt sleeves, sat on the edge of the table thinking how lucky it was that both father and mother were going away so the coast would be clear for a couple of hours. "Good! Now I can take down pop's gun and fire off a shot, without anybody's meddling interference," he said to himself.

But it was almost as if his father should have guessed the boy's thoughts for just as he was on the threshold and ready to start, he stopped short, and turned toward the boy: "Since you won't come to church with mother and me," he said, "the least you can do is to read the service at home. Will you promise to do so?" "Yes, that I can do easy enough," said the boy, thinking, of course, that he wouldn't read any more than he felt like reading.

The boy thought that never had he seen his mother get around so fast. In a jiffy she was over by the book shelf, near the fireplace, taking down Luther's Commentary, which she laid upon the table, in front of the window—opened at the service of the day. She also opened the New Testament, and placed it beside the Commentary. Finally she drew up the big armchair, which was bought at the parish auction the year before, and which, as a rule, no one but father was permitted to occupy.

The boy sat there thinking that his mother was giving herself altogether too much trouble with this spread, for he had

*From *The Wonderful Adventures of Nils*. Reprinted by permission of the publishers, Doubleday, Page & Co.

no intention of reading more than a page or so. But now, for the second time, it was almost as if his father were able to see right through him. He walked up to the boy and said in a severe tone: "Now remember that you are to read carefully! For when we come back, I shall question you thoroughly; and if you have skipped a single page, it will not go well with you."

"The service is fourteen pages and a half long," said his mother, piling it on, as it were. "You'll have to sit down and begin the reading at once, if you expect to get through with it."

With that they departed. And as the boy stood in the doorway, watching them, he felt that he had been caught in a trap. "There they go congratulating themselves, I suppose, in the belief that they've hit upon something so good that I'll be forced to sit and hang over the sermon the whole time that they are away," thought he.

But his father and mother were certainly not congratulating themselves upon anything of the sort; but, on the contrary, they were very much distressed. They were poor farmers, and their place was not much bigger than a garden-plot. When they first moved there, the bit of land couldn't feed more than one pig and a pair of chickens; but they were uncommonly thrifty and capable folk—and now they had both cows and geese. Things had turned out very well for them; and they would have gone to church that beautiful morning satisfied and happy, if they hadn't had their son to think of. Father complained that he was dull and lazy; he had not cared to learn anything at school, and he was such an all-around good-for-nothing that he could barely be made to tend geese. Mother could not deny that this was true; but she was most distressed because he was wild and bad, cruel to animals, and ill-willed toward human beings. "May God soften his hard heart and give him a better disposition!" said the mother, "else he will be a misfortune, both to himself and to us."

The boy stood there a long time pondering whether he should read the service or not.   Finally, he came to the conclusion that this time it was best to be obedient.   He seated himself in the easy chair, and began to read.   But when he had been rattling away in an undertone for a little while, this mumbling seemed to have a soothing effect upon him—and he began to nod.

It was the most beautiful weather outside!   It was only the twentieth of March; but the boy lived in West Vemmenhog Parish, down in Southern Skans, where the spring was already in full swing.   It was not as yet green, but fresh and budding.   There was water in all the trenches, and the colt's-foot at the edge of the ditch was in bloom.   All the weeds that grew in among the stones were brown and shiny.   The beech-woods in the distance seemed to swell and grow thicker with every second.   The skies were high, and a clear blue.   The cottage door stood ajar, and the lark's trill could be heard in the room.   The hens and geese pattered about in the yard; and the cows, who felt the spring air away in their stalls, lowed their approval every now and then.

The boy read and nodded and fought against drowsiness. "No!   I don't want to fall asleep," thought he, "for then I'll not get through with this thing the whole forenoon."

But somehow he fell asleep.

He did not know whether he had slept a short while or a long while; but he was awakened by hearing a slight noise back of him.

On the window-sill, facing the boy, stood a small looking glass; and almost the entire cottage could be seen in it.   As the boy raised his head, he happened to look in the glass and then he saw that the cover of his mother's chest had been opened.

His mother owned a great, heavy, iron-bound oak chest which she permitted no one but herself to open.   Here she treasured all the things she had inherited from her mother, and of these she was especially careful. Here lay a couple of old-time peasant dresses, of red homespun with short bodice and plaited skirt, and a pearl-bedecked breast-pin. There were starched white linen headdresses, and heavy silver ornaments and chains. Folks don't care to go about dressed like that in these days, and several times his mother had thought of getting rid of the old things; but somehow, she hadn't the heart to do it.

Now the boy saw distinctly—in the glass—that the chest-lid was open. He could not understand how this had happened, for his mother had closed the chest before she went. She never would have left the precious chest open with only him there.

He became low-spirited and apprehensive. He was afraid that a thief had sneaked his way into the cottage. He didn't dare move, but sat still and stared into the looking glass.

While he sat there and waited for the thief to make his appearance, he began to wonder what the dark shadow was which fell across the edge of the chest. He stared and stared and wouldn't believe his eyes. But the object, which at first seemed shadowy, became more and more clear to him; and soon he saw that it was something real. It was nothing less than an elf that sat there—astride the edge of the chest!

To be sure, the boy had heard stories about elves, but he had never dreamed that they were such tiny creatures. He was no taller than a hand's breadth—this one, who sat on the edge of the chest. He had an old, wrinkled and beardless face, and was dressed in a long frock coat, knee-breeches and a broad-brimmed felt hat. He was very trim and smart, with his white laces at the throat and wrist-bands, his buckled shoes, and the bows on his garters. He had taken from the chest an embroidered piece, and sat gazing at the old-fashioned handi-work with such an air of veneration that he did not observe the boy had awakened.

The boy was somewhat surprised to see the elf, but, on the other hand, he was not exactly frightened. It was impossible to be afraid of one who was so little. And since the elf was so absorbed in his own thoughts that he neither saw nor heard, the boy thought that it would be great fun to play a trick on him; to push him over into the chest and shut the lid on him, or something of the kind.

Yet the boy was not so courageous that he dared touch the elf with his hands; instead he glanced around the room for some-thing to poke him with. He let his gaze wander from the sofa to the leaf-table; from the leaf-table to the fireplace. He glanced at the kettles, then at the coffee-urn, which stood on a shelf, near the fireplace; on the water bucket, near the door; and on the spoons and knives and forks and saucers and plates, which could be seen through the half-open cupboard door. He looked up at his father's gun, which hung on the wall beside the portrait of the Danish royal family, and at the geraniums and fuchsias, which blossomed in the window. And last, he caught sight of an old butterfly-snare that hung on the window frame. He had hardly set eyes on that butterfly-snare before he reached over and snatched it alongside the edge of the chest. He was him-self astonished at the luck he had. He hardly knew how he had managed it—but he had actually snared the elf. The poor little chap lay, head downward, in the bottom of the long snare, and could not free himself.

At the first moment the boy hadn't the least idea as to what he should do with his catch; but he was very careful to swing the snare backward and forward, to prevent the elf from getting a foothold and clambering up.

The elf began to speak, and begged, oh! so pitifully, for his freedom. He had brought them good luck these many years, he said, and deserved better treatment. Now, if the boy would set him free, he would give him an old penny, a silver spoon, and a gold coin, as big as the case on his father's silver watch.

The boy didn't think that this was much of an offer; but it so happened that after he had got the elf into his power, he was afraid of him. He felt that he had entered into an agreement with something weird and uncanny, something which did not belong to his world; and he was only too glad to rid himself of the horrid creature.

For this reason he agreed at once to the bargain, and held the snare still, so the elf could crawl out of it. But when the elf was almost out of the snare, the boy happened to think that he should have bargained for large estates, and all sorts of good things. He should at least have made this stipulation: that the elf conjure the sermon into his head. "What a fool I was to let him go!" thought he, and began to shake the snare violently, so the elf would tumble down again.

But the instant the boy did that he received such a stinging box on the ear that he thought his head would fly in pieces. He was dashed—first against one wall, then against the other; finally he sank to the floor, and lay there—senseless.

When he awoke he was alone in the cottage. There was not a sign of the elf! The chest-lid was down, and the butterfly-snare hung in its usual place by the window. If he had not felt how the right cheek burned from that box on the ear, he would have been tempted to believe the whole thing a dream. "At any rate, father and mother will be sure to insist that it was nothing else," thought he. "They are not likely to make any allowances for that old sermon, on the elf's account. It's best for me to get at that reading again."

But as he walked toward the table, he noticed something remarkable. It couldn't be possible that the cottage had grown. But why did he have to take so many more steps than usual to get to the table? And what was wrong with the chair? It looked no bigger than it did a while ago; but now he had to step on the first rung and then clamber up in order to reach the seat. It was the same with the table. He could not look across the top without climbing to the arm of the chair.

"What in all the world is this?" said the boy. "I believe the elf has bewitched both armchair and table—and the whole cottage."

The Commentary lay on the table and, to all appearances, it was not changed; but there must have been something queer about that too, for he could not manage to read a single word of it without actually standing right in the book itself.

He read a couple of lines, then happened to look up. With that his glance fell on the looking glass; and then he cried aloud: "Look! There's another little one."

For in the glass he saw plainly a little, little creature who was dressed in a hood and leather breeches.

"Why, that one is dressed exactly like me!" said the boy, clasping his hands in astonishment. And then he saw that the thing in the mirror did the same thing. Thereupon, he began to pull his hair and pinch his arms and swing round; and instantly he did the same thing after him; he, who was in the mirror.

The boy ran around the glass several times, to see if there wasn't a little man hidden behind it, but he found no one there; and then he began to shake with terror. For now he understood that the elf had bewitched him, and that the creature whose image he saw in the glass was—himself.

The boy simply could not make himself believe that he had been transformed into an elf. "It can't be anything but a dream—a queer fancy," thought he. "If I wait a few moments, I'll surely be turned back into a human being."

He placed himself before the glass and closed his eyes. He opened them again after a couple of minutes, expecting to find that it had all passed over—but it hadn't. He was—and remained—just as little. In other respects, he was the same as before. The thin, straw-coloured hair; the freckles across his nose; the patches on his leather breeches, and the darns on his stockings were all like themselves, with this difference—they had become diminished.

No, it would do him no good to stand still and wait, of that he was certain. He must try something else. And he thought the wisest thing that he could do was to try to find the elf, and make his peace with him.

He jumped to the floor and began to search. He looked behind chairs and cupboards; under the sofa and in the oven, and he even crawled down into a couple of ratholes—but he simply couldn't find the elf.

And while he sought, he cried and prayed and promised everything he could think of. Nevermore would he break his word to any one; never again would he be naughty; and never, never would he fall asleep any more over the sermon. If he might only be a human being once more, he would be such a good and helpful and obedient boy. But no matter how much he promised, it did not help him the least little bit.

Suddenly he remembered that he had heard his mother say all the tiny folk made their home in the cowshed; and, at once, he decided to go there, to see if he couldn't find the elf. It was a lucky thing that the cottage-door stood partly open, for he never could have reached the bolt and opened it; but now he slipped through without difficulty.

When he came out into the hallway, he looked around for his wooden shoes; for in the house, to be sure, he had gone about in his stocking feet. He wondered how he should ever manage with these big, clumsy wooden shoes on the door-step. When he observed that the elf had been so thoughtful as to bewitch even the wooden shoes, he was more troubled than ever. It was evidently the elf's meaning that this affliction should last a long time.

On the old plank-walk in front of the cottage, hopped a gray sparrow. It had hardly set eyes on the boy before it called out: "Teetee! Teetee! Look at Nils goosey-boy! Look at Thumbie-tot! Look at Nils Helgersson Thumbietot!"

Instantly the geese and the chickens turned and stared at the boy; and then they set up a fearful cackling. "Cock-el-i-coo," crowed the rooster, "good enough for him! Cock-el-i-coo, he has pulled my comb." "Ka, ka, kada, serves him right!" cried the hens, and with that they kept up a continuous cackle. The geese got together in a tight group, stuck their heads together and asked: "Who can have done this? Who can have done this?"

But the strangest of all was, that the boy understood what they said. He was so astonished that he stood there as if rooted to the doorstep and listened. "It must be because I am turning into an elf," said he. "This is probably why I understand bird-talk."

He thought it unbearable that the hens would not stop saying that it served him right. He threw a stone at them and shouted, "Shut up, you pack!"

But it hadn't occurred to him before that he was no longer the sort of boy the hens fear. The whole henyard made a rush at him, and formed a ring around him; then they all cried at once: "Ka, ka, kada, served you right! Ka, ka, kada, served you right!"

The boy tried to get away, but the chickens ran after him and screamed until he thought he'd lose his hearing. It is more than likely that he never could have got away from them if the house cat hadn't come along just then. As soon as the chickens saw the cat, they quieted down and pretended to be thinking of nothing else than just to scratch in the earth for worms.

Immediately the boy ran up to the cat. "You dear pussy!" he said, "you must know all the corners and hiding-places here-

about! You'll be a good little kitty and tell me where I can find the elf."

The cat did not reply at once. He sat down leisurely, curled his tail into a graceful ring around his paws—and stared at the boy. It was a large black cat with one white spot on the chest. His fur lay sleek and soft, and shone in the sunlight. The claws were drawn in, and the eyes were a dull gray, with just a little, narrow, dark streak down the centre. The cat looked thoroughly good-natured.

"I know well enough where the elf lives," he said in a soft voice, "but that doesn't say that I'm going to tell *you* about it."

"Dear pussy, you must tell me where the elf lives!" pleaded the boy. "Can't you see how he has bewitched me?"

The cat opened his eyes a little, so that the green wickedness began to shine forth. He spun round and purred with satisfaction before he replied. "Shall I perhaps help you because you have so often grabbed me by the tail?" he said at last.

Then the boy was furious and forgot entirely how little and helpless he was now. "Oh! I can pull your tail again, I can," said he, and ran toward the cat.

The next instant the cat was so changed that the boy could scarcely believe it was the same animal. Every separate hair on his body stood on end. The back was bent; the legs had become elongated; the claws scraped the ground; the tail had grown thick and short; the ears were laid back; the mouth was frothy; the eyes were wide open and glistened like sparks of red fire.

The boy didn't want to let himself be scared by a cat, so he took a step forward. Then the cat made one spring and landed right on the boy, knocked him down and stood over him—his forepaws on his chest, his jaws wide apart over his throat.

The boy felt how the sharp claws sank through his vest and

shirt into his skin; and how the sharp eyeteeth tickled his throat. He shrieked for help as loudly as he could, but no one came. He thought surely that his last hour had come. Then he felt that the cat drew in his claws and let go the hold on his throat.

"There!" he said, "that will do for now. "I'll let you go this time, for my mistress's sake. I only wanted you to know which one of us two had the power now."

With that the cat walked away, looking as smooth and pious as when he first appeared on the scene. The boy was so crest-fallen that he couldn't say a word, but only hurried to the cow-house to look for the elf.

There were not more than three cows, all told. But when the boy came in, there was such a bellowing and such a kick-up, that one might easily have believed there were at least thirty.

"Moo, moo, moo," bellowed Mayrose. "It is well there is such a thing as justice in this world."

"Moo, moo, moo," sang the three of them in unison. He couldn't hear what they said, for each tried to out-bellow the others.

The boy wanted to ask after the elf, but he couldn't make himself heard because the cows were in full uproar. They carried on as they used to when he would let a strange dog in on them. They kicked with their hind legs, shook their flanks, stretched their heads, and measured the distance with their horns.

"Come here, you!" said Mayrose, "and you'll get a kick that you won't forget in a hurry!"

"Come here," said Gold Lily, "and you shall dance on my horns!"

"Come here, and you shall taste how it felt when you threw your wooden shoes at me, as you did last summer!" bawled Star.

"Come here, and you shall be repaid for that wasp you let loose in my ear!" growled Gold Lily.

Mayrose was the oldest and wisest among them, and she was the very maddest. "Come here!" she said, "that I may pay you back for the many times that you have jerked the milk pail away from your mother, and for all the snares you laid for her when she came carrying the milk pails and for all the tears which she has stood here and wept over you!"

The boy wanted to tell them how much he regretted that he had been unkind to them; and that never, never, from now on, should he be anything but good, if they would only tell him where the elf was. But the cows didn't listen to him. They made such a racket that he began to fear one of them would succeed in breaking loose; so he thought that the best thing for him to do, was to go quietly away from the cowhouse.

When he came out again he was thoroughly disheartened. He could understand that no one on the place wanted to help him find the elf. And little good would it do him, probably, if the elf were found!

He crawled up on the broad hedge which fenced in the farm, and which was overgrown with brier and lichen. There he sat to ponder how it would go with him were he never again to become a human being. When father and mother get back from church, there would be a surprise for them. Yes, a surprise—it would be all over the land; and people would come flocking from East Vemmenhog, and from Torp, and from Skerup. The whole Vemmenhog Parish would come to stare at him. Perhaps father and mother would take him along to Kivik, and show him at the market-place.

No, that was too horrible to think about. He would rather that no human being should ever see him again.

His unhappiness was simply frightful! No one in all the world was so unhappy as he. He was no longer a human being —but a freak.

Little by little he began to comprehend what it meant—
to be no longer human. He was separated from everything now;
he could no longer play with other boys.

He sat and looked at his home. It was a little log house,
which lay as if crushed down to earth, under the high, sloping
roof. The outhouses were also small; and the patches of tilled
ground were so narrow that a horse could barely turn around
on them. But little and poor though the place was, it was much
too good for him *now*. He couldn't hope for a better home than
a hole under the stable floor.

It was wondrously beautiful weather! It budded, and it
rippled, and it murmured, and it twittered—all around him.
But he sat there with such a heavy sorrow. He should never
be happy any more about anything.

And that is the way the adventures of Nils began. Far out
into the world he had to go and he travelled far and he travelled
wide before he saw his mother and father and found the elf again.
And all through his long, long journey little he stayed until he
grew big. But what is the secret of that I leave you to guess.

Little Diamond and The North Wind*

GEORGE MACDONALD

I HAVE been asked to tell you about the back of the North Wind. I am going to tell you how it fared with a boy who went there. He lived in a low room over a coach-house. Indeed, I am not sure whether I ought to call it a room; for it was just a loft were they kept hay and straw and oats for the horses. And when little Diamond—but stop, I must tell you that his father who was a coachman, had named him after a favorite horse—when little Diamond, then, lay there in bed, he could hear the horses under him munching away in the dark, or moving sleepily in their dreams. For Diamond's father had built him a bed in the loft with boards all round it, because they had so little room in their own end over the coach-house.

There was hay at his feet and hay at his head, piled up in great trusses to the very roof. Indeed it was sometimes only through a little lane with several turnings, which looked as if it had been sawed out for him, that he could reach his bed at all. Sometimes, when his mother had undressed him in her room and told him to trot away to bed by himself, he would creep into the heart of the hay, and lie there thinking how cold it was outside in the wind, and how warm it was inside there in his bed, and how he could go to it when he pleased, only he wouldn't just yet; he would get a little colder first. And ever as he grew colder, his bed would grow warmer, till at last he would scramble out of the hay, shoot like an arrow into his bed, cover himself up, and snuggle down, thinking what a happy boy he was. He had not the least idea that the wind got in at a chink in the wall, and blew about him all night. For the back of his bed was only boards an inch thick, and on the other side of them was the north wind.

*From *At the Back of the North Wind.*

THROUGH FAIRY HALLS

Now, as I have already said, these boards were soft and crumbly. Hence it happened that the soft part having worn away from about it, little Diamond found one night, after he lay down, that a knot had come out of one of them, and that the wind was blowing in upon him in a cold and rather imperious fashion. Now he had no fancy for leaving things wrong that might be set right; so he jumped out of bed again, got a little strike of hay, twisted it up, folded it in the middle, and, having thus made it into a cork, stuck it into the hole in the wall. But the wind began to blow loud and angrily, and, as Diamond was falling asleep, out blew his cork and hit him on the nose, just hard enough to wake him up quite, and let him hear the wind whistling shrill in the hole. He searched for his hay-cork, found it, stuck it in harder, and was just dropping off once more, when, pop! with an angry whistle behind it, the cork struck him again, this time on the cheek. Up he rose once more, made a fresh stopple of hay, and corked the hole severely. But he was hardly down again before—pop! it came on his forehead. He gave it up, drew the clothes above his head, and was soon fast asleep.

Although the next day was very stormy, Diamond forgot all about the hole. His mother, however, discovered it, and pasted a bit of brown paper over it, so when Diamond snuggled down the next night, he had no occasion to think of it.

Presently, however, he lifted his head and listened. Who could that be talking to him? The wind was rising again, and getting very loud, and full of rushes and whistles. He was sure some one was talking—and very near him, too, it was. But he was not frightened; so he sat up and hearkened. At last the voice, which, though quite gentle, sounded a little angry, appeared to come from the back of the bed. He crept nearer to it, and laid his ear against the wall. Then he heard nothing but the wind, which sounded very loud indeed. The moment, however,

 that he moved his head from the wall, he heard the voice again close to his ear. He felt about with his hand, and came upon the piece of paper his mother had pasted over the hole. Against this he laid his ear, and then he heard the voice quite distinctly. There was, in fact, a little corner of the paper loose, and through that, as from a mouth in the wall, the voice came.

"What do you mean, little boy—closing up my window?"

"What window?" asked Diamond.

"You stuffed hay into it three times last night. I had to blow it out again three times."

"You can't mean this little hole! It isn't a window; it's a hole in my bed."

"I did not say it was *a* window. I said it was *my* window."

"But it can't be a window, because windows are holes to see out of."

"Well, that's just what I made this window for."

"But you are outside; you can't want a window."

"You are quite mistaken. Windows are to see out of, you say. Well, I'm in my house, and I want windows to see out of it."

"But you've made a window into my bed."

"Well, your mother has got three windows into my dancing room, and you have three into my garret. Just open this window."

"Mother says I shouldn't be disobliging; but it's rather hard. You see the north wind will blow right in my face if I do."

"I am the North Wind."

"O-o-oh!" said Diamond, thoughtfully. "Then will you promise not to blow on my face if I open your window?"

"You shall not be the worse for it—I promise you that."

THROUGH FAIRY HALLS

"Well, I *can* pull the clothes over my head," said Diamond, and feeling with his little sharp nails, he got hold of the open edge of the paper and tore it off at once.

In came a long whistling spear of cold, and struck his little

naked chest. He scrambled and tumbled in under the bedclothes, and covered himself up; there was no paper now between him and the voice, and he felt a little—not frightened exactly—but rather queer; for what a strange person this North Wind must be that lived in the great house—"called Out-of-Doors, I suppose," thought Diamond—and made windows into people's beds! But the voice began again; and he could hear it quite plainly, even with his head under the bedclothes.

"What is your name, little boy?" it asked.

"Diamond," answered Diamond, under the bedclothes.

"What a funny name!"

"Diamond is a very pretty name," persisted the boy, vexed that it should not give satisfaction. "Diamond is a great and good horse; and he *sleeps* right under me. He's Old Diamond, and I'm Young Diamond; or, if you like it better, for you're very particular, Mr. North Wind, he's Big Diamond, and I'm Little Diamond; and I don't know which of us my father likes best."

A beautiful laugh, large but very soft and musical, sounded somewhere beside him, but Diamond kept his head under the clothes.

"I'm not Mr. North Wind," said the voice.

"You told me that you were the North Wind," insisted Diamond.

"I did not say *Mister* North Wind," said the voice.

"Well, then, I do; for mother tells me I ought to be polite."

"Then let me tell you I don't think it at all polite of you to say *Mister* to me. You can't say it's polite to lie there talking—with your head under the bedclothes, and never look up to see what kind of person you are talking to. I want you to come out with me."

"I want to go to sleep," said Diamond, very nearly crying.

"You shall sleep all the better to-morrow night. Will you

take your head out of the bedclothes?" said the voice.

"No!" answered Diamond, half peevish, half frightened.

The instant he said the word, a tremendous blast of wind crashed in a board of the wall, and swept the clothes off Diamond. He started up in terror. Leaning over him was the large, beautiful, pale face of a woman. Her dark eyes looked a little angry, for they had just begun to flash; but a quivering in her sweet upper lip made her look as if she were going to cry. What was the most strange was that away from her head streamed out her black hair in every direction, so that the darkness in the hayloft looked as if it were made of her hair; but as Diamond gazed at her in speechless amazement, mingled with confidence —for the boy was entranced with her mighty beauty—her hair began to gather itself out of the darkness, and fell down all about her again, till her face looked out of the midst of it like a moon out of a cloud. From her eyes came all the light by which Diamond saw her face and her hair; and that was all he did see of her yet. The wind was over and gone.

"Will you go with me now, you little Diamond? I am sorry I was forced to be so rough with you," said the lady.

"I will; yes, I will," answered Diamond, holding out both his arms. "Please, North Wind, you are so beautiful, I am quite ready to go with you."

"You must not be ready to go with everything beautiful all at once, Diamond."

"But what's beautiful can't be bad. I will go with you because you are beautiful and good, too."

"Ah, but there's another thing, Diamond:—What if I should look ugly without being bad—look ugly myself because I am making ugly things beautiful? What then?"

"I don't quite understand you, North Wind. You tell me what then."

"Well, I will tell you. If you see me with my face all black, don't be frightened. If you see me flapping wings like a bat's, as big as the whole sky, don't be frightened. If you hear me raging ten times worse than Mrs. Bill, the blacksmith's wife —even if you see me looking in at people's windows like Mrs. Eve Dropper, the gardener's wife—you must believe that I am doing my work. Nay, Diamond, if I change into a serpent or a tiger, you must not let go your hold of me, for my hand will never change in yours if you keep a good hold. If you keep a hold, you will know who I am all the time, even when you look at me and can't see me the least like the North Wind. I may look something very awful. Do you understand?"

"Quite well," said little Diamond.

"Come along, then," said North Wind, and disappeared behind the mountain of hay.

Diamond crept out of bed and followed her.

North Wind laughed merrily, and went tripping on faster. Her grassy robe swept and swirled about her steps, and wherever it passed over withered leaves, they went fleeing and whirling in spirals, and running on their edges like wheels, all about her feet. They were now climbing the slope of a grassy ascent. It was Primrose Hill, in fact, although Diamond had never heard of it. The moment they reached the top, North Wind stood and turned her face towards London. The stars were still shining clear and cold overhead. There was not a cloud to be seen. The air was sharp, but Diamond did not find it cold.

"Now," said the lady, "whatever you do, do not let my hand go." And as she stood looking towards London, Diamond saw that she was trembling.

"Are you cold, North Wind?" he asked.

"No, Diamond," she answered, looking down upon him with a smile; "I am only getting ready to sweep one of my rooms. Those careless, greedy, untidy children make it in such a mess."

As she spoke he could have told by her voice, if he had not seen with his eyes, that she was growing larger and larger. Her head went up and up towards the stars; and as she grew, still trembling through all her body, her hair also grew—longer and longer, and lifted itself from her head, and went out in black waves. The next moment, however, it fell back around her, and she grew less and less till she was only a tall woman. Then she put her hands behind her head, and gathered some of her hair, and began weaving and knotting it together. When she had done, she bent down her beautiful face close to his, and said:

"Diamond, I am afraid you would not keep hold of me, and if I were to drop you, I don't know what might happen; so I have been making a place for you in my hair. Come."

Diamond held out his arms, for with that grand face looking at him, he believed like a baby. She took him in her hands, threw him over her shoulder, and said, "Get in, Diamond."

And Diamond parted her hair with his hands, crept between, and, feeling about, soon found the woven nest. It was just like a pocket, or like the shawl in which gipsy women carry their children. North Wind put her hands to her back, felt all about the nest, and finding it safe, said:

"Are you comfortable, Diamond?"

"Yes, indeed," answered Diamond.

The next moment he was rising in the air. North Wind grew towering up to the place of the clouds. Her hair went streaming out from her, till it spread like a mist over the stars. She flung herself abroad in space.

Diamond held on by two of the twisted ropes which, parted and interwoven, formed his shelter, for he could not help being a little afraid. As soon as he had come to himself, he peeped through the woven meshes, for he did not dare to look over the top of the nest. The earth was rushing past like a river or a sea below him. Trees, and water, and green grass hurried away beneath. Chimney-pots fell, and tiles flew from the roofs. There was a great roaring, for the wind was dashing against London like a sea; but at North Wind's back Diamond, of course, felt nothing of it all. He was in a perfect calm. He could hear the sound of it, that was all.

By and by he raised himself and looked over the edge of his nest. There were the houses rushing up and shooting away below him, like a fierce torrent of rocks instead of water. Then he looked up to the sky, but could see no stars; they were hidden by the blinding masses of the lady's hair which swept between. He began to wonder whether she would hear him if he spoke. He would try.

"Please, North Wind," he said, "what is that noise?"

From high over his head came the voice of North Wind, answering him gently:

"The noise of my besom. I am the old woman that sweeps the cobwebs from the sky; only I'm busy with the floor now."

"What makes the houses look as if they were running away?"

"I am sweeping so fast over them."

"But, please, North Wind, I knew London was very big, but I didn't know it was so big as this. It seems as if we should never get away from it."

"We are going round and round, else we should have left it long ago."

"Please, would you mind going a little slower, for I want to see the streets?"

"You won't see much now."

"Why?"

"Because I have swept nearly all the people home."

But she dropped a little towards the roofs of the houses, and Diamond could see down into the streets. There were very few people about, though. The lamps flickered and flared again, but nobody seemed to want them.

Suddenly Diamond espied a little girl coming along a street. She was dreadfully blown by the wind, and a broom she was trailing behind her was very troublesome. It seemed as if the wind had a spite at her—it kept worrying her like a wild beast, and tearing at her rags. She was so lonely there!

"Oh! please, North Wind," he cried, "won't you help that little girl?"

"No, Diamond; I musn't leave my work."

"But why shouldn't you be kind to her?"

"I am kind to her; I am sweeping the wicked smells away."

"But you're kinder to me, dear North Wind. Why shouldn't you be as kind to her as you are to me?"

"There are reasons, Diamond. Everybody can't be done to all the same. Everybody is not ready for the same thing."

"But I don't see why I should be kinder used than she."

"Do you think nothing's to be done but what you can see, Diamond, you silly! It's all right. Of course you can help her if you like. You've got nothing particular to do at this moment; I have."

"Oh! do let me help her, then. But you won't be able to wait, perhaps?"

"No, I can't wait; you must do it yourself."

"I want to go," said Diamond. "Only there's just one thing —how am I to get home?"

"Well, though I cannot promise to take you home," said North Wind, as she sank nearer and nearer to the tops of the houses, "I can promise you will get home somehow. Have you made up your mind what to do?"

"Yes; to help the little girl," said Diamond firmly.

The same moment North Wind dropped into the street and stood, only a tall lady, but with her hair flying up over the house-tops. She put her hands to her back, took Diamond, and set him down in the street. The same moment he was caught in the fierce coils of the blast, and all but blown away. North Wind stepped back a pace, and at once towered in stature to the height of the houses. A chimney-pot clashed at Diamond's feet. He turned in terror, but it was to look for the little girl, and when he turned again the lady had vanished, and the wind was roaring along the street as if it had been the bed of an inuisible torrent. The little girl was scudding before the blast, her hair flying too, and behind her she dragged her broom. Her little legs were going as fast as ever they could to keep her from falling. Diamond crept into the shelter of a doorway, thinking to stop her; but she passed him like a bird, crying pitifully.

"Stop! little girl," shouted Diamond, starting in pursuit.

"I can't," wailed the girl; "the wind won't leave go of me."

THROUGH FAIRY HALLS

Diamond could run faster than she, and he had no broom. In a few moments he had caught her by the frock. But it tore in his hand, and away went the little girl. So he had to run again, and this time he ran so fast that he got before her, and turning round caught her in his arms, when down they went both together, which made the little girl laugh in the midst of her crying.

"Where are you going?" asked Diamond, rubbing the elbow that had stuck farthest out. The arm it belonged to was twined round a lamp-post as he stood between the little girl and the wind.

"Home," she said, gasping for breath.

"Then I will go with you," said Diamond.

And then they were silent for a while, for the wind blew worse than ever, and they had both to hold on to the lamp-post.

"Where is your crossing?" asked the girl at length.

"I don't sweep," answered Diamond.

"What *do* you do, then?" asked she. "You ain't big enough for most things."

"I don't know what I do do," answered he, feeling rather ashamed. "Nothing, I suppose. My father's Mr. Coleman's coachman."

"Have you a father?" she said, staring at him as if a boy with a father was a natural curiosity.

"Yes. Haven't *you?*" returned Diamond.

"No; nor mother neither. Old Sal's all I've got." And she began to cry again. "If she was my mother, she wouldn't lie abed and laugh to hear me crying at the door."

"You don't mean she won't let you in to-night?"

"It'll be a good chance if she does."

"Why are you out so late, then?" asked Diamond.

"My crossing's a long way off at the West End."

"We'd better have a try anyhow. Come along. You lead me," said Diamond, taking her hand. "and I'll take care of you."

433

The girl withdrew her hand, but only to dry her eyes with her frock, for the other had enough to do with her broom. She put it in his again, and led him, turning after turning, until they stopped at a cellar-door in a very dirty lane. There she knocked.

"I shouldn't like to live here," said Diamond.

"Oh, yes, you would, if you had nowheres else to go to," answered the girl. "I only wish we may get in."

"I don't want to go in," said Diamond.

"Where do you mean to go, then?"

"Home to my home."

"Where's that?"

"I don't exactly know."

"Then you're worse off than I am."

"Oh no, for North Wind—" began Diamond, and stopped, he hardly knew why.

"*What?*" said the girl, as she held her ear to the door, listening.

But Diamond did not reply. Neither did old Sal.

"I told you so," said the girl. "She is wide awake hearkening. But we don't get in."

"What will you do, then?" asked Diamond.

"Move on," she answered.

"Where?"

"Oh, anywheres. Bless you, I'm used to it."

"Hadn't you better come home with me, then?"

"That's a good joke, when you don't know where it is. Come on."

"But where?"

"Oh, nowheres in particular. Come on."

Diamond obeyed. The wind had now fallen considerably. They wandered on and on, turning in this direction and that, without any reason for one way more than another, until they had got out of the thick of the houses into a waste kind of place.

THROUGH FAIRY HALLS

By this time they were both very tired. Diamond felt a good deal inclined to cry, and thought he had been very silly to get down from the back of the North Wind; not that he would have minded it if he had done the girl any good; but he thought he had been of no use to her. He was mistaken there, for she was far happier for having Diamond with her than if she had been wandering about alone. She did not seem so tired as he was.

"Do let us rest a bit," said Diamond.

"Let's see," she answered. "There's something like a railway there. Perhaps there's an open arch."

They went towards it and found one, and, better still, there was an empty barrel lying under the arch.

"Hello! here we are!" said the girl. "A barrel's the jolliest bed going—on the tramp, I mean. We'll have forty winks, and then go on again."

She crept in, and Diamond crept in beside her. They put their arms around each other, and when he began to grow warm Diamond's courage began to come back.

"This *is* jolly!" he said. "I'm *so* glad!"

"I don't think so much of it," said the girl. "I'm used to it, I suppose. But I can't think how a kid like you comes to be out all alone this time o' the night."

She called him a *kid*, but she was not really a month older

than he was; only she had had to work for her bread, and that so soon makes people older.

"But I shouldn't have been out so late if I hadn't got down to help you," said Diamond. "North Wind is gone home long ago."

"You said something about the north wind afore that I couldn't get the rights of."

So now, for the sake of his character, Diamond had to tell her the whole story.

She did not believe a word of it. She said she wasn't such a flat as to believe all that bosh. But as she spoke there came a great blast of wind through the arch, and set the barrel rolling. So they made haste to get out of it, for they had no notion of being rolled over and over as if they had been packed tight and wouldn't hurt, like a barrel of herrings.

"I thought we should have had a sleep," said Diamond; "but I can't say I'm very sleepy after all. Let's go on again."

They wandered on and on, sometimes sitting on a door-step, but always turning into lanes or fields when they had a chance.

They found themselves at last on a rising ground that sloped rather steeply on the other side. It was a waste kind of spot below, bounded by an irregular wall, with a few doors in it. Outside lay broken things in general, from garden rollers to flower-pots and wine-bottles. But the moment they reached the brow of the rising ground, a gust of wind seized them and blew them down hill as fast as they could run. Nor could Diamond stop before he went bang against one of the doors in the wall. To his dismay it burst open. When they came to themselves they peeped in. It was the back door of a garden.

"Ah, ah!" cried Diamond, after staring for a few moments "I thought so! North Wind takes nobody in! Here I am in master's garden! I tell you what, little girl, you just bore a hole in old Sal's wall, put your mouth to it, and say, 'Please, North

Wind, mayn't I go out with you?' Then you'll see what'll come."

"I daresay I shall. But I'm out in the wind too often already to want more of it."

"I said *with* the North Wind, not *in* it."

"It's all one."

"It's *not* all one."

"It *is* all one."

"But I know best."

"And I know better. I'll box your ears," said the girl.

Diamond got very angry. But he remembered that even if she did box his ears, he mustn't box hers again, for she was a girl, and all that boys must do, if girls are rude, is to go away and leave them. So he went in at the door.

"Good-bye, mister," said the girl.

This brought Diamond to his senses.

"I'm sorry I was cross," he said. "Come in, and my mother will give you some breakfast."

"No, thank you. I must be off to my crossing. It's morning now."

"I'm very sorry for you," said Diamond.

"Well, it is a life to be tired of—what with old Sal, and so many holes in my shoes. When I think of it, though, I always want to see what's coming next. Good-bye!"

She ran up the hill and disappeared behind it. Then Diamond shut the door as he best could, and ran through the kitchen-garden to the stable. And wasn't he glad to get into his own blessed bed again!

437

The Renowned and World-Famous
Adventures of Punch and Judy

"Ladies and gentlemen, pray how you do?
If you all happy, me all happy too.
Stop and hear my merry little play,
If me make you laugh, me need not make you pay!

Squeak! Sque-eak!" Here's old Mr. Punch again, with his great hooked nose, and his hooked chin, and his peaked cap, and his fat stomach and his slender little legs and his smile, smile, smile! Old Mr. Punch and his wife, Judy, and the baby who is always being thrown out of the window, and Toby, the dog, and the hobby horse and all the rest of the well-known, widely travelled and world-famous performers in the puppet show.

There's hardly a corner of the world Punch and Judy haven't visited, and they've been sending men, women and children into gales of laughter from Boston to Paris, from China to Peru, for nobody-knows-how-many hundreds of years. So you see Punch and Judy are people of renown.

A hundred years ago, in any great city of Europe or America one might have seen set up in some public place, a little movable box of a theatre in which all the actors were wooden dolls—puppets or marionettes, as they are called. Sometimes these puppets were made to move about and go through the action of the play by means of wires attached to their heads; sometimes the man who gave the show stood inside a box below the little stage and wore Punch and Judy on his hands, which were covered from sight by the clothes of the puppets. He would use his thumb and middle finger to move the arms and his forefinger for the head. Then Mr. Punch, and Mrs. Judy, and the baby, and the hobby horse, and the distinguished foreign gentleman who couldn't speak English, and the rest would go through their parts with much spirit, while the show-man made up the words they were supposed to speak to each other, as the play went on.

Some of the puppet shows in London remained always in one place and were so loved by the people that real actors and singers at the opera complained because their play houses were empty while everybody crowded to see the puppet shows. There was even one droll show-man who trained a little pig to dance with Mr. Punch and squeak as if he were singing in imitation of one of the great Italian opera singers of the day.

Other puppet shows, instead of remaining always in one place, were carried about, both in town and in the country, on the backs of strolling showmen. These were particularly popular at country fairs, where they drew great crowds of merry, laughter-loving people. One man would carry the theatre itself on his back, and the other the box in which the puppets were packed. The first man would blow a little tin whistle and the second a trumpet to attract people's attention, and wherever they found a crowd gathered together or saw signs of interest, they set up their theatre and gave a performance. As soon as

Mr. Punch showed his ridiculous hooked nose between the curtains and gave the squeak that always announces his appearances, the people began to laugh, and they never left off laughing till the show was over. One of the men would pass about among the on-lookers and collect pennies during the play, and then off they would go to find another crowd.

The puppet shows came to England from Italy, but long, long, before that time, in the year 1000 B. C. or thereabouts, it is said that a puppet show-man gave a performance before the Emperor of China. That august gentleman had never heard of a puppet show and he thought that the dolls must be live men who dared to make faces at him. At last, becoming angry at their grimaces, he ordered all their heads off! The show-man with great difficulty was able to persuade the emperor that the actors were only dolls, whereupon, not only did he escape punishment, but was rewarded for his cleverness by being made official puppet show-man of the Chinese Empire.

Since Mr. Punch first appeared in the world the story about him has been little changed, although it was part of the show-man's business to make up new lines for the characters to speak as the play went on. Mr. Punch has been from the beginning and still is, the most ridiculous, absurd, impossible old rascal and villain in the world! He beats his wife, lays everybody else out with his stick, and flings his baby out the window quite unconcerned about it all, ever smiling, ever dancing and singing, without a pang of sorrow or regret. In the end he comes off victorious and conquers all his enemies without ever once being punished for his sins!

Once a very serious-minded show-man was so disturbed at Punch's always coming off victorious in spite of his evil deeds, that he made bold to change the ending of the play, and have Punch meet his just punishment, but O me! and O my! the crowd round about wouldn't have it—not at all. They pelted the poor man and his show with mud and drove him away.

So you see we shall have to take Mr. Punch just as he is and for what he is—a joke, not a real man at all, but a delightfully droll and absurd wooden puppet.

This is the Punch and Judy show as it has been given with slight variations for hundreds of years.

As the curtains are drawn back Mr. Punch is heard singing down below the stage,

> *"I dreamt that I dwelt in marble halls*
> *With vassals and serfs by my si-hi-hide!"*

All of a sudden up he pops like a jack-in-the-box, calling for his wife Judy. Instead of Judy, in comes the little dog Toby.

Punch says, "Hello, Toby! Who called you? How you do, Mr. Toby? Hope you very well, Mr. Toby."

"Bow, wow, wow!" says Toby.

"I'm glad to hear it, Toby! What a nice, good dog you are! Good Toby! Good Toby!"

At that Toby snarls, "Arr-rr! Arr-rr!"

"What, Toby, you cross this morning? You get out of bed the wrong way upwards?"

"Arr-rr! Arr-rr," answers Toby.

Punch puts out his hand cautiously to coax the dog. "Good doggie! Good doggie! Be a good doggie and me give you some pail of water and a broomstick for supper!" Toby snaps at his hand. "Toby, you're one bad dog! Get away with you!" and he strikes at the dog with his stick. Just at that moment Mr. Scaramouch, the owner of the dog, rises from below the stage and Biff! he receives the blow intended for Toby on his head.

"Ow-wow!" squeals Mr. Scaramouch, "I shall make you pay for my head, sir!"

"And I shall make you pay for my stick, sir!"

"I haven't broken your stick!"

"And I haven't broken your head!"

"You have, sir!"

"Then it must have been cracked before!"

"Hello," cries Mr. Scaramouch, spying Toby, "why, that's my dog Toby. Toby, old fellow, how are you?" Toby barks.

"He isn't your dog!" cries Punch.

"He is!"

"No, he isn't."

"He is, I tell you! A fortnight ago I lost him."

"And a fortnight ago I found him!"

"We'll soon see whether he belongs to you!" shouts Mr. Scaramouch. "You shall go up to him and say, 'Toby, poor little fellow, how are you?'"

"Very good!" agrees Mr. Punch, and he goes up to Toby, saying, "Toby, poor little fellow, how are you?" Toby snaps at Punch's nose.

"There you see that shows the dog is mine!" yells Scaramouch.

"No!" cries Punch, "it shows he's mine!"

"If he's yours, why does he bite you?"

"He bites me because he likes me!"

"Nonsense!" cries Scaramouch. "We'll soon settle which of us the dog belongs to. We'll fight for him. Now don't you begin till I say 'Time!'"

Punch knocks Mr. Scaramouch down and Scaramouch howls, "That wasn't fair!"

"It was fair!" cries Punch, "I didn't hit till you cried 'Time'."

"I never did!" goes on Mr. Scaramouch. "I only said, 'Don't begin till I say 'Time.'" Punch knocks him down a second time. "There you said it again!"

Scaramouch roars, "Toby, come help your master." The dog springs forward. Seeing this Punch begins to squeal, "No, no! Call off the dog! It isn't fair! You didn't say 'Time!'" Toby barks furiously and seizes Punch by the nose.

"Oh dear! Oh dear!" squeaks Punch, "my nose! my poor nose! my pretty little nose, my beautiful nose!" He tries to shake off the dog, but Toby still clings to his nose as he dances wildly around the stage. "Murder! Fire! Thieves! Call off your dog!"

"Very well," says Mr. Scaramouch, "come along, Toby!"

Toby lets go and the two leave the stage.

"I wouldn't have that dog as a gift," says Punch, nursing his nose and calling once again for Judy.

Judy comes in, in a frilled cap, with a hooked nose and hooked chin, just as ugly as Mr. Punch. "Well, what do you want now I've come?" says she.

"Ah," says Punch in a wheedling tone, "what a pretty little creature! Ain't she one beauty? Why, I want to dance with you, my duckie!" They dance. At the conclusion of the dance Punch hits Judy over the head with his stick.

"You villain," cries Judy, "how dare you strike me? Take that!" and she slaps him in the face.

"Ah," says Punch, stroking his cheek, "she is always so playful! Bring me the child, Judy! Bring me the child!"

Judy goes and brings back the baby which she leaves with Punch. He dandles the child in his arms and sings:

> *"Dancy baby diddy;*
> *What shall daddy do widdy?*
> *Sit on his lap,*
> *Give it some pap;*
> *Dancy, baby, diddy."*

"What a pretty baby it is," he croons, "little duck! Never was such a good child!"

The Baby cries, "Mama-a-a-a!"

Punch thumps the child with his stick.

"Go to sleep, my pretty!" he cries.

Baby cries louder, "Mama-a-a-a!"

Punch whacks him harder still, singing, "Hush-a-bye! Hush! Hush! Hush-sh-sh!"

Baby yells "Ya-a-ah!" and catches hold of Punch's nose.

"Murder! Let go!" howls Punch. "Go to your mother, darling,"—and Biff! he throws the baby out the window. Then he sings, smiling and unconcerned:

> *"I dreamt that I dwelt in marble halls,*
> *With vassals and serfs by my si-hi-hide!"*

At that, in comes Judy.

"Where's the boy?" she cries.

"Why, didn't you catch him?" asks Punch.

"Catch him?" says Judy. "What have you done with him?"

"Oh," cries Punch, "I just threw him out the window! Thought you might be passing and catch him."

"Oh you horrid wretch!" shrieks Judy. "You shall pay for this!" She hurries out, comes back in a moment with a stick, and hits Punch a resounding blow on the head, continuing then to pound him. "I'll teach you to drop my child out the window!"

"Ow-wow," howls Punch. "I'll never do it again!"

"I'll teach you! I'll teach you!"

"Then I be teacher too!" cries Punch. He takes the stick from Judy and knocks her flat with a blow, then he goes on singing:
> *"I dreamt that I dwelt in marble halls,*
> *With vassals and serfs by my si-hi-hide."*

In comes a policeman brandishing his club.

"Hollo! Hollo! Hollo! Here I am!" cries the policeman.

"Hollo! Hollo! Hollo!" answers Punch. "Here I am too!" and he whacks the policeman over the head!—

"Do you see my club, sir?" shouts the policeman.

"Do you feel my stick, sir?" answers Punch.

"Take your nose out of my face, sir!"

"Take your face out of my nose, sir!"

"Pooh!" cries the policeman.

"Pooh!" answers Punch.

"You have committed a crime, sir," says the policeman, "and I am come to take you up."

"And I am come to knock you down!" retorts Punch. Whack! He lays the policeman flat and goes on singing and dancing as before. Then he gets a great sheep bell and begins to shake it all about the stage. There enters a foreign servant dressed in outlandish livery.

"Mr. Punch," says the servant, "my master he say he no lika de noise."

Punch mimics him, "Your master he say he no lika de noise! What noise?"

"Dat horrid, bad noise! He'll no have more noise near his house!"

"He won't, won't he?" and Punch runs about the stage shaking the bell as loud as before.

"Get away I say wid dat horrid, bad bell," says the servant.

"Do you call that a bell," says Punch, "it's an organ!"

"I say it is a bell, a horrid bad bell!"

"I say it is an organ!" and Punch pounds him with it. "What you say it is now?"

"Ow-wow! Stop! Stop! It is an organ!" cries the servant.

"An organ? I say it is a fiddle!" Punch offers to pound him again.

"It is a fiddle," agrees the servant.

"I say it is a drum," yells Punch.

"It is a drum," agrees the servant.

"I say it is a trumpet," yells Punch.

"Well, so it is a trumpet; but bell, organ, fiddle, drum or trumpet, my master he no lika de music."

"Not like my sweet music?" says Punch. "I'll teach you to like sweet music!" and he pounds the servant about the stage with the bell till he runs away. Then comes in the distinguished foreign gentleman himself, who, being unable to express himself in English, says very solemnly,

"Shallaballah!"

"Why don't you speak English?" asks Punch.

"Shallaballah!" answers the foreign gentleman.

"Then I'll hit you with my stick," says Punch.

"Shallaballah!" says the foreign gentleman.

Punch hits him over the head and he falls to the ground. Then Punch sings as before:

"I dreamt that I dwelt in marble halls
With vassals and serfs by my si-hi-hide!"

Suddenly the image of all Mr. Punch's evil deeds in the form of a ghost peeps around a corner of the stage and whispers,

"Booh!" then disappears again.

Punch throws up his arms in alarm and says, "Ah, ah! I didn't do anything! It wasn't me!"

At that, all the people whom Punch has laid out on the stage rise straight up in the air, point their fingers accusingly at him, and float away.

"Oh dear! Oh dear!" cries Punch, "a horse! My Kingdom for a horse!" Suddenly his hobby horse comes prancing in. Punch tries to mount him in order to run away but the horse rears up and throws him.

"Oh dear! Oh dear!" moans Punch, from the ground and then in comes the Hangman. The Hangman says:

"Mr. Punch, you are my prisoner! You have broken the laws of your country!"

"Broken the laws?" whines Punch picking himself up. "I couldn't break 'em. I never touched 'em!"

"I have come to string you up," says the Hangman.

"Oh dear! Oh dear! Spare me! I've a wife and sixteen small children! What will they do without me?"

Nevertheless the Hangman produces a rope with a noose at the end, and this he throws over the limb of a tree.

"Come here!" says he.

"I can't," wails Punch. "I've a bone in my leg!"

"Then I must fetch you!" The two struggle and the Hangman takes Punch over to the tree.

"Put your head in here," says the Hangman, showing the noose.

"I don't know how! Show me!" whines Punch.

"Why it's easy! Just like this," says the Hangman. He puts his own head in the noose to show Punch how. Punch quickly pulls the rope and strings up the Hangman. "Oee! Oee!" he squeaks and begins to sing again. At that the ghost rises slowly.

"You are come for," he says in a hollow voice.

"Oh dear! Oh dear! What for?" cries Punch.

"To be carried off for your evil deeds, to the land of Bobbety Shooty."

The ghost approaches, still repeating in his hollow voice, "To be carried off for your evil deeds, to be carried off. To be carried off."

"That for my evil deeds," cries Punch. He hits the ghost himself on the head and biff! that's the end of the ghost. Then he jumps on his hobby horse and rides away, singing:

> "Right tol de rol, it serves him right,
> Now all my foes are put to flight,
> Ladies and gentlemen all, good night,
> To the freaks of Punch and Judy!"